A Pa
Affair

Three powerful, passionate men
Three intense love affairs

Three exciting, glamorous romances from three bestselling Mills & Boon authors!

In January 2009 Mills & Boon bring you two classic collections, each featuring three favourite romances by our bestselling authors…

A PASSIONATE AFFAIR

The Passionate Husband by Helen Brooks

The Italian's Passion by Elizabeth Power

A Latin Passion by Kathryn Ross

TAKEN BY THE BOSS

His Very Personal Assistant by Carole Mortimer

In the Banker's Bed by Cathy Williams

The Takeover Bid by Leigh Michaels

A Passionate Affair

THE PASSIONATE HUSBAND
by
Helen Brooks

THE ITALIAN'S PASSION
by
Elizabeth Power

A LATIN PASSION
by
Kathryn Ross

All the characters in this book have no existence outside the imagination of the author, and have no relation whatsoever to anyone bearing the same name or names. They are not even distantly inspired by any individual known or unknown to the author, and all the incidents are pure invention.

Harlequin Mills & Boon Limited,
Eton House, 18-24 Paradise Road, Richmond, Surrey TW9 1SR

The Passionate Husband, The Italian's Passion and *A Latin Passion* were first published in Great Britain by Harlequin Mills & Boon Limited in separate, single volumes.

ISBN: 978 0 263 87123 4

05-0109

Printed and bound in Spain
by Litografia Rosés S.A., Barcelona

THE PASSIONATE HUSBAND

by

Helen Brooks

Helen Brooks lives in Northamptonshire and is married with three children. As she is a committed Christian, busy housewife and mother, her spare time is at a premium, but her hobbies include reading, swimming, gardening and walking her old, faithful dog. Her long-cherished aspiration to write became a reality when she put pen to paper on reaching the age of forty, and sent the result off to Mills & Boon.

CHAPTER ONE

'I BET YOU'RE the only woman in the room who hasn't noticed the hunk with she who must be obeyed. Right?'

'What?'

Marsha raised startled emerald-green eyes, and the small plump girl standing in front of her sighed resignedly. 'I knew it. The whole place is buzzing with curiosity and there's you—as serene and cool as always.'

'Nicki, you know better than anyone else I need the facts and figures for the Baxter slot at my fingertips for the meeting tomorrow,' Marsha said patiently, reaching for the glass of fizzy mineral water at her side and taking a sip. 'As my secretary—'

'I'm talking as your friend, not your secretary,' Nicki responded smartly. 'This is supposed to be a little get-together as a reward for the current ratings and all our hard work, and you're the only one not taking advantage of the free food and booze. Don't you *like* champagne, for goodness' sake?' She wrinkled her snub nose at the hapless mineral water.

'Not particularly,' Marsha answered truthfully. It was a vastly overrated beverage in her opinion. 'And I like to keep a clear head when I'm working.'

'Ah, but you shouldn't *be* working,' Nicki pointed out triumphantly. 'It's once in a blue moon that the powers-that-be acknowledge what a great team they've got below them. Can't you take a few minutes to enjoy the moment?'

Now it was Marsha who sighed. When Nicki dug her

heels in she could be formidable. This made her an excellent secretary in some respects, but, as there was a distinct mother hen quirk to her extrovert personality, it could also be irritating.

Nicki was only three years older than her, at thirty, but the other woman appeared positively matronly most of the time. She was also loyal, trustworthy, hard-working and discreet, and Marsha counted herself fortunate to have Nicki in her corner in the cut-and-thrust world of television, the sector in which she had decided to make her career.

She gave mental affirmation to this last thought now as she said, 'Okay, okay, you win. One glass of champagne to keep you happy won't hurt, I guess.'

'Great.' Nicki's round pretty face beamed as she surveyed the slim delicate woman sitting on a sofa in a quiet recess of the bustling room. 'I presume you are coming out of your hidey-hole to drink it?'

'Hardly a hidey-hole, Nicki,' Marsha said drily. The recess was in full view of at least half the room where the drink and nibbles get-together was being thrown, and she'd had every intention of being sociable for a while once she had finished working. Now, stifling a sigh, Marsha rose to her feet, smoothing a lock of silver-blonde hair away from her face as she followed Nicki into the throng of animated noisy folk whose conversation had risen and ebbed like the tide for the last hour or so.

'So, where's the hunk, then?' Marsha glanced round the crowded room as Nicki handed her a glass of sparkling champagne. 'Penelope can't have eaten him already.'

Penelope Pelham was a top executive at the television company they worked for, with a well-deserved reputation for ruthlessness in every sphere of her life. It was an accepted fact that one would consider appealing to Penelope's kindness and compassion in the same way as a great white shark's.

Gossip had it that Penelope ate men up and spat them out in the same way she did any employee unfortunate enough to fall foul of her temper, and no one doubted this was true.

Marsha had never had cause to cross swords with the beautiful flamboyant brunette since she had started working for the television company some twelve months before, but that didn't mean she wasn't as wary of the other woman as everyone else. Penelope was powerful and influential, and the force of her dominant personality was impressive.

'Janie says they've just disappeared into Penelope's office with strict instructions from the lady herself they're not to be disturbed. Mind you, for once I have to say I see eye to eye with Penelope. If I had got my claws into a man like that, I'd want to be alone with him every moment I could get.'

Nicki gave a ridiculously hammed-up leer and Marsha began to laugh. She took a sip of the effervescent drink and found it to be surprisingly good. The bigwigs had pulled out all the stops for once. Normally the odd work do like this consisted of cheap plonk and sandwiches curling round the edges.

'Come and get some food.' Nicki was on a roll now, and Marsha didn't object when she was pulled over to the loaded table at the far end of the room. Knowing they were all expected to attend this gathering at the end of the working day, she'd skipped lunch in an effort to get the Baxter story under her belt. Now, as she looked at the very nice spread, without a curling ham sandwich in sight, she found she was hungry. Ravenous, in fact.

'Ooh, I just love kebabs, don't you?' Nicki was busy stocking up her plate. 'And this flan is delicious. And just *look* at those desserts. Janie had a free hand so she ordered them from Finns.'

Janie was Penelope's secretary, and Nicki had made it her business to strike up a friendship with the other woman—when Janie had started working for the company six months before—on the premise that you could never have too many friends in high places. Marsha wasn't sure if she agreed with this somewhat machiavellian viewpoint, but it was undoubtedly useful to have a secretary with her finger on the pulse, albeit second-hand.

'I presume you've asked Janie for the dope on the hunk?' Marsha asked idly, filling her own plate as she spoke and then picking up her glass of champagne and making her way over to a couple of vacant seats.

'Uh-huh.' Nicki demolished two bulging pastry *hors d'oeuvres*, licking her lips and rolling her eyes in appreciation, before she added, 'She didn't know anything.'

Marsha nodded. If she was being honest she would have said she wasn't in the least bit curious about Penelope's new man-friend, but she didn't want to hurt Nicki's feelings. Her secretary had been happily married to her childhood sweetheart for the last eleven years, but that didn't stop Nicki being a romance addict who read every book and saw every film with even the tiniest bit of amorous intrigue in it.

Marsha knew she had greatly disappointed the other woman when she'd made it clear, a few weeks after starting work at the company, that she wasn't interested in the opposite sex. And, no, she'd hastily added when Nicki's expression had made it clear what she was thinking, she wasn't interested in the female sex either! She had made the decision to concentrate on her career and only her career some time ago, that was all.

A few months later, when the two women had become friends as well as work colleagues, Marsha had admitted her decision had something to do with a man—once bitten, twice shy—but hadn't elaborated further. It said a lot for Nicki's strength of will that she had never brought the subject up again, merely confining herself to the odd remark about some dishy man she or her husband knew who had recently become single again, or pointing out that *everyone* indulged in one or two blind dates in their lives. Marsha normally responded to such obvious wiles by ignoring them and changing the subject.

'How come,' Nicki said thoughtfully, 'you can eat like you do and not put on a pound of weight? It's not fair.'

'I did miss lunch.' It was said gently. Nicki ate the equivalent of a three-course meal every lunchtime, and there was always a bag of sweets in her desk drawer which was replaced daily, not to mention hot sausage rolls from the canteen mid-morning, and cakes or biscuits mid-afternoon.

Nicki grinned. 'I wish everyone was as tactful as you, but I do so *enjoy* my food. And then there's those evenings when the urge to pig out is just irresistible, and chocolate just sort of leaps up and waves its hands. Know what I mean?'

'Marsha has never particularly cared for chocolate. Now, coconut ice is something else. I've known her to eat a pound or so of that all to herself in one sitting.'

The deep voice behind them was relaxed and cool, but as Marsha's head shot round she saw the sculptured features of the tall man standing with Penelope could have been carved in granite. Admittedly the hard mouth curled at the edges with something which could have been described as a smile by those who did not know better. But Marsha did know better. And how. She fought for control, willing herself not to stutter and stammer as she said, 'Taylor. What a surprise.'

'Isn't it?' The startling tawny eyes with their thick black lashes were fixed on her shocked face. 'But a pleasant one…for me, that is.'

'You two are obviously already acquainted,' Penelope drawled sweetly, her smile not quite reaching the blue eyes set in a face which was faintly exotic and very lovely. Marsha noticed the way the other woman's hand had tightened on Taylor's arm in an instinctive predatory gesture which said volumes.

She drew in a long, body-straightening breath and squared her shoulders. So that was how it was. But she should have known, shouldn't she, with Taylor's reputation? 'We knew each other once, a long time ago,' she said clearly, her tone dismissive. 'Now, if you'll excuse me, I've some work to finish—'

'Once? Oh, come on, Marsha, you'll have these good folk believing we were ships that passed in the night instead of man and wife.'

Nicki's mouth had dropped open to the point where she looked comical, but no one was looking at her.

Marsha's clear green eyes widened infinitesimally, even as she told herself she should have expected this. Taylor being Taylor, he wouldn't let her get away with snubbing him. A vein in her temple throbbed, but her voice was quiet when she said, 'Goodbye, Taylor.'

'You were *married*?' In any other circumstances Marsha would have enjoyed seeing the ice-cool Penelope dumbfounded.

'Not were, Penelope. Are.' Taylor's voice was as quiet as Marsha's had been, but the steely note made it twice as compelling. 'Marsha is my wife.'

'Until the divorce is finalised.' She had turned, but now she swung back as she shot the words at him. 'And that would have happened a long time ago if I'd had my way.'

Her voice had risen slightly, calling forth one or two interested glances from people around them who hadn't heard what had been said but who recognised anger when they heard it.

'But…but your surname is Gosling, isn't it?'

Penelope was staring at her as though she'd never seen her before, and in spite of the awfulness of the moment there was an element of satisfaction in being able to reply, 'Gosling is my maiden name. Personnel are aware of my marital status—albeit temporary.' She flashed a scathing glance at the tall dark man at Penelope's side. 'But when I said I prefer to be known as Miss Gosling on a day-to-day basis they saw no reason to object.'

'This is most irregular.' Penelope had recovered her composure and her tone was frosty. 'I should have been informed.'

Marsha could have said here that her immediate boss, Jeff North, was fully aware of her circumstances, but she wasn't about to get into a discussion on the rights and wrongs of it all with Penelope. Not with Taylor standing there with his eyes fixed on her face.

The brief glances she'd bestowed on him had told her he was as devastatingly attractive as ever. He had never been textbook handsome, his appeal was too virile and manly for that, but the hard, rugged features offset by tawny cat eyes and jet-black hair radiated magnetism. And the strong, tough face was set above a body which was just as vigorous, its sinewy muscles and a powerful frame ensuring women everywhere gave him a second glance. Or three or four or more.

This last thought made Marsha's voice every bit as cold as Penelope's when she said, 'Possibly. Now, if you'll excuse me?' And she left without a backward glance.

It wasn't until she got in the lift and attempted to press the button for the third floor that Marsha realised how much her hands were shaking. She stood stiff and straight until the doors had glided to, and then leant limply against the carpeted side of the lift, her stomach swirling. Taylor—here. What was she going to do?

And then the answer came, as though from somewhere outside herself. Nothing. You are going to do nothing, because nothing has changed from how things were this morning. He is not in your life any more. He can't hurt you.

But if that was true why was she feeling as though her whole world had collapsed around her right now? The world she had carefully built up over the last months?

Shock. The answer was there again. Shock, pure and simple. It was so unexpected, seeing him like that. You were unprepared, taken off guard. But that doesn't mean you aren't over him.

The lift had stopped, and now the doors opened again, but for a moment Marsha stood staring blankly ahead, her mind racing. She wasn't over him. She'd never be over him. You didn't get over someone like

Taylor. You just learnt to live with the pain that it was over.

'Enough.' She spoke out loud, the courage and self-respect which had enabled her to leave him in the first place coming to her aid. 'No snivelling, no crying. You've cried enough tears to fill an ocean as it is.'

Once in the office she shared with Nicki, Jeff North's room being separated from theirs by an interjoining door, Marsha sat down at her desk with a little plump. Of all the places in all the world, why was Taylor here? And *was* he Penelope's new lover? The thought brought such a shaft of pain she pushed it to the back of her consciousness to think about later, once she was home. For now she had to get out of this place with a semblance of dignity, and she'd do it if it killed her.

It was at that point she realised she'd left her handbag, along with the papers she'd been looking at when Nicki had pounced on her, downstairs in the alcove. She muttered something very rude before leaning back in the seat and shutting her eyes for a moment. Great, just great. She'd have to go and retrieve everything, which would totally ruin the decorous exit she'd just made.

Footsteps brought her eyes snapping open and her back straightening, but it was Nicki who emerged in the doorway, and she was clutching the Baxter file and Marsha's handbag. 'You forgot these,' she said awkwardly. 'Are you all right?'

'Sort of.' Marsha managed a weak smile. 'Thanks for these.'

'All in a day's work.'

Marsha had expected a barrage of questions the next time she saw Nicki, but when the other girl sat down at her own desk and began packing her things away, all she said was, 'They've gone, by the way, Penelope and your—and him.'

'Right.' She'd explain a little tomorrow, but tonight she couldn't face it. 'I'm off too. We'll talk in the morning, Nicki,' she said, rising to her feet and reaching for her jacket. It was her brisk boss tone, something Marsha used rarely, but when she did Nicki knew enough to take the hint.

Once she was in the lift again, a thousand butterflies began to do an Irish jig in Marsha's stomach. What if Nicki was wrong and he was waiting for her in Reception? She wouldn't put it past Taylor. She wouldn't put *anything* past Taylor Kane.

Reception was the usual madhouse at this time of night, but it was Taylorless and that was all Marsha asked. She responded to a couple of goodnights, raising a hand in farewell to Bob, the security guard, with whom she often had a chat when she was working late and it was quieter. He regaled her with tales of his six children, who had all gone off the rails in some way or other and who drove Bob and his long-suffering wife mad, but tonight Marsha felt she would swap places with them like a shot.

Once outside, in the warm June evening, Marsha looked about her, only relaxing and breathing more easily after a few moments of scanning the bustling crowd. Everyone was walking fast and every other person was talking into a mobile phone. Irate drivers were honking car horns, there was the occasional screech of tyres and the odd person or so was dicing with death by ignoring pedestrian crossings and throwing themselves in front of the rush hour traffic. A normal evening, in fact.

It was too warm for the jacket she'd worn that morning, and now she tucked it over her arm as she began to walk past Notting Hill towards Kensington. Somehow she couldn't face the jam-packed anonymity of the tube or a bus tonight. It would take a while to get to her tiny bedsit deep in West Kensington, but the walk through Holland Park was pleasant on an evening like this, and she needed some time to collect her whirling thoughts and sort out her emotions. And then she wrinkled her small straight nose at the thought. Since when had she ever been able to get her head round her feelings for Taylor?

'I had a feeling you'd walk.'

Her pulse leapt as the deep voice at her elbow registered, and in that moment she knew she had been expecting him to make an appearance. She didn't turn her head, and she was pleased her voice was so cool—considering her racing heartbeat—when she said, 'Clever you.'

'How are you, Fuzz?'

His pet name for her caused her traitorous heart to lurch before she quelled the weakness. Fuzz had come into being on their second date, when he had said he thought goslings were supposed to be all fluff and down, his eyes on her sleek shiny hair. She'd smiled, answering that fuzz and feathers weren't compulsory, and from that moment—whenever they were alone—he'd whispered the name in a smoky tone which had caused her knees to buckle. But that was then and this was now. Her voice tight, she said, 'Don't call me that.'

'Why? You used to like it.'

His arrogance provoked her into raising angry eyes to meet his gaze, and she knew immediately it was a mistake. He was too close, for one thing. She could see the furrows in the tanned skin of his face, the laughter lines which crinkled the corners of his eyes. She caught her breath, steadying herself before she said, 'I'm glad you used the past tense.'

He shrugged, a casual easy movement she envied. 'Past, present, future—it's all the same. You're mine, Fuzz. You've been mine from the first moment we met.'

For a moment the urge to strike out in action as well as words was so strong it shocked her, but it acted like a bucket of cold water on her hot fury. Men like him never changed, she knew that, so why had she expected any different? Everything about Taylor whispered wealth and power and limitless control. She had married him knowing he was dangerous, but she had hoped she'd captured his heart. She had been wrong. 'I don't think so, Taylor. We'll be divorced soon, and that is the end of the road.'

'You think a piece of paper makes any difference one way or the other?' He took her arm, pulling her to a stop as he encircled her with his arms. 'This nonsense has to stop. Do you understand? I've been patient long enough.'

His height and breadth dwarfed her slender shape, and the familiar smell of him—a subtle mixture of deliciously sexy aftershave, clean male skin and something that was peculiarly Taylor—sent her senses reeling. *Control, control, control.* He was a past master of it—she had learnt it day by painful day in the months they had been separated. She couldn't let all that agony be for nothing. She ignored the longing which made her want to melt against the hard wall of his chest, saying instead, her voice clipped, 'Let go of me or I'll scream my head off. I mean it.'

'Scream away,' he offered lazily, but she had seen the narrowing of his eyes and the tightening of his mouth and she knew she had scored a hit.

She remained absolutely rigid and still in his arms, her eyes blazing, and after another long moment he let her go. 'You're still not prepared to listen to reason?'

'Reason?' She forced a scornful laugh, taking a step backwards and treading on some poor man's toe with her wafer-thin heels. His muffled yelp went unheeded.

'Yes, reason. Reason, logic, common sense—all those worthy attributes which seem to be so sadly lacking within that beautiful frame of yours,' he drawled, deliberately provocative.

Marsha gritted her teeth for a moment. He was the one person in all the world who could make her madder than hell in two seconds flat. 'Your definition of reason and logic is different from mine,' she said scathingly. 'I go by the *Oxford Dictionary*.'

'Meaning?'

'Meaning I don't hold with your clarification that reason means a promiscuous lifestyle where anything goes, and logic says you only begin to worry if you are caught out.'

He surveyed her defiant face expressionlessly, the magnificent tawny eyes glittering in the tanned darkness of his face. After an eternity, and very softly, he said, 'I see.'

Marsha stared back at him, determined not to let him see the quiet response had taken the wind out of her sails. She had been married to this man for three years, eighteen months of which she had been separated from him, but she'd had no idea how he would react to what she had said. Which summed up their relationship, really, she thought wretchedly. And was one of the reasons why she had left him and would never go back. *That and the other women.*

Her small chin rose a fraction, and now her voice had

lost its heat and was icy when she said, 'Good. It will save me having to repeat myself.'

'You look wonderful.' It was as though her previous words had never been voiced. 'Businesslike…' His gaze roamed over her curves, neatly ensconced in a jade-green pencil-slim skirt and a blouse of a slightly lighter hue. 'But still good enough to eat,' he added as his eyes returned to hers once more.

Marsha ignored the way her body had responded to the hunger in his face and concentrated on maintaining her equanimity. 'Don't try the Kane charm on me, Taylor,' she said coolly. 'I'm immune now.'

'Is that so?' His hand came up to tuck a strand of her hair behind her ear, his fingers lingering for a moment at her neck and setting off a chain reaction she knew he could sense. 'I don't think so.'

She hated him: his arrogance, his supreme confidence in his mastery over her mind, soul and body… She caught the bitterness, forcing it down where the astute amber eyes couldn't see and taking a deep hidden breath before she said, 'Then you must believe what you like. It really doesn't matter any more. In a month or so we will be divorced and free agents, and—'

'The hell we will.'

She ignored the interruption and hoped she hadn't revealed her composure was only skin-deep. 'And we can put the past behind us,' she finished evenly.

'You really think I will just let you walk away from me for ever?' He raised dark brows. 'You know me better than that.'

'I have never known you.' She had answered too quickly, her voice raw for a moment, and immediately she knew her mistake. She had to be calm and collected in front of him; it was her best defence. 'Just as you never really knew me,' she added quickly. 'We both thought each other was someone different. That was our mistake.'

'*Our* mistake?' The dark brows rose even higher. 'Did I hear correctly? You're actually admitting you're capable of being wrong occasionally?'

She would have given the world to sock him right on the jaw. Her neck and shoulders were stiff with the effort it was taking to remain poised and dignified, but she conquered the desire to wipe the slight smile off his face, although not without some gritting of teeth. When she could trust herself to speak, she said sweetly, 'I've nothing more to say to you. Goodbye, Taylor,' turning on her heel as she spoke his name.

It was only a moment or two before she realised he was walking alongside her. 'What are you doing?' she asked frostily.

'Walking you back home.' He didn't actually add, Of course, but he might as well have.

'I don't want you to.'

'Okay.' He stopped, but as she walked on, head high and heart thumping a tattoo, he called, 'I'll pick you up at eight, so be ready.'

'What?' She whirled round, causing a middle-aged woman with a huge bag of shopping to bump into her. When she had finished apologising she marched over to where Taylor was standing, arms crossed, as he leant against a convenient lamppost. 'Are you mad?' she asked in a tight voice.

'Me?' The innocence was galling. 'It was you who nearly knocked that poor woman off her feet.'

'You know what I mean.' She glared at him, wondering how she could have forgotten quite how attractive he was. There were very few men with truly black hair, but Taylor was one of them, and the contrast between his eyes and hair had always been riveting. Brushing this traitorous thought aside, she continued, 'I have no intention of having dinner with you, Taylor. Not today, not tomorrow, not ever. We're getting a *divorce*, for goodness' sake.'

He smiled. Marsha caught her breath. His smile had always affected her, like warm sunshine flooding over a stormy sea, possibly because he did it so rarely. Not genuine smiles anyway. 'Then what are you so afraid of?' he asked silkily. 'I'm merely suggesting we have dinner together, not that we finish the evening in bed.'

Her pulse jumped and then raced frantically as her body remembered what it had been like to be in bed with this man. To be loved, utterly and completely. To be consumed by him until all rational thought was gone and all that existed was Taylor. But then it hadn't been love, had it? At least not as she interpreted the word. Love and marriage meant commitment, faithfulness and loyalty as far as she was concerned, and she was blowed if she was going to apologise for feeling that way. 'I'm not afraid,' she said shakily. 'Don't be so ridiculous.'

'Then have dinner with me. For the time being at least we are still man and wife, Fuzz. Can't we try to be civilised?' His eyes were searching hers in that old way she remembered from when they had still been together. He had always looked at her like this in moments of stress or importance, as though he was trying to see the inner core of her, the essence of what made her *her*.

Marsha blinked, breaking the spell the glowing tawny colour that circled fierce black centres had wrought. She clutched at a reason for refusal. 'What about Penelope?' she said. 'Won't she mind?'

'Penelope?' He repeated the name as though he didn't have the faintest idea who the woman was, and then he said softly, 'Penelope Pelham is a business colleague, that's all. I'm quoting for new sound equipment and a load of stuff and she is my contact.'

Oh, yes? Who was kidding who? It had been as plain as the nose on her face that Penelope had decided Taylor was her next bedfellow. Kane International might well be putting in a tender for the new equipment they had all heard was being acquired, but if Taylor's firm won the work it would be because he had provided proof that his equipment was the best in more ways than one. Marsha blinked again. That last thought was not like her—but that was Taylor all over, she thought irritably. Bringing out the worst in her. 'I don't think dinner is a good idea,' she said firmly.

'It's an excellent idea,' he said, even more firmly.

'I'm trying to say no nicely.' She eyed him severely.

'Try saying yes badly.'

He was so close his warm breath fanned the silk of her hair, and for a moment she wanted to breathe in the smell and feel of him in great gulps. Instead the intensity of her emotion acted like a shot of adrenalin. 'It might surprise you, Taylor Kane, but you can't always have what you want,' she said steadily, the blood surging through her veins in a tumult.

'Not always, no.' This time he didn't smile. 'But tonight is not one of those times. Eight on the dot. I'm quite prepared to break the door down if you play coy.'

She was so surprised when he upped and walked away that for a good thirty seconds she was speechless. Then she called after him, oblivious of the passers-by, 'You don't know where I live!'

He turned just long enough to say, 'I have always known where you are, every minute since you've been gone.' And after that she found she was unable to say another word.

CHAPTER TWO

WHEN Marsha opened the front door of her bedsit a little while later, it was with the disturbing realisation that she couldn't remember a moment of the walk home. Her head had been so full of Taylor and their conversation, not least his ridiculous presumption that she would eat dinner with him, that the stroll she normally so enjoyed at the end of the working day had been accomplished on automatic.

Her bedsit was on the top floor of a three-storey terraced house, and in the last twelve months since she had been living in it Marsha had made it her own haven, away from the stress and excitement of her working life. She stood on the threshold for a moment, glancing round the sun-filled room in front of her, and as always a sense of pleasure made itself felt.

The room had been a mess when she had first viewed it, the previous occupiers having been a pair of young female students who clearly had never been introduced to soap and water or cleaning materials in the whole of their lives. She had scrubbed and scoured and cleaned for days, but eventually, after plenty of elbow grease and some deep thought on what she wanted, she had begun to decorate.

First she had stripped the old floorboards, which had been in surprisingly good condition, and once they were finished, she'd known how to proceed. She had painted the whole bedsit in a palette of gentle shades of off-white and cream, which harmonised with each other and the different tones of wood in the floorboards, before splashing out on organdie curtains for the two wide floor-to-ceiling windows, along with ecru blinds which she only pulled at night when it was dark and she was getting ready for bed.

The small sitting and sleeping area was separated from the kitchen by a sleek and beautiful glass breakfast bar, which Mrs Tate-Collins—Marsha's elderly landlady, who lived in the basement along with her three cats—had had installed in each of the three bedsits when she'd had the house converted after her husband had died. The *pièce de résistance* for Marsha, however, and the thing which had really sold the bedsit to her when she had first viewed it, was Mrs Tate-Collins's forethought in providing a tiny shower room in a recess off the kitchen. It was only large enough to hold a shower, loo and small corner washbasin, but all the other bedsits she had viewed at the time had necessitated a walk along a landing to a communal bathroom.

Once she had bought a sofabed, TV and two wooden stools for the breakfast bar, which served as her dining table, Marsha had left the bed and breakfast she had lived in since her split with Taylor and moved into her new home, adding touches like the ecru throw and tumbled cushions of soft ash-gold, stone and cream for the sofa as she had lived there.

The slim built-in wardrobe to one side of the front door, which held all her clothes, meant she had to be selective in what she bought, and the kitchen was only large enough to house the smallest of fridges, along with the built-in hob and oven, but Marsha didn't mind the lack of space. The bedsit was her retreat, somewhere she could shut the rest of the world out whenever she wanted to.

Her miniature garden was in the form of a Juliet balcony opening out from the windows, and although it could only hold one small wicker chair, along with a profusion of scented plants, she spent a good deal of her free time there in the warmer months, reading, dozing and looking out over the rooftops.

She loved her home. Marsha walked across to the windows now, opening them wide and letting the scents from the small balcony drift into the room. And now Taylor was going to come here, and that would spoil everything. She did not want him in her hideaway. She didn't want him in her *life*.

The hum of evening traffic from the busy main street beyond the cul-de-sac the house was situated in was louder now the windows were open. Normally Marsha didn't even hear the sound, so used had she become to the background noise. Tonight, though, it registered on her consciousness, and she found herself wondering what Taylor would make of the bedsit. The downstairs cloakroom in his lovely home deep in Harrow was about the same size as her entire living space.

'I don't care what he thinks.' She spoke out loud, flexing her shoulders as though to dislodge a weight there. 'And there is absolutely no way I am going out to dinner with him.'

So saying, she roused herself and walked into the kitchen, fixing herself a mug of milky chocolate which she took out on to the balcony. She sat down with a sigh, curling up on the big soft cushion in the wicker chair as she gazed out into space, a frown between her eyes.

Thirty minutes later and she had had a shower, and her hair was bundled under a soft handtowel as she stood surveying her meagre wardrobe.

She was only going to dinner with him to prevent a scene, she assured herself silently. A scene which would undoubtedly occur if Taylor did not get his own way. But this was strictly a one-off, something she would make perfectly clear to him, as well as letting him know she was counting the days until the divorce when all ties would be cut for good.

She pulled a pair of slinky, slightly flared pants in a misty silver colour from the wardrobe, teaming them with a bolero-style silk jacket in pale green. They were the newest items of clothing she possessed, bought for a cocktail party she had attended a month or so before. After placing the clothes on the back of the sofa she walked over to the full-length mirror on the back of the wardrobe door, staring at herself long and hard for a moment or two.

How could Taylor imagine, even for one single second, that there was any hope for them after what he had done? But then she *had* walked away from Taylor, rather than it being the other way round, something he would have found insupportable. To her knowledge, no woman had ever ended a relationship with him before—it had always been Taylor who had ditched them. Which was probably why his ego had been big enough to think he could have his cake and eat it.

This last reflection brought Marsha's lips into a thin line as she pictured the 'cake' in question. Tanya West—a voluptuous redhead with the body of Marilyn Monroe and the face of an angel. And according to Susan, Taylor's sister, Tanya hadn't been the first little dalliance he'd indulged in since his marriage.

She whipped the towel off her head, beginning to blow dry her hair into a soft silky bob and all the time denying the hurt and anger which had flared up at the thought of the other woman.

She was still denying it when the buzzer next to the door sounded forty minutes later. Pressing the little switch, she stared at Taylor's face—small and very far away—as she said, 'I'll be down in just a second.' She didn't open the front door of the building, deciding he could think what he liked.

One last swift glance in the mirror told her she was looking cool and controlled, despite the way her heart was pounding, and she offered up a quick prayer that the illusion would hold during the time she was with Taylor. He had to understand she wasn't the same gullible fool who had been so besotted with him she hadn't seen what was in front of her nose. She had thought he'd accepted that when she had left him and refused to see him eighteen months ago, especially in view of the fact there had been no objection from his solicitor—to her knowledge—when she had filed for divorce.

Locking the door of the bedsit behind her, she made for the stairs, careful how she descended in the high strappy sandals she was wearing, and it was as she approached the ground floor that she heard the unmistakable sound of Taylor's voice talking to someone inside the house. Someone had let him into the hall. She froze for a moment on the stairs, her ears straining to hear whom he was speaking to.

Mrs Tate-Collins. As Marsha identified the other voice she raised her eyes heavenwards. Her landlady was a sweetie-pie, but the elderly lady really belonged in a powder and crinoline age, where men were gallant and noble and all women were prone to attacks of the vapours. Mrs Tate-Collins had told her once of her privileged upbringing and her private education at home and then an establishment for well brought up young gentlewomen. When Marsha had said she had been raised in a children's home after her single-parent mother had abandoned her when she was two years old the other woman had stared at her as though she was a creature from another planet. Not that she hadn't been sympathetic, Marsha qualified, but it had been plain the other woman was out of her depth with such an alien concept. How Mrs Tate-Collins was going to cope with finding out Miss Gosling was really Mrs Kane, Marsha didn't know.

'Ah, here she is, Mr Kane,' Mrs Tate-Collins trilled as Marsha came into view. 'And looking very lovely.'

Marsha gave what she hoped was a neutral smile. 'Thank you,' she said directly to the other woman, before glancing at Taylor, whereupon the smile iced over. 'I told you I'd be straight down,' she said evenly. 'There was no need to come in.'

'Oh, I was just on my way across the hall after seeing Miss Gordon when your young man rang,' Mrs Tate-Collins chimed in before Taylor could speak, turning to him as she added, 'That's the lady who lives on this floor, you know, the poor thing. She had a fall the other day and it has shaken her up a little, so I took her a drop of soup and a roll to save her having to think about supper. She is getting on a bit, bless her.'

Marsha saw Taylor gaze into the lined face of the small wizened woman in front of him, who looked ninety if a day, but his voice was perfectly serious when he said, 'That was kind of you, Mrs Tate-Collins.'

'Shall we go?' It was clear Taylor hadn't got round to mentioning their marital status, which suited her just fine, and she was anxious to get him out of the door before her landlady started another cosy chat. 'Goodbye, Mrs Tate-Collins,' she added briskly.

'Oh, goodbye, dear.'

It was a little surprised, but in view of the fact Marsha had gripped Taylor's arm with one hand and opened the front door with the other, virtually pushing him on to the top step, she really couldn't blame her landlady.

'She'll think you can't wait to have your wicked way with me.' Once they had descended the eight steps and were on the pavement Taylor raised an amused eyebrow at her.

Up to this moment she had successfully fought acknowledging how drop-dead gorgeous he looked, but as her heart missed a couple of beats she said stiffly, 'Mrs Tate-Collins would never think anything so vulgar.'

'Really? I thought she had a little twinkle in her eye.'

Any female, whatever her age, would have a twinkle in her eye when she looked at Taylor. That was the effect he had on the whole of womankind. 'I think not,' she said crisply. 'And before we move from here I want to make it perfectly plain that I have agreed to this meeting under sufferance, and only because I want the divorce to go through with the minimum of disruption.'

Taylor surveyed her silently, his customary stern expression now in place. 'Feel better now you've got that off your chest?' he asked mildly after a very long moment.

Marsha shrugged. 'I just wanted you to know, that's all,' she said, wondering why she suddenly felt like a recalcitrant schoolgirl.

'Believe me, Fuzz, I was never in any doubt,' he said drily. 'You are nothing if not straightforward.'

Which was more than could be said for him.

She hadn't spoken, but the words must have been

plain to read on her face because he next said, even more drily, 'Especially when you say nothing at all.'

'So, in view of that, why are we doing this?' she asked a touch bewilderedly. He hadn't contacted her in almost eighteen months, so why now, with the divorce just weeks away?

'Because it's time.'

He had always been good at those—the cryptic one-liners. Right from when she had first met him she had known he was an enigma, but she had thought she'd found the key when he'd asked her to marry him just weeks after they had first been introduced at a dinner party by a mutual friend. Love. She had mistakenly imagined he loved her as she loved him—*had* loved him, she corrected immediately. *Had.*

The warm evening was redolent with the faint smells of cooking from various open windows, along with the strains of a popular chart hit and bursts of laughter from the house next door. Marsha watched Taylor wrinkle his aquiline nose. 'Shall we go?' he asked quietly, his eyes tight on her face.

She would have liked to have said no and turned on her heel, but it really wasn't an option. She nodded, allowing him to take her arm as they walked a few steps to where his Aston Martin was parked. He had changed the model in the last eighteen months, she noted silently, although the other car had only been six months old when she had left him. This one was sleek and dark and dangerous—very much like Taylor.

He opened the passenger door for her, and she slid into the expensive interior with a gracefulness she was pleased about, considering the way her stomach was jumping and her legs were trembling. That was the trouble with Taylor, she thought irritably. However much she tried to prepare herself, he always got under her skin.

Once he had joined her in the car, she steeled herself to glance at him as though his closeness bothered her not at all. 'Where are we going?'

'Surprise.' He didn't look at her, starting the engine and then manoeuvring the powerful car out of the close confines of the parking space. Her eyes fell on the thick gold ring on the third finger of his left hand, and again her heart lurched. Did he wear his wedding band all the time, or had he donned it specially for this evening? she asked herself, before answering in the next breath, what did it matter anyway? The ring was just an item of jewellery if the commitment it was meant to signify wasn't there. Her own hands had been ringless from the moment she had walked out of their house and out of Taylor's life.

The car purred along the busy London streets, passing numerous pubs and wine bars where folk were sitting outside drinking or eating in the dying sunshine. In the interim between leaving university and meeting Taylor Marsha had often enjoyed summer evenings with friends in this way, but since the breakdown of her marriage she hadn't wanted to go back to the old crowd. She still saw one or two of them occasionally, but it wasn't the same—not for her. They were still all relatively fancy-free and into having a good time, but she felt she had passed that stage and couldn't go back—certainly not while she was still legally a married woman anyway. Stupid, maybe, she admitted a trifle bitterly, considering the way Taylor had behaved, but she couldn't help it.

She glanced down at her hands, which were tight fists in her lap, and forced her fingers to relax, uncurling them one by one as she breathed deeply and willed her pulse into a steady beat. 'I don't like surprises,' she said clearly, as though Taylor had just spoken that moment rather than all of ten minutes ago. Ten minutes of ragged vibrating silence.

She kept her gaze on the windscreen as the tawny eyes flashed over her tight profile before returning to the road ahead. 'Shame,' he drawled smoothly.

'So, where are we going?' And then, as the car made another turning, she knew. He was taking her home! No, not home—home was now her tiny sanctuary in West Kensington. 'Stop the car please, Taylor,' she said as evenly as she could.

'Why?'

His tone was so innocent she knew she was right. 'Because you told me you were taking me out to dinner,' she said stonily.

'I am.' He gestured with one hand at the immaculate dinner suit he was wearing.

'Taylor!' She paused, warning herself to take care not to lose her temper and give him the satisfaction of winning. 'I recognise where we are,' she said more calmly. 'This is a stone's throw from Harrow.'

He nodded, totally unrepentant. 'That's right, and Hannah has been like a dog with two tails knowing you were dropping by tonight.'

Dropping by? Was the man mad? And then the thought of the buxom, middle-aged housekeeper who had mothered her from the first moment she had been introduced to her melted Marsha enough for a lump to come into her throat. She bit down on the emotion, saying, 'I have no intention of going to your home.'

'Our home, Fuzz.' His voice was suddenly dangerous. 'And although you might be able to cast people off as though they have never existed, Hannah can't. Mad as you were with me, it wouldn't have hurt you to have dropped her a line or arranged to meet her somewhere. Even a phone call would have been something. You damn near broke her heart.'

She couldn't stand this. Didn't he know that any reminder of him, however small, had crucified her in the early days, and if she had seen Hannah all her resolve to be strong and make a new life would have been swept away? She had missed the woman who had become the only mother she had ever known nearly as much as Taylor. And then, because she was working on sheer emotion, and without the necessary protective shields in place, she spoke out the thing which had hurt her as much as his betrayal with Tanya. 'If you were so concerned about Hannah's feelings, why didn't you contact me after I'd left?' she bit out harshly. 'You're a fine one to talk about casting people off.'

'I don't believe I'm hearing this,' he growled, raking back his hair with an angry gesture which spoke volumes. 'I came home after three days in Germany which had been pure hell to find you already packed and waiting to leave. You came at me all guns firing and accusing me of goodness knows what, and when I tried to make you see reason you walked out of the door. I followed you to your car to prevent you leaving and you slammed the door on my hand, breaking several bones in the process.'

'That was an accident,' she defended quickly. 'I said so at the time, if you remember. I didn't know you'd got your hand in the way of the door.'

'It didn't prevent you from driving off though, did it?' he reminded her heatedly.

Marsha took a moment to compose herself. He was

turning this all round, as though she was the one who had had an affair! 'Hannah was there to take care of you—'

'Damn Hannah,' he said furiously, as though he hadn't just accused her of being unfeeling. 'I drove after you, if you remember, and do you recall what you said when we stopped at those traffic lights? If I didn't stop following you, you'd drive into a wall. Tell me you didn't mean that.'

She had meant it. She had been so desperate and hurt that night it would have been a relief not to have to think or feel ever again.

He nodded grimly. 'Quite,' he said, as though she had just confirmed what he'd said out loud. 'So I let you go. Call me old-fashioned, but I thought I'd rather see you alive than dead.'

'Call *me* old-fashioned, but I always thought there were two in a marriage, not three—or more.'

She saw a muscle in his cheek twitch at her direct hit, but his voice was suddenly much calmer when he said, 'Tanya again.'

She ignored that, continuing, 'And my point still remains the same. You did not contact me after that night.'

'Not physically, maybe, but surely the letter counts for something?'

'Letter?' She hadn't received a letter and she didn't believe for one moment he had written one. Whatever game he was playing, she wasn't going to fall for it.

'Oh, come on, Fuzz,' he said wearily. 'Don't pretend you didn't receive my letter.'

His tone brought her temper to boiling point once more. 'I *never* pretend,' she said hotly, 'and I don't lie either. I did not receive a letter, although if I had it would have made no difference whatsoever to how I felt—feel. You had an affair with Tanya West and there had been others before her. I have that on good authority. You shared a double room in Germany reserved under the name of Mr and Mrs Kane. Don't lie to me about that because I phoned the hotel myself to check.'

'Tanya was my secretary and only my secretary,' he ground out, swinging the car round a sharp corner at such speed Marsha had to stifle a little scream. 'The room in Germany was booked in error. She had the double and I took the only other bed in the whole damn place, due to the conference, and spent three nights sharing a twin with a huge Swede who looked as though he weight-lifted for his country and snored like hell. I told you that on the night you left and reiterated it in the letter.'

'Then why was I put through to Tanya when I asked for Mr Kane after the receptionist had confirmed the double room?' Marsha asked as icily as her raw nerves would allow. The way he was driving they would be lucky to see another day.

'I've told you, the room was booked in error. The Swede kindly allowed me to share his room when the hotel asked him, but the room was in his name, not mine. Maybe the receptionist you spoke to hadn't been informed of what had happened. It was one of the biggest conferences of the year, damn it, and the place was heaving.'

He must think she was born yesterday.

'You don't believe me.' As he accelerated to pass a staid family saloon she sat tensely silent because there was nothing more to say. 'I gave you telephone numbers to ring in that letter, and not just the hotel. I had the Swede's business card. I also made you a promise, because of the way you had reacted that night in the car, that I wouldn't try to force you to see me until you were ready, and being ready meant an apology and a declaration of trust.'

The *nerve* of him. Even if all this with Tanya was a mistake—and she didn't think it was for a moment—what about the other liaisons Susan had told her about? Taylor bought silence from people, but he hadn't been able to buy Susan's. Susan had been her friend as well as her sister-in-law, and the episode in Germany had been too much for the other woman to ignore. Susan had sworn her to secrecy at the time, making her promise she wouldn't tell who it was who had informed on him—mainly because Susan's husband worked for her brother and their livelihood depended on Taylor's favour. Well, she hadn't betrayed Susan eighteen months ago and she wasn't about to do so now, much as she would have loved to fling his sister's name into the arena.

She took a deep pull of air. 'If the letter said you wouldn't contact me until I was ready to apologise and trust you, why are we here now? I don't trust you, Taylor, and I would rather walk through coals of fire than apologise to you.'

He muttered something under his breath before saying, his voice curt, 'I am not going to allow you to wreck both our lives, that's why. Not through foolish pride.'

Pride? If they hadn't been travelling at such speed she would have been tempted to knock his block off, she thought poetically. As it was she contented herself with saying scathingly, 'I've salvaged by life and it's a good one, so speak for yourself.'

'I don't believe you.'

They were now in territory she recognised as being a street or so away from where Taylor's palatial home dwelt, so in view of her safety, and everyone else's within the immediate vicinity, she waited until the car had actually passed through the open gates and was travelling up the scrunchy drive before she said, 'That's your problem.'

He brought the car to a standstill at the bottom of the wide, semi-circular stone steps which led up to the front door, and Marsha forced herself to look about her as though her heart didn't feel as though it was being torn out by its roots. She had been almost demented with bitterness and pain when she had last left here, and certainly in no state to drive. She had hoped if she ever saw this place again she would be able to look at it with a measure of peace in her heart, but it wasn't the case. She felt nearly as wretched with misery as she had then.

Taylor hadn't answered her before he slid out of the car and walked round the bonnet to open her door, and now, as she took the hand he proferred and exited the Aston Martin, the haunting fragrance of lavender teased her nostrils. A bowling-green-smooth lawn bordered both sides of the curving drive, and the huge thatched house was framed by two cooper beech trees, their leaves glowing in the last of the sunlight, but it was the tiny hedges of lavender which ran from the bottom of the largest step in a wide half-moon shape right up to the corners of the house which produced the most evocative memory.

It had been this perfume which had remained with her the first time she had ever visited the house, on her second date with Taylor, and which had scented their nights in their big billowy bed when they had made love till dawn with the windows open to the scents and sounds of the night.

The pain which gripped her now wasn't helped by the warm contact with his skin, which sent a hundred tiny needles of sensation shivering up her arm, and as soon as she was standing she extricated her hand from his.

'You loved this place when the lavender was out.' Taylor spoke quietly, his eyes tight on her pale face.

Her green eyes shot to meet hot amber. He had waited and planned to bring her here when the conditions were just right for maximum effect. She could read it in his face even if his words hadn't confirmed it. The words she hissed at him would have shocked the motherly Hannah into a coma.

Taylor surveyed her flushed face thoughtfully. 'Are you sure that last suggestion is anatomically possible?'

She glared at him. 'You are the most manipulative, scheming, cunning man I've ever met.'

A corner of his mouth twitched. 'Thank you. I think you're pretty exceptional too.'

Suddenly the anger and resentment left her body in a great whoosh of sadness and regret for what might have been if he had been different. Or maybe if *she* had been different? If she had been bright and beautiful and sophisticated, like the women he had dated before he'd met her, maybe then he would have continued to love her and wouldn't have needed anyone else. Maybe then she would have been enough for him?

She wasn't aware of the expression on her face, or the droop to her mouth, so when he said, very softly, 'I want you back, Fuzz. I don't want a divorce,' she stared at him for a moment, her breath catching in her throat at the matter-of-fact way he had spoken.

'That…that's impossible; you know it is.' She took a step backwards away from him, her eyes wide.

He shook his head. 'No, it isn't. It's incredibly simple. I tell my lawyer to go to hell and you do the same with yours.'

'Nothing's changed,' she protested shakily.

'Exactly.' He eyed her sternly.

'What I mean is—'

'I know what you mean,' he interrupted. 'What *I* mean is I was faithful to you before you left and I've been faithful since. No women. Not one. That's the bottom line.'

She stood straight and still, her chin high and her body language saying more than any words could have done.

He stared at her a moment more before saying quietly, 'When I find out who whispered the sweet nothings in your ear, they'll wish they'd never been born. Who was it, Fuzz? Who wanted to destroy us so badly they fed your insecurities with the very thing you most feared?'

'What?' She reached out to lean against the car, needing its solid support. If he had yelled at her she could have taken it in her stride, but the almost tender note in his voice frightened her to death. 'I don't know what you're talking about. I'm not insecure. Just because I'm not the sort of woman to turn a blind eye to—'

'Insecurities which came into being when your mother dumped you in the hands of the social services,' he interrupted again, his voice flat now, and holding a ruthlessness which was more typical of him. 'Insecurities which grew in that damn awful place you were brought up in and which crippled you emotionally. The ones which told you no one could love you or want you or need you, not for ever anyway. Why would they when the one person in all the world who should love you beyond life gave you away like an unwanted gift?'

'Stop it.' Her face was as white as lint. Even her lips had lost their colour. 'Why are you doing this?'

'To kick-start the process of making you wake up,' he said, no apology in his tone. 'I'd been waiting eighteen months for it to happen naturally before I realised I could wait eighteen years—or eighty. I'm not that patient.'

'I hate you.' She stared at him, wounded beyond measure by the things he had said.

'No, you don't,' he said evenly. 'You just think you do.'

She was saved having to make a reply when the front door opened on a delighted screech of her name. 'Marsha! Oh, Marsha, honey.' Hannah's plump bulk fairly flew down the steps, and the next moment Marsha was enfolded in a floral scented embrace that took the breath out of her lungs.

'Don't throttle her, woman.'

She was released to the sound of Taylor's mordant voice and Hannah moved her back a little, staring into her face as she said, 'You're thinner. You're too thin. You're not eating enough.'

'Oh, Hannah.' It was as if she had only seen her the day before, Marsha thought wonderingly. The last eighteen months had been swept away in a moment of time and now she couldn't prevent the tears flowing as she said, 'I've missed you.'

Hannah hugged her again, and there was no reproach in her voice or manner when she said, 'Not as much as I've missed you, child.'

They clung together a moment longer before Taylor's

voice brought them apart once more, saying, 'Much as I hate to mention it, I'm starving. Can we continue the reunion inside?'

'Oh, you, thinking of your stomach at a time like this,' Hannah chided smilingly through her own tears.

Marsha walked up the steps and into the house with her arm in Hannah's, and once in the beautifully light-oak panelled hall the Jamaican housekeeper pushed her in the direction of the drawing room, saying, 'The cocktails are all ready. You go in and sit down a while, and I'll call you through in a few minutes.'

'Thank you, Hannah.' It was Taylor who answered, taking Marsha's arm as he led her into the gracious rose and pale lilac high-ceilinged room which had French windows opening out on to the grounds at the back of the house.

Marsha knew what she would see if she walked over to where antique lace was billowing gently in the slight breeze from the garden. Clipped yews bordering an old stone wall, in front of which was a manicured lawn enclosed by flower beds, and behind it a splendid Edwardian summerhouse now used as a changing room for the rectangular swimming pool of timeless style that Taylor had installed ten years before, when he had bought the house.

She walked over to one of the two-seater sofas dotted about the room and sat down before she said, 'You should have told me you were bringing me here.'

'You wouldn't have agreed to come,' he answered quietly, a silky note in his voice.

'So you tricked me. Clever you.' It was acidic.

He poured a pale pink cocktail, and then one for himself, and it was only after he had handed her the tall fluted glass and sat down himself opposite her that he said, 'Why is it easier to believe lies than the truth? Have you ever asked yourself that?'

'Meaning regarding you and Tanya, I suppose?' she said flatly.

He sat back in his seat, studying her over the rim of his glass. 'Has it never occurred to you that you might be wrong about all this?'

Hundreds, thousands of times, but wishful thinking didn't stand up when confronted by harsh reality. She would never forget the churning of her stomach when she had made that call to Germany, or the sickening feeling when the hotel receptionist had put her through to Taylor's room and the bright, fluttery voice of Tanya had answered. 'No.' She swallowed. It was hard to lie with his eyes on her. 'I might be a fool but I'm not certifiable.'

'I see.' He set down his drink and then steepled his fingers, his gaze never leaving her face for a moment. 'Then we won't waste any more time tonight discussing it. Drink your cocktail.' And he smiled the smile which lit up his face. The rat. The low-down, cheating, lying, philandering rat.

Marsha stared at him, the misery she had been feeling replaced by a healthy dose of anger. How dared he sit there smiling like the cat with the cream when he had all but destroyed her eighteen months ago? Without taking her eyes from his, she set her glass down with a little touch of defiance. 'Is Tanya still working for you?' she asked baldly. He was not going to dictate what they discussed and what they didn't, not after kidnapping her!

'Of course.' He undid his dinner jacket as he spoke, slipping it off and slinging it across the room to another sofa, before loosening his tie so it hung in two thin strands on either side of his throat.

'Of course.' She put a wealth of sarcasm into her voice.

He picked up his glass again, draining it before he added, 'But only for the next month or so, unfortunately. I shall be sorry to lose her; she's a damn good secretary and they don't grow on trees.'

'She's leaving you?' Marsha raised fine eyebrows in what she hoped was a mocking expression. 'Dear, dear. A better offer?'

'Not exactly.' He stood up, moving across to her and handing her her glass again. 'Drink up. There's time for another before Hannah calls us through, and I've ordered a taxi for later.'

She accepted the glass simply because she felt she needed the fortifying effect the alcohol would have on her nerves. It tasted heavenly, but Hannah had always been able to mix a mean cocktail. After two sips, she said, 'If it's not a better offer, why is she going?' Lovers' tiff?

'She's having a baby at the end of September.'

Marsha drank deeply, using the action as an excuse to break the force of his eyes on hers. 'Thank you.' She held out the empty glass with a brittle smile. 'That was lovely.'

'Wasn't it?' he murmured softly. He strolled over to the cocktail cabinet, his movements easy.

Marsha wondered whether Hannah would support her if she demanded to leave. So this was why he had made the move after all this time? Tanya was pregnant. By him? The pain which sliced through her was too severe to continue down that path, so she brushed the possibility aside until she could consider it when she was alone.

'I think her husband wants a little girl; he has two boys from a previous relationship,' Taylor continued with his back to her as he poured two more drinks. 'But I guess all that matters in the long run is that the child is healthy.'

She sat very still as he turned and walked back to her, accepting the drink from him with a slight inclination of her head. So Tanya was married? When had that happened? The other woman had been a Miss when she had left Taylor. Had Tanya been seeing Taylor as well as the man who was now her husband at the time of the Germany trip? Did her husband know she had been more than just a secretary to Taylor at one time? A hundred questions were buzzing in her head, but she couldn't ask any of them.

She raised her head as Taylor took the chair he had vacated, and for a moment her gaze met his. Her breath caught for a second at the look in his eyes. It was brief, and instantly veiled, but for a moment she had seen the inner man, the man she had known in the intimacy of their bed. The vital, vigorous, dynamic lifeforce which was Taylor, a force which let nothing and no one stand in the way of something he wanted. It was this magnetic power which had made her flee that night eighteen months ago, before he had had a chance to convince her that black was white, before that dark, dangerous energy of his reached out and smothered all rational thought and sense.

Contrary to what she'd expected, Taylor said nothing more as they sat and sipped their drinks in a silence which was fairly shrieking. The rich scents from the garden were drifting into the room on the warm breeze and a summer twilight was beginning to fall. The sounds of the birds as they began to settle down for the night and the drone of lazy insects about their business were the only intrusion.

Marsha resisted glancing Taylor's way. She could feel he was watching her, his long lean body stretched out indolently in a very masculine pose, the amber eyes hooded and intense. He hadn't moved a muscle, and yet the very air around them had become sensuous and coaxing. He could do that, she thought crossly, willing herself not to fidget in spite of the ripples of sexual awareness which had caused her nipples to flower and harden and her mouth to become dry. He could seduce by his very presence alone, and it was galling to have to recognise that his power over her body was just the same as it had always been.

She stared into her cocktail glass, determined it wouldn't be her who would break the silence. And she wouldn't mention Tanya West—or whatever her name was now—again either. Pregnant… The rush of emotion was so strong she had to purposely relax her fingers or risk breaking the stem of the glass. There had been a time when she had ached to have Taylor's baby, and it had only been his insistence that they have some time enjoying each other together first that had prevented her from stopping taking the Pill. Of course she hadn't been aware that Taylor was busy 'enjoying' other women too, she reflected sourly.

A minor commotion in the garden involving a great deal of frenzied squawking brought Taylor out of his chair in one smooth, fluid movement. To Marsha's absolute bewilderment, he bent down behind a sofa close to the open French doors, re-emerging a second later with what looked like a child's water gun.

'Taylor?' The question she'd been about to put to him was lost in the furore as he leapt out into the garden, firing as he went in a very personable imitation of James Bond. A moment later a loud yowl was added to the hubbub in the garden.

'Got him.' As Marsha joined Taylor outside, curiosity having got the better of her, he turned to her, satisfaction written all over his handsome face. 'A couple more soakings and he'll get the message.'

'Who will get what message?'

'The neighbourhood tom. He's after the resident blackbird's fledglings in one of the yews. The water doesn't hurt him, but it sure as hell dents his pride when he skulks off like a drowned rat. Any day now and his male ego will acknowledge he can't take any more of this.'

And Taylor would know all about male ego. Marsha was about to voice the thought when a blackbird sailed by their heads in what looked suspiciously like a victory dance. Taylor called after it, 'Right on, buddy! He doesn't stand a chance.'

This was the man who had started and built up a multi-million-pound business before he was thirty. Marsha felt she knew what Alice had felt like in Wonderland.

'Listen.' As she went to speak Taylor moved his head on one side, listening intently.

'What?' she whispered. 'Is the cat back?'

'No.' He grinned at her, slinging the gun over his shoulder as he turned towards the house. 'Hannah's calling us for dinner.'

CHAPTER THREE

THE dinner was wonderful, but Marsha had known it would be. Hannah was an excellent cook. As course followed delicious course, accompanied by a wine which was truly superb, Marsha was aware that Taylor had set himself out to be the perfect dinner companion.

He talked of inconsequential things, his manner easy, but Marsha kept reminding herself she wasn't fooled by his lazy air and lack of aggression. This was Taylor, and she forgot it at her peril. She had lived with this man for eighteen months, and known him for nearly nine months before that, and one thing that time had taught her was that he was single-minded and unapologetically ruthless when he wanted something. And right now that was her.

The dining table had been intimately set for two, complete with candles and roses and scented napkins. In spite of her bulk, Hannah glided in and out with each course, her face beaming whenever Marsha glanced at her but otherwise uncharacteristically silent.

A cold-blooded seduction scene, Marsha told herself, and Taylor had used his charm to obtain Hannah's assistance. What had he told the housekeeper about their break-up? Certainly not the truth; she would bet her life on it.

It was after dessert—a velvety, luxurious, smooth chocolate terrine topped with fresh cream and strawberries—that Marsha decided enough was enough. She had just related an amusing incident which had happened that day at work and he had laughed, the hard angles of his face breaking up into attractive curves. The danger signals had gone off big-time.

What was she *doing*? she asked herself furiously. How on earth had she managed to get herself into this ridiculous position? Taylor had re-entered her life with all the finesse and thoughtfulness of a charging bull elephant, and she had let him get away with bullying her into having dinner with him. And in their marital home at that! She needed her head looking at.

'What's the matter?'

She looked up to meet Taylor's unreadable eyes, trying to disguise the sudden panic in hers by keeping her face deadpan. 'I'm sorry?' she asked coolly, through her whirling dismay.

'Correct me if I'm wrong, but I suspect we're suddenly back to square one.' The dark brows had drawn together. 'Why?'

Did he have any idea how powerfully attractive he was? Marsha moistened dry lips.

But of course he did, she answered silently in the next moment. Born in a high-rise slum to a mother who drank and a father who was rarely around, Taylor had used his devastating looks, charm and rapier-sharp intelligence from an early age.

He had left home at fifteen, started his own sound equipment business at eighteen, with money he had begged and borrowed, and at twenty had been in a position to give Susan—who was four years younger than him—a home, after their mother had died of a drink-related problem and their father had taken himself off for good.

At the tender age of twenty-three he'd had his first million under his belt and more had followed. He was a self-made man, now thirty-five years of age, with a name which was both respected and feared for the ruthlessness it embodied.

But he had never been ruthless with her. The thought came from nowhere, and she countered the weakening effect it had on her resolve. Not outwardly anyway, but then secret affairs were the worst sort of ruthlessness. Susan had been sure there had been others before Tanya, but even if there hadn't, one infidelity was one too many.

'I've no idea what you are talking about,' she said crisply. 'We're not "back" anywhere. We've never moved in the first place. You asked me to dinner because—' She stopped abruptly. Why exactly *had* he asked her?

'Because I wanted to be with you?' he suggested smoothly.

'Because you wanted us to part in a civilised way.' She remembered civilised had been in there somewhere.

'Making it up as you go along.' He smiled, but it didn't reach the magnificent tawny eyes. 'Nothing changes, I see.'

She glared at him. If anyone in this room suffered from a severe aversion to the truth, it wasn't her. 'Now, look here—'

'No, *you* look, my sweet, headstrong, perverse wife.' He had risen with one of the swift animal-like movements characteristic of him, and before she could react he had drawn her to her feet, both hands gripping her elbows as he held her in front of him. 'I intend to talk this through.'

'I don't want to talk,' she protested, angry at the way his nearness was affecting her equilibrium. 'There's nothing to say and no need to talk.'

'Maybe you're right at that.' His eyes had locked on hers, drawing her into the glowing amber as he filled her vision. 'Action speaks louder than words, isn't that what they say?'

She had arched back, but in one expert movement he had drawn her into him, his mouth coming down quickly on hers.

She struggled, but it was like beating herself against solid stone as he held her with the force of his body, his mouth plundering hers. She knew she was fighting herself as much as Taylor—the second his lips had touched hers she wanted him with a passion which frightened her more than anything else could have done. This was the man who had betrayed her, broken her heart and then sailed back into her life as though he had every right to be there. She couldn't, she mustn't, give in to him.

But the desire was as it had always been from the first moment she had met him—clean and hot and senseless. He was the master of the senses, her senses, whether she liked it or not, she thought desperately. He always had been.

The kiss was deep and potent, the taste and smell of him spinning in her head as she fought for control of the need which was raging through her flesh. It had been so long since she had been in his arms like this, and desire was a fire inside her which was spreading however she tried to dampen it down.

His mouth was urgent and hungry, but not cruel. Nevertheless, as she managed to jerk her head away for an instant, she gasped, 'You're hurting me. Let me go.'

Even as his mouth claimed hers again she felt him tense and knew her words had registered. For a moment he continued to hold her, so she could feel every inch of his powerful body, and then, with a low groan, he wrenched his mouth from hers. He was breathing hard, the trembling she'd felt in his body mirrored in hers. She was conscious of his chest rising and falling under the fine linen shirt as he fought for control for one more second, and then suddenly—regretfully—she was free. And now she was fighting an almost overwhelming craving to fling herself into his arms again.

She instinctively hid behind attack being the best defence. 'How dare you manhandle me?' She ignored the hot, insistent flow of desire flowing through her shaking limbs. 'You try anything like that again and I swear I'll scream the place down. Maybe even Hannah would think twice about working for a man who forces women.'

He surveyed her for what seemed like an eternity without speaking, his hands now thrust into the pockets of his trousers. 'Methinks the lady protests too hard.' And then he smiled, as if amused.

He had to be the most infuriating man ever born. Why couldn't he get angry at what she had just said? Instead he stood there looking immensely pleased with life, the arrogant, two-timing, conceited swine. She tried to match his composure when she said, 'Don't flatter yourself, Taylor. I'm counting the minutes, let alone the hours until I'm free of you for good.'

His smile disappeared. She would have liked to have felt triumphant, but merely felt sick at heart. To think they had come to this when it had been so *good*.

The entrance of Hannah, with a tray of coffee and the special shortcake she made—which was utterly delicious and melted in the mouth—silenced further sparring.

Hannah glanced at them both but made no comment,

although the atmosphere was such you didn't need to be the brain of Britain to work out all was not well. Whether the housekeeper had noticed her swollen lips and tousled hair, Marsha wasn't sure, but if she had Hannah was being the soul of discretion—which wasn't like her.

Marsha had sat down as the door had opened, but Taylor remained standing by her chair until Hannah left the room again, at which point he walked over to the window in the dining room and stood looking out into the dark night.

Marsha looked down into her glass and wondered if the excess of wine she'd consumed was making her maudlin. But it wasn't the alcohol. It was the sight of Taylor looking good enough to eat that had her forcing back the tears. She wanted to be over him, she *needed* to be over him, so why couldn't she manage her feelings as she'd learnt to manage the rest of her life?

She could feel the tension within mounting and wondered how much more of his silence she could take. But she wasn't going to speak first. Silly, maybe, perhaps even childish, but she needed every small victory she could get with Taylor.

'Fancy taking our coffees outside?' He turned as he spoke, his tone so perfectly normal and matter-of-fact that Marsha could have floored him. Here was she, tied up in knots and suffering the torment of the damned, and he was Mr Cool.

She shrugged nonchalantly, lifting her eyes to meet his. 'If you like, and then I really will have to go. I've an important meeting first thing tomorrow.'

'Oh, yes?' He raised enquiring eyebrows as he walked over to the table and lifted the coffee pot.

'Jeff—he's my boss and one of the producers—wants

me to discuss ideas for a documentary we've been looking into. His researchers have given me reams of information, but I need to pull it together and sell the concept overall.'

She was unaware of how animated her voice had become as she talked about the work she loved, but he had stopped filling the coffee cups and was giving her his full attention as he said, 'You're his assistant, I take it?'

She nodded. It had been a huge boost to her self-esteem when she had snatched the coveted job from a host of other hopefuls, some of them internal applicants, mainly because Jeff had remembered her from her pre-marriage days. She had come across his path whilst on a training scheme for people who were expected to rise to become producers or managers for a different television company, and although the contact had only been fleeting he had obviously been impressed with her.

It had been her decision, along with a little gentle persuasion from Taylor, to leave the other company after her marriage, mainly because the sort of hours and commitment the five-year training scheme involved could be very antisocial, and she had wanted to be with her new husband as much as possible. In hindsight, it was a decision she bitterly regretted.

Her first at university, in English and Communication Studies, had meant constant hard work and dedication, but it had lifted her into the realm of high-calibre graduates. This had given her a ticket on to the training scheme, at which only a mere handful of the thousands who applied each year were successful. And then she had thrown it all away. But for the lucky break with Jeff she could well have found herself making the tea and sweeping up rather than back in the hub of things.

'I'm pleased for you, Fuzz.'

His quiet voice brought her out of her thoughts and her eyes focused on his sombre face. She stared at him, knowing that certain something which had always used to sizzle between them was still there and hating the power it gave him. She made her voice cool when she said, 'Really?' putting a wealth of disbelief in the one word.

'Uh-huh. Really.' He had crossed his arms over his chest, studying her with those strangely beautiful tawny eyes which had always seemed to look straight into her soul.

'Forgive me, but I find that difficult to believe,' she said, allowing her gaze to freeze.

'I do—forgive you, that is,' he returned comfortably. 'Mainly because I understand now just how fragile and insecure you are beneath that beautiful, resilient exterior.'

Insecure again. If he said that word once more she wouldn't be held responsible for her actions!

'It was a mistake for you to give up your career when we married, but I didn't realise that until it was too late. You needed the sense of self-worth it gave you. I thought I would be enough for you, that I could give you everything you needed, but it was too soon.'

'Cut the psychoanalysis, Taylor,' she said stonily. 'The mistake I made was trusting you; it's as simple as that.'

'Nothing is simple where you are concerned, as I've learnt to my cost.' He finished pouring the coffee as he spoke, seemingly totally unconcerned by her declaration. 'I always thought someone was innocent until proven guilty in this country.' He turned suddenly to face her for an instant. 'Where's your proof, Fuzz?'

Her body jerked as if she had been stung, but although she eyed him hotly she said nothing.

'You won't even do me the courtesy of allowing me to challenge the person who caused the breakdown of our marriage.'

'You can challenge Tanya any day,' she bit back swiftly.

'Tanya is as innocent as I am of all charges.' It was laconic. He placed the cups, sugar and cream, along with the shortbread, on the tray Hannah had left propped against the table. 'Shall we?' He waved his hand towards the garden before picking up the tray.

She walked past him out of the room, continuing down the hall and into the drawing room, whereupon she made her way out of the French doors. The automatic lights clicked on as she stepped on to the patio area beyond which the lawn lay. The sound of the small fountain falling into the lily pond at the side of the patio reminded her of many happy meals eaten alfresco, but she resolutely refused to dwell on the memory.

She walked across to the wicker table and ticking-cushioned chairs she and Taylor had chosen together just after their marriage, when she had persuaded him that eating outside was fun, sitting down facing the yews and old stone wall. The flower beds were a riot of colour, their scent adding to the beauty all around her, and the sky was black velvet, pierced with stars.

She didn't speak as Taylor placed the tray on the table and sat down, but as he went to add cream and sugar to her cup she said, 'I take mine black now, thank you.'

He quirked a brow. 'The cream and sugar queen?'

'We drink coffee all day at work, and I've got used

to it black.' It was a silly thing, but she was pleased she'd surprised him.

'I can see I mustn't assume anything,' he drawled mockingly, making her feel as though she was being puerile for the sake of it.

But she *had* changed in the last eighteen months, she thought militantly, and drinking her coffee black was the least of it. 'Quite so,' she responded evenly, as though she hadn't caught the inflection in his voice, and she ignored the slight smile twisting his lips with an aplomb she was proud of.

There were six chairs grouped round the table, but he had chosen to sit in the one next to her rather than opposite, as she had expected, and now he was so close his shoulder was almost brushing hers. With an effort, Marsha relaxed her body, determined not to give him the satisfaction of knowing how tense she was.

Some moments had ticked by before she said, 'What did you mean when you said you'd known where I was every minute since we split up?' It had been at the back of her mind all evening, she realised now with a dart of surprise as she heard herself speak.

'Exactly that.'

She wasn't going to let him get away with being so succinct. 'That's not an answer,' she said, finishing her coffee.

'Of course it is.' He turned his head, the amber light on her face, but she kept her gaze on the shadowed garden. 'You didn't really think I would just let you walk out of the house and my life, did you?'

Her stomach trembled. 'Who…? How…?'

She didn't know quite how to put it, but he seemed to understand what she was trying to say. He shifted slightly in his chair, his long legs stretched out in front of him, and as she caught a faint whiff of his aftershave a hundred nerves went haywire.

'I employed someone, okay?' he said mildly.

No, not okay! *Mega* not okay. 'You *employed* someone?' she said, so shrilly a number of birds protested in the trees surrounding the garden as their slumber was interrupted. 'You had me watched? Like...like a criminal?'

'Don't be childish,' he said calmly as her eyes met his. 'I wanted to make sure you were all right, that was all. You are my wife, my responsibility.'

'The hell I am!'

He clicked his tongue disapprovingly, shaking his head at her. She deeply regretted there was no coffee left in her cup to fling at him. 'I would like to leave now.' She stood to her feet, her eyes blazing.

'Sure.' To her absolute amazement, Taylor rose lazily. 'The taxi's been outside for the last few minutes. I didn't think you'd want to be too late on a working day.'

'Who was he? This guy you had spy on me?' Much as she would have liked to storm off with her nose in the air, she really wanted to know.

'He was a she, and from one of the most reputable firms in the country.' He looked at her squarely. 'And there was no question of spying. She merely checked now and again that you weren't in any trouble, that everything was okay. That was it.'

'And who I saw and where I went and with whom?' Indignation lit her eyes and flushed her cheeks.

He was magnificently unperturbed. 'Of course. You are my wife.'

'We are *separated*.'

'You're still my wife, Marsha.' The use of her name

checked her even more than the tone of his voice, which had suddenly chilled.

She looked into amber eyes which had become as dangerous as those of a big cat, and just as hard. 'I shall never forgive you for this,' she said shakily. 'To have me watched, put under surveillance as though *I'm* the one in the wrong—' She wished with all her heart she *had* met someone in the last months, gone out on a date or two, flirted a little—anything to puncture that giant ego.

'Then it is merely another crime to be added to the list, yes?' He shrugged as though bored.

'And you obviously don't care about any of your crimes, right?' she snapped, furiously angry with his offhand manner and lack of remorse.

'If you are referring to my supposed affair with Tanya, I plead innocent to all charges, remember?'

She glared at him, wondering how it was that he could so get under her skin, even when she knew exactly what he was playing at. She ought to be able to ignore his arrogance, but it grated on her unbearably. 'I want the bloodhound called off.'

'I doubt the very attractive woman concerned would appreciate being labelled a dog.'

He was laughing at her! She stared into the hard face, quivering with righteous indignation. 'I can think of worse things to call her,' she said forcefully.

'I don't doubt it.'

'Does she know the sort of man she's working for?'

'I think so.' He was regarding her lazily. 'More to the point, do you?'

'Only too well.'

'Now, *that* I doubt.' He caught her upper arms in his hands, holding her in front of him and looking deep into her eyes as he said, 'But before I'm finished you will know, Marsha. That's a promise.'

'Let go of me.' She stood rigid in his grasp, glaring furiously up at him. 'I don't appreciate being subjected to brute force.'

'Brute force?' His eyes pierced her with laser brightness. 'There's times I wonder what planet you're on.'

His complete refusal to accept any blame for his actions made her see red. 'You're the lowest of the low—you know that, don't you?' she hissed bitterly. 'I hate you—'

Anything else she might have said was cut off by the simple expedient of his mouth on hers. She knew enough not to struggle this time, willing herself to show no feeling at all as he brought all his sexual experience to the fore in a kiss that was tender and erotic and deep in turn. He gently probed her mouth until her lips parted for him of their own volition as resistance drained from her, in spite of all her efforts to remain unmoved.

He was just too good at this, she thought feverishly. He always had been. In the early days she had been enchanted to find a man who kissed like Taylor, who made it into an art. The trouble was it had left her with no defences, no barriers to the response he could always bring forth with seemingly effortless skill.

She knew she was melting against him, and yet she could no more have stopped her body's response than she could have stopped breathing, and the past and the present were forgotten as the magic that was his mouth took her senses. Taylor shifted his stance slightly to take more of her weight, one arm going round her waist and the other moving to take a handful of her hair as he pulled her head back gently for greater access to her mouth. The position and feel of him brought a torrent of memories to mind, and all of them good.

His tongue curled round hers, probing in a way that sent tremors throughout her whole body, and then his mouth moved to one earlobe, nibbling gently. Heat was flowing in her veins, intensified by his tongue as it traced a delicate path in and around her ear in a sensual pattern that had her legs trembling.

Her eyes were closed now, colours and sensation merging as she gave herself utterly to the bewitching assault. She could feel his arousal, hard against her softness, and it added to the pleasure she was experiencing. Her body felt as if it was one hot, sensual nerve.

'You're so beautiful, so delicious.' The soft whisper came at a time when he was caressing her aching breasts with sure fingers, each light touch sending electricity bolts right down to her toes. 'I could eat you, devour you.'

And she wanted him to. She couldn't stop her hips moving against him in an invitation that was as old as time, and moans shuddered through her body as the scent of him surrounded her in an intoxicating bubble.

He was powerfully muscled, without an ounce of surplus flesh, his body hard and uncompromisingly male, and as her hands roamed over his wide shoulders and strong chest her desire reached fever pitch. She felt the cool night air on her breasts and realised he must have undone the tiny mother-of-pearl buttons on her jacket without her being aware of it. But it was when his hands cradled her breasts, his fingers having pushed the filmy lace of her bra out of the way, that she found the strength to push him away.

'No.' She took a step backwards, her legs shaking so

much she felt they wouldn't hold her. 'I don't want this.'

He made no move towards her, merely raising a dark eyebrow as he said, 'That's not what your body is saying.'

She stared at him, forced to admit to herself that her whole body was so sensitised by his lovemaking that every move he made registered on her nervous system. 'I'm not saying that I'm not physically attracted to you,' she said carefully, 'but that is something quite different.'

'You've lost me.' He sounded tolerant, and she didn't trust that. Tolerance was not one of Taylor's attributes.

'We're no longer an item, Taylor. That's what I'm saying,' she said firmly.

'We never were an "item", Fuzz. We were married, remember?' He didn't sound quite so tolerant now. 'Or should I say we *are* married.'

She did up the buttons on her jacket as swiftly as her trembling hands would permit, furious with herself for giving in so easily to what was clearly a ploy on his part. He thought he only had to turn on the charm and she would fall at his feet, she thought caustically, ignoring the little voice in her head which added nastily that he was quite right.

'I think it's high time I went home.' She raised her chin as she spoke, desperate to hide the burning sense of shame that had flooded every part of her.

'You are home.'

'You know exactly what I mean.'

'You mean you want to go back to that lonely little box you inhabit, right?'

She reared up like a scalded cat at the insult to the home she had so carefully put together. 'You say the taxi is waiting?' she asked, with a cool dignity she was very pleased about afterwards, when she thought about it.

'That it is.' The amusement was back in his voice, and nothing could have been more guaranteed to hit her on the raw.

'Then thank you for dinner,' she said icily, 'but I really do have to leave now.'

'I'll tell Hannah you're leaving. You *were* going to say goodbye to her, weren't you?' he added disparagingly.

'Of course I was.' She frowned at him, hurt that he could suggest otherwise. 'I've no quarrel with Hannah.'

'She'll be most relieved to hear it,' he drawled mockingly.

'I hate you.'

'That's the third time you've said that today. Are you trying to convince me or yourself?'

CHAPTER FOUR

MARSHA awoke very early the next morning, before it was light, after a sleep which had been troubled and restless. After making herself coffee, she took a mug out on to the balcony along with her duvet, snuggling under its folds as she sat and watched the dawn break.

Taylor had insisted on accompanying her home in the taxi the night before, despite all her heated protests, but contrary to her expectations hadn't done so much as hold her hand on the journey back to the bedsit. After telling the driver to wait, he had escorted her to the door of the building—again with her protests ringing in his ears—and then up the stairs to her floor.

She had faced him defiantly then, waiting for the move she'd been sure he would make after that scorching kiss back at his house in Harrow, but he had merely nodded to her without smiling once she had opened her front door, wished her goodnight and left.

Which left her where? she asked herself now, her tired eyes searching the pink and mother-of-pearl sky in front of her as though it could provide an answer. Had he admitted defeat? Was he going to leave her alone now she had made it crystal-clear how she still felt?

She drained the mug, setting it down on the floor beside the chair before letting her head fall back against the cane as she shut her eyes. She *was* right about all this—him, their marriage, Tanya, everything—wasn't she? But of course she was. She had to be. The misery of the last eighteen months couldn't be for nothing. He had slept with Tanya in Germany, even if he hadn't done so before, and from what Susan had said there had been a before. Several befores.

But he had seemed so…plausible. She opened her eyes again. The hum of traffic and sounds from the street beyond the cul-de-sac were louder now the city had begun to wake up and go about its business. But then he'd always been able to make anyone believe anything. That was one of the gifts he had which had shot him from obscurity to extreme wealth in such a short time.

She wriggled restlessly, drawing her cold toes into her hands under the duvet. The day was due to be another hot one, but the morning air was decidedly cool.

She still loved him. The truth which had haunted her sleep wouldn't be denied in the harsh light of day. She would always love him. The love which had been such a blessing when they were together and happy would forever be a millstone round her neck. And because she loved him so much she could never go back to him.

She rose, her movements jerky with pain, and, leaving the duvet on the chair, strode back into the room to make herself another coffee.

She had been aware of Taylor with every cell in her body last night, and that alone told her she had to be strong. She had done her days and nights of weeping for what might have been. That was over. Maybe if she had been a different type of woman, one who was able to turn a blind eye to her man's little liaisons, perhaps, or if she hadn't loved him quite so much, things might have been different. As it was, he would destroy her.

She didn't intend to live the rest of her life looking about her for the next notch on Taylor's bedpost to emerge, or, worse still, become like one or two women she'd known in the past, who had gone through their partner's pockets every night looking for signs that they were playing away from home.

She cupped her cold hands round the hot mug of coffee, inhaling its fragrance even as the chill within deepened. She had had her time of being naive and starry-eyed, of thinking that there really was such a thing as happy endings in this tough, dog-eat-dog world, but she knew better now. And she would not make the same mistake again.

Taylor had left her without a word last night, and that was for the best. She saw that now. He had got to her despite all her efforts to keep him at bay, he had breached the wall she had built around her emotions as easily as he had always done, but she would make sure it did not happen again. She wasn't quite sure how she would manage it, but she would—if they met again, that was.

She drank the coffee scalding hot, sitting at the breakfast bar, before marching on to the balcony and retrieving the duvet from the chair.

Once the bedsit was put in order, she showered and washed her hair, making up her face quickly and expertly before dressing in a pale lilac cotton suit with a boatneck jacket and short pencil-slim skirt. She didn't normally dress so formally for the office, but with the forthcoming meeting in mind she knew it would be expected.

It was still only half-past six when she left the house, but she wanted to clear her head by walking to work, and arriving so early would give her plenty of time to be word-perfect for the meeting at ten o'clock.

It was a beautiful morning, the streets already spangled by sunlight but the chill of the night causing the city air to smell clean and fresh for once. It was on mornings like these that she and Taylor had eaten breakfast in their bathrobes on the patio, the twitter of the birds and the drone of the odd aircraft overhead mingling with their laughter and the smell of warm croissants, fresh from Hannah's oven. She hadn't been able to enjoy a croissant since she had left.

She frowned, annoyed with herself for letting the memory intrude on the morning. She had to be focused on her work and nothing else, she knew that, so no more mawkish thoughts. She nodded determinedly at the declaration, striding out with renewed purpose.

Her steps slowed fractionally as she approached the television building, inner turmoil reasserting itself as she faced the prospect that her marriage would soon be the current news on the gossip grapevine. But she couldn't worry about that, and it was no one's business but hers after all. She would explain to Nicki, she owed the other woman that, but other than with her secretary she would not discuss the matter, should anyone have the temerity to raise it.

Once in her office she kicked off her high-heeled shoes, hung her jacket on the back of her chair, and within moments had become immersed in all the Baxter paperwork.

Nicki arrived prompt at eight-thirty, at which time Marsha suggested they lunch together and have a chat, but other than that she continued to pore over the files on her desk.

At ten she sailed into the meeting, looking confident and self-assured, and by half-past she knew she had won everyone over—everyone except Penelope, that was. The other woman's cold blue eyes had been the first thing she'd seen when she had entered the boardroom, and after Penelope had cut her dead when she had smiled at her, Marsha knew she wasn't the flavour of the month.

'I just don't know if we should take on a conglomerate like Manning Dale on such…scant information.' Penelope looked round the table reflectively, her thin eyebrows raised. 'We don't want another lawsuit thrown at us so soon after the last one. I mean, how do we *know* the big boys stepped on Charles Baxter to make him sign away his business? And even if—*if*,' she emphasised, her scarlet-painted lips lingering on the word for a moment, 'they did, it doesn't necessarily follow they've done the same thing before. What we have here is a number of statements, all from people with axes to grind.'

'I disagree,' Jeff North said firmly, his face rather than his voice expressing some surprise that Penelope was taking this tack on what to him was a cut and dried matter. 'From the facts and figures Marsha has presented this morning it's obvious dirty deals have shadowed Manning Dale's success from day one, but this last scam with Baxter ended in a man's death. We need to bring this into the public arena. That's what we're here for.'

'Hmmm.' Penelope glanced at the other top executive in the room, who was effectively Jeff's boss. 'Do you think Marsha has collected enough data, Tim? My fear is that her…enthusiasm for the story has made her a little slapdash.'

Timothy Cassell joined his hands in front of him on the table, studying them for a second or two before he looked up. He had worked with Penelope for more than a decade and knew her very well. For some reason she was gunning for Jeff's assistant, and when she was like this she could be as awkward as blazes. The story was a good one, and they all knew it, but delaying it for a week or two on the pretext of collecting more information wouldn't be the end of the world. Certainly he had no wish to get on Penelope's bad side. They had a policy of 'you scratch my back and I'll scratch yours' which had worked exceedingly well over the years.

He cleared his throat, avoiding looking at Marsha's burning face as he said, 'See what else you can find out, by all means, and we'll look at it again in a couple of weeks. Now, is there anything else while we're all together?'

'Well, yes, this new equipment we've been looking at? I've got the quotes in now, and one in particular is most attractive. Kane International?' And then, as if suddenly realising she was speaking out of turn, Penelope turned to the others in the room, saying sweetly, 'Thank you, everyone. I don't think we need to keep you any longer.'

'What was all that about?' Once they were in the lift, returning to their more lowly floor, Jeff scratched his head in bewilderment as he glanced at Marsha's hot face. 'There's enough information in this lot to satisfy anyone.'

'I think it's my fault.' Marsha had decided that prevarication was pointless. 'Penelope found out I was married yesterday, and was offended she hadn't been informed of the full situation before.'

'You told her?'

'Not exactly.' Marsha took a deep breath. 'The Kane of Kane International is my husband, Jeff. He was here yesterday with Penelope.'

'Ah…'

Much as she would have liked to say Penelope's spite had not affected her, Marsha sat and seethed for the rest of the morning. She had been unfairly criticised and held up as negligent and it was all Taylor's fault, she told herself furiously, refusing to acknowledge the little voice inside which said she was being a mite unfair. But if he hadn't announced they were married yesterday to all and sundry Penelope wouldn't be any the wiser right now and the Baxter story—the first project Jeff had given her sole responsibility for—would be in the bag. His pique at her attempt to cold-shoulder him at the cocktail party yesterday had resulted in her looking a fool this morning in front of everyone. It just wasn't *fair*. But then when had fairness ever been in Taylor's vocabulary? She loathed him, absolutely and utterly *loathed* him. Penelope too. If ever a pair were made for each other, they were.

By lunchtime Marsha had the beginnings of a major headache drumming away behind her eyes, and was as tense as piano wire. She was aware of the small hurried glances Nicki had been giving her ever since she and Jeff had returned from the meeting, but hadn't given her secretary a chance to engage her in conversation once she had informed her that the Baxter story was not yet approved.

Now, as Nicki said carefully, 'We can do lunch another day if you'd rather, Marsha?' she suddenly felt enormously guilty.

'No, not at all.' She forced a smile. 'And I'm sorry for being like a bear with a sore head all morning. Come on, let's go now—and if we're late back, who cares?'

'Fighting talk.' Nicki grinned at her.

To make up for her reluctance, Marsha decided to treat Nicki to lunch at Lyndons—a plush little restaurant a short taxi ride away. Once they had arrived, and were seated at a table for two with an open bottle of wine between them, Marsha relaxed back in her seat with a long sigh. 'Wine in the lunch hour,' she said ruefully. 'I'm slipping, and dragging you down with me.'

'Drag away,' Nicki said with relish as she took a hefty swig at her glass. 'And don't worry about the Baxter story. Everyone knows it's a good one and that Penelope is just having one of her turns.'

'It's the reason for the turn that's bothering me more than the story,' Marsha said soberly.

'Him?' Nicki was nothing if not intuitive.

Marsha nodded. Suddenly she found herself telling Nicki all of it—something she hadn't planned to do at all. She even related her upbringing in the children's home, the two failed attempts at being adopted, which had occurred mainly because she had been convinced her mother would come back for her, her inability to make close friends after her best friend at the home had been adopted and had never contacted her again—the whole story. This between mouthfuls of smoked salmon salad with potato rosti and horseradish cream, followed by lemon chicken and wild rice with courgette strips and peppers. She finished as they were waiting for the dessert menu.

'Wow…' Nicki had shaken her head at regular intervals throughout the account. Now she astounded Marsha by leaning over the table and hugging her with such genuine warmth and sympathy it brought tears to Marsha's eyes. 'And you're still only twenty-seven.'

Nicki hadn't meant to be funny. Whether it was the other girl's face, which was so concerned it was comedic, or the amazed note in Nicki's voice, or yet again the half-bottle of wine, Marsha wasn't sure, but she was relieved to find herself laughing rather than crying. 'I feel decades older,' she admitted ruefully. 'Especially today. I was just getting my life back and he has to turn up again.'

'Some men are like that,' Nicki said, with her vast knowledge of just one. 'Especially when they look as good as he does. They think they just have to snap their fingers and women fall into their lap like ripe plums.'

'He doesn't even have to snap his fingers,' Marsha said truthfully.

Dessert was a wonderful caramelised lemon and orange tart, which they followed with coffee and the restaurant's special homemade truffles. By the time Marsha paid the bill, she knew she had found a wealth of affection and friendliness in the other woman.

She had never had a sister, she reflected as the two of them walked out into the bright sunny afternoon, but if she had she could imagine her being just like Nicki.

It was as they were riding back in the taxi that Nicki said thoughtfully, 'You *are* absolutely positive that this person who told you about Tanya and said there had been others couldn't have had an ulterior motive for lying?'

Marsha nodded. It was the same thought which had occurred to her more than once since last night, but each time she had known she was clutching at straws. She didn't know why she had not told Nicki it was Taylor's sister who had informed on him—it was the only thing she had kept back. Perhaps it was because she had promised Susan she wouldn't divulge her name to Taylor, although there was no chance of Nicki ever telling him.

'You don't have to say a name, but was it a woman?' When Marsha nodded again, Nicki frowned. 'Having seen the man, I'd say there could be an element of doubt there, then.'

Marsha dragged in a deep breath and expelled it resignedly. She'd have to tell her or Nicki would be like a dog with a bone. 'It was his sister, Susan,' she said quietly. 'And she adores him and he, her. So, no motive.'

Nicki glanced at her, her frown deepening. She said nothing, but suggested volumes.

'What?' Marsha stared at the other woman.

'You've never lived in a family environment so you might have an idealised view of siblings,' Nicki said flatly. 'Believe me, being a sister or a brother doesn't automatically qualify you for instant sainthood. There's all sorts of undercurrents in the human psyche, and siblings can bring out the worst in other siblings. When I got a 2.1 at uni, and my sister got a 2.2 two years later, she didn't speak to me for six months.'

'We're talking marriage break-up here, Nicki. Not someone being miffed because of a grade in a degree.'

'Oh, believe me, I could tell you worse stories. Not about my sister,' Nicki added hurriedly, as latent loyalty kicked in, 'but rivalry and jealousy can be at their most intense in families.'

'He's been like mother and father to her all her life,' Marsha argued vehemently. 'She worships the ground he walks on. Even her husband has to take second place to Taylor.'

'Really?' Nicki wrinkled her nose. 'Unhealthy.'

'And she was great to me from day one. She was even my maid of honour.'

'Doesn't mean a thing,' Nicki stated evenly. 'Now, I'm not saying she lied, Marsha, but it's not impossible. Nothing is. At least consider the possibility.'

'Why?' said Marsha, and her brows came together in a perplexed frown at the other girl's doggedness.

'Because you still love him,' Nicki said very quietly. 'And being brought up as you were means there's a whole chunk of experience missing, and that makes you vulnerable.'

'Don't say I'm insecure,' Marsha warned fiercely.

'The word will never pass my lips.'

The rest of the day passed in a whirl of trying to catch up on what she'd missed in the morning as she sat and fumed at Penelope's cavalier treatment of her work. By seven o'clock everyone she normally worked with had gone, and the headache—which the wine had not improved at lunchtime and which she had kept at bay all afternoon with medication—was now a persistent drumming, sending hot flashes of pain into her brain.

When she emerged from the building into the warm June evening she winced as bright sunlight met her eyes, but a search of her handbag revealed she had left her sunglasses at home. Wonderful. The day had just got better and better and looked as if it was going to end on a high note, she thought darkly, the noise of the traffic seeming to roar through her aching head.

'Do you always work this late?'

Her pulse gave a mighty leap and she caught her breath, turning her head to see Taylor standing a yard or so to her right. He was dressed in black jeans and a short-sleeved shirt the colour of his eyes, and he looked wonderful. He smiled at her surprise, his strong white teeth a contrast to his tanned skin.

She thought about her answer for a second or two, instead of coming out with her first response of, What are you doing here? And, considering the headache and the sort of day she'd had, she was rather pleased with the coolness of her voice when she said, 'You should know, surely, with little Miss Private Detective keeping you up to date?'

'Ow.' The devastating smile turned into a grin in which there wasn't a trace of remorse. 'I should have expected that one.'

And he needn't try his charm on her either! He was going to get a nice juicy contract, courtesy of a plainly besotted Penelope, and she was going to get a couple of weeks of frustration, trying to dig up more data when everyone knew all avenues had been exhausted and it wasn't necessary anyway. A shaft of white-hot pain shot through her head and exploded out of her eyes, causing her to visibly wince.

'What's wrong?' The grin had vanished and his voice was soft and deep as he took her arm, drawing her out of the way of other pedestrians and shielding her with his body as they stood at the side of the building.

'Don't.' She shook off his hand, refusing the physical contact. 'It's just a headache, that's all.'

He took in her white face and the blue shadows of exhaustion under her eyes. 'How did the meeting go?' he asked quietly.

'Great.' She stared straight at him. 'Penelope accused me of slackness and implied I wasn't up to the job in front of everyone when she knows full well the story's a hot one. A none too subtle punishment for yesterday. Consequently the story's on hold for a couple of weeks.'

'That's not the end of the world, is it?'

This from a man who had to have everything flowing like clockwork in his work, down to the last 'i' being dotted the second he demanded it. 'Right now, yes, it is,' she said flatly. 'Not that I would expect you to understand for a minute. Your girlfriend is a nasty piece of work, and I resent being made to look a fool simply because I'm your wife—not that that will be the case for much longer.'

His expression altered as he absorbed her words. 'One, Penelope is not my girlfriend. Two, I understand your frustration perfectly. Three, you need a bath, then a light supper, followed by some medication to knock you out, and a cool dark room to sleep the effects off. Agreed?'

It sounded wonderful, but she wasn't about to tell him she didn't have the luxury of a bath in her tiny shower room, or that her fridge boasted nothing more than a wilting lettuce and half a carton of cottage cheese which had probably passed its sell-by date. 'Quite.' She nodded carefully. She wasn't too sure her head wouldn't fall off with any vigorous movement. 'So if you'll excuse me I'll be off home.'

'You don't intend to walk, feeling like you do?'

Not with Taylor in tow. 'I'm going to get a taxi,' she said tersely, his statement about Penelope a massive question mark in her mind. She needed to be somewhere quiet and *think*.

'No need.' He smiled sunnily. 'My car's parked over there. I can have you home in two jiffs.'

'Taylor, how can I put this? I don't want to ride in your car any more than I want to find you waiting for me when I come out of work.' It wasn't true, but he didn't know that. She watched two young girls who couldn't have been more than seventeen or eighteen do a doubletake as they caught sight of him, and hated him for it. Which made her fit for the funny farm, she thought wearily.

'You've a blinding headache and need to get home quickly. I have a car parked ten yards away.' He tilted his head expressively. 'Seems pretty straightforward to me.'

Lots of things seemed straightforward to him, but it did not mean that they were. She wanted to argue, but she was too tired, too muzzy-headed, too heartsore. Suddenly it seemed a whole lot simpler just to allow him to take her home and be done with it. 'Okay.'

'Okay?' He was surprised by the capitulation and it showed.

'I can appreciate logic when it's explained so well,' she said with veiled sarcasm, deciding however bad she felt she wasn't going to make it easy for him.

However, once she was in the safe confines of the car, and the rest of the busy, whirling, hellishly loud world was shut out, the temptation to shut her aching eyes was too strong to resist. The painkillers she had taken at regular intervals during the afternoon—probably *too* regular, she admitted silently—were telling on her. She felt leaden-limbed and exhausted, along with slightly nauseous and dizzy.

'That's right, shut your eyes.' Taylor's voice was no more than a soothing rumble at her side. 'I'll have you home in no time.'

She was not aware she had fallen asleep, but when she heard the murmur of voices and felt a gentle hand rousing her she looked up into Hannah's anxious face and realised she must have been out for the count. She also realised—a touch belatedly—that the home Taylor had referred to had not been her bedsit.

Through the pounding in her head, Marsha glanced out of the open door of the car and saw the steps leading up to Taylor's front door. She groaned. 'I want to go home.'

'You are home.' Taylor's face appeared at the side of Hannah's and it was grim. 'And you're not well. You were sleeping so deeply there I had to check your pulse a couple of times to make sure you were still breathing. What the hell have you been taking, anyway?'

'Just aspirin. And paracetamol. Oh, and one of the researchers gave me a couple of pills she takes for migraines.'

'Give me strength.' It was terse. 'I married a junkie.' And then, as Hannah whispered something, she heard him say, 'Flu, headache or whatever. She needs looking after.'

Marsha wanted to object when he lifted her bodily out of the car, but the effort it would take wasn't worth it. She was aware of Taylor carrying her up the stairs, and of then being placed in a comfortable bed which knocked the spots off her sofabed in the bedsit. But it was when she felt her shoes being taken off and then her jacket that she found the will to open her eyes and protest. 'Don't… I can do it.'

'Don't try my patience.'

'Where's Hannah?'

'Fixing an omelette.'

His hands were firm and sure, but not unkind—not until she tried to push him away, when he gave a none too gentle tap at her fingers. 'We're man and wife, for crying out loud. I've undressed you before.'

'That was different.'

'And how.'

She gave up. She couldn't argue. You had to be *compos mentis* to argue, and it had finally dawned on her that in her anxiety to stifle her headache and prove to all and sundry she was efficient and totally on the ball—whatever Penelope might imply—she had definitely overdone the medication.

Naked as the day she was born, she snuggled into fresh-scented linen covers and was asleep as soon as Taylor's hands left her body.

How soon she was awoken again by a quiet-voiced Hannah she didn't know, but the housekeeper gently plumped the pillows behind her after Marsha groggily sat up to take the tray the other woman was holding. 'You eat that all up, honey.' Once the pillows were sorted, Hannah stood back to gaze at her. 'I daresay you haven't eaten all day, huh?'

'I had a huge lunch,' Marsha protested weakly through the thumping in her head.

Hannah's three chins went down into her neck as her eyebrows rose in the universal expression of disbelief, but Marsha was not up to arguing. She stared down at an omelette done to moist fluffiness beside three thin slices of Hannah's home-cured ham, and knew she couldn't eat a thing.

Hannah, apparently, was not of the same persuasion. 'I'm staying right here till all that's gone,' she warned. 'Boss's instructions.'

'I'm not a child.' Marsha was stung into retaliation.

'Sure you're not, honey.' A fork was placed in her hand and Hannah beamed at her.

Marsha sighed and started to eat, surprised to find that she could clear the plate before sliding back down under the covers again. She was asleep before Hannah left the room.

CHAPTER FIVE

IT WAS the enormous sense of well-being which first registered the next morning as Marsha began to float from layers of soft billowy warmth. She was neither fully asleep nor fully awake, too comfortable and content to move or think. She just luxuriated in the deep tranquillity and peace her mind and body were resting in.

She sighed softly, the caress on her skin part of her dreamlike state and no more threatening than the stroking of a butterfly's wing. The pleasure was tantalising, teasing her senses with half-remembered stirrings which grew sweeter and more potent as she lazily embraced them.

Her body felt fluid, with heat beginning to pulse in time with the erotic rippling over her flesh, and she moaned, her half-open lips captured in the next moment in a kiss that was teasing and tangible. Suddenly she was wide awake.

'Good morning, sweet wife.'

She stared at Taylor, the thick curtain of sleep lifted but her mind refusing to accept for the moment that he was real. And then it all came rushing back—the headache, the pills, and the drive to the house—and she realised to her consternation that the covers were rumpled to one side and she was wearing nothing at all.

'You were touching me.' She made a grab for the duvet, horrified that he had been making love to her without her knowledge. Bringing the cover up to her chin, she eyed him hotly. 'That's despicable.'

He was sitting on the side of the bed and made no effort to deny the charge, merely smiling slowly as he said, 'You taste the same, like warm honey.'

Her heart was racing, less with anger than the pleasure his hands and mouth had called forth so effortlessly, which was still sending needles of desire into every pulse. 'You're the lowest of the low.'

'Why? Because I like to touch and look at my wife?'

'You knew I was asleep.' She glared at him, refusing to acknowledge how the smell and feel of him affected her. 'That's as bad as a peeping Tom.'

'Maybe.' If he agreed with her it didn't bother him an iota. 'But you looked so tempting lying there, and I've never pretended to be a saint. Mortal man can only take so much when confronted with Aphrodite at—' he consulted the gold Rolex on his tanned wrist '—eleven o'clock in the morning.'

'What?' The mention of the time deflected her wrath, as he had known it would. 'It can't be eleven o'clock.' She made a move to spring out of bed and then remembered she was naked. 'Why didn't someone wake me, for goodness' sake? I have a meeting first thing this morning, and a report which has to be on Jeff's desk by noon. I can't believe—'

'Calm down.'

It was the last straw. He could sit there as calm as a cucumber—or was it as cool as a cucumber? She couldn't remember now, but it was all the same—and act as though she should be pleased to discover she was hours late for the office. 'Where are my clothes?' she asked stonily, forcing herself not to give way and yell at him.

'In Hannah's tender care. She thought your suit needed pressing. Of course you have a wardrobe full, still in our room,' he reminded her innocently, before adding, 'How's the head this morning?'

'Fine. I told you last night, it was just a headache. If you had let me walk home—'

'You wouldn't have made it. Not with all the stuff you'd pumped into yourself.'

He made her sound like a drug addict, and she resented it bitterly—that and the fact that he was right. She looked into his face now and saw he was watching her intently, his eyes like polished amber, with a disturbing gleam at the back of them. She swallowed, feeling hot and flustered. 'Thank you,' she said grudgingly, 'for taking care of things.'

'My pleasure.' The carved lips twitched a little.

'But I need to phone the office and explain why I'm late.'

'You aren't late. You're having the day off because you are ill, probably because they are working you too hard. I phoned and spoke to Jeff first thing.'

She stared at him, her expression altering as she absorbed his words. 'You had no right to do that.' Her voice rose with her indignation. 'Not without asking me first.'

'You were asleep,' he pointed out mildly, 'and I thought you'd just thanked me for taking care of things?'

'This is different.' She wished he would stand up and move away. It was more disconcerting than she could express having him sitting inches away from her, fully dressed, when she was stark naked under the questionable protection of the bedcover.

'You would rather have let them think you just hadn't bothered to call in?' he asked with a puzzled frown.

She counted silently to ten. 'What exactly did you say?'

'Exactly?' He shut his eyes for an infinitesimal moment, as though he was trying to recall the conversation, but Marsha was not fooled. That computer brain forgot nothing—ever. 'Merely that you were taken ill last night and would not be fit to work today. I said I would phone before five this evening with an update,' he added helpfully.

Great. Just great. Now Jeff would be thinking all sorts of things—mainly about whose bed she had spent the night in—and she really couldn't blame him. Would he be discreet? She was not sure.

'Stop frowning.' His deep husky voice had laughter somewhere at the back of it, although the chiselled face was perfectly serious. 'You'll have wrinkles before you're thirty at this rate.'

'I have some already,' she snapped back curtly. And the odd grey hair, although she was not about to point that out.

'Not that I can see.' He bent forward on the pretence of looking more closely, invading her air space with the warmth and scent of his body.

The muscled strength that padded his chest and shoulders was very apparent under the thin silk of the shirt he was wearing, and Marsha had to force herself not to wriggle back against the pillows.

She would *not* give him the satisfaction of knowing how much he bothered her, she told herself furiously. But she wished she had had time to at least brush her teeth and wash her face before he had decided to come in. She tried to stop looking at his mouth. It was a very sexy, cynical mouth, and had always had the power to make her bones melt.

'If you would like to tell Hannah I'm ready for my clothes, I can at least make an appearance before lunch and work on the report for this afternoon,' she said stiffly.

'I wouldn't—like to tell Hannah, that is,' he said without moving an inch.

'Taylor, I'm going into the office today.'

'Marsha, you are not.'

His use of her Christian name warned her that, however calm and laid-back he appeared, he meant business, as did the glint in his eyes.

'This is quite ridiculous. You can't keep me here against my will and—'

Anything else she might have said was swallowed up as his mouth came down quickly on hers, a deft turn of his body bringing his hands either side of her slim shape as he pinned her beneath him. She wriggled and tried to fight him, only to realise that any movement brought the duvet dangerously close to slipping right down her body. She stopped squirming and immediately the kiss became subtly deeper, his mouth and tongue doing incredible things to her.

Heat was racing through her bloodstream and she felt the length and power of his arousal, her nerve-endings becoming sensitised as he moved his hips over her shape in a way which forced her to recognise his dominance. But his mouth was all persuasion. He probed, he sipped, he nipped, moving down from her lips when he felt her trembling submission and heard the little moans she couldn't hide, to rain burning kisses on her throat, her neck and the smooth silky skin beneath.

Her breath caught in her throat as he peeled the cover

back enough to expose the twin peaks of her breasts, his hands cupping and shaping the engorged flesh and his thumbs teasing her nipples into hard life even as his mouth took her gasps.

'I want to eat you alive.' His voice was a husky growl. 'Do you know that? Devour you…'

She had missed him so much. Even as the thought took shape a polite knock sounded on the bedroom door. 'Hannah.' With a sound deep in his throat, which could have been a groan or a sigh, Taylor straightened up, moving the cover up to her neck as she just stared at him dazedly. 'You were supposed to be drinking that—' he indicated a now cold cup of tea on the table at the side of the bed '—while she prepared your breakfast.'

As the knock came again, he said, 'Okay if she comes in?' brushing back a lock of her hair which had tumbled across her face as he spoke.

'Of course.' She jerked her head away from him, humiliation and self-contempt making her voice sharp. He clicked his fingers and she came to heel like an obedient puppy—was that what he was thinking? Why on earth had she allowed him to kiss her like that, caress and touch her? Why hadn't she resisted more forcefully?

His eyes narrowed slightly at the tone of her voice, but other than that he gave no sign that he was aware of her discomfiture, merely rising from the bed before he called for Hannah to enter.

Hannah fussed and babied her as she plumped the pillows for her patient and settled the tray on the invalid's lap, but Marsha didn't mind the other woman's attention. Hannah had been widowed in her native Jamaica after only fifteen months of marriage, the shock of her husband's death through drowning, when his fishing boat had been sunk in a storm, bringing on the birth of their first child over two months early. The baby, a little girl, had lived for an hour, and had been buried in her father's arms.

Hannah had told her the story one afternoon, shortly after Marsha had got engaged to Taylor, adding that for a long time afterwards she had—in her own words—gone a little crazy. Then, due to her youngest sister marrying a rich American, Hannah had been given the chance to move to the United States and take up residence in her brother-in-law's home when his housekeeper had walked out after a row with the new wife.

It had been a way of escape from the downward spiral of depression and increasingly strong medication, and Hannah had taken it, only to find she could fully sympathise with the previous housekeeper when she had worked for her sister for a little while. But she had stuck with the only chance she'd had of making a new life, and in due course, when the husband had entertained Taylor for a few days—the two men having met through a business deal years earlier and consequently become friends—had got to know the young Englishman.

When Taylor had offered her employment in England—with the blessing of her brother-in-law, who was getting increasingly irritated by the two sisters' altercations—Hannah had accepted on the spot, and the rest, as Hannah had said, was history. And whilst Taylor strongly objected to any attempts of Hannah to mother him, Marsha had instantly recognised the need the other woman hid beneath her bustling exterior. The housekeeper was the sort of woman who should have had a houseful of children to keep her busy, and as the affection between the older and younger woman had grown Hannah had made no bones about the fact that she was longing for the day when the patter of tiny feet would occur.

Once they were alone again, Taylor raised wry eyebrows at Marsha. 'She's as pleased as punch you're here.'

Marsha said nothing. She was half sitting up in bed, with the tray balanced on her lap and the duvet wrapped round her. She needed the loo, and she wanted to put something on before she ate, neither of which could be sorted until Taylor left.

If nothing else, Taylor was intuitive. 'You would prefer me to leave you in peace?' he said easily, apparently not in the least put out.

'Yes, please.' She was not about to mince words.

'Pity.' The tawny eyes touched her lips for a second, causing her flesh to tingle. 'You used to enjoy breakfast in bed with me.'

Memories of those times, when the coffee had invariably got cold along with the food whilst they'd indulged in a different sort of nourishment, brought the heat to her cheeks, but she managed a brittle smile. 'You've already eaten,' she pointed out evenly, 'and those times are in the past.'

'True.' He let his gaze sweep over her again. 'But only for the moment.'

'I don't think so, Taylor.'

'I know so.' His smile was confident and infuriating. 'We are man and wife, and I'm damned if I'll let some sick bozo smash everything. I was hoping you'd come to see the truth for yourself, but that was asking too much. No matter.' He moved closer to the bed, leaning over her with one hand on the headboard. 'You've proved you are more than capable of surviving without me, Fuzz. Okay? Now you can choose to be with me because you want to be. And you do want me, like I want you.'

He bent down, and she gave herself over to his kiss even as she berated herself for flirting with the danger of becoming vulnerable.

It only lasted for a few moments before he straightened, his voice cool as he said, 'Now, eat your breakfast, like a good wife, and put any thought of going into work out of your head. We are spending the day together, all right? I've put a very lucrative business deal on ice because of you, not to mention a couple of meetings and a discussion with my accountant.'

'Am I supposed to be grateful?' She eyed him hotly.

He smiled again and reached for her left hand, raising it to his lips as he kissed her ringless third finger. 'You might have discarded the visible evidence of our union, but you can't discard what is in here—' he touched the area over his heart '—so easily, my love. I know you. You're in every nerve and sinew, every breath.'

She snatched her hand back, her cheeks fiery. 'Then you should know I'm not the type of woman to accept adultery as part of the marriage contract,' she bit out furiously.

'I would never have married you if you were.'

Marsha stared at him. There was no mockery and no hesitation in his voice, and the questions which had risen to the surface after Nicki had expressed her doubts over the validity of what Susan had told her flooded in again.

Her fingers tightened briefly on the tray before she told herself not to be so silly. Susan had no reason to lie, not one. And Tanya was beautiful. Beautiful and clever and— And *married*? But that didn't mean anything. Taylor's secretary had not been married at the time she had been told of their affair; that was the point she had to concentrate on here.

'I'll make you eat every word of accusation, Fuzz. I promise you that.' There was darkness in his face now, and for a moment she felt a dart of fear. 'But that's nothing to what I'll do to the person who fed you such garbage. The mind games stop today, do you hear me?'

'Mind games?' She didn't have a clue what he was talking about.

He held her gaze for ever, until finally his square jaw released its tight clench. 'Eat your breakfast,' he said silkily. 'We'll talk later.'

And he turned and left the room.

Once Marsha had visited the *en suite* bathroom, pulling on one of the guest robes hanging on the back of the door before she left the gleaming marble surrounds, she found to her absolute amazement she was ravenous.

She demolished the plateful of eggs, bacon and sausages, the two slices of toast and blackcurrant preserve and the pot of coffee the breakfast tray held in indecent haste, before sinking back against the bedhead and staring straight ahead.

A bath. She nodded at the thought, refusing to think of Taylor until she was clean and groomed again. The tiny shower room in her bedsit was all very well, but a long warm scented bath would be sheer heaven, and if ever she had needed a touch of heavenly comfort it was now.

It was five minutes later, when she was engulfed in a sea of perfumed bubbles and trying to empty her mind of everything but the pleasure her body was experiencing, that she suddenly sat up with enough force to send water slopping over the side of the bath. Why hadn't

Taylor placed her in *their* bed last night? She had been out of it, she admitted, and hardly in a position to resist any overtures on his part, so why hadn't he taken advantage of the situation? Not that he would have forced himself on her when she was unwell, she didn't think that for a moment, but if she had been in their bed then this morning would have been a different kettle of fish entirely. To wake up beside him…

She sank down again, a frown crinkling her brow as she pondered the thought. When she had left him she had left practically every article of clothing and every personal item she possessed, and from what he had intimated this morning her clothes, at least, were still all in place. He could have used that as an excuse to have her in his bed. Not that Taylor had ever needed an excuse for something he wanted to do, she reflected acidly.

She raised one foot from beneath the foam, studying her scarlet-painted toenails thoughtfully. If they had woken up together the inevitable would have happened; he must know that. She had never been able to resist him, and he was fully aware of his sexual power.

Another half an hour of rumination brought her no nearer to an answer other than the obvious one—he hadn't wanted her to share their room again. As she rose from the now cool water she refused to let the idea hurt. They would no longer be married in a few weeks' time, and once she left this house today she would make sure she never set foot in it again. She didn't understand Taylor Kane, she had *never* understood him, and she wasn't about to waste any more time trying.

She flexed shoulders which should have been relaxed after the amount of time she had been lying in the water but were taut and tense, and then proceeded to dry herself with a big fluffy towel. It was as she was smoothing scented body lotion on every inch of skin that she stopped suddenly, gazing into the mirror in front of her. She needed to talk to Susan. Her heart began to thud as she accepted the notion which had been hammering away at the door of her mind ever since Nicki had expressed her doubts about the other woman's motives.

A sound from the room outside, and then a knock on the *en suite* door jerked her out of her musing. She whipped the bath towel round her, folding a smaller one turban-style round her wet hair, before padding across and opening the door.

'Hi.' Taylor smiled at her. 'I was beginning to think you'd drowned in there.'

'It was nice to have a bath for a change.' And at his raised eyebrows she explained, 'I only have a shower at home.'

There was a quick, almost imperceptible change in his expression. 'This is your home.'

Marsha brushed past him, ignoring the swift reaction of her body to his nearness. She paused in the middle of the bedroom, turning to face him as she said, 'Are my clothes ready now?'

'No.' He offered no more explanation before he said, 'But, like I said earlier, you have a wardrobe full of things in our room. Come and select what you want to wear.'

She stiffened. It was bad enough being in her old home in one of the guest rooms; she didn't know how she would handle entering the room where they had enjoyed so many hours of love and tenderness and passion. But she couldn't let him see that. He would regard it as weakness and play on it accordingly. 'Fine.' She raised her chin and aimed a level stare.

Taylor's mouth twitched. 'Personally, I think you look great in what you're wearing now,' he said easily, his eyes going to her head. 'Sort of…eastern, harem-like.'

Marsha ground her teeth at the implication. No doubt he would just love to have his own little bevy of beauties dancing at his beck and call, but she was blowed if she'd be one of them. 'I hardly think a handtowel wrapped round one's head deserves such a comment,' she said coolly.

'Perhaps not.' He tilted his head, and now the amusement crept into his eyes. 'But a man can dream, can't he?'

She had no intention of continuing down this path, and she wished she had taken the time to put the towelling robe back on when he had knocked. It was infinitely more reassuring than a towel. Battling a number of emotions, none of which were clear, she said, 'My clothes?'

'Of course.' He turned, opening the bedroom door and then bowing slightly. 'When you're ready, ma'am.'

Even though she had prepared herself for the moment when Taylor opened the door to their bedroom, Marsha felt something akin to an electric shock travel down each nerve-end as she entered the big spacious room. The windows had been flung wide open, and the scent of lavender from the grounds below was sweet. Her eyes were drawn to the huge bed which dominated the cream and coffee-coloured room, but she forced herself to remain blank-faced as she marched across to her walk-in wardrobe.

Everything was just as she had left it, she noticed, down to the last pair of shoes on the racks below her clothes—and the perfume she had worn during her marriage—a madly expensive extravagance first bought on honeymoon—still lingered in the air.

She swallowed hard, keeping her back to the room as she selected a light pair of trousers and a short-sleeved top, along with a bra and pair of panties. There were several pairs of sandals at one end of the wardrobe, and she chose a low-heeled style suitable for a working day. She still intended to go into work that afternoon, but she wasn't about to announce it again until she was ready to leave.

'Thank you.' After closing the wardrobe door she nodded at Taylor, who was leaning against the far wall, strong muscled arms crossed over his chest and a faintly brooding expression on his face. 'I'll see you downstairs, shall I?'

'What do you feel? Coming in here again, I mean.'

'What?' He had taken her completely by surprise. Her eyes flickered with momentary panic, quickly controlled. She shrugged carefully. 'It's a beautiful room,' she said steadily.

'That's not what I asked,' he countered coolly.

'How do you think I feel?' She found herself glaring at him now and warned herself to tread warily. No show of emotion, no challenges. 'A little sad, I guess,' she added quickly.

'A little sad?' Something flashed in his eyes at her words. 'A little sad as in having your guts torn out by their roots, or the sort of feeling you would have when watching a weepy movie?'

'Taylor, I don't want to do this.'

'Tough.' He took a step nearer and instinctively she brought the clothes up to her chest. 'We've done it your way all through this and where have we got?' His eyes locked on hers, anchoring her to the spot. 'I want to know what you are thinking for once, damn it. All through our marriage—right from when we met, in fact—I've had to pull what you're thinking out of you like a dentist extracting a tooth. I'm sick of it.'

She stared at him, her eyes hot as her temper rose. 'I didn't ask you to bring me here,' she shot at him furiously, 'and if you're so sick of me, wouldn't it be best for both of us if I left right now?'

'As always, you don't hear what I'm saying.' He reached her in one fluid movement, gripping her shoulders as he said, 'I'm sick of the lack of communication, not you. There's a difference there, if you'd open your eyes to see it. I never wanted a clinging vine who couldn't say boo to a goose and lived in my shadow, but you're something else. It's like there's an invisible wall round you, and however high I climb I never get to the top. You've never really let me in, have you? Not in all the months we were together did I ever feel I'd breached the guard you keep round the real you.'

'And that's why you slept with Tanya?' she flung at him bitterly. 'Because I didn't fall at your feet and worship you like all the others?'

'Give me strength! Listen, woman, will you? This is about me and you, not Tanya or anyone else. From the day I met you I've never looked at another woman. You're enough—more than enough,' he added scathingly, 'for any man to handle.'

'I don't believe you.'

'No, and do you know why you accepted those lies about me and our marriage so easily? Because you are frightened of the truth.'

'You're crazy,' she said harshly, aware she would have bruises where his hands were gripping her.

'About you? I must be, to put up with all this stuff

and nonsense. You are petrified of letting go and giving me everything. That's the crux of all this. If you trust me absolutely I'll let you down—that's what you've told yourself from day one. And then, surprise, surprise, you were told exactly what you were waiting to hear—I'd fallen from grace. I was having an affair. It must have been music to your ears.'

'That's a hateful thing to say.'

'But this is Taylor talking, remember? The low-life, the scum who was fooling around just eighteen months after he had promised to forsake all others for the rest of his life.'

'You're hurting me.' She was rigid and as white as a sheet under his hands.

'Damn it, Marsha.' His muttered oath had all the power of a shout, and she almost winced before she controlled herself. But he had released her.

He stepped backwards a pace or two, as though he didn't trust himself not to take hold of her again, and then, slowly and deliberately, he slipped his hands into his pockets. 'You still believe, without a shadow of a doubt, that I'm guilty as charged?' he asked in a flat grim tone which frightened her far more than his rage.

Did she? The answer was there without her having to think about it, and she spoke it out without considering her words. 'I don't know what to think any more. I was sure…' She hesitated. 'I mean, why would anyone make something like that up?'

He shook his head, his eyes mordant. 'How long have you got? Come on, Fuzz, you can't pretend to be that naive. There's a hundred reasons why people turn sour.'

But it was your sister. Your *sister*. For a second she thought she had actually spoken the words out loud, but when his expression didn't alter she knew the shout had just been in her mind.

'I hoped when you'd had time to think about all this you would begin to question—at least that. If you couldn't trust me, surely that wasn't too much to ask, was it? But there was just silence. No contact, no phone calls, no answer to my letter. So I told myself to be patient, to wait. We loved each other and no one could take that away. Hell!' It was bitter. 'And I called *you* naive.'

Marsha stared at him for a moment before turning her head aside. She had the terrible feeling deep inside that everything had shifted again. Just when she had trained herself to get through each twenty-four hours without him he was back in her life, turning over all the stones to examine the dirt beneath. And she didn't want to do that. It had nearly killed her, leaving him, but she had managed to crawl through the weeks and months since, and that was something.

She shut her eyes, her hands clenching into fists at her sides. 'Why are you doing this?'

'Because someone has to. You would actually throw away everything we had without fighting for it. I realise that now. So it's up to me to fight for both of us. Who was it? Who talked to you?'

'I…I can't say. I promised.'

He swore, a savage oath. 'You promised me more. Remember? Love, honour, cherish, in sickness and in health? You owe me a name, damn it.'

'Taylor, I—'

'A name, Marsha. Then maybe we can start to get to the bottom of this. If I'd had my head screwed on I'd have done this months ago, instead of assuming you could actually reason like any sane human being.'

It opened her eyes and brought her head up. She was so angry she wanted to stamp and scream like a child. He was intent on blaming everything on her, even when the evidence against him had been stacked to the sky. He would never know how much she had suffered when she had made that call to the hotel and heard Tanya speak in her sexy little-girl voice from their room. 'You don't want to know who it was,' she said tightly. 'Take it from me.'

'I do.' His eyes were boring into her and his face was harder than she had ever seen it, unreachable.

She stared at him, Susan's name hovering on her tongue even as her mind raced. If she told Taylor his sister had betrayed him, what would it do to his and Susan's relationship? Smash it for ever. He was not the sort of man to forgive; she knew that. Whether Susan's accusation was true or not, he would cut her out of his life with the ruthlessness that had got him to where he was now. And that would mean Dale, her husband, would lose his job, perhaps even their house, because no one would pay Dale what Taylor paid him.

Of course if Susan had lied she deserved all that and maybe more—but if she hadn't…? And Taylor? What would it do to him? He loved his sister; she was all the natural family he had. Oh, what should she do? She was in a no-win situation here and so was he, if he did but know it. Tough as he was, his sister occupied a very special place in his heart, as he did in Susan's. That was what made this whole thing so impossible. Susan *had* to have been telling the truth…didn't she?

'I'm sorry, Taylor.' She kept her eyes steady despite the growing darkness in his face.

'I see.'

No—no, he didn't see, but what could she do? She

would have to go and see Susan as soon as possible. Maybe talking to her would settle some things. 'I…I can't tell you. I would if there was a way, but—'

'Forget it.' His tone was final and very cold.

'Forget it?' Her mouth had opened in a little O of surprise.

'Go and get dressed, Marsha.' He stood aside, his face closed against her.

In spite of herself she reached out her hand, touching his broad chest in a helpless little gesture that carried a wealth of pleading in it. He didn't move a muscle, merely watching her with narrowed amber eyes that were as cool and unemotional as the resin they resembled.

When her hand fell back to her side she turned swiftly and walked across the room without looking at him again, making her way to the guest room on legs that trembled. Once inside she locked the door, her eyes burning with unshed tears and the lump in her throat threatening to choke her. It was over. The look in his eyes had told her so.

She walked across to the bed and sank down on it, still holding the clothes in her hands. He didn't want her any more. He had said he was sick of her and the last minute or two had proved it. She ought to be pleased.

She pressed a hand to her mouth, the tears falling hot and fast as she rocked to and fro in an agony of grief, feeling more desolate than she had ever felt before.

Five minutes later and she had pulled herself together sufficiently to pick up the telephone and request a taxi-cab. After washing her face she dressed quickly, running a comb through her hair and applying some lipstick—the only item of make-up she had with her.

She couldn't countenance an afternoon in Taylor's company; she felt too raw. Okay, it might look as if she was running away—and maybe she was, she admitted wretchedly—but this was pure self-survival. Reaching for her handbag, she extracted a little notebook and scribbled a quick message to Hannah, promising the older woman she would ring her soon and arrange for them to meet up somewhere. Then, feeling like someone in a bad drama on TV, she crept carefully downstairs and out of the front door, hurrying down the drive.

She was so relieved to see the taxi waiting just beyond the entrance to the drive she could have kissed the small balding man behind the wheel. Instead she clambered in quickly, giving him the address of the bedsit and then changing her mind in the next instant and telling him to take her straight into work. If Taylor came after her—and it was a big if, considering how they had parted—she would rather have the security of a work environment than be all alone at the bedsit.

She didn't begin to breathe freely until they were well on their way, and right until she actually walked into the building she felt as though at any moment a hand would tap her on the shoulder or a deep unmistakable voice would call her name. But then she was in the lift, being transported to her floor, and she knew she had done it.

And, strangely, in that moment she felt more miserable than ever.

CHAPTER SIX

'WHEN do you think he'll realise the bird has flown the nest?'

Nicki placed a steaming mug of coffee in front of her as she spoke, and Marsha took a careful sip of the scalding liquid before she said, 'He must know by now.'

'Worried?'

'No.' Marsha's fingers tightened on the mug. 'Why should I be? He doesn't own me, and I'm blowed if I'll let him tell me whether I can come into work or not.'

'Good on you.' Nicki was all approval. 'He ought to be crawling on his hands and knees begging forgiveness for the way he's treated you.'

Marsha looked up from the coffee, her eyes narrowing. She might be wrong, but hadn't Nicki changed tack somewhat from yesterday? Then she had been urging her to give Taylor the benefit of the doubt. Now she sounded as if she'd like to punch him on the nose. 'What have you heard?' she asked flatly.

'Heard?' Nicki flushed a deep pink as she sat down at her own desk, fiddling unnecessarily with some papers as she said, 'What makes you think I've heard something?'

Marsha didn't bother to reply, merely raising her eyebrows and lowering her chin while she waited for the other woman to look up.

There was a pause before Nicki glanced at her. 'It's just something Janie said, that's all.'

'Which was?'

Nicki wriggled uncomfortably. 'Penelope has swung the contract for Kane International and he—your husband—is taking her out for a meal to celebrate.'

Marsha shrugged. 'It's a free country,' she said, as lightly as she could.

'Dinner at the Hot Spot.'

Marsha took a moment to steady her voice. 'We're separated, Nicki. He's allowed to see anyone he wants.' The Hot Spot was the latest big sensation with London's jet set: a nightclub where you could dance the night away and even get breakfast in the morning. No one went there just for dinner.

Nicki sniffed a very eloquent sniff. 'I've never liked tall dark men,' she said flatly. 'Especially when their egos match their…hat size.'

'I've never seen Taylor in a hat.'

The two women stared at each other for a moment before they both smiled weakly. 'I'll get you a sandwich while you get stuck into that report,' Nicki said quietly.

'Thanks.'

The rest of the day passed without incident. Nicki insisted Marsha have dinner with herself and her husband, and after a pleasant evening in their Paddington flat they drove her home, waiting outside until she waved to them from the bedsit window to say all was well. Their concern was sweet, but made Marsha feel slightly ridiculous. Taylor wasn't violent, for goodness' sake, or dangerous—not in an abusive sense anyway. She knew he would rather cut off his right hand than raise it to a woman. She very much doubted his pride would allow him to try and see her again anyway, outside of the divorce court.

She slept badly that night, tossing and turning and drifting into one nightmare after another until, at just gone six, she rose from her rumpled bed and had a long warm shower. Thank goodness it was Friday and she had the weekend in front of her to get a handle on all this. She needed to be able to take a long walk in the fresh air and get her thoughts in order.

She always thought better out in the open. It was a hangover from her childhood and teenage years, when she had liked nothing better than to escape the confines of the dormitory and communal dining hall and wander about in the grounds of the home, staying out until she was found and brought back by an irate assistant.

It was during those times that she had eventually come to terms with the fact that it was probably her fault she had been returned to the home twice when adoption attempts had fallen through.

She had told herself so often the story of how her mother would come back for her—arms open wide as she tearfully told her daughter how much she loved her—that she had been unable to separate fact from fiction. She couldn't not be there when her mother came, she had determined, and so—much as she hated it—she couldn't live anywhere else.

It was after her best friend had left the home and forgotten all her extravagant promises to write and visit that she had begun to face the prospect that just wishing for people to behave a certain way didn't mean it was going to happen. But by then it had been too late.

She had been labelled withdrawn and difficult, and was no longer a cute little girl, but a gawky youngster approaching teenage years with braces on her teeth and spots on her chin.

By the time the ugly duckling had turned into a diffident and shy swan she had learnt she could rely on no one but herself. If she didn't expect anything of anyone she wouldn't be disappointed, and if she didn't let anyone get near they wouldn't be able to hurt her. Simple.

Only it hadn't worked that way with Taylor. From the second she had seen him she had wanted him; it had been as clear and unequivocal as that. Not that she hadn't known it was madness.

She turned off the shower, wrapping a towel round her and walking through into the main room. Sunlight was already slanting golden shafts into the room and the day promised to be another warm one.

Yes, she'd known it was madness, she reiterated as she dried her hair. Deep inside she'd continually asked herself how serious he was about relinquishing his love 'em and leave 'em lifestyle. Did he want her for a lifetime? Did he need her as she needed him? Could she handle the complex being that was Taylor Kane? Would he grow bored with marriage or, worse, her? Those questions had plagued her from day one.

'Who fed your insecurities with the very thing you most feared?' Taylor's words came back to her with piercing suddenness, causing her hand to still before she threw the hairdryer on to the sofa.

He had insisted on his innocence that night eighteen months ago and he was still insisting on it. Had he sent her a letter giving the telephone number of this stranger who had allowed him to share his room in Germany? It was easy for him to say so now, when so much time had elapsed, and surely it was more than a little farfetched to think the letter had got lost in the post?

The ring of the telephone right at her elbow made her jump a mile, and she put a hand to her racing heart before glancing at her watch. Six-thirty. Who on earth was calling her at six-thirty?

She refused to admit she was expecting it to be

Taylor, but the minute she lifted the receiver and heard his voice her heart galloped even faster. He had spoken only her name, his voice even, and she couldn't tell what sort of mood he was in.

'Hello, Taylor.' She was pleased to hear her voice betrayed nothing of what she was feeling.

'Did I wake you?'

Prevarication seemed the best response. She wasn't about to let him know she had been up with the birds because he had invaded her dreams as well as every waking moment. 'It *is* six-thirty in the morning,' she said coolly. 'I don't normally rise before seven.' Which was true.

'I couldn't sleep.' His voice was warm and soft and did the craziest things to her nerve-endings.

Marsha breathed out very slowly. 'Most people reach for a book rather than the phone in that situation.'

'I'm not most people.'

Now, that was definitely the truest thing he had ever said! She stared at the painted wall some feet away, trying to work out where he was coming from. He didn't sound mad, but he had always been able to conceal anger very well. 'What do you want?' she asked carefully.

'You.' It was immediate. 'But I'll settle for breakfast.'

In his dreams! She forced a sarcastic laugh. 'I don't think so.'

'No?'

'No.'

'Oh, well, I guess I can throw stones at Mrs Tate-Collins's window and see if she's in the mood for warm croissants. Say what you like, but I think I might be in with a chance there.'

She stared at the receiver as she tried to assimilate the implication of what he had just said. 'Where are you, exactly?' she said flatly.

'Exactly?' The pause was deliberate. 'Well, if we're talking exactly, I'm on the second paving slab to the left of the steps which lead up to the front door of your building.'

He was *outside*? For a second she was tempted to tell him to go ahead and wake Mrs Tate-Collins, but knowing he would almost certainly call her bluff restrained her. She didn't want him sitting in the basement telling Mrs Tate-Collins all the ins and outs of this ridiculous situation, as he knew full well.

She tried one last time. 'Go home, Taylor.'

'No chance.'

She dipped her head, shaking it irritably before she said, 'Doesn't what I want count for anything?'

'Absolutely not. We've done it your way over the last months and what have we got? No nearer to sorting anything out and even more tangles in the web.'

'I could get a restraining order. That way you wouldn't be able to keep harassing me.'

'You could try.' It was mordant. 'But I doubt if any court in the land would agree that offering you dinner, giving you a helping hand when you were sick and then calling by with breakfast constitutes harassment.'

She took a deep breath to combat the anger his supremely confident voice had aroused. He took the biscuit for sheer arrogance. 'I'll open the front door.'

'Thanks.'

Sixty seconds later a light knock announced his arrival. She had just had time to pull on a pair of cream cotton combat trousers and a sleeveless top, but with her newly washed hair shining like raw silk and her skin fresh and clean from the shower she felt more than able to hold her own. She didn't rush to answer the door, waiting for a moment or two before she pulled it open.

Taylor was standing with a box in his arms, his smile lazy and his amber eyes reflecting the golden sunlight from the landing window. 'Good morning.' He waited for an invitation to enter.

She inclined her head, refusing to let him see what his presence did to her. He was wearing black jeans and an open-necked black denim shirt and he looked magnificent. 'Come in,' she said grudgingly.

He quirked a brow at her tone but said nothing, walking past her and then standing just inside the room. 'This is great.' He couldn't quite disguise his surprise.

'I like it.' She had opened the balcony windows first thing, and now he walked across the room, after depositing the box on the breakfast bar, standing and looking out over the rooftops for a moment or two.

Turning, he said, 'Did you have to do much when you first moved in?'

'Quite a bit.' It felt very strange, having him stand in her little home, and to cover her agitation she began to unpack the box of food he had brought as she detailed her additions and alterations to the bedsit.

He had brought warm croissants, as he had said, along with a selection of preserves in tiny individual jars, and cold cooked meats, cheese, hard-boiled eggs and potato salad. Melon, kiwi, grapefruit, mango and other fruits—all ready prepared and sliced in containers—along with a variety of cereals and fresh orange juice made up the box, at the top of which lay a deep red rose, its petals still damp with the morning dew.

Marsha made no comment about the rose, placing it to one side. It seemed safer.

'Do you really mind me bringing breakfast round?'

He had come up behind her, his breath warm on the back of her neck. She was not fooled by the gentle persuasive tone. He was using the Kane charm, and it could be lethal on occasion. 'Actually, yes.' She used the excuse of fetching plates and bowls to put a few feet between them.

'Why?'

She turned, her hands full, and found herself facing his chest. He had moved as lightly and swiftly as a cat. 'Because this is my home and I prefer to invite callers.' As he made a move to take the crockery from her she said, 'I can manage, thank you.'

'I'm sure you can.' He took it, nevertheless, setting it down on the breakfast bar and then perching on one of the stools which he had pulled out further into the room. 'But there's more to life than managing, surely?'

She warned herself not to get drawn into this. 'You know what I meant.'

'And you know what I meant. I've existed, not lived, the last eighteen months. Tell me you haven't done the same.' He raked back his hair as he spoke and the simple action created a surge of sexual need inside her she couldn't believe.

'I've been fine. I *am* fine.' She stared straight at him, refusing to blink as she lied.

'You're getting better at lying, but you'll never really master the art,' he said comfortably.

'I see the giant ego is still alive and healthy.'

'However, I would say you've improved beyond measure with the putdowns.'

He had an answer for everything, impossible man. She had promised herself she wouldn't show any emotion, but now her green eyes glowed like an angry cat's as she glared at him. 'You're the only person who ever affects me that way,' she said, without thinking about her words.

She saw the tawny gaze widen for a second and realised what she had said. 'No one else is as rude or pushy as you,' she qualified quickly.

He stared at her, his expression carefully masked but with a slight smile playing at the corners of his mouth which was more annoying than any challenge. 'Relax, Fuzz. I'm not about to leap on you and have my wicked way. This is just breakfast, okay?'

Too true it was. Did he really think she would just fall into his arms like a ripe plum if he made a move? She raised her chin. 'I didn't expect to hear from you again after the way I left the house.'

'Yes, you did,' he argued softly. 'You knew I wouldn't be able to keep away from you.'

'You managed it fairly successfully for eighteen months.' She had intended her words to be barbed, but they merely sounded faintly woebegone.

'I've told you why. You needed to face certain issues and work them through so you could see the truth for yourself and make the first move to reconciliation.'

'Well, that didn't work, did it?'

He smiled. 'I do occasionally get it wrong. That ought to please you.'

She shrugged, picking up one of the fruit containers, only to have it taken out of her hand in the next moment. 'Look at me, Fuzz,' he said quietly, his voice gentle. 'I mean *really* look at me. Can't you see I've been in hell the last months? Don't you know I've been half crazy?'

As he spoke, he stroked the back of his fingers across

her cheek, his other arm enclosing her into the warmth of him. 'Don't.' It was feeble and they both knew it.

'The touch, the feel, the smell of you.' His voice was even softer, the amber eyes mesmerising. 'I've thought of nothing else. When you were in that wretched little bed and breakfast I used to come and park a few doors away late at night, just so I could be in the same vicinity as you. How's that for crazy? And then when you moved here if I picked up the phone once to call, I did it a thousand times.'

'Why didn't you follow through?' she asked weakly.

'I thought I was doing the best for us, for our future. Those gremlins that dog you have got to be brought into the light and destroyed. Oh, Fuzz…' He took her mouth in the gentlest of kisses, his tenderness beguiling her utterly. 'You're perfect, don't you know that? Everything I could ever want.'

This time when his mouth fastened on hers the pressure was more intense, and now both arms held her to him. He was kissing her in the way she remembered, a way which made her body ache for him. His hands roamed up and down the silky skin of her arms before moving one strap of her top aside so his lips could caress the smooth flesh of her shoulder. She shivered and his attentions increased. Her arms instinctively lifted as he raised the bottom of the top and pulled it over her head.

'Beautiful…' It was a throaty murmur as his hands cupped and moulded the full mounds of her breasts, his thumbs playing over the hard peaks of her nipples. 'Ravishingly beautiful.'

When his mouth took what his hands had just admired, she couldn't help arching back, a moan escaping her lips as hot sensation curled like electricity from the tip of her left breast right into the core of her. She dug her fingers into his shoulders, her legs trembling so much she couldn't hide how deeply he was affecting her.

When his hands moved to the clip on her trousers she was beyond protest. His own clothes followed hers a moment later until they were both naked, their skin warm and moist. She inhaled the clean smell of his lemony aftershave, its sharp tang mixed with his own musky scent to produce an erotic perfume that was pure Taylor. She had so missed him... It was the only thought she was capable of.

There was a fire inside her as he explored her mouth and body with a slow, pleasure-inducing enjoyment which brought them both to the peak of arousal. And she touched him, running her fingers over the hard-muscled lines of his powerful body, across the broad, hair-roughened chest and the solid bridge of his shoulders.

There was an infinite hunger inside her which only the feel of him deep in her innermost being could assuage, and when at last he thrust into her molten body her muscles contracted to hold him tight in the silken sheath. She was leaning against the smooth cool wall now, but then he raised her with his hands on her bottom, forcing her long legs to wrap themselves around his hips as their bodies entwined still closer.

When the release came its explosion took them both into a shattering world of light and colour and sensation in which time had no meaning. There was no past and no future, and even the present consisted only of the swirling heights to which they had risen. Passion was the master, and it was all the more powerful for being denied so long.

Her head was resting against the hard column of his throat as he cradled her against him, the furious pounding of his heart beginning to diminish as he placed small burning kisses on her brow.

It wasn't until he gently lowered her feet to the floor that she began to think again, but even then she was so wrapped up in his arms as he continued to hold her close against him that the full import didn't register. 'I love you, sweetheart.' His voice was muffled above her head but warm with lingering passion. 'Never doubt that for a moment.'

She continued to rest against the lean bulk of him, but now reality wouldn't be kept at bay. She had allowed Taylor to make love to her. No, not just allowed it—encouraged it, begged for it, she admitted silently, feeling numb with shame.

'This is where you say you love me too.'

The beginning of her reply was lost in his kiss as he bent his head, but after a moment or two the lack of response must have got through to him. He raised his head, his eyes taking in her mortified face. 'We're married, Fuzz,' he reminded her evenly. 'It's okay to say you love me.'

He was saying it was okay for much more than that, and they both knew it. 'We—we're separated,' she protested faintly.

He held her away from him for a second, his gaze conducting a leisurely evaluation of the space between them. 'So we are,' he agreed lazily, his voice deep with throaty amusement. 'But I can soon remedy that again, if you so wish?'

In spite of herself her body tingled where his eyes had stroked, and now her face was scarlet. For months she had been fiercely telling herself that she was able to make a new life in which Taylor played no part. She was a career woman now; she was going to concentrate on that and that alone. Men, romance, sex—she didn't want any of it. There were too many complications, too many compromises, too much heartache. And what had happened to all her grand thoughts and principles? Taylor had happened. He had crooked his little finger after eighteen months of silence and she had flown into his arms like a homing pigeon. It was her worst nightmare come to life.

'We shouldn't have done this.' She pulled herself free, yanking the throw off the sofa and wrapping it round her. 'It will only complicate things.'

'I doubt they could get more complicated,' he said mildly.

'Of course they can.'

He didn't contradict her this time. He simply stood there, stark naked and faintly amused as he surveyed her frantic face. After a moment he said, very calmly, 'I don't know about you but I'm starving. Shall we eat?'

Shall we eat? She stared at him, her cheeks pink and her hair ruffled. Men were a different species, they really were.

'Fuzz, you haven't done anything wrong.' It was said in tones of insulting patience, the sort of voice one used with a child who was being particularly silly. 'We've just enjoyed one of the most natural pleasures known to man—and woman.' She went even pinker, as he had meant her to. 'Besides which we *are* man and wife, for crying out loud. Or had that little fact slipped your mind with it being so long?'

Nothing about Taylor had ever slipped her mind. 'The…the divorce.' Had he made love to her just to put a spanner in the works? She wouldn't put it past him.

She wouldn't put *anything* past him. 'Will it make a difference if the solicitors find out?'

'I tell you what, I won't tell if you don't.' His face had closed against her as she had spoken, and now he bent to retrieve his clothes, beginning to dress with lazy grace.

She watched him miserably, more confused than she had ever been in her life. She loved him. She had never stopped loving him even when she had told herself she hated him for what he had done. But did she trust him? Did she really believe he had just been Tanya's boss and that was all? Did she know, deep in her heart, that there had never been any other women since he had met her? The answer sent a bleak chill through her, quelling any words of appeasement.

Once he was dressed he looked at her, no expression on his face now. 'I can't carry you kicking and screaming out of that place of shadows you inhabit and into the real world,' he said quietly. 'And I can't show you any more clearly how I feel. You're destroying us—you know that, don't you? Throwing away something which should have lasted for a lifetime and beyond. I know what your mother did was tough, along with the rest of it, but sooner or later you have to make up your mind whether anything at all is worth fighting for. If it is, we should be at the top of the list.'

'I didn't ask you to come here this morning,' she said numbly.

'No, you didn't.' He nodded his agreement. 'But I came anyway, so that should tell you something. And don't say it was because of what we've just done either. If it was just sex I wanted there are any number of women I could call on. That's the way of it when you are wealthy and successful. I don't want sex, Fuzz. I want to make love. With you. There's a hell of a difference there. Do you see that?'

She stared at him, her eyes huge. 'I don't know what to think any more. I'm—'

'Confused.' Taylor confirmed his understanding with a nod. 'But not knowing what to think is better than being sure of the wrong thing. Maybe there's hope for you yet.'

She couldn't return his smile. She felt raw and exposed and his last words had done nothing to calm her agitation. Taylor was the master of manipulation. Had this morning been an exercise in psyching her out? If so it had been an extremely rewarding one as far as he was concerned.

'Get dressed, Fuzz.' His smile was replaced by a sombre gaze. 'And I promise I won't touch you again this morning, okay? We'll eat, pretend this is just the beginning of a normal working day for an old married couple.'

'I'm not hungry.' She wondered why the bedsit seemed to have shrunk since he had walked into it.

'You still need to eat.'

She wanted to argue, but she had the horrible feeling she might burst into tears if she did. Gathering up her clothes, she said, 'I'll just have a quick shower,' and scuttled across the room, closing the door of the shower room firmly behind her and then locking it. Her body felt sensuously replete, the core of her throbbing faintly with a pleasant ache and her breasts full and heavy as she showered before dressing. She eyed herself in the small mirror before leaving the tiny room and groaned softly. She had the look of a woman who had just been made love to, sure enough. She was going to have to make up very carefully once he had gone.

She took a deep breath and lifted her head, opening the shower room door and walking briskly into the main room. And then she stopped dead. It was empty. He'd gone. She glanced about her as though she expected him to leap up from behind the sofa, and then she saw the note on the breakfast bar. Walking across, she picked it up, holding the rose which he had slanted across one of the pages from the message pad she kept near the telephone.

Sorry, urgent call on my mobile means I've got to cut and run. We'll talk later. T

Marsha sank down on one of the stools, her heart thudding. T. Not even 'love T'. And surely he could have waited a few minutes until she'd showered and dressed? Had he regretted making love to her? Or had he thought it would be easier on her if he left before she came out? She had said she wasn't hungry, but—

Stop it. The command in her head was strong. No amount of rationalising would give her the answer. Only Taylor could do that, and she couldn't ask him. She put down the note and the rose, staring at the deep red petals for a long time. She had let Taylor into her mind and her body this morning; she'd gone against everything she had told herself over the last eighteen months and had given him goodness knows what message. She was stark staring mad.

Coffee. She nodded to the thought. She was going to have a cup of strong hot coffee and then force herself to eat some of this food. She would need to be fully in command of herself when she went to see Susan this morning. The time had come. Or perhaps it was long overdue. Eighteen months overdue. If nothing else she should have insisted on seeing Susan and Dale once the initial shock had subsided. She realised that now. So perhaps, as Taylor had said, there was hope for her yet? But it wasn't hope for herself she wanted, it was hope for them.

She frowned to herself, hating to admit just how much she needed him. From the moment he had come into her life, like a powerful, inexorable force, she had known she would never love anyone else. Taylor was part of her, he was in her blood, her bones, and whatever she did to try to forget him it didn't work.

It had been so good when they had first been married… She let her mind wander back to those golden days in a way she hadn't done for a long time because it was too painful. She had adored him, had been over the moon that a man like Taylor—sophisticated, handsome, wealthy, powerful—had noticed her. Not just noticed her but fallen madly in love with her if he was to be believed. And he had been so gentle, so tender with her.

She pushed back the silk of her hair, her eyes cloudy with the memories which were crowding in.

Right from their first date it had been enough to be together; they hadn't needed anyone else. In fact it had been something of a sacrifice when they had shared their time with other people, even old friends. They had practically lived in each other's pockets before they were married, their relationship so intense it had disturbed her when she stopped to think about it. Which wasn't often. Not with Taylor by her side, filling every moment, every thought, every breath.

She sighed deeply, her body still holding the tingling awareness of their lovemaking and her breasts full and heavy with the remnants of passion.

She had told him they shouldn't have made love, but it had seemed the most natural, the *right* thing to do. So where did that leave her?

Up the creek without a paddle. An old saying of the home's matron, a severe, grey-haired lady with the name of Armstrong, came to mind. Matron Armstrong had been a Yorkshire lass, and full of such little gems, but she had been kind beneath her grim exterior. Marsha could still recall when the second set of prospective parents had returned her to the home, making no effort to hide their disappointment in her, and the way Matron had whisked her into her quarters once they had gone, feeding her hot crumpets and jam by the fire and talking long and hard about how stupid some grown-ups could be. Yes, she had been a nice woman, Matron Armstrong.

She sighed again, gazing round the bedsit as though the little home she had created for herself would help her sort out her confusion. Why did she still, knowing all she knew about Tanya—or at least thought she knew, she corrected, trying to be fair—ache for his touch, his love?

Because she loved him in a way she could never love anyone else.

The thought thrust itself into the forefront of her mind, causing her to lower her head as she made a sound deep in her throat.

She sat quite still for some minutes before raising her head, and now her mouth was set in a determined line, her eyes narrowed. She would go and see Susan and bear whatever came of their meeting, good or bad. She owed it to herself to do that, even if she didn't owe it to Taylor.

CHAPTER SEVEN

SUSAN'S large, faintly ostentatious house was gently baking in the morning sun as Marsha paid the taxi driver. As he drove off she turned, standing and looking at the building for a moment.

The small select estate of three-year-old executive style properties was all manicured green lawns, pristine flower borders with not a petal in the wrong place and pocket-size back gardens without a bird in sight. Windows gleamed, drives were immaculate and the odd silver birch tree—the only trees which had been planted by the builders in the middle of every other front lawn—were neatly trimmed and perfect. Marsha found it hard to imagine that real flesh and blood people lived in such uniform perfection.

She had telephoned Susan earlier that morning, and it was clear the other woman had been keeping an eye out for the taxi as the front door suddenly opened. 'Marsha.' Susan smiled at her. 'How lovely to see you. Do come in.'

As Marsha reached her sister-in-law she was briefly enfolded in a cool perfumed embrace, and then she was in Susan's elegant cream and biscuit hall—the same colour scheme being reflected throughout the five-bedroomed house.

'Come through to the sitting room,' Susan continued, leading the way into the large and expensively furnished room Marsha remembered from when she had still been living with Taylor. Brother and sister had had a few altercations over the price of several items, not least the three two-seater cream leather sofas, the cost of which had run into six figures. Dale's salary—as Taylor's general manager—should have been able to cover the mortgage and the cost of any necessary new furniture or appliances when they had moved from their more modest house just after Marsha and Taylor had wed, but neither Susan's husband nor her brother had expected her to go on a spending spree as she had. When Susan had come crying to Taylor that she couldn't keep up the repayments on various items he had taken the debts and paid them, but not before he had made it very clear he wasn't happy with her wild squandering of what was essentially his money.

Susan had argued and cried and sulked, taking herself off for a weekend to a health farm at the height of the dispute, but with the debts all paid off and her new home furnished exactly the way she wanted she had soon been herself again—with Taylor, at least. With Dale she had seemed a little distant.

It was through this fracas that Marsha had seen Taylor's relationship with his sister was more father to daughter than sibling to sibling. One night when the dust had settled he had explained to her that their father had been such a transitory figure in their lives, even before their mother had died, that he had taken on the responsibility of Susan from childhood. It had explained a lot. Susan's adoration of her big brother and Taylor's indulgent humouring of his sister's sometimes excessive demands had fallen into place.

'I've missed you.' Susan placed a beringed hand on Marsha's arm once they were sitting in air-conditioned comfort. Mrs Temple—Susan's daily—bustled in a moment later with a tray of coffee.

Once the two women were alone again Susan leant forward, her light brown eyes—which were a washed-out version of Taylor's deep tawny orbs—uncharacteristically warm as she said, 'How are things, Marsha? What have you been doing with yourself?'

Marsha gave a brief description of her job and her home, to which Susan listened intently. Taylor's sister had never aspired to further education and she had left school at sixteen, working for a few hours a day in a flower shop before her marriage to Dale, when she had been just over twenty-one. At that point she had given up work entirely.

'And do you enjoy your job? Are you happy?'

There was something of an urgency to Susan's tone, which surprised Marsha. She looked at her sister-in-law, her smile soft at the other woman's concern as she said, 'Yes, I love my work. It's challenging and rewarding and every day is different.'

'But are you *happy*?'

Marsha took a sip of her coffee to give herself time to think. She had never worn her heart on her sleeve and she wasn't about to start now, but she couldn't in all honesty say she was happy, not even before Taylor had burst into her life again and turned everything upside down. She was satisfied with the life she had carved out for herself of necessity, and with that satisfaction had come more self-respect than she had ever had before, along with a belief in her own strength and fortitude, but happy? Happiness was Taylor. Joy was Taylor.

She took a steadying breath as she placed the delicate bone china cup on its fragile saucer. 'Happiness is different things to different people,' she prevaricated quietly, 'but can I tell you why I came today?'

'It's something to do with Taylor, isn't it?' It was more a statement than a question.

'He's told you he came to see me?' Marsha found she was faintly surprised. Susan and Taylor were very close, but somehow she had imagined he would keep the last few days quiet until they had sorted things out one way or the other.

Susan nodded, her eyes fixed on Marsha's face. 'He…he said you're still determined not to go back to him. Is that true?'

Again Marsha prevaricated. 'Susan, I just need to check a few things with you. Some of what he said—' She stopped abruptly. She really didn't know how to put this. 'He's adamant he never slept with Tanya or anyone else, not then and not since we've been separated. Could you have got it wrong?'

Susan continued to stare at her before bringing her lids down over her eyes as she reached for her own cup. 'You phoned the hotel yourself,' she said flatly.

'I know.' Marsha's stomach lurched. She had been banking on a ray of hope; she realised that now. 'Taylor said the booking was made in error—the double room for him and Tanya, I mean. He said he took the only other available bed in the place and shared a twin with another man at the conference. He maintains he wrote me a letter explaining everything—'

'Marsha, what do you want me to say?' Susan had set her cup down and now her face was tight as she raised her head again. 'You made the decision to leave him at the time and I don't see what's changed.'

Marsha returned her gaze for a long moment, then sank back against the sofa, putting a hand to her forehead. She had been clutching at straws; she saw that now. Susan was trying to be kind by not rubbing it in, but it was clear the other woman had no doubts about Taylor's infidelity. 'I…I want to believe him, I suppose,' she said throatily, tears welling up despite all her efforts to control herself.

'Oh, I'm sorry, Marsha, really.' Suddenly Susan was beside her, hugging her. 'But you've just told me what a great life you've made for yourself without him. You'll be all right. You will. You're so brainy and beautiful and…and nice.'

As her sister-in-law's voice broke and Susan began to cry with her, Marsha knew she had to get her equilibrium back. She should never have come here today. It could serve no useful purpose—simply opening the old wound until it was raw and bleeding.

She drew back a little from Susan with as much aplomb as she could muster, her voice still husky with tears as she said, 'It's me that's sorry, Sue. I've come here and upset you, and after all you did for me. It must have been hard, loving Taylor as you do, to tell me about Tanya and everything. Look, I ought to go.'

'No, no, don't.' Susan sounded almost desperate. 'Stay for a bit, please. Here, have some more coffee; you'll feel better.'

She couldn't feel any worse. Marsha dredged up a smile from somewhere as she nodded.

'I have missed you, Marsha, so much. I mean it.' Susan pushed back her hair from her damp face.

'Not with your busy social life, surely?' Marsha attempted to bring things back to normal, her voice brighter. Susan and Dale lived in a social whirl that would have made her giddy. She and Taylor had liked to go out quite often, dancing the night away at nightclubs, having and going to dinner parties or to the theatre, but they had also enjoyed quiet romantic dinners at home together, or weekends when they saw no one. Susan and Dale, on the other hand, rarely had an evening at home, and when they did it was usually because they were throwing a dinner party.

Susan shrugged now. 'Quantity of friends doesn't necessarily mean the quality is right,' she said, so bitterly that Marsha was shocked out of her own misery.

'Is anything wrong?' She placed a hand on Susan's arm.

'Lots. But then no one's life is perfect, is it?' Susan's smile was brittle now, and she made a show of pouring two more cups of coffee, removing herself back to her own seat as she did so.

The conversation was a little stilted from that point on, with Marsha telling Susan more about the TV company and the way things worked, and Susan responding by talking about the latest drama or film she'd seen.

It was as Marsha stood up to go that Taylor's sister reached out her hands again, taking Marsha's in her own as she said, 'You haven't told Taylor it was me? I mean, you haven't let anything slip that might give him an idea? He's so...'

As her voice faded away, Marsha acknowledged that she knew what Susan was trying to say. Her smile was crooked as she shook the other woman's hands gently. 'Of course I haven't. I gave you my word, but I wouldn't do that to you anyway,' she reassured her softly. 'We're friends, aren't we? More than friends—family.' For a little while longer, at least, until the divorce was finalised.

Susan's eyes flickered and then filled with tears, and for the umpteenth time since Marsha had come to the house the other woman surprised her by hugging her tight. Susan had never been physically demonstrative in all the time Marsha had known her, not even with Dale. The only person she had ever seen Susan hug of her own volition was Taylor, and even then it would be brief.

Marsha frowned over the other woman's head. There was definitely something wrong, and it was serious; she could sense it. She tried one last time. 'Sue, are you feeling all right? You don't seem yourself.'

Susan drew back immediately, brushing her face with the back of her hand. 'Thanks, but I'm fine,' she said, smiling now. 'It's just so nice to see you, that's all.'

She couldn't force a confidence if Susan didn't want to discuss it. Marsha smiled back, bringing a teasing note to her voice when she said, 'You just miss those shopping trips you used to drag me on, that's all.'

'We had fun, didn't we?' Susan said wistfully.

'Lots of it.' For the first time Marsha noticed that Susan's slimness bordered on the extreme. Taylor's sister had always been a fitness addict, spending hours at a local gym she belonged to, but now she appeared positively scrawny.

Marsha had phoned for a taxi some minutes earlier, and when the two women opened the front door it was just pulling up outside. 'Good timing.' Marsha smiled at her sister-in-law, determined to leave on a brighter note. 'It was good to see you again. Take care of yourself, won't you?'

Susan nodded. 'You too. I wish you would let me drive you back.'

'No need.' To be truthful, she needed to be by herself. 'And if I talk to Taylor I won't mention I called today. Okay?'

Susan nodded. 'Goodbye, Marsha.'

She had just sat down in the taxi and was leaning

forward to shut the door when Susan was at her elbow again. 'Could we meet occasionally?' she asked, with the urgency Marsha had noticed once or twice before. 'Have lunch, that sort of thing?'

Marsha didn't know what to say. This meeting had torn her heart out by its roots all over again, but it was clear that their relationship was important to Susan.

The only way she had been able to cope when she had first left Taylor was to cut herself off from her old life completely, and she was feeling like that once more. The pain was raw, but if Susan needed her...

She reached out her hand and took Susan's cool fingers in hers. 'In a little while, okay?' she said quietly. 'I need to make Taylor understand we can never get together again, that it is really over once and for all. Once the divorce is through I'll feel...easier about everything. But we will meet then, if that's what you want.'

She had tried to prevent it, but her eyes had filled up again as she spoke, and now Susan's face was distraught as she murmured, 'I shouldn't have asked.'

'Of course you should.' Marsha squeezed the other woman's hand one last time before settling back into the taxi. 'We're friends, and friends are always there for each other, whatever's happened.'

Susan shut the taxi door without saying anything more. As the vehicle drew away Marsha waved, but the other woman barely responded, although just as they turned the corner out of sight Taylor's sister was still standing at the bottom of the drive, staring after the car.

Marsha shut her eyes, letting out her breath in a deep sigh. So much for hope. She had been stupid to think Susan would say anything other than what she had eighteen months before. She didn't know why she had come now. As she'd told Nicki, Susan was Taylor's sister and she loved her brother devotedly. It must have been a real battle of divided loyalties for her.

She had to accept that it was really over, that there weren't any Prince Charmings left in the world who would ride in on their valiant steeds and rescue the fair maiden from whatever assailed her. Real life was different; *people* were different. People like her mother, her best friend. People like Taylor.

But she had thought he was special. It was the cry of a child in her heart. He had made her believe in happy ever after and that wasn't fair. None of this was fair. She had thought they would create their own family—not straight away, but in time. A family that would be a secure unit, strong, and who would do anything for each other. She didn't want to be alone the rest of her life.

No snivelling.

The voice in her head brought her up sharp, and she answered it by sitting up straight.

'All right, love?'

She became aware of the taxi driver's eyes on her in his mirror and she nodded quickly. 'Yes, thank you.'

'Only you look a bit under the weather, if you don't mind me saying so.'

'I'm fine.'

'Course, there's a lot of this flu about, you know. The wife went down with it a couple of weeks ago, and two of the kids are off school now. Mind, I reckon the little 'un is playing the wag. Don't like school, the little 'un.'

Marsha nodded, trying to be polite but wishing he would just drive the cab.

He must have got the message, because thankfully the rest of the journey progressed in silence.

She had rung Jeff at home first thing that morning, explaining that something unexpected had come up and she would like to take a day's holiday, if that was possible. 'Problems?' he had asked, and when she'd merely replied that they were personal ones he'd told her there was no need to use up any holiday time but, depending on how long it took to get things sorted, he would appreciate even an hour or two at the end of the day if she were able.

She found she was glad of this now. Her job was hectic and demanding, but that was exactly what she needed. The thought of going home to the empty bedsit filled her with dread. She would get to the office just before lunchtime and make sure she did not leave until she was too exhausted to do another minute. That way she might be able to sleep when she got home. Tomorrow was another day and she would think about everything then. For now it was enough to get through with her emotions so lacerated.

She had been an idiot when Taylor had called this morning. She had underestimated her own strength to resist him, but she wouldn't make the same mistake again. Her hands bunched together as she remembered their embraces, her cheeks flushing with humiliation at how easily he had beguiled her. From now on he could threaten to wake the whole street and she would not let him in. But it wouldn't come to that anyway. Tomorrow she would arrange to meet him somewhere anonymous, a wine bar or something similar, and she would make it abundantly clear the divorce was going through come hell or high water.

She caught her breath as her heart twisted. Behind

her closed eyelids she could picture him on the screen of her mind. His long lean tanned body as it had looked that morning, the broad muscled chest, flat stomach and hard powerful thighs, his hands—brown and long-fingered—and his mouth. Oh, his mouth… Sensuous, coaxing, possessing the power to send her delirious with desire. How was she going to manage without him? How would she ever get through the rest of her life, knowing he was in the world—walking, eating, breathing, loving—but not with her?

Stop it. She opened her eyes with a snap, furious at herself. She had got by the last eighteen months and she would do so again. Taylor Kane was not the be all and end all; she had to remember that. He might be fascinating and sexy and tender and magnetic, but he was also ruthless and arrogant and hard when it suited him. The same qualities that drew her to him drew other women, and she wasn't about to live her life ruled by jealousy, eaten up by it. This had to be a clean sharp cut which severed any fragile links still hanging between them.

She turned her head to gaze unseeing out of the window. Of course she would always love him, always carry a thousand regrets for what might have been, but she mustn't let him know that. She had thought she would grow old with him, loving him and being loved in return, but it wasn't to be. There would be no babies, no little Taylors with dark hair and tawny eyes…

Again she jerked herself out of her thoughts by sheer will-power. She must not let her mind stray for one moment. She had to keep absolute control over herself or she would end up a gibbering idiot! She had made the only decision she could eighteen months ago and nothing had changed. She couldn't spend her life wondering when he would tire of her completely, when one of his other women would capture his heart, mind and soul. Living alone for the rest of her life would be preferable to that.

The thought mocked her, especially because, having seen him again, she wasn't sure if it was true. If she thought there was a chance she might hold him she would take it.

But not at the cost of your own soul. She sat up straighter, her mouth setting in a grim line. And that was what it boiled down to. She wouldn't let herself become a victim, the sort of woman who put up with intolerable indignities in the name of love.

'Here we are, miss.'

As the taxi drew up outside the TV building Marsha scrambled out, giving the man a handsome tip to make up for being such an uncommunicative passenger.

She had made a life for herself and it was a good one. It *was*. It would have to be enough.

CHAPTER EIGHT

'MARSHA. I didn't expect you today.'

Nicki beamed at her as she walked into the office, which was a slight balm to her sore feelings. At least her secretary liked her, she thought with a heavy dose of self-pity which she wasn't about to apologise for in the slightest. 'I sorted things out quicker than I expected,' she said quietly.

'Sorted things out?' Nicki frowned. 'Jeff said you'd come back to work yesterday too quickly and weren't feeling great again today.'

Bless him. Marsha felt a brief warm glow in the leaden ball of her stomach. People could be so nice on occasion. 'Well, I'll stick to that officially, then. Unofficially—' she bent down closer '—I took your advice and went to see Taylor's sister.' She wasn't about to tell even Nicki of the early-morning breakfast scenario.

'And?'

'Nothing. She was very sweet and very upset, but that's all. The truth is the truth when all's said and done.'

'Pants.'

'Quite.'

Marsha seated herself at her desk and pulled a wad of papers in front of her. There was nothing more to be said.

When Nicki brought back half the canteen's stock of food at lunchtime Marsha ate a rather pitiable-looking ham sandwich and apple at her desk, but she had to force the food down. Jeff had popped his head out just after she had got into the office, declaring himself immensely pleased to see her, after which he had deposited a slim file in front of her, ordering her to stop all other work immediately. Marsha was not fooled by the width of the file. Thinking up ideas for new and interesting programmes was testing enough, but often necessitated a minimum of paperwork. Translating the idea into a programme within a budget, often with the impending broadcasting date just ahead, was the really hard work. After glancing through the paperwork she knew she would be working all over the weekend.

She had just returned to her desk, after a visit to the studio where the programme would be shot, and was immersed in a wad of possible facts and figures when Nicki leapt in front of her. 'Could you sign this please?' she said loudly, adding in a low hiss, 'Penelope and *him* are in the corridor outside.'

Marsha's stomach curled, but she had the presence of mind to keep her head down as she reached for the blank piece of paper Nicki had thrust on her desk.

Every nerve-end prickling, she waited for the door to open. She wasn't disappointed. Penelope sailed in first, in a cloud of cloying perfume, her tone pre-emptive as she said, 'He's in, I take it?' and made for Jeff's door.

'Just a moment, Miss Pelham.' Marsha was on her feet and in front of Jeff's door quicker than a dose of salts. She ignored the dark figure behind the other woman as she said, 'If you would like to take a seat, I'll just check Mr North is free.'

Penelope halted, swirling on her high heels as she said to Taylor, 'Really!' But she didn't press her case, knowing full well it was exactly how she would have expected her second in command to have acted.

Marsha knocked on Jeff's door, slipping inside and closing it again before she said evenly, 'Miss Pelham and Mr Kane are outside.'

'What?' Jeff had been deep in an intricate and soaring budget which had been giving him a headache for days, but as her words registered his eyes cleared. He disliked Penelope every bit as much as he liked Marsha, and he thought this Kane fellow needed his head testing. He didn't know what had gone on in the marriage—it might have been six of one and half a dozen of the other, though he doubted it—but for the guy to rub Marsha's nose in it with Penelope was downright cruel. And he had a pretty good idea what the 'personal business' Marsha had spoken about earlier involved. 'You okay?' he said softly.

Marsha put out her hand, turning it from side to side as she said, 'So, so,' her smile shaky.

'You know you're far too good for that bozo, don't you? Let Penelope get her claws into him for a while. He'll soon wish he'd never been born.'

Marsha's smile was more natural this time. 'Thanks, Jeff. I'll show them in, shall I?'

He nodded. 'And get Nicki to bring some coffee in, would you? Penelope takes hers with arsenic.'

'Oh, Jeff.' The kindness was a little too much, coming at a time when her composure was fragile to say the least. As the smile wobbled and her bottom lip trembled Jeff was round his desk in a shot.

'Hey, come on. No guy is worth your tears. Now, then—there's plenty out there who would give their right arm to be with you.'

He put a comforting arm round her shoulders, digging

in his pocket for a crisp white handkerchief with the other. He handed it to her with a wry smile. 'Chin up,' he said gently. 'Don't give either of them the satisfaction of seeing this bothers you.'

'I'll try.'

'That's my girl.'

'Oh, I'm sorry. Are we interrupting anything?' Penelope's cool voice from the doorway brought Marsha's blonde head and Jeff's brown one swinging round as though connected by the same cord.

Neither of them had heard the door open, but Penelope was standing staring at them, her eyes aglow, with Taylor filling the space behind her. Marsha gave an inward groan, but to give Jeff his due he maintained the stance for a second or so more, removing his arm from her shoulders almost leisurely as he said, 'We'll talk later, Marsha. Okay? Now, perhaps if you'd like to get Nicki organising that coffee…?'

'Certainly.' Taking her cue from Jeff, she raised her chin, speaking to the two in the doorway but keeping her eyes on Penelope's feline face as she said, 'If you'd like to take a seat?'

She let them come into the room before she made any effort to pass them, but even though she didn't glance at Taylor she could sense the dark waves emanating from the tall figure. Just as she shut the door she heard Penelope say in an overt whisper, 'Jeff, I'm so sorry. I had no idea. I thought Marsha was merely announcing us. If we've embarrassed you in any way…'

She might have known Penelope would turn the knife a little. Marsha took a deep pull of air as she stood outside the closed door, staring across the office.

'I couldn't stop her, Marsha.' Nicki was standing by her desk, her plump face agitated. 'She muttered something about she wasn't going to be kept waiting for anyone, and then just opened the door before I realised what she was doing.'

'Don't worry, Nicki, it wasn't your fault.' Marsha's voice was soothing, but she was working on automatic.

What on earth had it looked like in there to Taylor? She imagined their stance from his eyes. Nothing short of a clinch, that was what. Rats! She walked across to her desk, her tone preoccupied as she said, 'They want coffee, please, Nicki.'

As the other woman bustled off Marsha gazed down at the papers on her desk, but she wasn't seeing the figures in front of her. This was all she needed! Damn Penelope. It wouldn't make any difference that it was well-known Jeff was madly in love with his wife and a devoted family man; Penelope would have her last pound of flesh with this one.

She wrestled with what she could do or say until Nicki returned with the coffee, but once her secretary was seated at her desk again Marsha told herself she had to clear her mind and concentrate on the job in hand. She had very little time to organise everything, and all the agonising in the world couldn't turn back time. Taylor would have to think what he liked, and if any gossip started circulating Jeff was the sort of person who would nip it in the bud, Penelope or no Penelope.

It was only ten minutes later when the interjoining door opened, and although Marsha's stomach turned over she deliberately took her time about raising her eyes, keeping her expression calm and serene.

'I need to talk to you.' Taylor had stopped by her desk, Penelope by his side, and Marsha thought the other woman would burst a blood vessel when he turned his head, saying, 'I'll be along shortly, Penelope.'

'Fine, fine.' It was an immediate recovery, but Penelope was good at those.

Jeff, too, had paused, and now he said, 'We're going along to discuss a few items in this proposal with Tim. Can you cope here, Marsha?'

He was asking about more than the office and they were all aware of it. Marsha nodded, her voice steady as she said, 'Of course, but don't forget your appointment at four o'clock.'

'I won't.'

As Penelope and Jeff left Marsha turned to Nicki, who was all agog whilst pretending to work. 'I'm going to be here late tonight, Nicki. Could you pop down to the canteen and get something for my tea? A salad or sandwiches will do—something like that. I'll settle up with you when you come back.'

'Sure.' Nicki rose immediately, but not before she had given Taylor the once-over, her face unmistakably hostile.

It was Taylor who spoke first when they were alone. He perched on the edge of her desk, bringing well-cut trousers tight over hard male thighs as he said, 'She doesn't like me.'

'What?' It hadn't been what she'd expected.

'Your secretary. She doesn't like me.'

'Well, there has to be the odd female or two who are immune to your charms, surely?' Marsha said with a lightness she was proud of, considering the circumstances.

He eyed her steadily. 'Like to explain what that—' he indicated the office behind him with a jerk of his head '—was all about?'

A hundred sharp rejoinders burned on her tongue, but she didn't voice any of them. She stared at him for a moment or two, as though his words were taking time to filter through. 'I assume by ''that'' you mean the friendly arm round the shoulders?'

'Is that what it was?'

'Jeff is very happily married with two children. He is also a very nice man, who is a friend as well as my boss.'

Dark eyebrows rose. 'I've known several very happily married men who have the family-man image down to a fine art and also an obliging mistress on the side,' he said coolly.

'I don't doubt for a minute you are acquainted with that side of life,' she shot back tightly, 'but Jeff isn't.'

He shifted slightly and her senses went haywire. His suit jacket was open, revealing a crisp white shirt and a patterned navy tie, and as she watched he undid the first two or three buttons of the shirt, pulling his tie loose. It was a perfectly ordinary action and there was no call for the rush of sexual tension that sent electricity into each nerve and sinew.

'Penelope informs me you got this job on Jeff's recommendation.' He was still speaking in the conversational tone he had employed since he had left Jeff's office, but Marsha had lived with him too long not to know that he was the master of control and an expert in giving nothing away.

'I met him briefly when I was working for a different company before we were married,' she said, in a tone which stated that all this was none of his business. 'When I applied for the job here he recognised me. That's all.'

'And he made sure you got the position under him.'

There was a definite insinuation there, but she mentally shrugged off the insult. 'He believed in me, yes.'

'Penelope seems to think he does more than believe in you.'

'Really?' From somewhere was coming the strength to deal with this in a way she would have thought beyond her. 'Again, that doesn't surprise me. When one's morals are akin to a bitch in heat it must be difficult to recognise decent men and women.'

He leant forward, studying her with those clear orbs of amber light which were as penetrating as sunlight into a shadowed corner. 'So there is nothing going on between you and North?' he asked softly.

'No, there isn't.'

'Good.' He straightened, his arms crossed in front of him. 'I wouldn't have liked to have to make him see the error of his ways.'

Her head whipped upward. She just couldn't believe what a hypocrite he was. She glared at him, her voice frosty when she said, 'Have you got a replacement ready for Tanya yet?' her voice as double-edged as his had been moments before.

'Of course.' If he was aware of what she was implying he gave no sign of it. 'Tanya has been training her for three months now.'

'*Tanya* has?'

'Most adeptly.'

He smiled, and Marsha wanted to hit him over the head with her table lamp. 'Sheila Cross is fifty and re-entering the workplace after nursing her husband with terminal cancer for three years. She held a very impressive position with one of my competitors before her husband was taken ill, but when she became available for work again they implied she was too old. Their mistake, my gain. She might be a grandmother of two, but she's sharper than any twenty- or thirty-year-old. She'll keep the rest of the staff on their toes.'

Her eyebrows had risen at his unexpected elucidation. Ridiculous, *absolutely* ridiculous, in view of what she had had confirmed that morning by Susan, but she found she was immensely glad there wasn't going to be another sumptuous young thing pouting in front of him, with her notebook and pencil at the ready and her skirt up to her thighs.

She surveyed him now, her green eyes revealing more than she knew. 'Do you believe me, about Jeff?' she asked after a moment.

'Of course.'

He spoke so easily she knew it was true, and for some reason she found it annoyed her. Which was so crazy, so absolutely illogical, that she didn't understand herself at all. She didn't want him to be jealous, did she? she asked herself silently, and then was horrified with the answer.

'I'm sorry I had to shoot off this morning,' he said very quietly. 'I would have liked to stay and eat with you.'

Her cheeks began to burn in spite of herself. She tried to forget how magnificent he had looked and how good it had been, but it was hard with him so close.

'I phoned this morning, but they said you were unwell. When I called round at the bedsit Mrs Tate-Collins said you had gone out.'

There was an enquiry in his tone. Marsha felt her strength waver for a moment, then she told him the truth. 'I needed to go and see someone.'

'Someone?'

He was too close. She needed to distance herself a little or she would never be able to say what had to be said. If she could have chosen she would have picked a different place and a different time, but it hadn't worked out like that. She stood up, walking across to the window and then turning to face him again. He was watching her intently and he hadn't moved.

'I needed to go and see the person who told me about you and Tanya,' she said very clearly. 'I had to know if they could be wrong.'

'And?'

'They weren't.'

He remained perfectly still. 'I think I'm in a position to be the best judge of that.'

'They said—'

'*Who* said?' He stood up in one fluid angry movement, before controlling himself with visible effort. 'Who the hell is this person who seems to be able to convince you black is white? Damn it, I'm your *husband*. Your husband, Fuzz. My word ought to mean more than some nobody on the fringe of your life.'

'I'm sorry, but I believe them.' She met his fury steadily, knowing it would be fatal to weaken now. 'They have no reason to lie.'

'Then they are mistaken, if they aren't lying,' he ground out savagely. 'Either way they need straightening out.'

'Like you would have straightened Jeff out if we had been having an affair?'

'What does that mean?'

Her hand went to her throat, her fingers pulling at the flesh there before she forced herself to lower it to her side. He had often told her that one of the secrets of his success story was his ability to read the body language of his opponent. 'You bulldoze anyone who stands in your way—either that or you use your charm to manipulate and coerce them into submission,' she said flatly. 'But I won't allow you to do that here.'

'Charming.' He was furiously angry, more angry than she had ever seen him, and she was glad they weren't alone at her bedsit. 'You paint a great picture of me, sweetheart. I'll give you that.'

'You've told me often enough you came up the hard way.'

'The hard way, yes. Lying, cheating or double-crossing, no. I don't defraud or fleece some poor sucker who doesn't know what day of the week it is. Hell, if you thought I was like that why did you marry me in the first place?'

'Because I loved you.' She spoke without thinking, without realising that she was in effect confirming she had thought all those things of him. Which she hadn't—she really hadn't, she told herself in the next moment as she watched his face change into a man she didn't recognise.

'Well, now I know where I stand.' Instead of the previous white-hot fury, his voice and eyes were as cold as ice and without expression. 'Your opinion of me couldn't be much lower, could it? A shark, a twister, the sort of conman who is without conscience both in his personal life as well as his business enterprises.'

'I didn't mean that.' She had gone too far. She would have known that even if his whole being hadn't shouted it.

'That's exactly what you meant,' he said tersely. 'Damn it, I poured out my heart to you. I told you about all of my past and my dreams for the future. I didn't keep anything back. I thought if I told you how much I loved you you would begin to believe it. I wanted you to understand we had the kind of love that would last for ever, the kind that means intimacy and commitment and happy ever after. Everything you'd missed out on. Kids, grandchildren, growing old together. Laughing, crying and maybe even grieving, but always together. Always closer than our own skins. You were part of me, Fuzz. You were knitted into the marrow of my bones.'

Past tense. He was using the past tense. She stared at him, a sense of terrible finality gripping her.

'And all the time you had this secret opinion of me.'

'No—no, I didn't.'

He ignored her as though she hadn't spoken. 'I told you how it was with my mother and dad, how they made our lives a living hell. She married him because she was pregnant with me and immediately regretted it. Drink was the way she escaped from him and from reality and he knew it. Knew it and couldn't take it. She thought he was nothing and eventually he came to believe that himself. And do you know why? Because he loved her. If he hadn't loved her so much he would have fought back better, but she was all he ever wanted. Funny that, don't you think?'

He smiled, a terrible smile. 'Like father, like son? But I'm not going to go the same way as him, Fuzz. I'm not going to end my days wallowing in the gutter because the woman I love despises me. I'm worth better than that.'

'I don't despise you.' She was so shocked she could hardly speak, and even to her own ears her voice was feeble.

'That's not how it reads from where I'm standing.' His voice was low and harsh. 'You won't tell me who fed you that garbage in the first place, you give me no chance to defend myself—what's that if not contempt?

I married you knowing I couldn't wipe the first twenty-four-odd years from your psyche, but I thought what we had would survive anything that came against it. I was wrong.'

Struggling for calmness, Marsha said, 'Listen to me. You have to listen to me. I don't despise you. I've never despised you. I love you, Taylor.'

'Not enough.' His anger had collapsed, and in its place was grim intent. 'Not enough to trust me. Not even enough to phone that guy who gave me a bed. Did you think I'd bought him too? Forced and manipulated him like I apparently do with everyone else? Is that why you didn't pick up the phone *and call him*?'

'I told you, I didn't get your letter.'

'And so you were content just to cut your losses?'

'It wasn't like that.' If he knew the pain she'd suffered, the agony of wanting him so badly she'd been prepared to crawl on her hands and knees some cold lonely nights to find him…

'We had it and we lost it, and I still don't know the hell why.'

She flinched visibly, trying to think of something to say to take the dead look out of his eyes and failing utterly. She had blown it. Whatever happened now, she had blown it, and it was only in this moment of absolute truth that she could say in all honesty that she believed in him. Somehow, *somehow* there had been a mistake. Susan had listened to the wrong person, or maybe Tanya had lied, or perhaps someone else outside of the family had had something to do with all this. Whatever—he hadn't betrayed her. Only now there was no joy in the knowledge because she knew he would never have her back.

'I made love to you this morning.'

Every word was like a sword-thrust straight through her heart, but now she stood silent and still, knowing she deserved all this and more.

'Love, Marsha. We didn't have sex. We didn't mate like two animals who don't know any better. When I took you it was because I loved you—mind, body, soul and spirit. Every inch of you, the good and the bad, the weak and the strong. I would have died for you, don't you know that?'

'I…I believe you now,' she said with a desperation she made no attempt to hide. 'I do, Taylor.'

'No. Let's have truth between us if nothing else. You are convinced I slept with Tanya, and others besides, and this last little while it's Penelope I'm suppose to be bedding. Right? You married one hell of a stud, Fuzz. When did I get the time to sleep with all those women when we were still together anyway? Didn't you stop long enough to ask yourself that? You know how it was between us. We couldn't keep our hands off each other. Why would I have looked at anyone else?'

'I know, I know.'

The strains of a tuneless rendering of a popular chart hit from the corridor outside the office announced Nicki's imminent and tactful return, and now Taylor straightened, his voice deep and flat when he said, 'Goodbye, Marsha.'

What could she say to convince him to stay? How could they work this out? Coherent thought, let alone speech, seemed to be beyond her. She stared at him, watching as he opened the door just as Nicki returned. He brushed past the other woman without so much as a backward glance.

Nicki came in and shut the door behind her, depositing the goods from the canteen on Marsha's desk but saying nothing before she reached out her arms and hugged her. 'You'll be all right. You *will* get through this,' she murmured against her hair.

'I've made the worst mistake of my life, Nicki.' Strangely she had no desire to cry; the shock and pain were too deep for such relief. 'Somehow Susan was wrong.'

'Did you tell him it was her who told you?'

She stared blankly into the concerned face in front of her. 'I don't think it would have made any difference. He hates me, Nicki. I could see it in his eyes.'

'Oh, Marsha.'

They looked at each other and it was clear that for once Nicki didn't know what to say or do. Marsha glanced down at her hands, numbly noting how badly they were trembling. 'I must get on with some work.'

Nicki swore softly. 'Leave all that,' she said firmly. 'There are more important things at stake here than some old television programme.'

And this from a girl who lived and breathed her work. Marsha forced a smile, but it was a shaky one. 'You don't understand.' She shook her head, seating herself at the desk again as she added, 'How could you, when I don't understand myself? Somehow it's gone from bad to worse. All I know is it's too late, Nicki. Much too late. And at least I can handle this—' she indicated the papers littering her desk '—even if I make such a mess of everything else.'

'Maybe he'll come round?' Nicki was ever hopeful, that was one of the things Marsha liked about her, but today she knew her secretary was on a loser. 'Men do sometimes, when they've had a chance to think about things. My hubby often comes in with a bunch of flowers or a box of chocolates when he's been a pig.'

'But Taylor hasn't been a pig. I have.'

'Well, give *him* a bunch of flowers or a box of chocolates, then. Eat humble pie. It might not taste too good at the time, but it's very beneficial afterwards.'

'If it was as simple as that I'd do it like a shot, but it's not. He's given me loads of chances and I've blown every one.'

'But if he loves you?' Nicki argued. 'Try once more.'

Marsha shook her head. 'You don't know him,' she said quietly. 'When he makes up his mind about something he's like a solid force, immovable.'

Nicki sighed deeply, plumping herself down at her desk.

Poor Nicki. Marsha glanced at her secretary's woeful face. She so wanted this to end like one of the films or books she devoured so avidly, but this wasn't fiction.

She had lost Taylor.

CHAPTER NINE

MARSHA didn't leave the office until it was nearly dark. When she stepped outside the building the air was warm and moist, the smell of traffic fumes still heavy in the air although the rush hour was long since past. She stood for a moment flexing tired neck muscles. She felt utterly spent. And she would have to be back at her desk early in the morning both tomorrow and Sunday. So much for a relaxing weekend. But she didn't mind. She would rather be doing something than having time on her hands, the way she was feeling.

Tired as she was, she decided to walk home, and by the time she reached the bedsit it was quite dark. Once inside she kicked off her shoes, turning off the main light and clicking on a small lamp to the side of her TV. A shower. She nodded mentally to the thought. A long cool shower and then a cup of milky chocolate and bed.

The swirling in her stomach which had been with her since the confrontation with Taylor had prevented her from eating the salad and ham and egg flan Nicki had brought from the canteen, and when, after leaving the shower and pulling on her nightie, she felt light-headed, she knew she had to eat something. She forced down a couple of slices of toast along with the chocolate drink, and she was just finishing the last bite when the front door buzzer connected to her bedsit sounded.

Her heart jumped, and then raced like a mad thing. Taylor? Surely it could only be him at this time of night? She was shaking as she pressed the intercom, but her voice sounded quite normal when she said, 'Hello? Who is it?'

'Me—Taylor. Listen, Marsha, it's Susan. She's in hospital. She tried…' There was a pause before he continued, 'She tried to kill herself tonight.'

'What?'

'Dale found her. He's with her now, but she's upset and she's asking for you. Could you—?'

'I'll be down straight away.' She threw off the nightie, reaching for some clean underwear and pulling on a pair of jeans and a light top. She didn't even stop to brush her hair, grabbing her handbag and keys and racing down the stairs after she'd shut her front door.

When she opened the door to the building Taylor was standing waiting for her, his face drawn and grim. She wanted to fling her arms round him, but everything in his posture warned her not to. Whatever had gone on with Susan, it hadn't altered anything with regard to them, she realised.

The Aston Martin was double parked in front of the house, and as they walked towards it he said, 'I'm sorry about this. Did I wake you?' his voice horribly formal.

'No, I was late leaving work. I've only just got in and had something to eat.'

He nodded, opening the passenger door for her as they reached the car and then shutting it before walking round the bonnet. She watched him, her heart thudding. He looked ill, grey, but no wonder. Surely Susan couldn't have tried to take her own life? She had everything to live for.

As Taylor slid in beside her she said, 'There must be some sort of mistake, surely? Susan wouldn't have tried to kill herself.'

He started the engine, and it was only when he had pulled out of the cul-de-sac and into the main thoroughfare that he said flatly, 'Dale was going to Germany on some business for me this afternoon, but when he got to the airport he realised he'd left an important file he was working on at home at the house. He tried to ring Susan, but after a while thought she was either talking to someone for a hell of a time, or had taken the phone off the hook. Either way, he couldn't do without the file. He arranged to catch an early-morning flight tomorrow and called in somewhere for a meal and a cup of coffee before going home. He found her stretched out on their bed with an empty pill box beside her and half a bottle of whisky gone. She doesn't even normally drink whisky.'

'But why? Does he know why?'

'Apparently things haven't been right between them for a couple of years. They've been trying for kids more or less since they were married, with no results, and five years ago they started IVF, again with no results. Dale said Susan became obsessed by the idea of having a baby, it was all that mattered to her, so what does he do two years ago? He has an affair with his secretary.'

He made her jump by suddenly thumping the steering wheel so hard it must have hurt his hand. 'He maintains it was over as soon as it was started but Susan found out somehow. I could kill him, Marsha. If he hadn't looked like death warmed up tonight I swear I'd have strung him up then and there at the side of her bed.'

'Oh, Taylor.' She didn't know what to say. Why hadn't Susan told them? But then why should she? she answered herself in the next moment. It was none of their business what went on with Susan and Dale.

'She took it hard. He says he's been trying to make

it up to her ever since, but things have been bad. I guess the new house, the spending and the rest of it was all a consolation for having no kids, and she could just about get by with that, but when he had this affair she realised she'd got nothing.'

He was gripping the wheel so hard his knuckles shone white, his face dark with the rage he was trying to control.

'But she's going to be all right?' she asked faintly.

He nodded. 'But it was touch and go for a while. They've pumped her stomach, and she was out of it most of the time, but as soon as she came round enough to realise she hadn't succeeded in what she'd tried to do she kept asking for you. She wouldn't talk to Dale or me and she was getting hysterical, so I said I'd come and fetch you.'

'Did she leave a note, anything like that?' She couldn't believe this was actually happening. It was like a drama on TV, not something that happened to nice ordinary folk like Susan and Dale.

'I don't think Dale noticed anything, but then as soon as he saw her he realised what she'd done and panicked. He phoned the ambulance and then me, and dragged her downstairs, apparently, trying to make her walk and come to. I was at a dinner party in Sevenoaks, so I went straight to the hospital. I guess Dale will find out from Susan if she left a letter anywhere.'

Sevenoaks. Penelope had a penthouse pad in Sevenoaks. Marsha refused to dwell on the thought; there were more important things to hand. 'Do you know why she wants to speak to me?' she asked carefully. She had only seen Susan that morning after all. But she couldn't reveal that or Taylor would undoubtedly put two and two together.

He shrugged. 'She's barely lucid, poor kid.'

They drove in silence after that, and never had Marsha so bitterly regretted that they weren't still living together as man and wife. She desperately wanted to comfort him, to kiss the tautness of his mouth and tell him everything would be all right, but she had forfeited the right to do that for ever.

He had been absolutely right in all he had said since he had found her again. She *should* have stayed around long enough—when he had got home from Germany after that disastrous weekend—to dot the 'i's and cross the 't's if nothing else. And she should never have promised Susan that she wouldn't reveal who had told her about Tanya. She had accused Taylor of engaging in adultery and then refused to listen to any explanation because she had believed immediately he was guilty. Remorse rose like gall in her throat.

She hadn't believed in him and she hadn't trusted him. And why? He had hit the nail on the head the morning after he had taken her home when she had been ill. She had been waiting for him to let her down, like everyone else had in her life to date. She had never really given Taylor all of herself because she hadn't dared to, and the more she had come to love and rely on him, the more it had terrified her. She was a mess. A twenty-four carat mess.

By the time they drew into the grounds of the hospital Marsha felt less than the dust under his shoes. As Taylor helped her out of the car his touch was impersonal and his manner remote, the change in him heaping coals of fire on to her head.

She wanted to weep and wail and give way to the grief she was feeling, but now was not the time, and so she took refuge in the stoic reserve which had sustained her all through her difficult childhood and teenage years and beyond.

Once they had been admitted into the hospital she walked through the hushed, dimly lit corridors at Taylor's side with her head high and her heart breaking. She could cry for what might have been when she was alone, but for now she would conduct herself with dignity, if nothing else.

When they reached the small private room off a main ward where Susan had been taken, Taylor knocked once and opened the door, holding it for Marsha to walk through but not entering into the room himself. Dale was sitting by the side of the bed, and she saw immediately Taylor hadn't exaggerated how he looked, but all her sympathy was for the slight figure lying so still in the hospital bed. Susan's thin body barely made a mound under the cotton sheet covering her and she had her eyes shut, but as soon as Taylor spoke, saying, 'Has she said anything?' her eyes shot open.

As Dale shook his head, Susan said weakly, 'Marsha, oh, Marsha,' big teardrops beginning to trickle down her white face.

Marsha was aware of Dale standing to his feet and leaving the room, of the door being gently shut behind the two men, but as she took the too thin body in her arms, and Susan's sobs shook them both, her only thought was for the young woman who was her sister-in-law. She sat on the edge of the bed, rocking Susan gently as she murmured soothing words of comfort, and it was a long time before the storm of weeping faded to hiccuping sobs and finally to the odd gasp or two.

'Here.' Marsha reached for a big box of tissues on the bedside locker, lifting Susan's chin and mopping her face. 'That's better.'

As she smiled into the tragic face Susan surprised her by gripping her hand, her voice low and desperate as she said, 'Marsha, I've done an unforgivable thing. I left some letters before I—' She shook her head from side to side. 'Dale didn't see them, but he will when he goes home.'

'Susan, whatever it is, it can't be bad enough for you to do this,' Marsha said gently.

'It is.' Susan stared at her with puffy swollen eyes. 'I'm so ashamed. I wish they had let me die.' She turned her head to the side, fresh tears trickling down her face.

The bolt of lightning came from nowhere, causing Marsha's whole body to become still. She moistened her lips with her tongue before she said, 'You made it up—about Tanya.'

Susan's body jerked. 'You knew?' she whispered.

'Not until this moment.'

'He…he never did anything, not with Tanya or anyone else.'

Susan was gripping her so hard she would have bruises, but the pain didn't register. As she stared into Taylor's sister's eyes, Marsha had a strange feeling come over her. For a moment she almost felt as though she was suffocating, and it was an enormous effort to say, 'Why did you do it?'

'I don't know, not really. I think I was a little deranged at the time, but that's no excuse, I know that. Dale…Dale had an affair with his secretary—'

'I know. He told Taylor tonight,' Marsha cut in.

'He did?' Susan wiped the back of her hand across her face but still held on tightly to Marsha with the other one. 'It made me feel…like nothing. Less than nothing. I couldn't have a baby and now my husband had been with someone else, *slept* with her. There was only

Taylor in my life who loved me, that's how I felt, but now he had you I wasn't really important to him like I used to be. Everything had changed.'

'Susan, Taylor's always loved you. You're his sister. His own flesh and blood.'

'But you would give him babies, children and grandchildren, and I would get more and more pushed out.'

'That would never have happened.' Marsha stared into the other woman's eyes, the pale orbs filled with misery and looking far too large for the elfin face.

'I know that now, I knew it soon after you had left Taylor, but it was too late by then. I couldn't say what I had done. He used to come and see me and rage against the person who had told you such lies, say what he'd do to them when he found out who it was. He will never forgive me, Marsha. He'll hate me now.'

Marsha looked at her, torn between pity and anger and pain and regret and a hundred other emotions besides. Struggling to put her own feelings aside for the moment, she said, 'Taylor could never hate you, Susan.'

'He could for this. From the moment he met you he worshipped the ground you walked on, and even before I knew you I was so jealous of you. But then… Well, you were so nice, and we got on so well.' Susan swallowed. 'And then I found out about Dale. I…I felt it must be my fault that he had wanted someone else. I wasn't good enough or pretty enough. I went on medication from the doctor but it didn't seem to help. I couldn't sleep, couldn't eat. I used to get up in the middle of the night when Dale was asleep and walk round the neighbourhood, wondering why all the other women in all the other houses could keep their men and I couldn't.'

Marsha reached out her hand and stroked a lock of

damp hair from out of Susan's eyes. 'Why didn't you tell someone?' she said softly. 'If not me, then Taylor.'

'Taylor would have beaten Dale to a pulp, and then there was Dale's job. It would have become impossible for him to continue working for Taylor and then where would we have been? But the main reason was...' Susan lowered her eyes, her voice becoming nothing more than the faintest whisper. 'I felt so humiliated, so ashamed—about Dale wanting someone else, the fact I couldn't have a baby, everything. I...I didn't feel a woman, Marsha, just a thing. An ugly, fat, barren thing.'

That was why Susan had become fanatical about working out at the gym and dieting, Marsha thought, not long after she and Taylor had married. 'You should have told me,' she said gently.

'I've never been good at sharing my feelings at the best of times,' Susan admitted pitifully. 'With Mum like she was there was no time for anything like talking or discussing any troubles. I can never remember her hugging or kissing me in the whole of my life. And of course Dad was never around, and on the rare occasion he was he was too busy fighting with Mum to take any notice of me or Taylor.'

'Oh, Susan.' Marsha's eyes were dry but she was crying inside. For the small bewildered and hurting child trapped in Susan's body, for Dale, who clearly hadn't got a clue how to handle the emotional volcano he had married, for Taylor, for herself. Susan's jealousy had led Taylor's sister down a lonely twisted path to a place where the outcome had been devastating for everyone.

'I've told Taylor everything in the letter I've left.' Susan was clutching at her again, her whole being begging for absolution. 'And there's one for you and one for Dale too. I've explained about your letter, the one that Taylor wrote you just after you had moved out and were living in that bed and breakfast.'

'You took it?'

'He told me what he was going to do, and so the morning after he'd posted it I said to Dale I was going jogging early. I hung about across the road from where you were staying and when I saw the postman I jogged over to him and pretended that I lived there. I asked if there was anything for a Mrs Kane and he handed me the letter. It was as simple as that.' Susan rubbed at her damp face. 'It's amazing how if you're deceitful enough you can fool nice people, isn't it?'

'And you made the reservation in Germany.' It was a statement, not a question, but Susan answered it anyway.

'I knew the hotel, because Taylor uses the same one every year when he goes to the conference, so it was just a matter of phoning and changing the two single rooms Tanya had booked for one double. They didn't even ask for an e-mail or anything to confirm.'

'And so you waited until they'd gone to Germany and then came and told me.' Marsha stared at the girl she had thought of as the sister she had never had.

Susan nodded, her voice husky from the effects of the treatment she had had as she said, 'I can't believe I did all that now, I really can't, but it was strange. One thing led to another and it was like I was on some kind of a high, like I was proving I wasn't so stupid and worthless somehow. When I got the letter that day I went to the gym in the afternoon and worked out for hours I had so much adrenalin.'

'Have you still got the letter?' Marsha asked numbly.

Susan shook her head. 'I was worried Dale might find

it. He has thought it's been the affair that has been between us for the last year or two, that I would never forgive him, but it wasn't that. How could I tell him what I'd done to you and Taylor? He would have despised me.'

'Do you still love him?' Marsha asked quietly. She couldn't sort out her own feelings, they were too confused and raw, but the fact that Susan had tried to take her own life and was clearly ill was at the forefront of her mind.

What Susan had done once she could do again, and although a therapist might be able to help her in the long term, she needed forgiveness right now more than anything. It wouldn't help anyone to rant and rave.

'Yes, I love him.' The words were softly spoken through trembling lips. 'And I can see why he had the affair. I pushed him away with the baby thing. I got so that having a child was all-important and I forgot I had a husband with needs of his own. The way it's been since I split you and Taylor up I've expected Dale to walk many times. He's certainly had good reason to, but he hasn't. He has been blaming himself for the affair; I've been blaming myself for what I've done to you and Taylor…'

Her voice trailed away and she shook her head. 'Can you ever forgive me, do you think? I know you won't straight away, but do you think you can in time?'

'I forgive you now.' How could she do anything else with that skeletal body and those agonised eyes in front of her? Whatever Susan had done, she had paid a high price the last eighteen months. Marsha reached forward, hugging Susan again as she reiterated, 'I mean it, Sue. I forgive you, okay? But you must promise me you'll get help.'

The thin body stiffened for a moment, and then Susan relaxed against her. 'A psychiatrist? Someone like that, you mean?' she whispered.

'Whatever it takes. If you talk to the doctors here they will be able to guide you to the right person, I'm sure. Do you promise me you'll do that?'

'I promise. And everything will be all right between you and Taylor now, won't it? Now you know the truth? You can be like you were before,' Susan pleaded, her voice muffled against the silk of Marsha's hair.

Susan was still such a child at heart. Marsha was glad Taylor's sister couldn't see her face at that moment, and she cleared her countenance of all expression as she drew away.

Susan thought all she had to do to put things right for them was to confess, and then the last eighteen months would be wiped away. But it wasn't as easy as that. Irreparable damage had been done—something Taylor had made clear today. In fact it really did not matter now who had told the lies about Tanya; they had gone past that. She hadn't given Taylor even a tiny measure of trust or commitment of the heart, and he knew it. If he had been with Penelope tonight, who could blame him?

Susan was still staring at her, so now she forced a smile, saying, 'Things will work out, Sue, but for now just concentrate on getting well, okay? Look, I'm going to go now, but I think you ought to tell Dale and Taylor yourself.'

'Not Taylor.' Susan clutched at her again, her grip surprisingly strong for one so frail. 'I could tell Dale, but I just couldn't look at Taylor's face, I couldn't.'

'I think you owe him that.'

'I'll tell Dale first,' Susan said after a moment or two.

'And then perhaps he will stay with me and we'll tell Taylor together?'

Marsha nodded, rising from the bed as she said, 'I'll send Dale in, shall I?'

'Yes, please.'

When Marsha turned and looked at her sister-in-law again before opening the door, Susan's fingers were working at the bedcover like a very old woman. She was ill, there was no doubt about it, Marsha thought as she smiled a goodbye, and she did feel sorry for her, but it was hard to believe that someone she had thought she knew could set out to be so horribly destructive.

Taylor and Dale were sitting in the small waiting room a stone's throw away, and as Marsha walked in she felt you could have cut the atmosphere with a knife. It was clear Taylor had spoken his mind about a few things, and when she told Dale that Susan wanted to see him he couldn't get out of his chair quickly enough.

'Do you mind if I sit down a moment?' Marsha said quietly.

There was a cold light in Taylor's eyes as he looked at her, waving his hand for her to take the seat his brother-in-law had vacated, but just at that moment Marsha felt if she didn't sit down she would fall down. She knew it hadn't really sunk in yet—Susan actually attempting to end her life besides her amazing confession—but the strange calmness and self-control which had been with her while she'd spoken with her sister-in-law was slipping away. It had probably been born of shock, she acknowledged, but at least it had helped her not to say anything she would regret later.

'How is she?' Taylor's voice was no warmer than his eyes.

'Calmer.'

'Would you like a cup of coffee?'

They were talking as though they were practically strangers and it hurt. 'No, thanks. I must be getting home in a minute.'

'I'll take you.'

As Taylor made to rise to his feet Marsha said hastily, 'No, it's all right, really. Susan said she wanted to speak to you in a little while and you ought to be here. I can get a cab.'

'As you wish.'

He really didn't care one way or the other, Marsha thought, the jagged edge of pain banishing the last of the anaesthetising calmness. He had cut his losses and moved on mentally. What would he feel when Susan admitted she was the instigator of the gigantic tangle their lives had become? He would forgive his sister, the hardest heart couldn't hold out against the pathetic creature Susan had become, but would he feel her loyalty to her sister-in-law was laudatory or otherwise? She really didn't know.

'Taylor? Earlier, at the office, I never meant to imply you would cheat or defraud someone. I've never thought that.' She had to take this one last chance to try and make him see how sorry she was. 'I was mixed up and terribly off beam about everything, I know, but—'

He interrupted her quietly but grimly. 'Excuse me if I'm wrong, but what's adultery if not the ultimate cheating?'

She stared at him, desperately trying to find words to explain how she felt. He had accused her of not loving him enough, but the truth of the matter was that she loved him too much. 'I meant what I said this afternoon, about believing you,' she said at last. She hoped he would remember she had believed him before Susan had told her what she'd done.

He raked his hair back, his jaw tense. 'Marsha, let's not do this, okay?'

'But you have to listen to me.'

'Why? Why do I have to listen to you?' He banged his fist on the coffee table in front of him as he spoke, making her jump a mile. His eyes blazing, he bit out, 'You've never listened to me. Not when you first found out about this supposed affair and not since. How do you think I could have made love to you if I had touched someone else? How do you think I could have done that? And this morning, after what we had shared, you still didn't believe me. You preferred to take the word of someone else and you wouldn't even give me their name.'

'There were good reasons for that.'

He went on as if she had not spoken. 'I don't believe you didn't receive my letter, Marsha. Whether you ripped it up unread, I don't know. That's more than possible, the state you were in, I suppose, and it would explain why you didn't ring the number I'd given you. Or maybe, like I said earlier, you thought I'd bought myself out of trouble by paying the guy to lie for me? Whatever—it's history now, and I'm sick to death with it all.'

With her. Sick to death with her, he meant. White as a sheet, Marsha stood to her feet. 'I had better go.'

Through clenched teeth he said, 'Yes, I think you'd better.'

Let me not fall at his feet and beg and plead with him to love me again. Let me walk out of here and out of his life with some semblance of dignity.

She had reached the door and begun to open it when he said, 'Marsha?'

'Yes?' She kept hold of the door as she turned her head.

'Thank you for coming to see Susan tonight.'

She inclined her head in acknowledgement before stepping out into the corridor and shutting the door carefully behind her. His voice had been flat, all the hot anger gone, and somehow it convinced her more than anything else that had gone before that he really had washed his hands of her.

When she climbed into the black cab and a cheery voice said, 'Well, hello there. It's you again. Remember me, love?' Marsha almost groaned out loud.

Instead she tried to look pleasant when she said, 'Yes I remember.'

'I picked you up this morning.'

'Yes, I remember.'

'You don't look any less peaky, if you don't mind me saying so.'

She did mind, she minded a lot, but it wasn't this poor man's fault her world had fallen into pieces around her. 'I've got a headache.'

'Oh, yes? The wife has headaches. Blimey, does she have headaches. Sick with it and everything.'

'Really?' Please shut up. Please, please shut up.

'Mind, she has them sometimes for convenience an' all. Know what I mean?' He chuckled to himself, apparently oblivious to the lack of response in the back. 'But she's a good woman and I wouldn't change her. Six kids we've got. You got any kids?'

'No, I haven't.'

'Married?'

Just. 'Sort of.' She didn't know why she added, 'I'm getting a divorce soon, actually.'

'Oh, yes?' He shook his head. 'You look too young to have to go through that, and he must be a silly so-an'-so to let a nice girl like you go.'

Marsha found herself provoked into saying, 'The divorce is my fault, actually.'

'Is that so?' There was silence for a moment. 'But you don't want it?'

She was startled into looking up and meeting the eyes in the mirror again. 'Who says?'

'Me.' She could tell he was grinning. 'You learn a lot about human nature when you drive a cab.'

She said nothing to this, hoping he would take the hint.

He did. Right up until she got out to pay the fare. 'Thanks, love.' She hadn't given such a generous tip this time, but he didn't seem to mind. 'And, look, if you don't want that divorce, you tell him, right? You march up to him and tell him straight. Things can't be worse than they are now, can they? So what have you got to lose apart from a little pride? And pride makes a cold bedfellow.'

Marsha found herself smiling with genuine warmth. 'Thank you,' she said quietly.

'You going to take my advice?'

'I might.'

'The next time I pick you up I shall ask, mind.' He chuckled again, before revving the engine and disappearing in a cloud of exhaust fumes.

CHAPTER TEN

WHEN Marsha let herself into the bedsit she didn't bother to put on the main light, preferring the muted glow from the lamp at the side of the TV, which she had left on while she was out. She walked over to the sofa, sitting down and remaining in the same position for long minutes in a kind of stupor.

Eventually she glanced at her watch. One o'clock in the morning. She had to get to bed. But she still didn't move. She felt exhausted, both mentally and physically, but she knew she wouldn't be able to sleep.

When the telephone rang five minutes later the one name in her head was Taylor, so it was with crucifying disappointment that she heard Jeff say, 'Marsha? Is that you?'

She rallied enough to say, 'Who else would it be at one o'clock in the morning?' in a fairly normal voice, continuing, 'What on earth are you ringing for at this time?'

'I'm sorry to wake you—' he didn't sound sorry, more excited '—but we've had one hell of a breakthrough with regard to the Baxter story. There's an old boy who used to work for Manning Dale, their chief accountant, and he's prepared to spill a few very tasty beans. Seems Baxter was a friend of his at one time and he's just found out about his death. One of our researchers made contact with him purely by a fluke, but it looks like it'll pay dividends. The problem is…' Jeff paused for breath '…the window of opportunity is extremely narrow. This guy, Oswald Wilmore, is going to see his son in Australia for six months and they'll be travelling round the Outback and so on. If we don't nail a few facts now we can forget it.'

'When does he leave?'

'The flight departs Heathrow in twelve hours' time. Now, as this has been your baby all along, I wondered if you wanted to go and see him. Otherwise I shall leave in the next ten minutes. The researcher's with him as we speak. Apparently they've been sharing a bottle of whisky,' he added drily.

'Where does this Oswald live?' Marsha asked weakly. What a night! And to think earlier she'd thought the most arduous thing she'd be doing this evening was drinking a mug of milky chocolate before going to bed!

'The near side of Watford. Do you want to do it?'

Penelope's beautiful feline face floated in front of her eyes. 'You bet,' she said, with more enthusiasm than she had ever thought she'd feel again after the last caustic hour with Taylor.

Jeff spent another five minutes filling her in with a list of dos and don'ts, and then she found herself flying round the bedsit, collecting everything she would need after phoning for a taxi.

Fifteen minutes later she was sitting in a cab on her way to Watford, all exhaustion burnt up in the flood of adrenalin coursing through her body. Oswald had apparently agreed to say what he had to say on camera, so a small crew were meeting her at the old man's house, along with one of the presenters. If Oswald really was prepared to dish the dirt on Manning Dale it would be a tremendous scoop. Marsha thought briefly of

Baxter's widow, a gentle woman with sad eyes, and hoped Oswald wouldn't chicken out at the last minute.

He didn't. Apparently he had been with Manning Dale from its beginnings, the founder having been a personal friend. Some years before he had retired, and after his friend had died, the man's sons, who were now in charge, began sailing very close to the wind. By then Manning Dale had become a corporation, formed by the merging of separate and diverse firms and—in Oswald's own words—a monster intent only on satisfying its lust for more and more power. Ethics, codes of practice, morality, personal conscience had all become dirty words to those at the reins.

'You nail the blighters—all right, love?' Oswald said in an aside to Marsha whilst the others were loading equipment back into the van. 'My old friend would be turning in his grave to think his lads had done the dirty on Charles Baxter. And don't forget, if you need me to come back and say anything more I'm willing. What's your second name, by the way, in case I need to talk to you while I'm gone?'

'Marsha Kane.' It was out before she thought about it, probably because Taylor had been there at the back of her mind all the time, and she hastily added, 'But my working name is Gosling. Marsha Gosling.'

'Kane?' The elderly man nodded. 'Unusual name. I don't suppose you're any relation to Taylor Kane of Kane International?'

Marsha stared at him. 'He's my husband,' she said faintly.

'Is that so? Well, I watched your husband build up his business from when he was a young whippersnapper. Success stories like that get talked about in business, you know, and I admired him. Oh, yes, I admired him all right. If my friend's sons had been like Kane we wouldn't be having this conversation right now. A hard man, mind, but fair with it. No skeletons in the cupboard there. But of course you'd know that better than most, eh?' He smiled at her, quite unaware he was turning the knife in the wound of her burning guilt.

'Thank you, Mr Wilmore, but we really have to be going now.' She had backed away from him as though he was the devil, rather than an upright seventy-year-old pillar of the establishment.

'Oswald, dear. Call me Oswald.'

Marsha was having a lift back to the TV offices with the presenter, who had come up in her own little red convertible. Bobbie was a bubbly redhead with inch-long eyelashes and a very firm idea of where her career was going and how to get there. She oozed confidence, along with plenty of sex appeal, if the cameramen were anything to go by, and was witty, bright and articulate. Marsha felt like someone's aged grandmother in comparison.

This was the sort of woman Taylor should have married, she told herself during the eternity of listening to Bobbie's conquests near and far on the journey back. The presenter would never imagine for a single moment that the man in her life was going to leave her, neither would she be crippled by self-doubt and diffidence. The world was Bobbie's oyster, and because she always expected a pearl to be lurking under the shell it invariably was.

Oh, Taylor, Taylor. Now the urgency of the interview was over the pain and self-recrimination she had been keeping at bay by working flooded in, along with the exhaustion twenty-four hours without sleep had induced.

Bobbie, on the other hand, seemed to get more animated and buoyant the nearer to base they got. On at least two occasions Marsha seriously considered jumping out of the car when they stopped at traffic lights, Bobbie's chatter having reached a pitch which had become unbearable. Only the thought of how much pleasure Penelope would get from such a story stopped her.

But then, at last, the building was there in front of them, and when Bobbie suggested she drop her off before she went and parked Marsha didn't argue.

It being a Saturday morning, Marsha knew Nicki and quite a few others wouldn't be in. Jeff, however, had been planning to come in and work on the material he had given her yesterday, so she intended to drop off the notes she'd gathered and brief Jeff on Oswald before going home to bed.

As she walked into her office Jeff's door opened and her boss's head peered round the aperture. 'Come on in here. I've got the coffeemaker from home going,' he said jovially, all smiles. As well he might be. The programme was going to be a winner. They'd all known it before Oswald, but now top viewing figures were a dead cert, Marsha thought as she followed him into the much larger room.

'You look rough,' was Jeff's opening remark.

'Thanks very much,' she said tartly. 'Considering I've been on the go for twenty-four hours and missed umpteen meals, I think I look pretty good.' She hadn't looked in a mirror for hours, but she wasn't about to tell him that. Neither was she going to confide that it wasn't lack of sleep or food that was the problem, but a six-foot-something man with eyes the colour of dark honey.

'Sit down.' He pushed her down into the big leather

chair opposite his own, the desk between them, and poured a cup of coffee from the machine perched on a little table next to him. It tasted wonderful.

'What's this?' He had placed a large brown bag in front of her, and when she opened it she found four rounds of bacon sandwiches.

Jeff produced a bag of his own as he said, 'Present from the wife. She reckoned you might be a bit peckish by the time you got back here.'

'How nice of her.' Marsha was really touched.

'She thinks I work you too hard.'

'She's right.'

'Fill me in on what you've got, and then we'll have another cup of coffee and eat.'

'See what I mean?' Marsha said ruefully.

'Slave is in your job description. Now, shoot.'

When she had finished telling him everything Jeff lay back in his chair and laughed out loud. 'We've got 'em tied up tighter than the hangman's noose. I'd like to see Penelope's face when you tell her what you've got.' He pushed the bag towards her. 'Now, eat up or the missus will think you don't like her food.'

They were on their second cup of coffee, Marsha's shoes having been discarded so she could flex her aching toes and an inch-thick bacon butty in her hand, when footsteps outside followed by a sharp knock at Jeff's door brought her straightening in her chair. The next moment Taylor was standing in the doorway. He was wearing the same dinner suit he'd had on at the hospital, now crumpled and creased, his five o'clock shadow had passed midnight and his hair was rumpled and most un-Taylorish. Marsha thought he'd never looked so handsome.

'I've been looking for you,' he said to her, after the

briefest of nods to a surprised Jeff. 'You weren't at the bedsit, and Mrs Tate-Collins didn't know where you had gone.'

'There was a rush job. Jeff phoned me last night when I got in from the hospital.' She couldn't move, couldn't think, and even to her own ears her voice was flat.

'Susan told me everything.'

He obviously expected her to make some response, but the numbness was holding. She felt weird, cold and shivery, frozen to the core of her being. She dared not hope that his being here meant anything. Her hopes and fears had had such a see-saw of a ride the last few days before finally being shattered beyond repair.

The silence between them stretched until it was painful, vibrating with tension as their eyes held, and it was Jeff who eventually couldn't stand a second more. 'Marsha's been in Watford since the early hours,' he said much too loudly, in an effort to be normal. 'The wife's provided bacon sandwiches all round and there's plenty. Care for one?'

For a moment she thought Taylor wasn't going to reply, but as she finally managed to wrench her gaze from his he turned to Jeff, his voice still very quiet when he said, 'Thank you. I'd like that.'

'Here.' When Taylor still continued to remain exactly where he was, just inside the room, Jeff stood up, moving one of the spare guest chairs from the far wall beside Marsha. 'Sit down, won't you? How do you like your coffee?'

Taylor seated himself, his eyes on Marsha again. 'Black, please,' he said absently.

Although she had her eyes centred on the mug in her hand, Marsha was aware of every inch of the long lean body next to her. She was horrified to find she was trembling, and drank half a mug of coffee scalding hot in an effort to still the shivering within.

After Jeff had placed a mug of coffee and a bacon sandwich in front of Taylor, he said, 'I've just got to pop out for a minute. Too much coffee. You know how it is…'

Neither of them acknowledged his going, but he hadn't expected them to.

'I didn't know where you had gone,' Taylor said softly when they were alone.

'I had to go on a rush job,' she repeated, her voice little more than a whisper.

'You can't have had much sleep.'

'No.' She found she couldn't raise her eyes to his. 'I haven't had any.' There was another pause, and then she said, 'How's Susan?'

'She was asleep when I left. Dale is going to stay with her and bring her home once the doctor has been later today.'

'So she'll be all right?'

'Eventually. They think she had a kind of breakdown round about the time she told you—' He stopped abruptly, shaking his head before he continued, 'Anyway, she needs help, that's for sure. She weighs next to nothing, and Dale told the doctors she roams about the house most nights because she can't sleep. He's been trying to get her to see a doctor for months. Having said all that, I have to admit if it was anyone but Susan I'd say she's got exactly what she deserves for what's happened to us.'

'But it is Susan,' Marsha said gently, meeting his eyes.

He stared at her, his gaze moving over each feature

of her face. 'You really don't bear her any ill will, do you?' he said, a touch of wonder in his voice. 'She said you'd forgiven her, but I thought it might be just because you didn't want to upset her last night.'

'Of course I've forgiven her.' For you, if nothing else.

'Thank you. Look, do you want that?' He gestured to the sandwich hanging limply in her hand.

She shook her head. She had thought she was hungry when she'd walked into Jeff's office, but now the whirling of her stomach made eating impossible.

'How soon can you leave here? We have to talk. You know that, don't you?'

She swallowed hard. He hadn't given her any ray of hope that he had softened regarding her treatment of him, but nothing on earth would have stopped her leaving with him. 'I've already told Jeff all he needs to know.' She placed her mug on the table. 'We can leave right now, if you like.'

He nodded. 'I do like.'

'I'll just write a note explaining that we had to go and I'll see him Monday morning.'

She found her hands were shaking as she scribbled a quick message, and she was vitally aware of Taylor on the perimeter of her vision. The ruffled hair and crumpled clothes were so at odds with his usual immaculate appearance it was disturbing, mainly because he obviously hadn't taken the time to go home and shower and change before he came to find her. But that didn't necessarily mean anything, she warned herself in the next moment as her heart leapt and raced. But, against all her efforts to stifle it, hope had risen again.

Her heart continued to thud alarmingly as they left the office and travelled downwards in the lift to

Reception, and it was after she had smiled and waved a goodbye to Bob that a thought struck her. 'How come Bob let you through without ringing my office first?'

Taylor reached in his pocket and produced one of the slim security passes all the employees were issued with. 'Kane International is supplying and installing that new equipment, remember? Penelope thought it would be a good idea if I could pop in at any time.'

Marsha just bet she did. Hope fizzled and spluttered and died again.

The Aston Martin was parked in one of the top executives' slots in the car park, which was so like Taylor that Marsha would have smiled if she'd been able. Taylor opened the passenger door and she slid inside, grateful to be sitting down again because she really was feeling most peculiar.

'You're worn out.' As Taylor joined her in the car the tawny gaze moved over her face.

Well, at least he hadn't said she looked rough, as Jeff had, even though it was obviously what he was thinking. She nodded, turning to glance at him and then finding her eyes held by his. The hard, handsome face was grim, his gaze holding her own with a searching intensity as he spoke. 'There's no excuse for the things I said to you.'

'What?' It was the very last thing in the world she had expected him to say.

'I should have known you wouldn't take the word of just anyone about Tanya, that there had to be something vital in the fact you wouldn't reveal a name. And the letter…'

'No, I can see why you wouldn't believe I hadn't received it,' she said quickly. 'The chances of it being lost or something were so small. It's me that's done everything wrong. I didn't trust you when I should have—'

'How could you?' He interrupted her bitterly. 'Susan orchestrated everything, down to the last nut and bolt, and she knew how vulnerable you were—knew your background. She played on your fear of being rejected, hitting all the right buttons. I still find it hard to believe my little sister was capable of such cruelty.'

'She wasn't in her right mind,' Marsha said softly, hating to see the pain etched in the rugged features and knowing the torment he was going through.

'She was sound enough to ring the hotel and change the booking before she told you, and also to intercept that letter.' His voice broke and he raked back his hair with a savage movement which spoke of his inner frustration and anger.

'Taylor, you have to remember it wasn't the real Susan at that time,' Marsha said, working through her own resentment at what his sister had done even as she spoke. 'The real person, the one you know and love, is the woman who has been racked with guilt ever since. She told me how she felt when she found out about Dale's affair—worthless, less than nothing, not even a woman. She couldn't have babies and now Dale didn't love her like she'd thought he did. That's how she was feeling. And…'

She took a deep breath, knowing she was going to probe a painful wound. 'And if I had trusted you, like I should have, none of what she did would have succeeded. But believe me on one thing, please. It wasn't that I didn't love you enough; it was that I loved you too much. It frightened me to know you were my world, my everything. I just couldn't believe someone like you would want someone like me for the rest of our lives.'

'Oh, my love.' He moved in his seat, leaning over her and taking her mouth as he pulled her hard against him. It wasn't a gentle kiss, it was one born of need and frustration and pain, but it was a lover's kiss, long and deep and hungry, and it left her physically and mentally shaken to the core.

'You're my everything—you know that, don't you?' he murmured against her lips as the kiss ended. 'I've been in hell since you left, crazy half the time, angry, tortured by thoughts of you with someone else. I just couldn't believe you wouldn't come back to me, that you wouldn't work out for yourself how much I loved you, that I could never betray you.'

'I'm sorry. I'm sorry.' His words were like little burning darts in her heart. She had hurt him so much. How could he still want her?

'No.' He put a hand to her lips and she was touched beyond measure to see it was shaking. 'It was me that was wrong. I should have known you were still too damaged by what had happened in your past to have confidence in yourself as a woman. We hadn't had enough time together before the attack came. Maybe if it had happened five or ten years down the road, when we'd had children and our family unit was strong, it might have been different. As it was, I expected too much.'

'It was your right to expect I should trust you,' she said, her tears like tiny diamonds as they hung on her lashes.

'Maybe.' He gathered her to him again. 'But what has right got to do with anything? I should have understood better, loving you like I do. It was only when we got so close to the divorce that I realised you really weren't going to come back. Then I panicked.'

'You did?' She stared at him, eyes wide and still glittering with tears. She couldn't imagine Taylor panicking about anything.

'Oh, yes.' He touched her mouth gently with the tip of a finger. 'I knew I couldn't live the rest of my life without you, so I had to do something—swallow my foolish pride, get off my butt and make you see the truth. I knew you loved me—' he managed to sound both magnificently arrogant and uncharacteristically humble '—but that clearly wasn't going to be enough to persuade you to come back. When I heard about the possibility of tenders for equipment at the company where you worked it was perfect. I could hassle you at work and at play. Of course I hadn't reckoned on the formidable Penelope.'

She couldn't believe she was in his arms, so close she could feel the thud of his heart with the tips of her fingers where they rested against his shirt. 'She likes you.' She looked into his eyes, remembering the painful jealousy she had felt. 'She had you lined up as her next conquest.'

'I'd sooner mate with a praying mantis.' Penelope was dismissed and put out of the way as their lips fused again, seeking each other greedily before at last Taylor lifted his head reluctantly. 'Any more and I'll take you right here in full view of the world,' he said huskily. 'Are you coming home?'

Home. The word sang in the quintessence of her mind, provoking such emotion that she could only nod her answer.

As the engine roared into life she found she was tingling with anticipation, her skin alive from the tips of her toes to the crown of her head, even as her brain still grappled with the fact that her misery was over.

Neither of them spoke on the way back to the house. All the threads could be unravelled later. For now it was enough that they were together again.

As the car pulled up on the drive the front door opened immediately, Hannah's bulk nearly filling the doorway. Marsha saw the housekeeper's eyes widen at the sight of her, but she merely met her on the steps, putting her arms round her in a bear hug which took her breath away as she said to Taylor, 'Dale phoned a few minutes ago. The doctor has been and said Susan can leave, so he's taking her home. He explained a little of what's gone on.'

'We'll talk later.' As they stepped into the hall Taylor patted Hannah's arm. 'Okay? For the moment we're going to sleep. Marsha hasn't slept in over twenty-four hours, and I only had cat naps at the hospital. If anyone phones, tell them I'm in bed with my wife and can't be disturbed.'

Hannah beamed.

They climbed the stairs hand in hand, but when Taylor opened the door to their bedroom and they walked into the beautiful room Marsha felt suddenly shy. Hannah had opened the windows, and the perfume from the lavender bushes was warm in the air, the huge bed with its soft billowy covers dominating the room as always. For a moment she felt like a bride again, and it was a strange feeling.

'Shower or bath?'

'What?'

Taylor smiled, reaching for her unresisting body and bringing her into the haven of his arms. 'Shower or bath before we turn in?'

She thought of the massive corner bath where they had loved so many times before. 'Bath.'

He left her to start the bath running, returning almost immediately to where she was still standing, slightly dazed by the swiftness with which everything had changed. She was home, home with Taylor, and the nightmare was over.

She didn't have time to think anything more. He covered her lips with his in a kiss of such hunger that all lucid thought fled and she gave herself up to pure sensation. She melted against him, sliding her hands over the rippling muscles in his back as she pulled him even closer. They fitted together so well, curves dissolving into hard angular male planes like a perfect jigsaw. How could she have stayed away so long?

'I've dreamt of this for eighteen months,' he murmured hoarsely. 'Eighteen months of cold showers.'

'There was the other morning,' she protested faintly, the words more of a sigh.

'That's not like having you here, where you belong. I want to undress you, touch and taste you, tease you. I want to wake up beside you and know I only have to reach out my hand and you are there, soft and silky at the side of me. I want…' His mouth kissed the tiny pulse racing wildly at the base of her throat. 'I want everything.'

He undressed her slowly, kissing every inch of her skin as he did so, peeling her clothes from her with an enjoyment he made no effort to hide. She gasped as the slightly callused pads of his fingers stroked across her engorged breasts, the peaks hard and aching, and then smoothed down over her flat stomach to her thighs.

His tongue left its teasing of her lips and his mouth began an exploration of where his fingers had touched, and now she pulled at his clothes, anxious to have nothing between them. When his clothes had joined hers, her breath caught in her throat at the beauty of him—tall, wide-shouldered and lean-hipped, strong and totally male.

'Come on, wench.' He caught her up in his arms, carrying her into the bathroom, where he laid her gently in the silky warm foaming water. She raised her arms to his, bereft at the loss of the feel of him, and he laughed softly, joining her in the bath a moment later.

'Let me wash you.' He gathered some foam in his hands, running them over her shoulders and down her arms before he turned his attention to her breasts. His fingers traced an erotic path around her nipples, becoming tantalisingly slower until they reached the very tips.

'Think of all the baths together we've missed,' he whispered, before ducking his head to take possession of one taut peak. 'We'll have to stay in here for a month to make up for lost time.'

Taylor wasn't satisfied until he had washed every inch of her, stroking and caressing until the sexual tension in her body grew unbearable and she felt she would explode if he touched one more inch.

'How about you?' She swished backwards in the water, reaching for a bar of soap on the side of the bath. 'I'm not sure if you're clean enough to share my bed.'

'Scrub away.' He grinned at her, spreading his arms along the side of the massive circular bath as she moved towards him. She knelt over him in the water, lathering the soap between the palms of her hands before beginning to gently massage the tanned clear skin of his throat and neck, moving to the broad expanse of his muscled chest when she was done. She curled the rough smattering of body hair on his chest round her fingers, teasing and caressing before she stroked the small nipples.

It felt wonderful to be with him, and the last eighteen months faded into a bad dream as she grew accustomed to every muscle and contour of his body once again. The warm water, the hard male body and the ripples of pleasure causing each nerve-end to glow seemed like a dream, a dream she never wanted to wake up from.

When her hands moved down to his flat stomach she felt him tense, and she didn't prolong the agony, stroking and cradling his manhood as she murmured, 'I think this needs special attention.'

'And how.'

The next moment he had pulled her to her feet, his breathing ragged as he said, 'Let's go to bed.'

In spite of the fact that they were both exhausted their union was no quick, lusty coming together, but a long, slow reacquaintance with every inch of each other's bodies. The almost desperate urgency which had gripped Taylor at the bedsit was gone. Marsha was home and they had all the time in the world.

They touched and savoured, their hands and lips almost reverent as the enormity of what they had come through dawned afresh in the wonder of being together in their bed once more. They whispered words of love, promises that never again would they doubt each other or be apart.

Marsha felt drugged with pleasure as Taylor tasted and teased and nibbled the silky smooth skin of her throat, her breasts, her stomach, her body aching for a release only he could give. It was an enchanting journey back into their world, their secret world, where no one else could intrude.

When at last Taylor eased himself between her thighs she was moist and ready for him, accepting his swollen fullness with a little moan of pleasure. Even then

Taylor's control held for long minutes, until eventually the time was right. They both shattered together, going over the edge into a world of colour and light and sensation.

It was some minutes before either of them stirred, locked together in each other's arms as they were. Marsha raised her hand, touching Taylor's face as she traced a path over his chin.

'I should have shaved.' He opened his eyes and smiled ruefully.

'Later.' She snuggled into him, waves of tiredness washing over her like a warm tide. 'Everything can come later.'

And they slept.

Neither of them heard the telephone ring, or Hannah's voice informing Penelope, as per Taylor's instructions, that Mr Kane was in bed with his wife and couldn't be disturbed.

EPILOGUE

IT WAS June again, the sun blazing down out of a clear blue sky and the scent of lavender heavy in the air. Marsha adjusted her position in the big easy chair under the shade of an umbrella, smiling to herself as she watched Taylor and Dale splashing about in the pool with Susan and Dale's twin girls.

Who would have thought five years could make such a difference? she thought idly, glancing at Susan, fast asleep at the side of her. No one had been more surprised than Susan and Dale when, six months after Marsha and Taylor had got back together again, Susan had discovered she was pregnant.

The birth of the twins had transformed Susan. She had ceased seeing her therapist, throwing herself into motherhood with gusto and enjoying every minute of it, hectic though it had been at first. Night feeds, screaming babies, lack of sleep—nothing had got her down, and Dale, Taylor and Marsha had looked on amazed as the thin, sickly creature of the past had turned into a plump matron who took everything in her stride.

'I don't know who enjoys playing more. The twins or Dale and Taylor.'

Susan's voice at the side of her brought Marsha's head turning again, and she saw her sister-in-law was awake.

'Definitely Dale and Taylor.' She giggled, watching

as they each tossed a little screaming infant into the air before catching them again before they hit the water. 'I think—' She stopped abruptly, shutting her eyes and breathing fast for a few moments. When she opened them again Susan was starting at her anxiously. 'That was a strong one,' Marsha said calmly.

'You're having pains?' Susan sat up so quickly her lounger rocked. 'Why didn't you say? How long have they been coming?'

'An hour or two,' Marsha said serenely, rubbing her huge stomach as the pain left her. 'Don't worry. Most people aren't like you.' Susan had given birth to the twins within two hours from start to finish, nearly giving Dale a heart attack when they'd got stuck in traffic a mile from the hospital. He had practically collapsed with relief when they finally reached it, the first baby being born just ten minutes later. 'First babies take ages.'

'I'm telling Taylor.'

Taylor was out of the pool like a shot, and at her side in seconds. 'How strong are they? Have your waters broken? Are you timing them?'

Marsha looked at him fondly. He had come to every antenatal class, and she appreciated that, but he had been like a cat on a hot tin roof the last few days since she had gone past her due date.

'I'm fine,' she said gently. 'There's ages to go yet. We'll be able to have the barbecue as planned.'

Taylor said something very rude about the barbecue, and Dale, who had now joined them, with a little arm-banded figure on each hip, added, 'Susan was saying there was ages to go ten minutes before ours were born.'

'Only because we were stuck in traffic and I didn't want you to panic.'

'I'm taking you in.'

When Taylor spoke in that voice Marsha knew she had no option, so, grumbling loudly, she lumbered to her feet, plodding into the house but having to stop halfway when another pain hit.

She sat in the hall with everyone fussing over her, and Hannah scurrying about like a chicken with its head cut off collecting her hospital case and things, and within moments—or so it seemed—Taylor was back downstairs, changed and ready.

He looks flustered, Marsha thought in absolute amazement. She had never thought to see her cool, contained husband in a spin, but she was seeing it now.

'How many contractions since I've been upstairs?'

'One—and did you know you've got one black and one brown sock on?'

'Damn my socks. How far apart in minutes?'

'Five.'

'Five?'

'I think the beginning of the pains must have been the backache I've had the last twenty-four hours,' Marsha supplied helpfully. 'It sort of worked its way round into the front a couple of hours ago, and—Oooh…' This time the contraction was strong, very strong, and once it had died down Taylor gathered her up in his arms, despite her vehement protests, and carried her out to the car, his face white under its tan.

'It's okay.' When he joined her in the car, after stowing her case in the boot, Marsha put a comforting hand on his. 'Women have babies every day, you know.'

'You are my wife, and this is my baby, and it doesn't happen every day to me.'

'Shouldn't that be our baby?' she asked drily. 'And from where I'm standing it's happening to me, not you.'

'You know what I mean.'

She did, and she loved him for his concern. She would probably never see Taylor in full panic mode again—unless it was with subsequent babies—so she settled back to enjoy every moment of it.

When they arrived at the hospital Marsha hadn't had a pain in the last ten minutes, and when she told Taylor this, once he had parked and was helping her out of the car, he groaned loudly. 'Don't do this to me.' He put a hand on her stomach, patting it gently. 'Do you hear me in there? Your old dad can't take any false starts.'

'I don't think this is a false start, Taylor,' Marsha said, looking down at her feet. 'My waters have just broken.'

By the time she was lying in bed in one of the delivery rooms the pains were back to every five minutes, and Marsha was reflecting that Taylor was probably the only father who had managed to be presented with a cup of tea to steady his nerves before the event. In fact the two midwives who were dealing with the five mothers who had all decided to give birth at the same time seemed far more interested in Taylor than they did her.

All that changed as time went on. Three of the mothers had given birth to bouncing baby boys, the midwife who had taken over Marsha's confinement announced, and Mrs Dodds next door was due to produce any moment. It looked like Mrs Kane was going to be the last, didn't it?

Mrs Kane didn't care if she was the last or the first, as long as this baby got a move on, and Mr Kane echoed that sentiment with every fibre of his being. He wouldn't have believed someone as fragile-looking as Marsha could have the grip of a sumo wrestler, but he seriously wondered if she had broken his fingers—again.

Samuel Taylor Kane was born at five in the evening, and he made it a fivefold whammy for the male sex that day, according to the smiling midwife. When Marsha looked into the tiny screwed-up face, above which was a ridiculously thick mop of black hair, she fell immediately and hopelessly in love. As did his father.

Taylor sat on the edge of the bed with them, gazing in rapt wonder at the nine-pound bruiser who was his son, tears on his cheeks. 'I love you,' he said softly to Marsha, touching the baby's silky hair with a gentle finger. 'So much.'

'I love you too.'

'No regrets about giving up work?'

She smiled at him. The Baxter story had been the sort of scoop which had ensured she got noticed by the powers-that-be, and when she had been promoted to controller, with a very tasty salary increase, no one had been surprised. She had enjoyed the last few years, but when she and Taylor had started trying for a baby she had known she wanted to be at home with it full time. She needed to give this baby, and the ones to follow, all that she had never had. 'Not one.' She could always take up her career again later if she wanted to. For now being a wife and mother was supreme.

'Thank you for our son.'

'You did play a part in the proceedings.'

'Only the easy bit.' He grinned at her, looking more gorgeous than he had any right to when it was going to be another six weeks at least before they could make love.

'That's true.' She brushed the tears from her own face, wondering why it was you cried when you were more happy than you'd ever been in your life. 'We're a family, darling.'

'That we are,' he whispered, sliding an arm round her and pulling his wife and child into the shelter of his body. 'That we are.'

THE ITALIAN'S PASSION

by

Elizabeth Power

Elizabeth Power was born in Bristol, where she still lives with her husband in a three-hundred-year-old cottage. A keen reader, as a teenager she had already made up her mind to be a novelist, although it wasn't until around thirty that she took up writing seriously. Her love of nature and animals is reflected in a leaning towards vegetarianism. Good food and wine come high on her list of priorities, and what better way to sample these delights than by just having to take another trip to some new exotic resort. Oh, and of course to find a location for the next book...!

To Alan – for all your love and support.

CHAPTER ONE

HE WAS sitting alone at one of the waterside tables, looking out over the rustic platform that jutted out from the rocks. A man who had produced a ripple of excitement among the female bathers and had had pulses fluttering like the white fringes of the blue sun umbrellas he was now studying with such careless arrogance even before he had stepped out of his dinghy and come ashore.

Now, under the raffia canopy of the beach restaurant, with her sunglasses shielding her eyes from the bright Italian sun, Mel Sheraton's interest was unwillingly drawn to him.

Probably in his mid-thirties, olive-skinned. His strong black hair, combed straight back from a high forehead, reached almost to his shoulders, marking him at once as a man who flouted convention. She couldn't see his eyes because he too was wearing shades, but instinctively she knew that they would miss nothing, that behind them lurked a brain that was hard and shrewd. But it was that profile! Those well-defined cheekbones and that grim mouth and jaw, carved as the rocks to which the white Moorish houses of Positano—partially obscured by the jutting headland—clung dramatically, that filled her with a sudden, disquieting unease.

'OK. He's a dish all right, but you don't have to eat him all at once.' Karen Kingsley's words cut through Mel's absorption, bringing her attention back to the dark-haired young woman sitting opposite her.

'Who?' she parried, with a prudent sideways glance down across the umbrellas to the three young people who were splashing about in the sparkling blue water. Checking, as she had been doing ever since they had finished lunch.

'Oh, come on, Mel. If you hadn't noticed before, he's been looking at you ever since he arrived.'

When, Mel thought tensely, she had done her level best to ignore him. Even so, she had been aware of the power of his presence when, after securing his boat beside the little wooden jetty, he strode across the planking and mounted the steps to a table just metres from their own.

'Don't be silly,' Mel responded, lifting her glass to take a long draught of her mineral water. 'If anyone, he's been looking at you, not me.'

Karen had worked as a model until leaving England two years ago when, newly married, she had emigrated with her artist husband and was now devoting all her time and energy to his small and modern gallery in Rome. But Karen was outstandingly beautiful with her fine, patrician features and expensively bobbed hair, and her shorts and sun top emphasising her long, willowy limbs. Quite a contrast to what Mel considered were her own average features, a body that was unimpressively petite and mutinous auburn hair that went its own way even after the most expert attention.

'You know that's not true. And even if he had been remotely interested—which he isn't—he'd already have noticed the wedding ring and discarded me as unnecessary hassle,' Karen assured her. 'Don't tell me you're immune, not to someone like him, because I shan't believe it, not least because of the way you've made a point of deliberately avoiding looking at him all the time he's been sitting there.'

'Good grief!' Bright tendrils that refused to be constrained in their twisted topknot stirred faintly against Mel's startled face. Was it that obvious?

'Yes,' Karen emphasised in response to her friend's unspoken query, and they both burst out laughing.

Karen was a good friend, Mel thought. They had met

when the model had been promoting the newest sports saloon to come out of Germany in an advertising campaign undertaken by Jonathan Harvey Associates, of which Mel was Sales and Marketing Director. Karen had driven all the way down from Rome to join her here in Positano two days ago. Tomorrow, before the rest of the team arrived, she would be driving back and taking Zoë with her, leaving Mel free to devote her time and effort to the week's conference that she and Jonathan were hosting on the firm's behalf, and Mel couldn't help but feel enormous gratitude to her friend.

Out of the corner of her eye, however, she was aware that the little bubble of merriment just now had produced a subtle glance from behind those dark lenses, even though the man was still engaged in conversation with the waiter.

'I'm not immune,' she stressed more seriously, careful not to look his way. 'But I do have Zoë to think about.' Which was why she had insisted on having a couple of days here alone with the child, ahead of schedule. She didn't even feel guilty any more about putting Jonathan off when he had suggested flying out earlier, joining them today. Just self-contained, she thought resolutely, hardening herself to the caress of the sun on her neck and bare arms, the scent of suntan lotion, sweet herbs and the delicious aroma of barbecued fish. All of them were combining to try and make her drop her guard, forget the lesson she had learnt a long time ago, of how devastating the power of sexual attraction could be. It had cost her everything. Almost.

Instinctively, her eyes returning to the swimmers, Mel saw the twelve-year-old striking out, away from the others.

Any further and she would have to consider calling her back, she decided with an anxiety she knew wasn't entirely justified. After all, Zoë's two teenage companions, who were staying in the hotel, had promised to look after her. Besides, she wasn't that far from the shore, Mel assured herself in an attempt to dispel her unnecessary worries. And

Zoë was a brilliant swimmer. As Mel's sister Kelly had been…

A blade of something, long-buried and acute, sliced unexpectedly through Mel and, for a few moments, from the familiar shape of the girl's head and the trick of light and water that made the dark chestnut hair gleam almost black, Mel had a job convincing herself it was Zoë swimming out there and not Kelly.

The warm breeze passing through her white beach tunic nevertheless made her shiver, and mentally she shook the disturbing images away.

Momentarily off guard, her glance strayed to a pair of broad shoulders beneath the stretch fabric of a white T-shirt, down over bronzed, bare forearms to a fit, lean torso. From where she was sitting she was able to assess that his legs, exposed by dark shorts, were hair-roughened and strong, that his feet were lean and as bronzed as the rest of him in their very masculine flip-flops and without warning an unbidden excitement uncoiled in her stomach.

Then she glanced up, realised with shaming self-consciousness that the waiter had gone and that she was looking straight into those hidden, yet all-seeing, eyes, and for several eternal seconds she couldn't look away.

Caught in the snare of his regard, she felt the pull of a sexual magnetism so great that the animated conversations around her, the chink of glass, the ring of cutlery, seemed not to be part of her world. All that existed was the racing of her blood and that burning gaze she could feel as tangibly as the dappled sunlight through the raffia canopy as it moved over the soft curve of her forehead with its fine dark brows, over her small straight nose and full, slightly parted lips to the long line of her throat, emphasised by the wide slash neckline of her tunic. Down and down his eyes slid, making her startlingly conscious that she wasn't wearing a bikini top. After her swim in the hotel pool before lunch, she had popped up to the room she shared with Zoë and simply substituted briefs and the tunic for her wet swimwear. And now, because of that shiver—at least she tried convincing herself it was because of the shiver—she felt the betraying tingle of her breasts and realised that their hardened peaks were straining against the soft cotton. Though she couldn't see his eyes, she could feel them playing on her breasts, and suddenly his mouth quirked as though he thought himself solely responsible for their shocking betrayal.

Mortified, she turned sharply away, her heart hammering. She was being silly, she thought, shaken. It couldn't be…!

Hardly daring to think, turning her attention seawards in involuntary escape, she froze, colour draining from her flushed face.

'Oh my God!' she whispered, springing to her feet. 'Oh my God!'

'What is it?' Karen asked, but the query was lost beneath the scrape of Mel's chair on the stony surface and the clunk of her tumbler hitting the vinyl tabletop, spilling a pool of melting ice across it as Mel's knee struck one of the legs.

She wasn't even aware of it in her desperate bid for the terrace. Zoë was in trouble, she realised, sick with fear. The two teenagers who had sworn to keep an eye on her weren't even conscious of what was happening. The girl hadn't left the comparative shallows of the rocks and the boy was too preoccupied with his snorkelling to notice anything. But Zoë was trying to swim and, from the frantic splashing of her flailing limbs, was finding it almost impossible even to stay afloat. Mel heard her scream then, the sound ringing ominously across the bay.

'Zoë!' Mel shrieked, heading for the steps to the sundeck, but, quick to assess the situation, the man had reached them first.

He must have leapt to his feet an instant after she had,

Mel realised distractedly, and now he was clearing the wooden steps two at a time.

Fear tearing at her chest, Mel tried to keep up, failing miserably to match his speed as he raced across the platform and on to the jetty. She wasn't even aware of people stirring beneath the umbrellas, or that some of the bathers were already on their feet. Her attention was solely with the man who, poised for a fragmented second, was suddenly plunging into the sea, his body like a dark arrow, before he surfaced, tossing water out of his eyes, arms slicing through the water in a powerful front crawl.

With a mixture of horror and fascination, Mel watched the gap closing between the man and the child, blind and deaf to the onlookers behind her. The teenage boy, suddenly wise to Zoë's screams, had already started to swim out to her. But the man had reached her first and, with a sigh of weakening relief, Mel saw him catch the frightened girl in his capable arms and turn effortlessly with her back towards the shore.

'It's all right. She's all right.' Mel felt a gentle arm go around her shoulders. Karen's, she realised, only conscious then of the sounds of expressed relief coming from behind her on the terrace, of people drifting back to their loungers.

'I shouldn't have let her swim out there on her own. I shouldn't have let her,' Mel repeated, bitterly reproaching herself. 'I should have said "no" and not let her persuade me, not given in.'

'You can't wrap her up in cotton wool,' Karen stated philosophically. 'Of course you should have. She's a stronger swimmer than you are, and besides, she wasn't alone.'

'Wasn't supposed to be,' Mel grimaced, angry. She shouldn't have been stupid enough to trust anyone that young to look after Zoë, she thought, still blaming herself, rushing forward the instant the man lifted the coughing, limping child on to the jetty.

'Zoë.' Her arms going gratefully around the slim, sodden girl, she was oblivious to the man who was now hauling himself on to dry land. Water seeped through her thin tunic and, where the garment had slipped off one shoulder, ran coldly from Zoë's long dripping hair on to Mel's heated skin.

'It's all right. I'm all right,' was the coughed, almost impatient, response from the twelve-year-old. Zoë hated fuss, and Mel knew she wouldn't allow herself to be discouraged for long. 'I just got cramp...' But, as the girl tried to walk, her face twisted in anguish and quickly Mel urged her down on to the decking where, kneeling, she straightened the young limb and gently drew Zoë's left foot upwards towards her shin.

'There's no harm done.' The deep voice drifted down to Mel as she massaged the tightly bunched muscles in the girl's calf. A voice that, despite those Latin looks, uttered only perfect, unaccented English. A voice she would never have forgotten in a million lifetimes. For a few brief moments though, she hadn't realised he was there.

Now she became aware of the long, powerful legs planted firmly beside her, of the water running from him, around his tanned bare feet. He must have kicked off his shoes prior to taking that dive, Mel's brain registered, as it started to get back into gear. 'The leg will probably be sore for a day or two, but your sister's a plucky little lady. It might not be a bad idea to keep a close eye on her over the next few days. These cramps have a habit of recurring.'

Zoë, clearly beginning to feel more comfortable, was grinning at the man's obvious mistake, but right then Mel couldn't share the child's amusement.

Still struggling with self-recrimination, gratitude and now

a deepening dread, Mel placed the young foot gently down on the decking and rose swiftly to her feet.

'Thank you…' She couldn't go on, rendered speechless as she tilted her head to meet harshly sculptured features.

'Vann. Vann Capella,' he offered, obviously imagining that she was waiting for him to introduce himself. Not for one moment that she was stunned into silence by this unbelievable trick fate seemed to be playing on her.

Vann Capella. He hadn't even needed to tell her his name. If she had wanted to deny it before, as she looked up into his face and met the steel-blue eyes—devoid of the sunglasses he had obviously ripped off earlier—then she had to acknowledge it now. For the best part of fourteen years this man had haunted her dreams and, if she were honest with herself, even her waking hours. Never had she thought it possible their paths would ever cross again. Yet here he was, like a phoenix rising from the ashes of time to taunt her with the bitterest of memories.

Mel swallowed, nodded her head, stammered something like, 'Y—Yes. Well…thank you.' She wasn't even sure herself what she was saying. Whatever it was, it was inadequate after what he had done, she acknowledged absently, as sentences like *Fancy seeing you here!* and *I wasn't sure it was you earlier* piled into her mind. But, of course, she hadn't known him at all, had she? Not really.

Tremblingly, she put a hand to her temple, her face pale beneath the brightness of her hair. 'I don't know what to say.'

His smile showed a set of strong white teeth. 'I think you've said it all,' he returned with impeccable grace.

Briefly, those disturbing eyes flicked over the gold skin of her bare shoulder. Her tunic, dampened from clutching Zoë, had to be almost transparent, she realised, where it lay across the projection of her breasts, leaving their full roundedness apparent to his gaze.

But he hadn't recognised her! Relief made her knees almost buckle.

'Are you all right?' His hand was wet and warm on her bare arm. 'You've had a bit of a shock. Do you want to sit down? Can I get you a drink? A brandy or something?'

Mel shook her head, trying to restore her equilibrium. He was so close she could smell the heady musk of his body, mingling with the fresh salt tang of the sea. His T-shirt and shorts clung wetly to his muscled torso, making her too conscious of the way his skin would glisten beneath them like polished bronze, feel like soft warm leather…

'No!' Shocked by the lethal strength of his sexuality and even more by her awareness of it, Mel pulled sharply away. 'N—no, I'm all right,' she breathed, hoping he would think her confusion stemmed solely from what had happened out there with Zoë.

'You're sure?' His dark eyes were studying her, but with no sign of recognition.

'Yes,' she said, still fighting for her composure. 'Yes, I'm all right. Thank you. And thanks again for what you did for my daughter. We're both very grateful.'

'Your *daughter*?' She followed his surprised glance towards Zoë. The child was still sitting, massaging her cramped muscles, her cornflower blue eyes, shielded by a hand from the sun's glare, looking adoringly up at her rescuer.

'Everyone tells Mum she looks too young to have me.' Her face, like Mel's, was a perfect oval, but with thicker, well-defined brows and a determined mouth that was too strong to be called pretty just yet. 'But I don't mind. I think it's cool.'

'She's a bright kid,' the man commented, mouth tugging down one side.

Under normal circumstances, and with anyone else, Mel would have rolled her eyes and laughed, said something like

Tell me about it!, because Zoë was a precocious child, intelligent, spirited, with a mind of her own. Only these weren't normal circumstances. And this wasn't anyone else. This was Vann Capella. And the man had virtually just saved her daughter's life!

Momentarily reliving the terror that had seized her when she had seen Zoë struggling out there, Mel turned her head away, her eyes stinging with overwhelming emotion. It could have been a terrible tragedy if he hadn't been on hand to prevent it happening. It was ironic when she considered it. Not to mention his mistaking Zoë for her sister!

All through lunch he had been sitting there and she hadn't even realised it to begin with. Or had she? She wondered now. Had her subconscious acknowledged him even when she hadn't? Had her physicality recognised his even when her brain refused to, producing that shaming sexual response in her across the tables?

A heated flush stole across her skin. Biting down on her lower lip, she heard him say, 'Are you sure you're all right?'

Swiftly, Mel pulled up her wayward thoughts. 'Of course,' she said, a little too sharply, because, of course, he hadn't recognised her. And why should he? she thought. She'd been no more than a temporary inconvenience in his life. 'Thanks again. Now, I'm afraid we really must go.'

'Oh, Mum! Do we have to?' Zoë groaned, getting up rather tentatively. Clearly she was enjoying the man's company.

He shrugged, turning to Mel with lips compressing as though he had just found an ally.

Strung with tension, without any of her usual patience, Mel said, 'Yes, I'm afraid we must,' almost pulling her daughter with her.

'Perhaps we'll meet again,' he said, but he was smiling down at Zoë. 'And look after that leg.'

'I will.' Zoë beamed, evidently smitten.

A host of conflicting emotions raged through Mel. 'I'm afraid she's leaving for Rome in the morning,' she put in quickly. Then wondered if she had imagined the shadow that seemed to flit across his face.

'Pity,' he expressed, his shrug of regret bringing Mel's reluctant attention to the superb width of his shoulders, to the musculature of his chest beneath the clinging cotton, to the whole disturbing strength of his virility. 'At least stay long enough to tell me your name?'

Every nerve-end was suddenly zinging with a vibrant warning. Holding herself rigid, Mel felt the silence stretch away into timelessness. Behind her, on one of the sun beds, she heard someone cough, heard the familiar clinking sounds of a table being cleared up in the café, caught the shrill cry of a seabird as it homed in, somewhere high above the grey shingle of the beach.

She took a breath and, chancing it, uttered, 'Mel. Mel Sheraton.' Her pulse thumping, she saw his thick dark brows come together, but then his frown was lost in the blaze of his smile.

'Well, Mel Sheraton…' He dipped his head in an ornately gallant gesture. Having made no connection, she thought, relieved. 'I'm pleased to have been of service to you.' Then he was gone, striding down the jetty where, with a swift economy of movement, he scooped up his discarded shoes and glasses and stepped lithely into his boat.

'That was Vann Capella!' A disbelieving voice suddenly reminded her that Karen had been there all the time. 'I was going to tell you that before you raced off after Zoë. Vann Capella,' her friend continued to enthuse. 'And you turned him down flat!'

Against the sound of a high-powered outboard motor bursting into life, Mel took a steadying breath.

'He was only offering me a brandy, Karen. And only because of the state he could see I was in over Zoë.' And over seeing him again. Over dreading that he would recognise her. Over a lot of things she couldn't even begin to tell her friend. Or anyone, she thought, watching the dinghy streak across the open water, leaving a white trail of turbulence behind it. Not now. Not ever.

'He was offering you a lot more than that and you know it,' Karen said, her tone almost scolding.

'Who is he?' Zoë wanted to know as they moved back across the terrace. She was still hobbling, though not quite as badly now.

Something tightened in Mel's chest and the dryness of her throat made her swallow. She wanted to wake up from this nightmare. To leave Vann Capella where he belonged. Firmly entrenched in the past.

'Who *is* he?' Karen echoed, with an incredulous glance at Zoë, unaware of her friend's turmoil. 'He owns Capella Enterprises, a conglomerate of international companies that probably touch every commercial field you could mention. One of your self-made, well-on-the-way-to-becoming one of Britain's richest and most eligible millionaire bachelors, if you please!'

'Anyway, why don't you run along and get an ice cream?' Mel asked her daughter quickly.

The twelve-year-old shrugged. 'OK. I thought he was cool, though. For an old guy, that is.'

Karen laughed, though Mel only managed a half-hearted smile.

'That was cowardly,' her friend remarked when the child limped off. 'A man shows an interest in you and you won't even talk about him. Not even to tell your own daughter who she's just been rescued by. I'm sure she would like to have known that, before he became a colossus among business tycoons, he was the most dynamic member of the biggest thing in modern rock bands. What what it? Eleven, twelve years ago?'

'It would hardly have meant very much to her,' Mel responded, without bothering to correct the other woman. 'They disbanded before she was even born.'

'And there was some scandal over that, wasn't there? Didn't they have a rather unscrupulous manager or something? Wasn't he responsible for them losing a lot of money so that they ended up virtually penniless? All I know is,' Karen went on without waiting for an answer, 'when they broke up the other members of the band were never heard of again. While Vann came back as the uncrowned king of commerce, having settled all the band's debts single-handedly. Which was rather magnanimous of him. And now…!' She paused, her sigh of admiration saying it all. 'Vann Capella,' she breathed. 'Who would have believed it? Here?'

'Who would?' Mel said with more vitriol than she had intended, and felt the questioning glance Karen sent her way.

'He was right, you know. You do look rather shaken up,' she commented, as Mel, keen to avoid her friend's well-meaning regard, started swiftly up the steps to the restaurant. 'Are you sure you're feeling OK?'

'Perfectly,' Mel sighed. If only Karen would drop the subject!

'I suppose Vann sounded more universal on stage than Giovanni,' to her dismay Mel heard her friend continuing behind her. 'But he isn't wholly Italian, is he? His mother was English, wasn't she?'

'I don't know.' She could have been more helpful, Mel decided, reaching the table they had abandoned in such haste only a short while ago. It seemed like an age to Mel, though, as she stooped to retrieve the canvas bag by the side of her chair. 'I wasn't a fan.'

'Everybody was. Everybody still breathing,' Karen exaggerated, reaching for her own belongings. 'He used to look irresistible, dressed all in black, with that deep, sexy voice. And he didn't use it to sing so much as to whisper low sexy phrases over that bass guitar that used to seem to throb when he played it.' She gave a delicious little shiver. 'It was orgasmic! And yet he hated it, didn't he? The whole music scene. I remember him referring to himself during a business interview some years ago, when the interviewer tried to get him to talk about it, as an Anglo-Italian boy who had found himself in the wrong place at the right time. And that was it. End of subject. He was born to be a business entrepreneur. That's only too obvious. But at the time I could have died when he quit that band.'

Slipping a canvas strap over one shoulder, Mel glanced towards the ice cream bar where Zoë was still deliberating over a bounty of flavours, and grimaced. 'You and fifteen million other teenage girls,' she remarked, with a sharp stab of concealed emotion.

'Probably,' Karen agreed. 'And he still looks great now, only more so if that's humanly possible. I'll bet he doesn't suffer fools. And he probably eats women for breakfast!' The model rolled her eyes, sounding like the love-struck adolescent she had obviously been. 'They don't come much more dynamic-looking than that, do they?'

Mel glanced down at the ground. There was a dampened patch of flagstone from the water she had spilt earlier when she had bumped into the table leg. The glass had been removed, the surface wiped clean by the efficient staff.

'Looks aren't everything,' she said, aware now of the little purple bruise already forming on her knee.

'It's a darn good start.'

'A start for what?' Mel enquired suspiciously, folding her arms as she waited patiently for Zoë.

'Ooh, I don't know…' Karen's lips were pursed. 'Another chance meeting? One stupendous night or two? A raging affair?'

'I thought you were happily married.'

'I am, but I can still admire, can't I? I don't intend trading Simon in for anyone. I was thinking of you.'

Mel laughed, but without any trace of humour. 'Then think again.'

She moved away, looking seaward for a moment. Most of the diners had gone, either down to the beach, to the loungers, or via the dimly lit corridor cut through the mountainside, back to the lift and the funicular railway that would take them all the way back up to the cliff-top hotel. There was only one young couple left, sitting at one of the rear tables near the gaping cavern of the corridor and, without even looking at them, Mel could tell that they were very much in love.

Perhaps feelings like that could last a lifetime for some people, she thought, but, going by her mother's two marriages, she had strong doubts.

'I forgot. You don't go in for one-night stands, do you? Or any kind of commitment, for that matter,' Karen commented, as though wise to her friend's thoughts. 'In fact, in the two or three years I've known you, you've never got involved—I mean, really involved—with anyone. Despite Jonathan's efforts. Not to mention mine and Simon's! You won't give it a chance, Mel—not even with the most innocent of blind dates.' Concern showed in the taller woman's eyes as she studied her friend and said, 'But it obviously hasn't always been like that.'

A bubble of girlish laughter floated towards them from the ice cream bar. Zoë, chuckling over something the middle-aged waiter was saying. Probably she had told him about her cramp and having to be rescued, Mel thought, noticing that he had filled a cone with an extra large helping of ice cream for her. Charmed, Mel decided wryly. Manipulated by that special quality of Zoë's that nearly always guaranteed her daughter her own way.

'That was a long time ago,' Mel said.

'In that case it's time to move on. And turning down multi-millionaires is definitely moving in the wrong direction. You might have screwed up your chances good and proper. He might not be so interested if you bump into him again.'

'Which I'm quite sure I won't,' Mel said meaningfully. 'Anyway, I think he got the impression that both Zoë and I were leaving in the morning. And, even if he hadn't, he really isn't my type.'

'And what is? Someone you'll feel safe with, as you did with Zoë's father? Other men can do that, if you'll only let them get close enough to you. You've got to let your hair down. Live a little, Mel. Have some fun.'

'And you call having an affair with someone like Vann Capella living a little? It would seem more like emotional suicide to me.'

'Because you think you'd be just one in a long line of conquests? You're probably right.' Karen laughed, with sleek dark eyebrows raised. 'But what a way to go!'

'Whatever turns you on,' Mel said dryly, but couldn't control the crack in her voice, the strain she could feel in every tense feature. It was only then that she noticed Karen surveying her curiously.

'It's really personal with you, isn't it?' she whispered. 'You really resent him, don't you?' And, when Mel didn't answer, 'Care to tell me why?'

Mel turned away. The sea was calm now, with no sign of the turbulence left by the dinghy's departure, or of the underlying currents of pain and remorse that were surging through her.

'It's no secret,' she murmured, thinking it a bitter injustice that she should now be burdened with indebtedness to Vann Capella on top of everything else. 'It was in all the papers. He was the man responsible for killing my sister.'

CHAPTER TWO

THE rest of the team were already there when Mel walked into the long, airy conference room on Monday morning. A couple of dozen plushly upholstered chairs had been set out in double rows of four as she had instructed.

She made a swift check of everything else she had requested. Fresh flowers on the table at the front. The screen and projector for her visual presentation. The folders containing the company's welcome pack, the week's agenda, topics to be discussed and reviewed.

'You've certainly worked hard in putting all this together,' Jonathan remarked, coming over to her. He was flipping approvingly through one of the folders. 'Our clients can't possibly fail to be impressed.'

Tall, blond and in his early thirties, Jonathan Harvey was Managing Director of Jonathan Harvey Associates and Mel's immediate boss, although over the past year they had shared a few casual dinners out of office hours.

'I've got a good team,' she acknowledged, glancing over to where Jack Slater and Hannah Merrifield, two of her young sales managers, were busily putting the finishing touches to the venue with two other young executives from Marketing. 'You know me.' She laughed. 'I've just been lazing around.'

'As if!' Jonathan pulled a wry face, tossing the folder down on to the pile he'd taken it from. 'You might look as though you've just stepped out of one of our *Eternal Springtime* ads…' his gaze took in her vibrant, wayward hair, painstakingly secured in a French pleat, her fresh, youthful complexion that required only the minimum of make-up, and the silver-grey suit tailored to her slim, petite figure '…but I know you work harder than anyone.'

Which was encouraging at least, Mel thought, with a mental grimace, glad to be compared with the positive results of a teenage beauty product. Her head, though, felt delicate from two restless nights' sleep, the outcome of having bumped into Vann Capella down at the beach the other day. Refusing to dwell on that, however, as she had been trying rather unsuccessfully to do ever since, she came back to the present to hear Jonathan saying, 'I see I shall have to watch my own job if you carry on like this.'

Despite everything, mischief lit the green eyes that were emphasised by a smudge of grey shadow. 'You think I might be after it?'

'Who knows?' He sent her a wry glance. 'You're a daunting businesswoman, Mel.' And then, as though needing to remind her, 'Did you enjoy your two or three days playing full-time mother?' he asked.

Dear Jonathan, she thought. She liked and respected him. But even he sometimes had difficulty dealing with her single mother/company director status, perhaps feeling, in some weird way, somehow threatened by it.

'It made a nice change,' she said, because that was what he expected her to say. Not that the job of being a mother ever ended—or the concerns and anxieties of it anyway. But she didn't think he would wholly understand that. Besides, the first clients had started to filter in.

Swiftly, Mel gestured to the rest of her team, who moved over to the door to greet them. Opposite her, Jonathan had taken up his position beside the pretty, fair-haired Hannah who was handing out a welcome pack to each client.

Managing Directors. Chief Executives. Wives and partners. These were the higher echelons of their most favoured international clients. Mostly middle-aged or elderly men. Wealthy and successful, if the display of Mercedes, Jaguars and BMWs she could see parked on the scorching asphalt outside was anything to go by. Even as she looked, a black Aston Martin with tinted windows swung in and purred to a halt alongside the others, its subdued colour and low, sleek lines, symbols of understated luxury.

She was talking to a chatty elderly man about the subtleties of advertising when her eyes were suddenly drawn towards the door. Lips parted, shock numbing her, she could only look on in disbelief. Vann Capella!

He was shaking hands with Jonathan, just a few metres from where she was standing, and the blow of seeing him again coupled with his stupendous appearance reduced everything else going on in the room to a blur.

Though it wasn't strictly a formal affair, all the men wore dark suits, white shirts, ties—the uniform of the company man. But it was obvious Vann Capella had not seen fit to conform.

Tie-less, in a light beige suit and open-necked white shirt that contrasted sharply with his tan, his very detachment appeared to mock their stiff formality, so that he seemed the only one appropriately dressed for Positano's stifling heat. The gleaming ebony hair, sleek against his head, was fastened at the nape of his neck today, its severity only seeming to emphasise his hard masculinity. He looked everything he was. Rich and powerful and awesome. Probably one of the youngest men here, Mel calculated, and yet he dominated the room.

Then he looked over and saw her, and the space between them was suddenly detonated with a high and dangerous energy. For fleeting seconds Mel couldn't move, trapped in the snare of a regard that was fiercely intent. But the man who was chattering away beside her suddenly paused, waiting for an answer to a question she hadn't even heard, and quickly Mel pulled herself together.

Bluffing her way through an explanation she hoped made

sense, trying to show an interest she no longer felt, she was suddenly wishing she could be somewhere else. Anywhere but here in this room. With him.

As the clients took their seats, out of the corner of her eye she saw Vann do the same, and her only coherent thought was: what was he doing here? He hadn't arrived when the other clients had throughout the previous afternoon and evening, and his name certainly hadn't been on the guest list. So why had he turned up today?

She didn't know how she managed to get through the morning's agenda, deliver a clear, concise talk on Harvey's new campaigns and its winning promotions, answer questions, and generally appear anything but ruffled. She could only congratulate herself when the whole thing was over and she had managed to sail through it without looking a total fool.

Put it down to professionalism, she thought in wry mockery of herself, as she was reloading her briefcase at the close of the meeting. But all her hard-won competence couldn't stop the leap of her pulse when she glanced up and saw Jonathan leading Vann over to where she was standing, just as she was congratulating Hannah and Jack on the morning's success.

'Vann. I want you to meet my henchman and right hand, Mel Sheraton. Mel.' The MD was beaming like someone who had just landed a prize catch. 'Vann Capella.'

Jonathan, whom Mel had always thought strikingly good-looking, today appeared totally eclipsed by the taller man's overwhelming presence, while behind them Hannah was looking positively awestruck.

Heart thumping, every nerve went on to red alert as good manners forced Mel to accept the hand Vann extended to her.

'How's the water baby?' he queried softly, looking amused.

Not thinking clearly, aware only of that strong male hand clasping hers, for a moment she frowned, then realising, uttered, 'Fine. Fine, thanks.' Her throat felt tight and dry.

'But in Rome?'

Of course. She had told him that much, hadn't she? He didn't seem surprised, however, that she hadn't gone as well. Perhaps, she thought, he had known she was co-host of this conference when he had asked her name down there at the beach the other day, having a distinct advantage over her in that case.

'She's at the age when looking round boutiques is preferable to playing in rock pools,' she murmured unnecessarily, and in a daze heard Jonathan's voice, strung with curiosity.

'Do you two know each other?'

Vann, though, didn't even look his way. Teeth white against his tan, he was smiling down from his superior height and with almost mocking directness was asking, 'Do we, Mel?'

For a moment it was as though there were only the two of them in the room, those soft tones seeming to imply things that were overtly intimate. But the significance of his question rocked her, so that she swallowed, moistened her dry lips. Did he mean simply because of their meeting on the jetty the other day? Or had he recognised her?

In the circumstances, she did the only thing she could. She chose to ignore it and, smilingly, in a voice she prayed she could hold steady, gave Jonathan a résumé of Zoë's rescue.

'I was just quicker off the mark than you were, that's all,' Vann remarked, as though she would have been perfectly capable of his own life-saving abilities. But she could feel him studying the tense contours of her face as though he sensed her unease and was somehow intrigued by it and it was Jonathan who finally broke the awkward little silence.

'Vann's standing in for Austin Heywood, who hasn't been able to get here. Vann took over as Chairman of Heywood last week to try and rescue its Communications Division and, as he's only staying down the coast at his villa, he decided to come himself. He said he hoped we didn't mind.' A purely perfunctory gesture, Mel decided, because she had the strongest suspicion that whatever this mature, stupendous-looking trouble-shooter wanted he would take, regardless of who minded! 'I said we're only too pleased to have such an illustrious client in our midst. That perhaps he could instruct my staff in how to stay ahead of the game. Pass on his expertise and hope that his Midas touch rubs off on Harvey's!'

This produced a burst of laughter from the three of them, though Mel sensed that only Jonathan's was genuine.

So Vann had added yet another string to his remarkable bow! she thought, impressed, yet Jonathan's deference to his prestigious new client irritated her.

'I'm sure anything he could teach us would be worth knowing,' she murmured politely, nonetheless. After all, he was the customer—and a pretty impressive one—and her professionalism wouldn't allow her to be anything but courteous.

'I'll look forward to it,' he said, the smile he flashed her ripe with innuendo. There was, however, something predatory and watchful in the hard glitter of his eyes.

Had something unlocked his memory banks? she wondered, mortified. Did he have any inkling at all as to who she was? He couldn't possibly. Even so, seeing him again had swept the ground from under her. She felt hot and sticky, despite the comfortable coolness of the air-conditioned room. Her head had started to ache, and all she wanted to do was get away.

'Well, it's nice to have met you,' she lied, swallowing to ease the dryness in her throat. 'I'll look forward to talking to you again—' saying it because it was expected of her '—perhaps before the day's through.'

'Sooner than that,' Jonathan chipped in before the other man could say anything. 'Vann's agreed to join us all for lunch.'

All, meaning two of their agency's oldest clients and their wives. Her heart sank.

'How nice,' she responded with a forced smile, determined to keep anyone from seeing through the gloss of her professional veneer. Nevertheless, she could feel those steely eyes upon her and had the distinct feeling that, behind his cool smile, Vann Capella had guessed at the turmoil going on inside her, even if he didn't understand the reason for it.

Lunch was an informal affair, served on the hotel balcony with magnificent views of the mountains and the valley plunging to the sea. Way below them, Positano's quaint houses and colourful hotels huddled precariously on their terraced ledges, a miniature town above the glittering sapphire of the bay.

Business was discussed, and then leisure filled the conversation. The glories of local crafts, the nearby islands of Ischia and Capri. The archaeological phenomenon of neighbouring Pompeii.

'Clever people—these Romans,' John Squire, the eldest of the two client directors remarked. He was a portly, ruddy-faced man in his sixties, who kept slapping his equally rounded wife, Maureen, on the knee.

'Not clever enough to hold on to their empire,' said the other director, a thin, serious-looking man with glasses who was sitting next to Mel.

'That's because they didn't have Vann,' Jonathan said, from Mel's other side. 'If he'd been at the helm two thousand years ago, they would have conquered the universe.'

A chuckle went around the table, murmurs of agreement from the two older men.

'I don't believe my enterprises have yet strayed into the realms of space travel,' Vann commented smoothly, smothering their deference to him with laconic ease.

He had removed his jacket, as everyone else had, and was sitting across the table immediately opposite Mel so that it was difficult to keep her eyes from straying to the broad span of his shoulders, as it was to stop herself from blushing when he sent her a rather covert smile that excited as much as it disturbed.

'It could come,' Jonathan jested. 'There aren't many men who could grab the heart and mind of every young female in the civilized world and then go on to evoke the envy and admiration of every man in commerce and industry today. You were aware that Vann was the driving force behind—' He had been addressing the others but turned towards his prized client, clicking his fingers as if that could produce the name of the long-disbanded fivesome that was eluding him. 'Sorry about this. It was a long time ago…'

'Exactly,' Vann stressed with a smile that only derided that area of his life. 'A mere anomaly on my part. An aberration. Nothing more.'

As she had been, Mel thought with a sudden piercing hurt she hadn't expected to feel. A straying into unwise waters. Best forgotten. Easily dismissed.

She was glad when the appetising-looking and beautifully presented meal was over, because she couldn't actually remember tasting a thing.

'You weren't half as greedy as the rest of us, Mel.' Maureen Squire laughed as they were getting up from the table. 'Resisting all those tempting sweets! Is that how you manage to keep that lovely slim figure?'

This was the cue for everyone's eyes to swivel in Mel's direction, but it was only Vann's she was aware of, moving with silent assessment over her white sleeveless blouse and short straight skirt that seemed suddenly too short beneath his stripping regard.

'Mel could eat for England and never put on a pound.' It was Jonathan, unconsciously drawing greater attention to her sudden loss of appetite. She saw Vann's lips compress, felt his eyes rake disconcertingly over her face, narrowing, darkly perceptive.

'Perhaps you're working her too hard, Harvey. There was certainly no sign of gourmet tendencies today. In fact, England would have lost if it had been counting on her.'

Darn the man, Mel thought, for emphasising the fact, even though she felt that last quip had been a back-handed lob in response to Jonathan's somewhat indelicate remark. But this man had wreaked devastation on her and her family, and the strain of seeing him again had made her head throb. She didn't want to be here, enduring his calculating glances, having him defend her when he couldn't even remember who she was!

'He's right.' Above the sound of the low horn of a ferryboat drifting up to them from the distant harbour, Mel realised that Jonathan was still pursuing the subject of her appetite. 'You didn't eat much today. Not sickening for anything, are you?' Blond brows drawn together, he was shrugging into his jacket. There were some crumbs on one of the dark lapels.

'No, of course not,' Mel said quickly, aware of those hard masculine eyes still watching her. Vann had retrieved his own jacket, but it was hooked casually over one shoulder, and Mel tried not to notice how the crisp shirt pulled tautly across his chest. But complaining of a headache in front of clients was simply not done and so she said, 'It's probably the heat. I never feel much like eating in these temperatures.' She just wanted to get away, escape to her room, find some breathing space so that she could begin to decide how to handle this torturous and difficult situation.

Her chance came as the Squires and the other couple departed for an afternoon trip into town in the hotel's courtesy car. Before anyone could protest, Mel quickly excused herself, leaving Vann in the luxurious lobby with her senior colleague.

Her own room was dark and cool. The maid had been in to clean, drawing the curtains and turning on the air-conditioning unit.

Gratefully, Mel crossed to the *en suite* bathroom and changed into her cotton bathrobe. Her head was thumping and, coming back into the bedroom, she poured herself some iced water from the fridge and took a couple of painkillers before pulling back the curtains. Daylight spilled in, causing her to wince from the sudden brightness.

The dark rattan furniture gleamed and the snowy coverlets on the twin beds reflected the cleanliness of the mirror-polished floor-tiles. Now, though, without Zoë's few belongings lying around, the place seemed sterile and empty and, with a sudden crushing loneliness, Mel put down her glass, pushed open the French doors and went out on to the balcony.

All the rooms in the main hotel overlooked the bay. On plunging terraces, countless flights of steps and quiet paths, shaded by the stirring pink heads of oleander and bougainvillaea, gave access on to garden rooms built into the steep rock. In the distance, looking east, lines of orange sun beds decorated the dark shingle of Positano's main beach.

Way above, on the verdant mountainside, a wisp of grey smoke was rising from one of the farmsteads and, from somewhere in the valley, the thin, metallic sound of a church bell rang out the hour.

She had been looking forward to coming here, she thought, feeling the prick of angry tears behind her eyes.

Yet now she was simply dreading the week ahead, and all because of one man.

Vann Capella.

His turning up here had opened up all sorts of wounds and grievances she had thought soothed by time. But they were still there, like skeletons in a dark cupboard, waiting only for the door to be opened to burst out as fully fleshed demons again.

The fact that he didn't recognise her was a blessing in itself, and yet even that small relief had brought its flipside of hurt, anger and bitterness. But why should he have recognised her? she thought, trying to rationalize, trying to justify. She had only met him once, after all, and then she had been just a kid with dark tinted hair cut elfin short, and a boyish figure which in no way represented the more feminine curves she had developed from becoming a mother. Of course he hadn't recognised her. She hadn't immediately recognised him, had she? Not really. Not to begin with. And he had been a celebrity. His face constantly in some magazine or other. While she…she had been just a nobody…

Speared by an emotion she refused even to acknowledge, she pressed her palms against the wells of her eyes, telling herself she was being over-sensitive, that all she was suffering from was a rather large dose of hurt pride.

It was fourteen years ago! her brain screamed at her. *It's gone! Over with! Finished!* But the demons had been let loose, and with them the memories, unchained to torture and shame her.

It was around the time of her eighteenth birthday when the band had come to the city where she had lived with her mother and her sister. Kelly had been obsessed with the band, but particularly with their aloof and brooding lead singer. She had been fifteen years old, a normal, healthy, happy schoolgirl, and she'd eaten, drank, slept and breathed Vann Capella.

Mel remembered how the music coming constantly from Kelly's room had almost driven their mother to distraction. Sharon Ratcliffe, deserted by two husbands, had struggled to bring up her daughters single-handed. But their fathers' defection had produced a close-knit bond between the two girls when Mel, from the age of seven, had taken her four-year-old half-sister under her wing. Together, wrapped in the cocoon of warmth and affection their mother had woven around them, they had learnt a moral self-sufficiency that excluded any male, a strictly female fortress that no man could storm. Mel thought it laughable now how she had imagined her safe, secure world would last for ever. That was until the night of that fateful concert, and then all her illusions had been brutally shattered.

For weeks Kelly had talked about nothing but Vann and the concert her friend had managed to get tickets for. At eighteen, Mel had considered herself above it all. She had been studying at college, working in a café at weekends and holidays, had her own set of interests, friends. As far as she was concerned, raving over rock stars was something schoolgirls did, girls of Kelly's age and, though appreciating the band's music, Mel had thought Vann Capella both arrogant and morose. He had to be, she decided, to appear so mean and magnificent on stage and yet remain so indifferent, almost contemptuous of the mania he was generating among the female population with his image. The other members of the band joked, flaunted obvious good looks and flashed boy-next-door smiles. Vann, always brooding and silent, oozed raw, unadulterated sex.

Which was why Mel had stayed so unaffected by him and had resolved to remain so every time she had caught herself looking up, drawn against her will by the dark persona of the man staring down at her from her sister's bedroom walls. And why she hadn't felt the slightest bit envious when she and her mother had dropped Kelly off at her friend's house on the evening of the concert. Felt very little for that matter because, sitting there in the car, how could she have known she would never see her half-sister again? Because, carried along on a wave of hysteria, Kelly had died screaming over him.

A heart attack, the hospital had said. They had received flowers from the band's manager. Security had been adequate but could have been better, some official judged. People had made the right noises. It was no one's fault. No one, it seemed, was responsible. And, if that wasn't enough to deal with, Vann Capella's remarks, splashed across one of the tabloids only days after she had died, had seemed to tip Mel over a precipice.

It wasn't his problem. That was it, pure and simple.

Anger had warred with grief. She owed it to her sister to let him know exactly what she thought of his cold, insensitive arrogance. He had been oblivious to Kelly's innocent feelings about him, but Mel vowed he would certainly be made aware of hers!

They had been performing at the Albert Hall that night. It was their largest and last UK concert before their big Australasian tour. Mel had known it was her only chance.

She couldn't even remember how she had explained her intended absence to her mother. That she needed to distance herself from a suddenly suffocating household of far-removed cousins and consoling friends? That she needed some time on her own? Whatever, armed only with a map and her determination, she had got into her old, battered Mini and, driven by unreasoning emotion, had headed straight for the south-west.

She knew that she wouldn't have had a cat in hell's chance of getting to see, let alone confront, Vann in London. He and the band would be whisked away before the fans had even blinked. But, by a quirk of fate, a college friend whose brother was involved with the band's promotion had bragged to Mel weeks before about knowing where the band would be staying after their last performance. They were being flown out of London by helicopter to a remote country manor hotel near Bath.

It was well after midnight when she finally saw the sign for the Somerset village and turned the car through the gates, along the tree-lined drive of the exclusive hotel. It was January and the road conditions had been hazardous. Rain had turned to sleet, then snow. The Mini, always temperamental, had broken down during the journey and, after Mel's futile groping about under the bonnet, decided, inexplicably, to start again, so that she reached the Palladian mansion dishevelled and grubby.

Chandelier-lit windows gave her a glimpse of the sheer luxury inside, while outdoor security lighting illuminated several expensive cars parked on a crescent of shingle, and the helicopter-landing pad embedded in the manicured lawn.

Her hollow stomach churned with apprehension and hunger as the Mini rattled into a space between a Porsche and a Rolls Royce. She was exhausted and she hadn't eaten for hours. But justice for Kelly had her scrambling out of the car, carried her feet over the shingle. The sleet stung her face and her thin scoop-necked sweater, light jacket and jeans were inadequate protection from the biting wind.

Her entry to the house was forestalled by a concierge who had heard her car arrive and had come out to investigate. Did she have a booking? Was she a friend of someone staying there? He probably wasn't accustomed to being descended on, Mel remembered thinking later, by a drowned-looking female with an oil-smeared face and hands in the middle of the night.

Somehow, though, she got into the house, demanding to see Vann Capella, her eyes barely registering the eighteenth-century style décor and furnishings, the elegant floral displays, the exquisite Regency furniture.

Eventually, another man appeared. The hotel's manager, Mel realised from his authoritative tone and manner. Who did she want to see? Who had told her the band was staying there? He was afraid he couldn't divulge any information about guests. He asked what her business was and, when she refused to tell him, had suggested politely but firmly that he thought she should leave.

Her resolve to stay right where she was, and until the morning if she had to, finally galvanized him into action.

With cool formality he had asked her to wait and swiftly disappeared, but the tough-looking, cropped-haired man he returned with wasn't half as polite.

Who the hell did she think she was coming there demanding to see anyone from the band? How had she got hold of the information anyway? The pressure of his fingers bruised her arm as he hustled her towards the door. If she didn't go right there and then, he said, he'd call the police. It was only later that she had discovered he was Bern Clayton, the band's manager. For him, evicting just another pestering teenage fan was par for the course.

Angrily, Mel told him who she was, asserting that Vann *would* see her. She pulled forcibly out of the man's grasp.

'I'm Kelly Ratcliffe's sister,' she threw at him bitterly, as if that would make a difference, believing it with all her naïve confidence of what was right and wrong.

He said he was sorry about her sister, but if she wanted to make a case out of it then she'd better get in touch with her solicitor. It wouldn't do any good, he advised her, taking it out on Vann. So why didn't she be a sensible girl and run on home?

Close to spent, Mel clung to the little fight left in her.

'I'll wait,' she said, folding her arms to emphasise her intention.

'Have it your own way.' The man took his phone out of his pocket, began dialling the police.

And then from behind him came another voice, deep and resolute, brooking no resistance. 'I'll see her.'

It was the first time Mel had seen Vann Capella in the flesh. Neither his photographs, nor his television appearances, could capture the sheer presence of the self-assured youth who had become every girl's dark fantasy, or that powerful sexual aura he wore like a blazing shield.

Framed by the pillared doorway to one of the magnificent staterooms, he was taller than Mel had expected, that air of cold arrogance more daunting, that familiar detachment one of almost hostile rebellion. He was wearing a black vest top and trousers, with an unbuttoned denim shirt slung loosely over the top. He looked as though he had just dragged himself out of the shower, Mel thought, because the thick black hair, worn shorter then, was still damp. Not so much handsome as formidably attractive, even at twenty-two there was a physical force and strength behind that wide brow and proud nose, in the brooding mouth and uncompromising jaw line that set him apart as a born leader, making him a match for his elders and superiors alike.

'You!' Mel breathed at the same time as Bern Clayton swung round, swearing viciously.

'For heaven's sake, Vann!' he snarled. 'Are you mad?'

'Probably.' His whole manner defied the older man as he moved with lithe youthfulness away from the doorjamb. 'What is it to you, anyway?'

Mel sensed that there wasn't too much accord between Bern Clayton and probably his most money-spinning, if not his most manageable, client. But the manager wasn't giving up that easily.

'For goodness' sake! Think of the trouble you could get yourself into,' Mel heard him urge imperatively.

'Don't worry, Clayton. I'm sure you can sort it out for me,' Vann drawled in what was to Mel a dry, uncaring tone so that, driven by hurt anger and injustice, her temper finally snapped.

'And why not?' Somehow she found the strength to raise her voice to him. 'It isn't your problem, is it?' And then, triggered by something beyond her control, all restraint was suddenly deserting her.

Her behaviour was totally out of character, and afterwards would shame her as much as it surprised the two men. Afterwards, too, she would have time to consider how she must have appeared to Vann: a bedraggled waif flying at him like some manic, mindless shrew. At the time, however, she was scarcely even aware of the manager's arm shooting out to stop her, or of Vann thrusting it aside to take the full brunt of her anger.

She knew only the texture of his skin as her nails dragged down the hard bone of his cheeks and shadowed jaw, met the resisting strength of muscle beneath rough denim.

He caught her arms then, which left her clawing at thin air, and suddenly everything became too much. The room started to spin. Weak with exhaustion and lack of nourishment, she felt her legs buckle under her and, with a small sob, collapsed against his hard leanness like a limp doll.

CHAPTER THREE

WHEN the dizziness receded, and her brain started to function again, she was sitting, with her head bowed, on the silky brocade of a chaise longue. Beneath her feet was a thick carpet, softly illuminated by subdued lighting, and on which, planted firmly apart, was a pair of dark, very masculine shoes.

'Feeling better now?'

The deep, concerned voice brought Mel's head up, her gaze lifting from that confident stance to take in the whole length of Vann Capella's hard, rangy body.

Long legs, narrow hips and waist. Black singlet stretched tautly across a smooth, tanned chest. He had discarded the loose shirt, which he must have simply thrown on earlier, exposing muscular arms and shoulders and a lot of swarthy flesh. His drying hair was curling slightly now against his neck, as dark and untamed as a gypsy's. But it was those terrifyingly attractive features—the brilliance of his steely-blue eyes beneath their thickly arched brows and heavy lashes—that for a few moments held Mel in thrall, commanding as much as they were compelling. And he had asked her if she felt better.

Dry-mouthed, she nodded. She hadn't expected him to be so menacingly beautiful. Behind him, in pride of place among the elegant eighteenth-century style furnishings, was an enormous four-poster bed.

'Sorry,' he apologised, as she shot him a swift, censuring look. 'All the public rooms were occupied and in view of the…nature of your visit *and* your rather…delicate state…I thought you'd want some privacy,' he concluded.

Mel put a hand to her temple, trying to take things in. The elaborate room. The doorway giving her a glimpse of an equally elaborate bathroom. So this was his suite.

'I passed out?' She met his eyes full on now. They were clear and cold and penetrating.

'In some style,' he said, grimacing, and she noticed how cruel his mouth was. Cruel and hard and sensual.

The memory of her behaviour in the lobby, however, returned with shaming clarity, making her blush to think of it. 'And you carried me here?'

'As I said, I thought you'd want some privacy. But my motives weren't entirely unselfish. If I was going to be laid into,' he acknowledged, slipping his hands into his pockets, 'I didn't particularly relish the idea of an audience. Even if some members of the media think I shouldn't even sneeze without it making front page news.'

He sounded coldly cynical and not the least bit Italian. Vaguely, Mel remembered Kelly telling her that he had spent most of his life in England.

'All right. I shouldn't have attacked you,' she admitted, stopping short of a full apology. After all, he didn't deserve one, did he? 'But you asked for it.' Just thinking about what he had told the press started her anger brewing again. 'You're nothing but a callous, arrogant bastard! How do you think we felt reading what you said about Kelly? Dismissing her like that? And then going ahead with your tour like she was nobody? *Nothing!*' She was shouting now, but she couldn't help herself, unleashing her pain and anger with every syllable she threw at him. 'Didn't you care that she might just have a family who might be going through hell over what had happened? How would you have felt if the same—'

'Terrible.'

'—thing had…' Her sentence drifted away, that one word stunning her into silence. Open-mouthed, she stared up at him, her eyes dark hollows in the small pale oval of her face.

'Terrible,' he reiterated, though that harshly sculpted face was hard to read.

'So why did you say it?' she whispered.

Beneath his incredibly thick lashes, Vann's eyes were unfathomable, yet for a moment, held by the intensity of their penetrating regard, Mel's bones seemed to liquefy, but from something other than mere fatigue this time.

'I didn't.'

'What do you mean, you didn't?' Accusation stole into her voice again. 'I read it. So did the whole of Britain probably!'

'I'm sure they did.' A muscle pulled beside that cruel mouth. 'But one thing you learn in this business is never to put all your faith in everything you read. I was misquoted,' he expounded bluntly. 'What I did say was that Kelly had a problem. A heart defect.' It was something that hadn't been known until after she had died. 'That, tragic though it was, the band couldn't shoulder responsibility for what had happened. That it wasn't anybody's fault. It makes better reading to transcribe it as though I didn't care. Far more sensational. Sells more newspapers, too. But I didn't say it. Nor would I. I'm not entirely… What was it you called me? A callous, arrogant bastard?' A black eyebrow lifted in an almost self-denigrating manner. 'And I had to go ahead with the tour. Like it or not, I'm under contract. I've got commitments—responsibilities to other people. I'm sorry it happened,' he said, removing his hands from his pockets. 'And I appreciate how you feel. I'd probably feel the same way—maybe worse—if the situation were reversed. But it really wasn't anyone's fault.'

Feeling the weight of grief pressing on her chest, Mel couldn't answer. She looked down at her hands, studying them as though she hadn't seen them before. They were grubby from tending to the car.

It wasn't anybody's fault, he had said. All the time she had been concentrating her efforts on blaming Vann, confronting him, yet hearing his side of the story shook her convictions to the core. There seemed to be more than a ring of truth to it, a forthrightness behind that dark, enigmatic persona that came dangerously close to making her believe everything he said. But someone had to take responsibility! It wasn't enough, his trying to tell her that nobody was to blame!

'It should never have happened! It should never have been *allowed* to happen!' The tears she had held bravely back over the past few days threatening to overwhelm her, she jumped up, anger the only thing left holding her together as she vented her outrage and misery on bands, the Establishment, Vann for being who he was, lashing out in one last desperate tirade to try and ease the unbelievable pain inside her. 'You shouldn't be allowed to do what you do when you know what it does to girls like Kelly! It's all for the fame—the adulation! She was only fifteen years old, for God's sake! Just a kid! Just a sweet, innocent kid and you killed her! You all killed her!' Tears were gushing from her now. Helpless in her grief, she sank to the carpet, her clawed hands turning into fists, thrashing out at the chaise longue, at the world, only hurting herself as her hand struck something hard and wooden.

'For Christ's sake…!' Swiftly he came down on his knees, catching her hard against him, holding her fast so that she couldn't do herself any more harm, imprisoning her arms with the determined power of his. 'It's all right! It's all right! Come on! Come on! It's all right!'

She was crying hysterically, her sobs only muffled by the warm, cushioning strength of his shoulder.

Quickly he carried her over to the bed, sat down with her

between the draped curtains, still clutching her tightly to him, whispering soothing words, rocking her as one would rock a baby.

'Hush. Hush. It's all right. It's going to be all right.'

He rocked her until her racking sobs began to subside.

Gradually, as she calmed down, she became acutely conscious of those strong bare arms around her, of that smooth velvet chest beneath his vest and his intoxicating scent.

'Are you all right?' he asked as she stirred against him.

She nodded, pulling away from him, sitting up. 'I feel a mess,' she sniffed, raking her fingers through her hair. She grimaced as she looked down at her other hand.

'If you think they're bad…' He didn't have to finish. A wry glance at her face said it all. He gave a jerk of his chin towards the *en suite* bathroom, moving swiftly to assist her as she shrugged out of her jacket.

'Can you manage?'

'Yes.'

In the luxurious bathroom she splashed soapy water on her mascara-stained cheeks, patting them dry with a fluffy towel that smelt of his shower gel. Hopelessly then she tried to tug her hair into some sort of shape.

Her face in the glass looked drawn and pale, and her eyelids were red and puffy. Behind her, reflected in the mirror, beads of water still clung to the glass and tiles of the shower cubicle. From where he had been cleaning up before he'd come downstairs, she remembered, wondering if he had come down at once, or if he had given it some consideration.

Her tired thoughts running riot, she imagined him leaping under the welcome jets as soon as he'd stepped off the helicopter, drenched in perspiration after his performance. He would have looked ungovernable, his clothes clinging to him, would have been exuding a raw, animal aroma…

'Are you OK in there?' His deep voice brought her out of her disconcerting reverie.

She moved back into the bedroom, so tired she could scarcely walk straight. Vann was reaching for his shirt on the bed, tossing it down on to the chaise. He glanced towards her as she dropped down on to the white coverlet.

'I'd better go,' she said, reaching exhaustedly for her jacket.

As she made to get up, however, a determined hand was on her shoulder, pressing her gently back down.

'You're not going anywhere,' he stated firmly. 'You're not in a fit state to stand, let alone drive! I presume you drove here?'

Mel uttered a small sound of confirmation. 'I can't stay here,' she argued feebly. She had very little cash with her and her credit limit certainly didn't extend to the prices charged in a hotel of that calibre.

'You can and you will,' Vann asserted in a tone that defied argument and, with one fluid movement, was lifting her legs up, swivelling her round fully on to the bed. 'I'm taking responsibility for you tonight, so you can protest all you like. You're staying.'

'Then…where will you sleep?' she asked hesitantly.

His glance followed hers to the chaise.

'Well, I'm sure that would be the gallant thing to do,' he accepted wryly. 'But I'm far too exhausted for that. Oh, don't worry,' he added, seeing the startled look that darkened her eyes. 'I've just done the gig of my life. Given every ounce of mental and physical energy in the process. I've got none left for anything save getting a good night's rest.'

Already he was removing her sneakers, black hair falling loosely across his brow.

'When did you last eat?'

'I don't know.'

'Then I'll ring down for something.'

'I'm not hungry.'

'Maybe not, but you've got to eat.'

He reached down for the phone on the bedside cabinet, started tapping out some digits. As if he was really concerned about her, she thought, listening to him ordering room service. As if he cared…

'Why didn't you just throw me out?' she asked wretchedly as he came off the phone.

'As Bern Clayton would have done?' And, when she frowned, 'Our manager,' he went on to enlighten her. 'The guy you met downstairs. Contrary to what you might have thought…' He paused, black brows drawing together. 'I'm sorry,' he said. 'I don't even know your name?'

Those clear, penetrating eyes seemed to take her breath away. But she answered croakily, 'It's Lissa.' She was going through the fad of hating her name, and used the derivative she was currently demanding her friends and family call her.

'Well…Lissa…' On his lips it sounded rich and warm, unbelievably sensual. 'As I said, I'm not totally heartless.' He was walking away from her, towards the bathroom, the easy grace of his movements capturing her gaze without her even being aware of it so that she was totally unsettled when he suddenly turned, caught her watching him. 'And you're wrong. It isn't all gold and glory in this business. It's cutthroat and exploitative. And sometimes the superficiality of it all makes me sick!'

The vehemence of his words surprised her. She had thought he wallowed in his fame. Yet now…

She was still trying to come to terms with her new concept of someone she was beginning to realise she had misjudged when the food arrived.

'Just one more spoonful,' he urged ten minutes later when she was forcing herself to swallow the thick home-made vegetable soup he had ordered with a basket of warm crusty rolls. He was sitting on the edge of the bed where she sat, propped up against several plump pillows.

'I can't.' Tiredly she let her spoon drop back into the half-emptied bowl.

He leaned forward to inspect it. 'Well, I suppose you've eaten enough,' he conceded, taking the bowl from her, the movement causing a waft of his pleasant, elusive scent to impinge on her nostrils. He obviously hadn't shaved since before his performance, as all he had probably been planning to do after his shower was go to bed, and the darkening shadow around his jaw only added to that thoroughly untamed image. Just above, on one of his cheeks, were a couple of small red marks.

Where her nails had caught him, Mel realised, horrified.

'I'm sorry I scratched you,' she said, contrite.

His thick lashes came down in silent acknowledgement of her apology, black against the dark olive of his skin. Suddenly, though, those amazing eyes lifted, clashed unexpectedly with hers, making her pulse seem to stop and then double its rhythm.

'Did you tell your parents you were coming here?'

Mel swallowed. He was so unbelievably…perfect. 'No,' she answered. 'Anyway, I'm eighteen. I can do as I like.'

'So grown up.' His smile was the most disarming thing about him, she decided at that moment, because he didn't do it very often, and with a shocking realisation found herself wondering, in spite of everything, what that cruel mouth would feel like against hers. More soberly then, he said, 'None of us can do as we like. We all have some responsibility to someone or something.'

As he had said he had to others involved in the tour?

She wondered how she had ever thought him selfish and arrogant. Well, just a little bit arrogant maybe, but not cold or callous as she had thrown at him earlier. He was caring. Considerate. Tender, even…

Just thinking about how tender he might be in a totally different situation caused a funny little feeling in her stomach. Her heart was beating ridiculously fast as he stood up.

'Won't anyone be worried about you?' His eyes were faintly puzzled. 'Shouldn't you call them?'

She shook her head. 'I needed to be alone. To get away. Anyway, it isn't my parents. It's just Mum and—'

She brought herself up quickly. She wouldn't cry again. She wouldn't! Swiftly, she pressed her lids against her burning eyes.

'Get some rest,' he murmured softly, and she felt his hand, strong yet understanding, on her shoulder. 'You'll have more strength to deal with it after a good night's sleep.'

She was crying in her dreams. Running weightlessly through a flat, empty landscape, calling out because she had lost something precious, frantically searching every identical blade of grass. There was only one massive tree in a vast endless field and, reaching it, gratefully she sank back against it, grasping the sturdy branch that somehow lay across her chest. The sun must have been playing on its trunk and branches because she could feel its warmth against her, and she felt comforted, secure and safe.

She groaned in her sleep, a low, pitiful moan.

'It's only a dream.' The deep voice was filtering down through the leaves of the tree. 'It's only a dream. It's all right. You're dreaming. That's all.'

Her eyes fluttering open, for a moment, lying there in the darkness, Mel couldn't remember where she was. Then it all came flooding back. Kelly. The desperate drive. Meeting Vann…

As consciousness returned with all its cruel reminders, she uttered another involuntary groan, suddenly aware that the warmth she could feel wasn't the sun but a shadowy, naked torso leaning over her, and the branch lying across her wasn't a branch at all, but a strong masculine forearm gently shaking her.

'Are you all right?' Vann asked.

She wasn't, but she nodded, fully awake now. A sliver of cold moonlight peeping through a chink in the heavy curtains lent a satiny sheen to his skin. The arm that had roused her now lay along the length of his body, which was half-covered by the bedclothes, and Mel wondered, with a sudden dryness in her throat, if he had stripped off completely before coming to bed.

He must, however, have pulled the covers up around her after she had fallen asleep, because she was too warm in her sweater and jeans. Meeting some resistance as she tried to throw them back, she realised that it was Vann's body weight that was stopping them, that he himself was only covered by the bedspread.

Either he liked to sleep in the cool or had wanted to give her extra privacy, she decided, too haunted by her thoughts to feel grateful to him at that moment.

'She was all I had besides Mum,' she whispered, staring face up into the darkness. 'I keep thinking that if I'd been there—gone to that concert with her—it might not have happened. She wanted me to at first, and I wouldn't.'

'Don't,' he said.

'Don't what?'

'Don't torture yourself like that. You couldn't have prevented what happened.'

'But I keep thinking that if I'd given in to her wishes for once—hadn't been so selfish—'

'It probably wouldn't have made the slightest bit of difference,' he said. 'She did what she wanted to do—so did you—and if you could have the time over again you'd do exactly the same thing. It's only natural, what you're feeling. It's just one of the recognised phases of grief which we all have to go through when we lose someone.'

She turned to look up at him, her face a pale, perplexed oval in the moonlight. 'What phases?'

'Disbelief. Anger. Self-reproach. Killing while it lasts. But you learn to judge yourself a little less harshly in time.'

He sounded as though he'd had first-hand experience. As though he knew. What was it Kelly had said? Mel reflected, wanting to remember, rifling through her memory banks and her sister's interminable ravings about him. That his father had died from…What was it? A heart attack? And his mother from an overdose of something less than a year later when he was, what, only fourteen?

Mentally she winced from the depth of anguish he must have suffered, unable to dismiss it now as lightly as when Kelly had tried to stir her reluctant sympathies towards him.

'It just hurts,' she murmured and, on a shuddering little breath, '*So* much.'

The arm that had been resting in an arc above her head now slipped around her shoulders, comforting, like the tree in her dream, sure and strong and protective.

'The deeper you love the more it's going to hurt.'

'I wish I hadn't,' she said poignantly. 'I wish I didn't love anyone.'

He gave a soft chortle through the darkness. 'You don't mean that,' he assured her equally softly. 'It can only be good to have loved someone—have someone love you—that much. Not everyone's that lucky.'

Something in his voice made her wonder if he was referring to himself. She looked up at him questioningly, but his face was a series of dark angles and planes, made harder by the shadows.

'I suppose not,' she breathed, feeling an insidious tension stealing through her, a heat that sprang from more than just the cocooning warmth of the magnificent four-poster bed.

There was a vulnerability to his mouth as he gazed down on the paleness of her throat and the delicate collar-bones exposed by the wide slash-neck of her sweater and for a moment she wanted to reach up, touch the hard line of his jaw. Then his eyes lifted, locked with hers, and she felt she was drowning in two lonely pools.

'Tomorrow…' he said huskily, reaching across to trace a finger down the soft curve of her cheek '…you'd better give me your telephone number.'

'My…telephone number?' Trembling from his touch, she turned her face into his palm, felt its calloused warmth against the corner of her mouth. Breathing shallowly, unconsciously she tilted her chin, moulding her skull to the curve of that arm that felt so warm and comforting, felt so right…

But suddenly he was rolling away from her.

'I'd better get up,' he said.

It was as though a lifeline had been suddenly snatched away from her. She was back in that empty landscape. Lost. Desolate. Cold.

'Don't go!'

He had already tossed back the bedspread, but her small plea stalled him. Wearing nothing but a pair of dark briefs, he was looking at her over his shoulder, his profile harshly outlined.

'You don't know what you're saying,' he reprimanded softly.

Mel's throat contracted. 'Yes, I do.' As she had sat up her sweater had slipped off one shoulder, and her moon-bathed flesh was smooth and pale. 'I don't want to be alone.' In the silvered light she looked young and vulnerable, both of which contributed to a soft sensuality she wasn't even aware of. 'Please hold me,' she whispered.

The gentle curve of her face complemented the hard-hewn angles of his. Where her softness yielded, Vann's austerity seemed unrelenting and rigid. For a few eternal seconds his lashes lay darkly against the wells of his eyes. The lower line of his mouth was drawn tautly in check, and his body seemed caught in the grip of some tight constraint. But then his shoulders relaxed and, as though he had just lost a battle with himself, he released a long sigh and opened his arms to her.

'Come here,' he breathed, and even that sounded like a command.

Tentatively, Mel shifted her position, easing into his embrace. Beneath her cheek the contours of his chest felt like warm, cushioned velvet and she could hear the hard, heavy rhythm of his heart.

'You test a man's strength. You know that, don't you?' he said, again in that slightly scolding tone, that smooth chest expanding beneath her palm.

'Do I?' It was an innocent response, one Mel could hardly voice for the sensations ripping through her.

She had had boyfriends in her young life. Teenage boys whose semi-nakedness she had snuggled up to during innocuous kisses on a beach. A young male body wasn't entirely a mystery to her. But no one had ever affected her as Vann was affecting her now. Her body ached for even closer contact with his. Never, she realised with sudden startling intensity, had she needed this closeness with another human being so much.

His chin brushed her hair and she lifted her head, seeking more than the clasp of those strong arms around her, seeking his comfort, his strength, and with them total oblivion from her misery.

Growing bolder from her need, she did as she was aching to do and let her fingers stray to the rough stubble of his jaw, tracing the path where her nails had tried so viciously to wound. The texture of his skin sent something like a volt of electricity zinging through her. Unconsciously, his name tumbled from her parted lips.

For a second he dipped his head, his mouth a hair's

breadth from hers. But then strong fingers locked around her wrist, halting her caresses.

'You don't want to do this,' he said hoarsely.

'Do what?' she whispered, barely reasoning, knowing only that she wanted to give of herself, to take away the pain, the loneliness or whatever it was she sensed behind that cool detachment and, in doing so, find merciful obliteration in his hard strength.

'You know very well.'

'Yes.'

'And you don't care?'

'I don't want to care.'

'Because you're unhappy and overwrought.'

She knew he was right, but she couldn't accept it because his mouth was so close to hers that she could feel the feather-light touch of his breath fanning her skin, and because the intensity of his gaze seemed to be mesmerizing her so that all she could do was close her eyes against it.

'Please,' she uttered, her emotions laid bare on that one small, tremulous note.

She felt the tension in his body, heard the way his breath seemed to catch in his lungs. Then his mouth was covering hers, and with such intense fulfilment of her longing that she sobbed against his lips, glorying in the strength of the arms that were suddenly locking her to him, not in comfort now but in a hard, sensual demand.

Unused as she was to such raw, masculine passion, Mel met it nevertheless with a feverish urgency of her own. Her fingers revelled in the thickness of his hair, in the smooth rippling satin of his shoulders and the hard musculature of his back.

His mouth was devouring her with its hungry insistence, burning kisses along her cheek and jaw, over her willing mouth, moving with electrifying skill down the sensitised length of her throat. His hand had slipped under her top just above the low waistband of her jeans, its shocking warmth against her bare midriff causing her to suck in her breath.

With heart-stopping anticipation she felt his fingers shape the curve of her hip. She jerked against him with a small guttural cry as shock waves of pure pleasure cascaded through her lower body.

'Easy now. Easy,' he murmured against the slope of her bare shoulder, yet he sounded flattered by her sensitivity to his touch.

Her breasts ached beneath the confining fetters of her clothes and she strained against his naked warmth, the action bringing her into sudden contact with the extent of his own arousal.

'Yes,' he agreed breathlessly, his mouth burning over her throat, and he made short work of removing her top and the white balcony bra, exposing her small breasts and the curvature of her waist and hips to his hot gaze.

She wondered what he thought of her, how she compared with all the other girls he might have had his pick of and undressed like this. And then she remembered that he hadn't picked her or intended to sleep with her. But he must like her a little to have been so gentle with her when they'd met, she considered, because no one had ever shown such tenderness towards her before. She only wished she was more experienced and didn't suddenly feel so unsure of herself, especially when he moved to remove her jeans and her skimpy briefs, then remove his own, and she saw him in all his masculine glory. He was so utterly perfect, proud and confident in his nakedness.

But then, as if reading her thoughts, he murmured, 'You're beautiful,' before dipping his head to taste the sweet bud of one burgeoning breast.

Everything seemed to spiral in a dizzy haze of sensation. The touch of his hands on her body, his hard length nudging at her softness, that exquisitely suckling mouth. She could hear the sleet outside, beating against the windows, the harshness of the night emphasising the warmth and sensuality of the world within. The sumptuous draping curtains above them were like silent witnesses to their passion, absorbing her cries of pleasure and Vann's deeper groans of need. And all at once she was aware that she wasn't shy any more, but confident of her own sexuality, glorying in her naked femininity laid out before him on the sensuous bed.

'I haven't any protection,' Vann said, in a voice thickened by desire. 'I should have done something about it before. But I can get some.'

An icy chill swept across her body as he started to move away. Desperately she clutched at his arm. 'It's all right. It doesn't matter.'

He stopped, frowning down at her. 'You're on the Pill?'

She didn't answer. How could she, when the truth meant that he would leave her? And he couldn't leave her. Not now! Not for a minute!

In response she brought her arms above her head in a gesture of total surrender but with a rather uncertain smile, nervous suddenly of the unknown.

He inhaled sharply and came down to her again, taking her silence as a 'yes'. But he didn't enter her at once, making certain she was ready, kissing the places where his lips and hands had explored, while she sobbed and writhed beneath him, her untutored body hungering for the unleashed power of his.

When it came, she let out a shuddering gasp as anticipation dissolved into mindless sensation. There was no pain, just an abandoned, exquisite ecstasy as he pushed into her.

She lifted her hips, her body yielding easily to accommodate his, and then he was filling her, wholly and completely, taking her with him into eternal, timeless space.

Some time afterwards, snuggled up to him with her head

on his chest, she murmured, 'You understand, don't you? What it feels like?'

'Yes.' He didn't need to ask. He knew she was referring to his parents.

'You must have been devastated.'

'Yes.'

'What happened?'

He stirred slightly, his body tensing as though he were steeling himself against remembering. 'You wouldn't want to know.'

'Tell me,' she pressed softly, raising herself up to touch her tongue to the warm velvet of his shoulder. It tasted slightly salty.

'A mutual exchange of trust?' Cynicism filtered through the soft tones. 'Is that what intimacy does? Drags out your darkest secrets?' And before she could respond, feeling somehow reprimanded, as though she had touched on something far too personal, he was saying, 'I thought it was common knowledge my father drank himself to death and my mother killed herself.'

The bluntness of his statement made her flinch. 'Why?' she whispered, sensing the anguish behind those bitter words. 'How could she leave you like that?'

'I guess she just missed my father.' His breath seemed to tremble through his lungs. 'God knows why! They were never happy. Between her wanting England and his wanting Italy, sometimes they spent months at a time apart.'

'What happened to you?' She laid her head on his chest again, felt its warmth against her cheek, his arm flex around her. 'Who did you live with?'

He made a cynical sound down his nostrils. 'Whoever won.'

'Won?'

'Oh yes, they fought tooth and nail over that little issue. Do you know what it's like,' he breathed, 'feeling as though you're just a weapon for one parent to hurt the other one?' His hand was moving absently along her arm, stroking, idly caressing. 'I suppose they could have divorced. But ethics and a strict moral upbringing decreed otherwise, in spite of my father's drinking, his violence, although my mother didn't help herself on that score. She only provoked him, which made matters worse. But I came along too soon in their marriage and they never stopped reminding me of that fact. Sometimes I felt that they wouldn't have been in the mess they were in at all if it hadn't been for me. Most of the time I felt like a whipping boy for a double dose of resentment. Then, after they died, all I felt was guilt. Sheer, crucifying guilt!'

'I'm sorry,' she breathed, shocked by what he had told her, her heart swelling with tenderness and compassion for him. The image he portrayed on stage wasn't an image at all, but the real man, she thought. The detached, self-sufficient, lonely Vann. Inside this wild-looking youth there had been pain as great, if not greater than hers, she realised, even if it had been somewhat assuaged by time. And at least she had known love, security…

'I'm sorry,' she whispered again, her hand caressing the warm plane of his chest, and didn't need to ask him anything else. At some time or another she had read about the rest. The foster homes. The jobs he had had. Hard, undesirable jobs, demanding all his time and strength—until one night in a bar he'd picked up the guitar abandoned by someone who had just walked out of the band…

But she didn't want to think about that because, without her realising it, his hands had turned exquisitely arousing. Neither had she realised how hers were affecting him until she heard him groan. But suddenly he was rolling her over, taking control again, and with a small moan of acquiescence she was meeting his insistent passion, welcoming it with a need as desperate as his until she was lost again in an all-consuming conflagration of the senses.

An unfamiliar whirring sound woke her. Grey morning light filtered through the chink in the curtains, showing Vann's side of the bed to be empty. The dent in his pillow made her smile as she remembered their abandoned lovemaking.

Scrambling naked out of bed, she reached the window and peered through the curtains just in time to see the helicopter lift up and away into a sky leaden with snow.

A knocking on the door made her swing round. Vann!

With her heart leaping, she whisked the thick curtain around her. 'Yes?' she called out, breathless with anticipation.

But it was Bern Clayton who strode in, big and brazen in a grey track suit, stopping dead when he saw her shielding her nakedness in the room's expensive furnishings.

'Where's Vann?' she enquired, looking past him, as though expecting his dynamic young client to come striding in after him.

'Gone. What did you expect?' he told her ruthlessly. 'He's got a TV interview and then a plane to catch. If you wanted to say goodbye to him, I'm afraid you're a little too late.' Then, seeing her wounded eyes, he said with a little more compassion, 'Perhaps he didn't want to wake you. He told me to see that you had a good breakfast and everything you needed to get home.'

Home. And then she remembered that he had asked for her telephone number. Probably because he knew he would be making an early start.

'He said he'd contact me, but he doesn't know where to find me,' she realised, horrified. She would need to rectify that. 'He asked me to leave my number. If I write it down before I leave, will you see that he gets it? He asked me specifically, you see.'

The man's gaze went from her shielded nudity to the incriminating chaos of the bed. 'Was that before? Or after?' he enquired brutally.

Mel moistened her lips. What was he suggesting? She saw him shaking his head, saw the censuring pity in his eyes and felt a gnawing anguish deep in the pit of her stomach.

'You young girls are all the same,' he commented disparagingly. 'You're so naïve. You sleep with a man once and then think that gives you some special hold over him, some special privilege. But it doesn't. Particularly a man like Vann. I don't like to have to tell you this, sweetheart, and I'm sorry about your sister—we all are—but he was just trying to make you feel better. He probably didn't mean to hurt your feelings. But if you come here, making yourself available...' His extended hands said it all. From his expression she knew exactly what he thought of her.

'It wasn't like that,' Mel uttered, wounded by his cold cruelty, the way he was reducing the tenderness she had shared with Vann to little more than sleaze.

'What did you think it was? The real thing between you two?' he sneered, looking, with his close-cropped hair, like a club bouncer, used to dealing with unwanted customers. 'When you're older you'll realise not to take these things so seriously. It wasn't a wise thing coming here. Vann has his career. You could make things bad for him—and yourself—if this got out. Think how it would look. Here.' He was rummaging in a back pocket. 'The least we can do is pay for your petrol home.'

She shrank away from the notes he was suddenly thrusting in front of her. She felt like a prostitute being paid off, or some greedy opportunist being settled with for no further hassle.

Had Vann discussed her with his manager? She just couldn't believe that Vann would have told him anything about last night. But Bern Clayton had already told her that she was naïve.

Refusing to accept that Vann would have done such a thing, she said, 'If he did mean it, he won't know where to find me. If I write my telephone number down, would you give it to him?'

'If he wanted to find you, he'd find you all right. Numbers wouldn't be necessary.'

'Please,' she appealed, feeling a cold desolation washing over her.

He shook his head again, his expression suddenly one of pitying resignation.

'I'll give it to him,' he said. 'But that's all I can do. Leave it on the table before you go.'

So she had, enclosing not only her number but also a few brief lines, which, even now, nearly fourteen years on, made Mel cringe to remember. As did her foolish behaviour that night with Vann. It was something she didn't even want to think about, let alone admit to anyone else. She hadn't even told Karen everything when her friend had asked.

She had told her, of course, what had happened to her sister and about confronting Vann. She had even mentioned how she had collapsed from exhaustion, and had had to spend the night in his hotel. But it had been easy to withhold the full facts from her friend as Karen had been rendered speechless by the whole train of events. Because, of course, shortly after Kelly had died, unable to withstand the shock, Sharon Ratcliffe had succumbed to the same heart defect that had claimed her youngest daughter, leaving a stunned, bereft Mel to cope alone.

Six months later she read that the group had disbanded. She never heard from Vann Capella again.

CHAPTER FOUR

JONATHAN was chatting with several clients when Mel stepped out on to the terrace that evening. Because of her migraine she had skipped dinner, but now she had recovered enough to shower and dress for what was basically a welcome party for their guests.

'Mel. Glad you could make it.' Jonathan sought her out before she could join his group, his grey eyes wandering appreciatively over her.

Because lounge suits and cocktail wear were the order of the day, Mel had chosen a pale green crêpe de Chine strappy top with a low, curving neckline and sensuously fluid matching trousers that moved against her legs like a breath of air. Her hair she had left loose in a cascade of brilliant auburn, the overall impression, with her dark curling lashes, softly shadowed green eyes and burnished lips, one of unquestionable femininity.

'You look stupendous,' Jonathan breathed, impressed. 'You haven't got a drink. Let me rectify that.' He gestured to a passing waiter, deposited a cool glass of champagne into her hand.

'I need to talk to you—before anyone else does,' he said in a lowered voice, which explained his reason for singling her out, she realised, following his rather stealthy glance over her shoulder.

Her heart missed a beat when she saw Vann's dark figure dominating a small group of clients on the other side of the terrace. He had told Jonathan earlier that he couldn't make it for dinner, so she hadn't expected him to be here for the party. She could hear his companions laughing, see them hanging on his every word, totally absorbed in whatever it was he was saying, and Mel turned back to Jonathan, feeling as though someone had just sucked the air out of her lungs as she tried to make sense of whatever it was he was telling her.

'…overheard Vann telling Squire that he's testing the water with us as it were, obviously looking for reasons why he shouldn't stick with the agencies he's been used to.'

'It's his prerogative. He doesn't have to use us if he doesn't want to,' Mel responded, catching on. In fact, things would be far less complicated, for her at any rate, she thought, if he didn't. 'Only joking,' she assured Jonathan quickly nevertheless, seeing the dismayed look on the MD's face. Heywood was a huge national company, and he'd been worried about losing the account for weeks. 'We're the best, and all these people here—' she indicated the happily conversing élite of their clientele with a gesture of her glass '—know it.'

'And it's your job to make sure Vann does.'

A fine auburn eyebrow arched. 'Mine?' Beneath Mel's composed veneer a little twinge of pain made itself felt at the point where her head had throbbed earlier. 'Why mine? I would imagine *the* Mr Capella would be used to dealing only with top brass. You know, like yourself.' She was trying to sound casual, as though she didn't care one way or the other, when in fact the thought of having to involve herself with Vann any more than she had to was in danger of throwing her into a blind panic.

'Oh, come on, Mel,' Jonathan urged with a hint of impatience. 'Use your loaf. He might speak impeccable English, but he is half Italian with hot Latin blood in his veins. Therefore he's not averse to a pretty face. Besides…' he leaned towards her so as not to be overheard by anyone else, so close that anyone watching might have thought they were an item '…I think he fancies you.'

'Don't be ridiculous!' Mel returned hotly, disconcerted as well as outraged by what Jonathan was intimating.

'Be nice to him,' he warned.

Head cocked, Mel eyed her friend and colleague suspiciously. 'Nice to him?'

'You know what I mean.'

'I'm not sure I do,' she said.

'Oh, come on, Mel. Stop being deliberately obtuse. I don't mean sleep with the man. You don't really think I'm asking you to do that?'

She wasn't sure what he was asking, only realising that since meeting Vann here today she had been half-hoping she could use the shield of Jonathan's friendship to protect her from the man and from her own mixed feelings about him. But now it looked as though she wasn't even going to be able to do that.

'Just use that blazing charm of yours. You haven't exactly been in a rush to stick around and show him the sort of hospitality his reputation warrants and it's too important an account to louse up. Just don't do anything to ruffle his feathers,' he advised.

Taking a sip of champagne, hoping its effects would steady her nerves, Mel murmured, 'Are we dealing with a peacock?' Flippancy was the only tool she could employ to hide her agitation.

'No,' Jonathan reminded her grimly. 'More a sharp-witted, hard-taloned bird of prey.'

A shiver ran down Mel's spine as a cascade of silver notes sounded from the live band that had started to play under the awning that shaded the windows of the luxurious lounge bar. Jonathan's depiction of the man was over the top, but so was her response to it, she decided.

'I'll do my job,' she told him flatly, just before the tall, thin, quiet-voiced Jack Slater intruded apologetically, obviously wanting to speak to Jonathan, and gratefully Mel eased out of their orbit, welcoming a few moments alone.

Several couples were dancing to the slow instrumental melody filling the night air. Others were standing or sitting in small groups around the scattered tables, drinking champagne.

Mel knew the right thing to do was to approach the group nearest her, offer them refills, make them feel special, as important as they were to the agency. But after that unsettling exchange with Jonathan, and the knowledge that he was placing the responsibility of saving the Heywood account squarely on her shoulders, she needed breathing space to gather her wits.

Sure no one was watching her, she covered the few feet to the edge of the terrace and, with both hands cupping her glass, rested her arms on the cool, polished wood of the balustrade.

The warm breeze caressed her bare shoulders, fanning the loose fire of her hair. Lamps, strategically placed, lit the steeply-terraced gardens, beyond which the dark rocks plunged to the sea. In the night-shrouded bay strings of lights from several large yachts cast silver streaks across the water, but these were nothing compared with the thousands of twinkling lights from every house and hotel that made Positano glimmer with a breathtaking fairytale quality.

A stream of red tail-lights moving along the otherwise unlit coast road caught her attention and she followed its progress away from the town, beyond the ridge of dark land that formed the village of Praiano on the next headland, until it was lost from view.

'What lonely traveller needs the Madonna watching over him when he has you?'

Mel swung round, almost spilling her champagne.

From a distance, in an immaculate dark suit, Vann had looked devastating. Now, at close quarters, with that strong black hair worn loose, and contrasting starkly with the pristine white shirt, he turned her insides to jelly. Flouting convention, yet again he was tie-less, the open V of his shirt revealing the hard contrast of his skin, and the dark, corded strength of his throat.

Needing all her will to drag her gaze away from him, Mel glanced upwards to the sightseeing spot on the road above the hotel where the coach parties stopped to admire the view and take photographs and where, from her vantage point, the illuminated statue of the Madonna—like so many Mel had seen on the roadside since coming to Italy—gazed serenely down on the fairy-lit resort below them.

'I'm fallible,' Mel responded, meeting his eyes. 'She isn't.'

'And to put his trust in you, a man could lose his way?'

He was joking, but there was cynicism in his voice, too. Pointedly, Mel said, 'It depends on the man,' and took a swift draught of her champagne.

That dark head dipped in acknowledgement. 'Have you been along that road you seemed to be viewing so wistfully? Wishing what?' he asked. 'That you could be far away from here having fun, instead of having to pander to the likes of people like me?'

He was smiling, but Mel guessed there was a shrewd calculation going on inside that sharp brain.

'Contrary to how it looked, I do enjoy being with my clients.' She flashed him one of her most flattering smiles. 'It was unforgivable, I know, but I just couldn't help being enticed over by the view. I'm sure no one noticed.' This with a sideways glance that showed her clientele still laughing, chatting obliviously amongst themselves. No one except you, she thought with a little shudder. 'And no,' she said, answering his question. 'I haven't been any further south than Positano.'

Something like mockery touched the firm line of his

mouth. 'You should,' he recommended. 'Praiano's worth a visit—as are all the villages from here to Amalfi. You must let me show you. It's among the most—if not *the* most romantic drive in the world.'

It sounded glorious, but his startling offer, along with that disturbing adjective he had used in connection with it, gave rise to every instinct of self-preservation within Mel.

'That's very kind of you, but I'll be far too busy for much sightseeing,' she answered, trying to inject the right amount of regret into her voice, trying to ignore that crazy little part of herself that ached to accept.

'Too busy to keep the clients happy?' That mockery was still there, tinged with what? The slightest admonishment? 'I thought that was the whole purpose of your being here. In fact, I wouldn't mind betting that that was what that little pep-talk you seemed to be getting from your boss just now was all about.'

'Wouldn't you?' Mel hid her startled surprise behind a wary smile. Had he noticed Jonathan's covert glances in his direction? She turned her back on the magical view and, uncomfortably aware of Vann following her back into the hub of the party, tossed over her shoulder, 'You could lose your money—betting on a conversation you couldn't possibly have heard from the other side of the terrace.'

'I didn't realise you'd noticed,' he said silkily.

Blast him! Mel thought, trying to equate her memory of the worldly, yet vulnerable young man to whom she had once given herself so freely with this steel-hard, speculative sophisticate.

'Body language.'

'What?' Weaving her way through the throng, she spared a smile for the matronly but elegant Maureen Squire who was just joining her husband and another couple at one of the round tables.

'Body language,' that deep voice repeated. 'It can tell one far more than mere words ever could.'

Amidst the laughter and conversation, Mel turned round to face him. She felt safer now she wasn't so alone with him, wondering why that word should spring so readily to mind. 'And what did our body language tell you?' she prompted, green eyes meeting blue with something of a challenge.

'That you're more than professional colleagues.'

'That's not true,' Mel protested without thinking, glancing automatically towards the attractive blond man. One could hardly call a couple of platonic dinners a raging affair!

'In that case, dance with me.'

The soft command brought her gaze darting upwards to meet those crushingly familiar features, her every instinct screaming at her to refuse.

He doesn't know who you are! Nor did she want him to find out, she realised. Any more than she wanted to acknowledge that, after all these years, despite his lack of interest in her before, despite her hard lessons and her maturity, she was still hopelessly drawn to him. But to make an excuse would seem rude, she decided. After all, she had unwisely spurned his offer to take her sightseeing. Besides, Jonathan had told her to be nice to him for the account's sake. Out of the corner of her eye she was aware of the MD, ostensibly listening to Jack while sending odd glances her way. She didn't want any arguments with Jonathan on top of everything else.

Straightening her shoulders, steeling herself for the inevitable, she saw Vann's mouth quirk in response.

'Do I take that to be a ''yes''?' he asked, much too clever for comfort, totally aware of what was going on.

She met those steely eyes with a coolness she was far from feeling. 'You're very astute.' To her own ears it sounded more like an accusation than a compliment.

'I have to be.' He was relieving her of her glass, discarding it on an empty table they had to pass to reach the other dancers. 'I promise you this won't hurt,' he stated softly, taking her in his arms.

But it will! her brain screamed chaotically as she felt the warmth of his hand against the small of her back, pressing her close to him. *It will! More than you know!*

'Relax.' His voice, so familiar, was like the sensuous purr of a jungle cat. 'You're so tense.'

That's because I can't cope with this! Mel wanted to cry out, despairing that he should notice, and for a fleeting moment had to close her eyes against the devastating sensations running through her.

They had only shared one night. Yet with the first combined movement of their bodies, hers was awakening to the conscious knowledge of his, all her senses straining in recognition of the whole man—the lithe economy of his movements, his latent strength, that sweep of dark shadow around his jaw, the long-forgotten musk of his skin. He had taken her to Paradise and back again and she had paid for it over and over; through her guilt and shame that she could have succumbed so easily to the man who had robbed Kelly of her life; through the knowledge that he could as easily discard and forget her. Through…

The sudden flexing of that arm around her brought her eyes flying open to see him steering her out of the path of Jack and Hannah, who had just joined the dancers. Jack looked awkward, slightly uncomfortable on the dance floor, Mel thought, her gaze returning to Vann. There was an almost indiscernible furrow between his eyes.

'So what is Mel short for?' he enquired casually, although she had a feeling he had wanted to ask something else. 'Melissa?'

She nodded and he repeated it, and she was reminded

with a cruel jolt of the first time he had spoken her name, when it had lingered on his lips like a sacred prayer.

'It's a beautiful name.'

'Thank you.'

'Like the woman herself.' Before Mel could say anything, caught off guard by his remark, he went on, 'You said it was your friend who was taking your daughter to Rome.'

It was something he must have overheard her telling one of the others at lunchtime. Nevertheless, his abrupt change of subject surprised her.

'Yes.'

'Do I take it then that there isn't a Mr Sheraton?' And, when she hesitated, instinct warning her against having him cross the boundaries of her private life, 'You aren't wearing a wedding ring,' he stated. 'I couldn't help but come to the conclusion that there isn't. Well, is there?' he pressed relentlessly.

For a moment it would have been so easy to lie. To claim the safety of a husband as protection against her own reckless attraction to this man and this very disconcerting situation in which she was trapped. But he could find out the truth from Jonathan or any of the others if he chose to, so, treading carefully, she answered, 'Not any more.'

'Or any other serious relationship for that matter, despite what illusions your boss might have to the contrary.'

The highlights in her hair danced like fire as she inclined her head to ask pointedly, 'What makes you say that?'

The music was soft and dreamy and more couples were dancing now, but Mel noticed nothing but how the terrace lights made the clean thickness of his hair gleam like polished jet, and how the shadows, as he moved, made an enigma of the planes and angles of his face, strengthening its beautiful austerity.

'The way you were looking at me down there in that restaurant the other day.'

Mel's heart seemed to come up into her mouth. Why did he have to mention that?

'I thought you were someone I knew,' she said unthinkingly, and immediately could have kicked herself. That path was far too ill-advised to go down.

'Do you look at all the men you think you know like that?' he enquired, his tone softly censuring.

'Like what?' she queried, abashed. She knew only too well.

'I think we're both adults. I don't think I need to spell it out for you. But I will if you want me—'

'No!'

'So you do know what I'm talking about.'

His mouth was twitching in sensual amusement, those shrewd eyes watching the colour deepen in her cheeks, probably noticing the tension too that made her skin feel as though it were being stretched across her face as she struggled to find a way to excuse her uncharacteristic behaviour that day.

'Look, I'm sorry if I gave you the entirely wrong message,' she stressed, battling for composure, 'but I wasn't looking at you in any particular way. Now, can we drop the subject?'

A masculine eyebrow lifted in mocking scepticism, but all he said was, 'Certainly,' his compliance surprising her. She couldn't imagine him giving up on anything that easily.

'Let's talk about you,' she said. 'You didn't mention earlier that we were on trial.' The champagne was starting to take effect, but it was more from being in his arms and the unsettling turn the conversation had taken that was making her unduly careless, loosening her tongue.

'It's no secret,' he said. 'I'm quite satisfied with the companies I've been using. I've got a lot at stake. I need to know I'm getting the best. Heywood has been losing a lot of money.'

'May I ask what decided you on putting yours into it? Why you're so determined to pull it out of the mire?'

'Austin's an old friend of mine. Shares have hit rock bottom, as you'll be aware. Call it tossing a lifeline to a vessel in distress. But I'm not totally altruistic. Naturally, I do have my own interests at heart.'

'Naturally,' Mel repeated. The boy who had spent his childhood tossed around like a ship in a storm, and then been the victim of corrupt management, hadn't turned his fortunes around by letting sentiment dominate his hard-headed thinking. He had given her help when she had needed it. Solace, too, she thought, with a deep ache somewhere around her ribcage, but then he had moved on.

'And are you saying that perhaps we didn't do enough to prevent them sinking so low?'

'No. I think their problems were down more to bad management within the division, coupled with a downward trend in the market-place for the type of product on offer. If so, I shall be looking at upgrading. Developing a whole new product if possible.'

'Then you aren't just a silent partner.' As only this morning Jonathan had said he was. 'You're going to be actively involved in getting the company back on its feet?'

His eyes, shielded by those thick lashes, travelled lazily down over the serious oval of her face. For a moment they rested on the burnished amber of her mouth, before taking in the creamy slope of her shoulders, the gentle swell of her breasts revealed by the low neckline and softly he murmured, 'I am now.'

She wondered at the meaningful way in which he said that. Of course he couldn't have meant since coming here. Since meeting her. Nevertheless, an uneasy excitement stirred within her.

'I hear your company's among the best,' he commented. 'Not to mention your own record of success. Having seen your presentation this morning, familiarized myself with how you do things, I can see why. How long have you worked for Harvey's?'

Mel explained, skimming briefly over her five-year career with them, when she had joined as a sales executive, until taking a salaried directorship just over two years ago.

He was an attentive listener, his concentration solely on what she was telling him.

'And before that?' he enquired when she had finished. Clearly, he didn't believe in leaving any stone unturned.

'I had Zoë,' she said cagily, reluctant to revert to the subject of her personal life with him. 'I split my time between studying and working at home. Typing. Helping with promotional work. Generally keeping the wolf from the door. When she was old enough to go to school, I was able to devote more time to getting my career underway.'

'So…your husband's been off the scene for a long time.'

She hadn't intended to say anything to make him think she had done it all alone. Maybe it had been something in the tone of her voice, she thought. She hadn't set out to deliberately mislead him either, but she had, she realised, releasing the breath she wasn't aware she had been holding. She didn't know whether to feel grateful or ashamed. A bit of both, she decided when, taking her silence for affirmation, he went on, 'What happens to your daughter when you're working? Or are there other Karens in England waiting to whisk her off at a moment's notice?'

Something in his tone needled her, had her returning somewhat defensively, 'I spend as much time with her as I can. And I always make sure it's quality time. But I have to work to provide and Zoë knows that. I arrange my holidays around hers and, with the help of friends who also have children her age, we work something out. Besides, she's an independent child. She hates being tied to my apron strings.'

He laughed. 'Something I can't entirely envisage around that trim waist of yours.'

Mel felt her whole body tensing, suddenly conscious that the flimsy top, which only just reached the waistband of her trousers, had made it all too easy for his hand to slip beneath. She could feel that strong, warm hand against her lower back, feel it as erotically as when she had been naked with him…

Battling to bring her assailed senses under control, she said accusingly, 'You think I'm a hard-nosed career woman? With no time for a home and family?' Anger flared in her eyes, matching the burning highlights in her hair. 'Are you criticising me?' she enquired tetchily, unable to contain her pique because of the effect he was having on her.

Shadows chased across his face as they moved to the gentle music. 'I wouldn't dream of it,' he said. 'I admire what you do. What you've achieved under obviously very difficult circumstances. It's commendable. Shows courage and determination.'

'But?'

'Does there have to be a "but"?' he enquired smoothly.

There did, although he wasn't admitting as much, pulling her closer to steer her out of the path of another dancing couple.

Her nostrils dilated, greedy for the masculine scent of him, her body responding to the delirious thrill of his nearness. Being of Italian descent, he carried the blood of a very family orientated culture, which alone could engender his disapproval of her way of life. But, recalling what she did know about his background, she knew that there were other reasons for the high moral stance he was refusing to voice. She could almost feel the censure in the compression of his mouth, in the taut, uncompromising line of his jaw.

'You think it isn't an ideal situation for a child?' she went on, still defensive. 'That I wouldn't have liked something better for mine? Any mother would,' she added emphatically. 'But sometimes it just doesn't work out that way.'

'I was only surmising that it must be tough—combining a job like yours with motherhood—single-handedly,' he said in more placating tones.

'It's had its moments.'

'I can imagine.'

Can you? she thought with bitter poignancy. Could he know what it was like nursing childhood illnesses? To scrape and save and eke out an existence as she had done during those early harrowing years? Working all hours of the day and night between poorly paid jobs, swotting for her degree?

'So how old is she?' he asked. 'No. Let me guess. Around twelve. Right?'

Lifting her chin, Mel hesitated with a blind stab of pain at her temples. But, considering the length of time until Zoë's birthday, she pulled a face and said, 'Only just.'

'Only just twelve?' His strong features were crossed by amused curiosity. 'Or only just right?'

Warning bells were clanging inside Mel's head. She didn't want to be talking to him like this. He hadn't recognised her, but the longer she was with him the greater the chance of his linking her to that distraught teenager who had behaved so badly with him. So, with a nervous little laugh, losing what confidence she had, she said, 'It amounts to the same thing, doesn't it?'

A line appeared momentarily between those dark brows. Could he tell how keyed up she was? she wondered. But then he nodded and, with a rather speculative look, said, 'I suppose it does,' and let it go.

The music had stopped. Around them people were applauding the three-piece band. Automatically, they both joined in.

'Well, I really should mingle,' Mel was pleased to be

saying as the applause died away. A quick glance towards Jonathan showed him watching them both. For all his advice about her being nice to Vann, he wasn't looking particularly happy. 'I'll look forward to discussing your ideas during the coming week, but if there's anything you need before then—any questions you want to ask—'

'Well, yes,' he said, cutting across her invitation to call her or any member of her team. 'There is one.'

'Oh?' She looked up at him with a forced smile, immensely relieved, now that he had released her, to be back on a more formal footing with him.

'Have we met before?'

The unexpectedness of his question hit her like a bombshell. Under his hard examination she felt her stomach muscles knotting, her throat clog with more than just the humiliation of being recognised. But, if he couldn't remember, then she wasn't going to tell him, was her cowardly thought, and on a tight little laugh she said, 'I think I would have remembered if we had.'

For a moment those steely eyes seemed to strip away the layers of her composure, exposing her as the sham she was beneath the fine gauze of her defences. But then, mercifully, John Squire came up and slapped a hand on Vann's shoulder, asking if he would join them, and Mel quickly excused herself. As she left them to it, she wondered how many more episodes like that her nerves could stand.

CHAPTER FIVE

JONATHAN was in a petulant mood the following morning as he found Mel finishing a light breakfast alone, beside one of the open windows in the long, sunny dining room.

'I know I recommended that you were nice to him,' he began without any preamble, occupying the chair immediately opposite hers. 'But don't you think you were carrying things a bit too far? You even had Maureen Squire commenting on what a perfect couple you made,' he complained, clearly jealous.

'I only danced with him,' Mel stressed, wanting to forget about Vann Capella, how it felt being in his arms, those mortifying few moments afterwards. She was glad he wasn't staying at the hotel. That his villa was just along the coast so that he wasn't always around like their other clients to unsettle her, perhaps press the point of the drive she had successfully managed to wriggle out of. 'All things considered, I couldn't very well refuse, could I?' She cast a sidelong glance out of the window. Way down, on one of the terraces, someone was setting out the sun beds around the deserted blue oblong of the pool.

'You weren't just dancing. You obliterated the rest of us. What were you talking about so intently anyway?'

Mel felt like telling him to mind his own business. She had enough troubles on her plate without this conflict of interests with Jonathan to contend with as well. But it was his business. Or partly, anyway, she reminded herself, and so she said, 'His new ad campaign. Oh, and Zoë. We talked about Zoë.' It struck her suddenly that Vann had shown comparatively more interest in her daughter during the space of a few minutes than Jonathan had in all the time she had known him. 'Anyway, he'd know if I were leading him on just to keep Heywood's custom. He isn't stupid. Don't underestimate him, Jonathan.'

'Don't you either,' he warned, helping himself to a carton of fruit yoghurt from a selection in the centre of the table. 'He'd swallow you for breakfast and then spit you out without turning a hair.'

Tell me about it, Mel thought, glad when Hannah, dressed similarly to herself in shorts and sun top, chose that moment to come and ask whether she fancied a stroll into Positano.

As it turned out, it was just what she needed, Mel decided later, because the endless steps leading down between the houses and linking the quiet lanes—a shortcut from the winding mountain road—demanded all their concentration to negotiate. But eventually the steep route brought them, with a momentum that had them laughing, down into the very heart of the bustling little resort.

'What was it like to dance with him?' Hannah shook her by suddenly asking when they were sitting sipping fruit punches outside one of the beach cafés.

'Who?' Mel parried, stirring the beverage needlessly with her straw.

Hannah laughed. 'You know very well.'

Glancing at a slow-moving queue of tourists on the quayside boarding the ferry for Sorrento, Mel shrugged, feigning nonchalance. 'I was merely doing my job.'

Fairer-skinned even than Mel, the younger girl's face showed signs of a little too much sun, Mel noted, as Hannah laughed and said, 'Give me a job like yours any day. I'd sacrifice a year's salary for it!'

'Would you?' A wan smile hid Mel's inner anguish. She couldn't tell Hannah that because of Vann she had sacrificed far, far more than that.

'You weren't doing too badly yourself with Jack,' Mel

reminded her, needing to change the subject. She knew Hannah liked the amiable young sales manager, evident from the way that ultra-pale skin reddened still more.

As they walked up through the vine-covered arbour of the town's pedestrian thoroughfare they saw local artists displaying their talents beneath bright blossoms of bougainvillaea. Here, numerous craft bazaars and endless boutiques provided a shopper's paradise all the way from the main street, down past the cathedral with its imposing majolica dome—visible from any point of the town—to the last steep steps leading to the harbour cafés and the sea.

Reaching the point just past the main square where the hotel courtesy car collected guests who didn't fancy the arduous walk back, they both turned as a horn beeped loudly behind them. It was a battered little red Fiat, driven, Mel realised, by one of the waiters she had seen eyeing Hannah at the party.

'He wants to know if we'd like a lift,' the blonde told Mel, having rushed forward as soon as the car pulled up. Already the young man was opening the front passenger door.

'You go on,' Mel said. She had noticed a skirt in one of the exclusive little boutiques on their descent into town earlier and had promised herself a closer look on her return. 'I want to do some more shopping. I can get the bus back later.' And, to the pleased-looking Italian, 'Thanks, anyway.'

'Well, he's no Vann Capella,' said Hannah, climbing in. 'But beggars can't be choosers.' Mel was still laughing as the little car screeched away.

Taking her time, she reached the shop and was deliberating over a gold and bronze gypsy-style skirt that was hanging with a number of other bright garments around the doorway, when a voice behind her said, 'It wouldn't suit you more if it had been made for you. And the same garment would cost you twice as much in New York or Rome.'

Mel pivoted to see Vann smiling down into her face, the sheer impact of his presence bringing dismay and excitement warring together inside her.

'You—you weren't at the hotel this morning,' she said, trying to ignore that aura of strength and vitality about him, but realising hopelessly that she sounded as though she had been thinking about him.

'I had some business in town.' His eyes ran unashamedly over the strappy cotton top that showed off the roundedness of her breasts, the lemon shorts that displayed too much smooth, golden leg. But fortunately the middle-aged shopkeeper was approaching them, offering her help in heavily accented English. Vann responded in fluent Italian.

'I've told her you'll buy it.'

Mel looked at him in amazement. 'Do you always make up other people's minds for them?'

His mouth compressed in amusement. 'It saves a lot of time. Apart from which, I never could mistake that longing in a woman's eyes.'

I'll bet you couldn't! Mel thought, guessing that he probably hadn't meant it in the way it had sounded. But his presence was far too disturbing, the memory of last night, of that other night of passion she had spent in his arms, causing such a kick of desire in her that she felt her breasts tighten in undeniable arousal against her skimpy top, recognised the throb of need deep in her loins.

She couldn't look at him as she went up to the counter to pay for her purchase.

'*Signore*...' The woman was speaking so quickly that, with her limited knowledge of the language, Mel couldn't possibly understand. She looked questioningly at Vann.

'She wants to know if I'd like to purchase a complementing piece of jewellery for the love of my life,' he translated, still looking amused. Smiling, the shopkeeper was holding up a delicately crafted gold chain.

'I trust you put her straight. That we're not an item,' Mel retorted, too unsettled by the whole situation to share his amusement.

'Who said she was talking about you and me?'

Two bright spots of colour invaded Mel's cheeks. Of course, she thought, brought firmly down to size.

A dispiriting unease crept through her, which was ludicrous, she told herself firmly. After all, until the other day he had been safely buried in the past.

'Why do I get the impression you like wrong-footing people?' she tossed up at him as they were leaving the shop, the brightly coloured bag dangling from her fingers.

'I don't. Only when the music's playing a waltz and they try to tango with me.'

Mel's pulse quickened. 'Oh?' she queried cagily as they stepped into the sun-baked street. It was surging with people. 'I thought we were pretty much in step last night. Did I bruise your toes or something?'

'Forget it,' he drawled. 'Are you going back to the hotel?' And, without waiting for an answer, 'Come on. I'll give you a lift.'

His car was the black Aston Martin she had seen from the conference room window the previous day, parked in the small multi-storey car park across the street. The smell of its pale leather upholstery impinged on her nostrils as she sank into her seat, but her mind was screaming for a way out as the car growled out of the car park, climbing the hill out of town.

He was no fool, she thought. He knew she was hiding something from him, even if he didn't know what it was.

All you have to do is tell him! she urged herself. But she couldn't. She'd feel humiliated. An utter fool!

Common sense, however, warned her that he had known

deceit once before, and that he probably wouldn't take too kindly to finding himself a victim of it a second time.

I can't do this! she thought, panicking, wondering what Jonathan would say if he realised that putting responsibility for the Heywood account on her shoulders was like throwing a match into a powder keg. But the only alternative was to back out of the conference and the only way she could do that was to tell Jonathan the truth.

But that was out of the question, she decided, and, even if it weren't, she couldn't let this situation affect her professionalism. She valued her job and her clients, and she had no intention of letting one long-forgotten night—at least where Vann Capella was concerned—ruin all that she had worked for.

She was glad when they had climbed the hill and the car was swinging on to the hotel's sloping drive. The statue of the Madonna stood white and serene on her pedestal as they passed it, looking seaward over the vista, hazy from the midday heat.

'Apart from a brief talk this afternoon which, I'm afraid, I can't attend,' Vann said, applying the handbrake, 'I see from your agenda that there are no more talks or presentations taking place this week.'

Mel breathed an inward sigh. Was he saying he wouldn't have been able to attend those either? Did that mean she could unwind at last?

'That's right. You can all take time off for good behaviour.' Relief made it easy to laugh.

'In that case, as you aren't tied up, you won't mind if I monopolise your time tomorrow to toy around with a few ideas I have in mind for Heywood. You can give me the benefit of your expert advice and we can take in the coast at the same time. I'll pick you up at nine,' he stated, and that was it. Settled.

Mel felt as if she had been bulldozed as he drove away.

* * *

'You're kidding!' Karen exhaled when Mel rang to check up on Zoë the following morning, then went on to tell her friend about the bizarre coincidence in meeting Vann, that she was going to be out with him for most of the day.

'Wow!' Karen continued to exclaim, unaware of her friend's raging apprehensions. 'And I thought you were ringing to tell me Jonathan had asked you to move in with him and that you'd accepted.'

'Hardly,' Mel answered with a grimace.

'Still, he can't be very pleased,' her friend commented.

He hadn't been when Mel had told him, questioning her rather huffily as to why Vann couldn't discuss his affairs there at the hotel like everyone else. Mel had wanted to point out that he had virtually thrown her into Vann's arms in the first place, but decided to bite her tongue. Now all she simply said was, 'It's business, Karen.'

'Yeah?'

'Yes,' Mel stressed, but her friend wasn't listening.

'Wait until I tell Simon,' she enthused excitedly. 'Not to mention your daughter. She scarcely talked about anything else on the journey back. Do you want a word? She's sitting here on the floor watching— Oh no, she isn't. She—'

From Karen's abrupt silence it was clear Zoë hadn't waited before grabbing the phone. Now a rush of envy and disbelief met Mel's ears.

'You're never going out with him! Why couldn't *I* have stayed in Positano? You always get all the fun,' Zoë wailed. 'It's not fair!'

Quietly Mel reminded her daughter that she had expressly requested a week shopping with Karen in Rome, and that they would have seven fun days together when Mel came to collect her at the weekend, hiring a car and showing her more unexplored parts of Italy.

She came off the phone, however, feeling as though she

had compromised in one battle only to have to face another. This time with herself.

Still in her silk negligée, the cool femininity of her new skirt beckoned from the wardrobe, but after what Vann had said about it yesterday she had no intention of wearing anything that would give him the wrong message. Besides, she was going along with too much of what he wanted already, she thought hopelessly, donning a simple cotton wraparound skirt in a navy and turquoise print with a matching sleeveless shirt which she left open over a turquoise camisole.

Nevertheless, she couldn't contain the violent leap of her pulse when, waiting downstairs among the soft sofas and lush green plants around the reception area, she saw Vann's car pull up outside.

She reached the door just as he was pushing it open.

'*Buon giorno*,' he greeted her, turning her bones to jelly, unaware of how his softly-spoken Italian affected her. Or maybe he was, she thought, feeling that lethal blend of charisma and virility drawing her to him like a potent lure.

The pale grey T-shirt he wore with loose-fitting light trousers hugged his broad shoulders, accentuating the hard muscles of his chest. His hair gleamed black above that intellectual brow, accentuating the strong nose, the prominent bones of his cheeks and jaw.

'*Buon giorno*,' she returned, smiling, aware of his eyes wandering lazily over her, feeling the breeze fan her face, stirring the bright tendrils she had failed to capture in her loosely swept-up hair as she stepped out into the equally bright morning.

'You're probably the very first woman who's never kept me waiting,' he congratulated her, opening the passenger door.

'Did you think I would?' She watched him move around the bonnet, as lithe and supple as a great hunting animal. 'I'm a businesswoman, Vann. I learnt a long time ago that time is of the essence, and that to keep someone waiting is costly as well as rude.'

'Do you measure everything in terms of time and money?' he asked across the car's gleaming bodywork. It looked dark and sleek and powerful, just as he did.

'When I'm working, certainly. I would have thought a man in your position would know the importance of that.'

'Oh, indeed.' But he appeared to be mocking her as he joined her in the car. 'Let go, Mel.' His voice was suddenly soft, his features serious. 'Relax for a few hours.' Under his skilled direction the Aston Martin purred into life. 'That's the secret of succeeding. Work to the limit if necessary. But play as hard as you work.'

Feeling oddly chastened, Mel settled back against the pale leather, trying to do as he suggested while the car bore them down the winding mountain road and into the town once again.

The woman in the boutique where Mel had purchased her skirt the previous day was standing in her doorway. She waved to them as they passed. They both waved back.

'She recognised us. Or you,' Mel amended, thinking the latter more likely.

'She should. Her husband and I go back a long way,' Vann told her.

So they were probably used to seeing him with no end of different women, Mel thought, remembering their conversation in the shop the day before. Refusing to think about that, or anything concerning his private life, she absorbed herself instead in the sights and sounds of the popular little resort.

There was only one narrow road through and, just like yesterday, holidaymakers, ambled along it, walking in the road, browsing in shop windows, cameras hanging from shoulders. Several turned now and then to admire the sleek lines of the car. Someone laughed, shouting something in

Italian to someone else across the street. Car horns sounded, bringing Mel's attention suddenly to what was going on ahead.

They had met a little bubble of congested traffic, through which one of the town's single-decker blue buses was trying to manoeuvre. A small dog, standing on the footwell of the stationary motor scooter immediately in front of them suddenly hopped off, stretched its little legs with an interested sniff around the surrounding area and, as the traffic ahead started to move again, hopped back on with such precision timing it had both Mel and Vann laughing aloud.

'That would never be allowed in England!' she breathed, amazed.

'I'm not sure it's entirely legal here.' He grinned, amusement lessening the severity of those brooding features. He looked younger, more approachable somehow.

He turned suddenly and caught her smile, his blue eyes searching and intense. 'That's better,' he remarked, echoing her own thoughts about him, before giving his concentration to the road again.

Within minutes they had left the town behind them, travelling along a highway gouged out of the rocky cliffs. On their side of the road, unprotected by any railings, the cliff edge dropped away, plunging dramatically to the sea-washed boulders hundreds of feet below.

'What do they call that island?' Mel asked, glancing back towards Positano and the dark mound of land jutting out of the aquamarine water. A rich man's heaven. 'Does it have a name?' Someone at the hotel had told her that it had once belonged to the famous Russian ballet dancer, Rudolf Nureyev.

'It's one of several and they're called ''the Sirenuse'', or ''Galli isles''.' He spread tanned fingers contemplatively on the steering wheel before saying, translating for her, 'The Cocks. Roosters. So named because a sorcerer who was rather partial to fowl once agreed to build a castle for the local king in exchange for all the roosters in Positano. The king saw to it that they were all slaughtered and sent to the sorcerer, but one young girl didn't want to give up her rooster and so she hid it under her bed. Of course, when it crowed the next morning, the sorcerer, thinking the king had betrayed him, abandoned the project, which is why Positano has no castle.'

'Somehow,' she breathed huskily, with an unintentionally provocative glance at him from beneath her dark lashes, 'I think you're having me on.'

His eyes met hers for just a fraction of a second, but long enough to ignite a spark of something exciting and dangerous in Mel. 'Now why would I do that?' His mouth was twitching as he turned his attention to the road again. 'These old wives' tales often contain an element of truth.'

'OK, so it's true!' Mel laughed. She hadn't felt this light-headed in a long time. It was so good to be with him; it seemed so right, joking like this. Not at any time, since the day she had forced herself to accept that she'd never hear from him again, had she ever thought it possible. Despite her better judgement, she wanted to make the most of it. 'So what happened to the young girl?'

'The girl?' One of those broad shoulders lifted. 'Who knows? She wasn't important to the story.'

It was a flippant exchange—about a legend—but those dismissive words touched a raw nerve in Mel.

'I would have thought she was of paramount importance,' she strove to continue in the same light-hearted vein, but a sudden chill had settled around her heart.

Don't get on a too familiar footing with him, she warned herself. You aren't here to enjoy yourself with him. The fact that she had an overwhelming desire to do so didn't come into the equation. She hadn't been important enough for him to want to see her again all those years ago, understandably perhaps. She had meant nothing to him, after all. But even telling herself that at the time hadn't prevented the knowledge hurting beyond belief as, surprisingly, it still chafed now. And, if he did guess who she was, then she would have to face the double humiliation of his not only remembering what had happened between them, but realising she had misled him solely to cover up the shame she was still suffering because of it, and what could be more humiliating than that?

She'd be a fool to let him get under her skin a second time, she berated herself. Especially when she was in such control of her own life now—her own destiny. Her mother's life had been complicated in the extreme, and Mel was determined not to allow herself to be let down by men in the same way. She and Zoë were doing fine on their own, and that was how things were going to stay.

'You're looking very fierce.'

Vann's quiet observation shook her out of her disturbing reverie.

'Am I?' she responded, tension knotting her usually genial features. 'It's just all this...' A sweep of her arm indicated the breathtaking beauty of their surroundings. 'I've got a job taking it all in.' That part at least was true.

She couldn't remember having been on such a thrilling drive before and could understand now why he had referred to it as the most romantic in the world. The winding road, little more than two cars' widths in places, passed through white villages splashed with the reds and pinks of geranium, oleander and bougainvillaea. On their left hand side the mountains peered down like awesome giants, dominating everything over which they loomed. The lane in which they were travelling still hugged the cliff edge, where vineyards and citrus orchards and slumbering luxury villas with their clear blue pools, ornate balconies and bright shutters clung to the rocky coast. Here and there a sandy cove harbouring small boats could be reached by countless narrow steps leading between the houses, down through verdant gardens and olive groves to the very edge of the sparkling sea.

'I've never seen anything so beautiful,' she said.

'No,' he agreed rather heavily. And, when she darted a questioning glance in his direction, she realised from the mere meeting of their eyes that he wasn't talking about the scenery at all.

She looked quickly away, an insidious heat stealing through her. Careful, she warned herself again. Then let out a nervous little scream as a coach, coming straight at them over the white line of the northbound lane, forced Vann to steer sharply, bringing them precariously close to the cliff edge.

'Relax,' he advised, amused by her flushed cheeks and her tremulous little laugh. 'You're perfectly safe.' But she knew that already.

The Aston Martin's tyres seemed to suck the road and Vann's driving was impeccable—unlike the reckless, far too-talkative taxi driver who had terrified both Zoë and herself on the journey down from Naples. Mel trusted his judgement implicitly and those strong, capable hands turning the wheel. Those long, beautifully tapered hands that had once stroked and caressed her body, stamping their mark on her to such a degree that the experience had spoilt her for any other man, because no other man had ever quite been able to measure up…

The memory of that night rose, unbidden and unashamedly, assailing her mind and body with an acute hunger she didn't want to feel. But, against her prior warnings, she knew an immense joy at having shared this brief time with him, dizzy now, but from a surfeit of excited emotion rather than from the height at which they were travelling.

He started talking then about his ideas to salvage the company he was funding; ways to improve its image beside its competitors. He spoke with a knowledge of marketing and consumer psychology that left no doubt as to his expertise and the foresight that had earned him the hard-won success to which he had referred earlier.

In turn, he listened to her ideas, evaluating them against his own, applauding her suggestions in a way that filled her with an absurd pleasure, and, from the way he invited her to enlarge upon most of the concepts she was putting forward, she knew he was impressed.

They stopped for coffee in Amalfi. Set at the mouth of a deep gorge, it was the principal town along the coast, with an impressive cathedral presiding over red-roofed white houses and a trio of jetties reaching out into the glittering bay.

Tucking into deep wedges of lemon cake, they were still talking business when the waiter brought them their second cappuccino under the flapping canopy of the crowded beachside café.

'We make a good team,' Vann remarked, with a satisfied firming of his mouth. 'Perhaps I should engage you myself.'

He was only joking. Even so, as she savoured the tangy lemon icing, Mel's heart skipped a beat.

'You're just one of a number of clients with whom I'm happy to share my expertise,' she uttered amiably, trying to sound businesslike, trying not to appear so ridiculously affected by the thought of sharing anything with him, because she was. 'I love my job. You'd have to pay me a pretty hefty wage,' she went on to assure him dryly, 'to seduce me away.'

He looked at her over the steam of his cappuccino, those long fingers absently toying with a spoon in the delicious white froth.

'Who said anything about a seduction?' he drawled, and there was nothing vague about the way those penetrating eyes captured and held hers.

'I was speaking figuratively,' Mel stressed, disconcerted by the more intimate turn the conversation had taken. From the way his mouth quirked, he noted the tremor in her voice, the flush beneath the translucent freshness of her skin.

'How old are you, Mel?'

The simple question threw her. 'Thirty-one.' There was implied amazement in the arching of a thick eyebrow. 'How old did you imagine?' She had already worked out that he would be thirty-six.

'I guessed you had to be,' he said, 'to have a twelve-year-old daughter. Even if you do look less than twenty-five.'

Mel pulled a wry face, her senses unconsciously absorbing the sounds of conversation around them, the hiss of steam from the espresso machine at the far end of the café. 'Everyone says the same thing. I keep a portrait in the attic.'

Laughter creased the corners of his eyes. 'So the effects of all your sins are absorbed by the painting while you remain young and pure?'

'You like Oscar Wilde?'

'I admire his wit.'

'Oh, for a fraction of it!' Mel found she was agreeing, hugging a secret pleasure in the knowledge that they shared a literary interest. 'Anyway, who says I'm so young and pure?'

'Aren't you?' He smiled meaningfully. 'So I was wrong comparing you with the Madonna.'

'Very misguided,' she murmured, smiling back with unmindful provocation as she picked up her cup. The froth was soft and cool compared with the surprisingly hot coffee underneath.

'Careful,' Vann warned swiftly, but she had already burnt her tongue.

How could she keep her mind on anything? she despaired, her mouth smarting. With him sitting opposite her looking like the treacherous seducer in some Italian movie? Or some sculpted god of strength and virility with that aura of power he exuded and that disciplined fitness that had made every female head turn when they had walked to this table earlier?

She was no less immune, Mel thought, trying, as laughter from another table drew his attention for a moment, to drag her gaze away from his arresting profile.

Too late, though; he turned back and caught her hopeless fascination for him. His mouth tugged in the subtlest of acknowledgements.

'What happened with you and Zoë's father?'

'What?' Agitatedly she looked down at her own cappuccino, spooning the froth as he had done. 'Oh…' Still not looking at him, she shrugged. 'It didn't work out.'

'How long were you together?'

Mel placed her spoon back into her saucer, her movements slow and measured. She didn't want to talk about past relationships. 'No time at all,' she admitted at length. 'He left before Zoë was even born.'

Surprise etched the strong masculine features. 'So he didn't know her?' And when Mel shook her head, 'That's tough,' he said with genuine understanding.

'It was my own fault. I was young and impetuous,' she said, wanting to drop the subject.

'Too young for commitment, that's for sure.' The deep tones were censuring. 'And you've never been tempted to settle down with anyone else?'

He was taking a lot for granted, but Mel decided it was best left that way. At the end of the week she would be back home. Back to her comfortable, suburban flat and her safe, practical, uncomplicated existence. Somehow, it didn't seem very thrilling.

'Why should I?' she quizzed. 'I've got a nice home. A great job. Zoë.'

Those blue eyes were coolly speculative. 'Is it enough?'

Was it? He was holding a mirror to her life, she realised, and she didn't like it.

'Yes,' she answered, rather too determinedly. 'Contrary to what society still might expect, not every woman's ultimate goal in life is to finish up with a husband. Mine certainly isn't.'

From the way his eyebrow cocked, her less than complimentary view of the matrimonial state had made its mark. Lifting his cup, however, all he said was, 'Not even for your child's sake?'

'I couldn't do it solely for that reason. I have to think what's right for me, too.'

'Over and above your child's security?' She wasn't sure whether that hard glitter in his eyes was disapproval or not.

'No,' she argued defensively, colour creeping up her throat. 'And she is secure.'

Suddenly the magic of the morning had gone, swept away by his uncomfortably probing questions, her annoyed response to them and by a little wave of guilt, too. Guilt which, in spite of all her declarations to the contrary, made her question, and not for the first time, whether she was in fact acting fairly in depriving Zoë of a surrogate father. Whether by her staying single her daughter had missed out on a great deal. She remembered the phone call that morning, how disappointed Zoë had sounded not to be here, her protestations of life being unfair, that her mother had all the fun, only compounding the guilt Mel felt, then and now.

It was that emotion, more than anything else, that had her throwing back at Vann, 'You really don't approve of my lifestyle, do you?'

'I don't know enough about it to approve or disapprove,' he said in more placatory tones. 'I've learnt enough, though, to realise that if anyone asks about it you come over all defensive.'

'I do not!' She knew that with that heated retort she was

only cementing his opinion, but her feelings about him—about Zoë—were in too much danger of being laid bare to respond in any other way.

'Blame my Italian side for making me believe that a child is better off with two parents. It's my personal opinion that he or she gets a more balanced view of life. But it is only my opinion.'

'Well, you would think that, wouldn't you? Having—'

She broke off abruptly, realising her anger was making her careless, wishing she had bitten off her sore tongue when she saw him frown.

'Having…what?' he queried softly, sitting back, his cappuccino finished. As if he had a cast-iron stomach, Mel thought distractedly.

Unnerved by the intensity of his regard, she lifted her cup and gingerly took a sip of her coffee. It had cooled just a little. Unlike me, she thought, feeling hot and sticky beneath her brightly printed top and skirt.

'I'm not sure what I was going to say,' she bluffed. God! How could she have been so stupid?

With an elbow resting on the back of his chair, Vann's eyes had narrowed into slits, the stretched fabric of his T-shirt emphasising his muscular chest, the broad shoulders and strong upper arms.

'Where was it, Mel?'

Fazed by his question, she put down her cup, knocking the little silver spoon out of her saucer. Quickly she retrieved it. It left a small brown stain on the creamy cloth.

'Where was what?' she asked cagily.

'Where was it we met before?'

CHAPTER SIX

THOSE shrewd eyes were so intent that she couldn't meet them.

Studying the small vase of yellow flowers in the centre of the table, she said with an affected little laugh, 'Have you known so many women that you can't remember the ones you've met from the ones you haven't?'

'Answer me,' he commanded quietly, dismissing her question with almost contemptuous scorn.

'Well, if we had known each other before...' eyes guarded, stalling for time, she lifted her small chin, censure masking the pain behind every fine feature as somehow she found the courage to say '...it wouldn't be doing a lot for my ego to think I could be so easily forgotten.'

'I wouldn't be human if I'd forgotten *you,*' he breathed.

Oh, but you have! cried an injured little voice inside her. OK, she might have been just a one-night affair. And he must have had scores of women since. But all that didn't make it any easier to bear!

'I'll bet you use that line on every woman,' she accused lightly in an attempt to keep a tight rein on her emotions, and gasped from the sudden grip of iron around her wrist.

She hadn't even seen him move. Such was the speed of his reactions. But his mouth was grim and fiery anger leapt in his eyes.

'I don't go in for useless flattery,' he argued. 'I only know that something flared between us down there in that restaurant the other day—that you felt it as strongly as I did—until I spoke to you—or until you realised who I was—and then you closed up like a limpet on a rock. Why?'

'I told you,' Mel uttered, feeling hopelessly out of her depth. 'You got the wrong impression…'

'Is that why your pulse is racing crazily beneath my fingers? Or are you going to tell me I've got the wrong impression about that, too?'

Her gaze dropped to the dark thumb sensuously massaging her comparatively pale flesh, beneath which a thin blue vein beat its merciless betrayal.

What could she say? she thought despairingly. Her responses to him were as reckless as they had been nearly fourteen years ago and, being an experienced, red-blooded male, he had recognised that fact, even if he hadn't recognised *her.*

'It's just chemistry,' she murmured on a derogatory little note.

'And you're determined to resist it to the bitter end.'

It wasn't a question, because he already knew the answer.

'I don't want any complications,' she admitted truthfully.

Those dark-fringed eyes seemed to dissect her before his thumb stilled on the frantic little pulse, his hand fell away and she was free.

'I'll get this,' he asserted harshly, seeing her intention to pay the bill the waiter had unobtrusively left while they had been talking, plucking it out of her reach.

'You're my client,' Mel protested, taking out her credit card.

'And therefore a tax deductible expense?'

His tone implied that he didn't like being regarded as such. But, still trembling from the shock of his touch and determined to keep things formal between them, she said nevertheless shakily, 'Something like that.'

'Put your purse away,' he ordered, and so incisively that she decided it best to obey. Her confusion made her clumsy, however, and as she was replacing the little piece of plastic some of the contents in the wallet section of her purse slid out—her driving licence, the business card supplied by the taxi driver who had brought her from Naples, a little gold booklet of English stamps.

She caught them all before they could get away from her. Vann, though, was picking up something from the floor.

'May I?' Without waiting for a reply, he turned the little photograph over. It was one of Zoë and herself, taken the previous summer during a weekend trip to Weymouth. It showed Mel in a green bikini. Zoë was in shorts and a crop-top, with a baseball cap turned round the wrong way hiding her sleek, dark auburn hair. Arms around each other, they were both grinning broadly at the camera.

'Someone offered to snap the two of us while I was trying to take a picture of Zoë,' Mel explained, suddenly deciding the bikini was far too revealing now beneath such intense male scrutiny. He seemed almost transfixed by it, those thick lashes lowered, his mouth and jaw chiselled with an emotion that seemed to hold him in thrall.

Quickly Mel grabbed the photo, stuffing it with the rest of her errant belongings back into her purse.

'Ready?' Vann asked tersely, getting up.

She wasn't. She was still putting her purse away and she hadn't finished her cappuccino but she nodded.

'Then let's go,' he said, tossing a couple of notes unceremoniously on to the plate containing the bill.

Scrambling to her feet, Mel caught a glimpse of his face as he ushered her out of the café. She thought he looked pale, tight-lipped, angry, and she wasn't sure why. She only knew that his mood had changed and simply put it down to his male ego being deflated.

Well, that isn't my problem, she thought, following him back to the car, and heard the echo of those words printed in that national newspaper she couldn't count how many lifetimes ago. *It wasn't his problem.* Words that had lured her to him. Words he had denied and which denial she had been so ready to believe. Which, in spite of everything, she still believed, she realised, with a little shiver of desolation that had everything to do with the past, she assured herself, not with the present. But her conviction fell into a chasm of such emptiness she knew it was a lie.

They walked in silence to the car park, a piazza between the outstretched arms of two jetties, reaching out into the sapphire sea.

Now, as they climbed into the blistering heat of the car, Vann started the engine and threw on the air-conditioning switch, the blast of its fans obviating the need for conversation.

He still looked grim, she thought, grappling with her seat-belt as he turned and flung an arm across the back of her seat.

To reverse out, she thought, then realised that was the last thing on his mind as that arm and one jerk of his knee brought her down across his lap, those hard hands turning her to lie face upwards to take the harsh invasion of his mouth.

She murmured a strangled protest, her hands against the unyielding wall of his body, trying in vain to push him away. But his mouth was insistent and unrelenting, forcing hers to open with a determination she was equally determined to fight.

Yet that musky male scent and the hard warmth of his body were aphrodisiacs in themselves, even without the punishing pressure of his mouth, and all at once her resistance snapped.

With a small moan of defeat, her arms slid up around him, drawing him down to her, inviting his kiss to deepen, to quell this need that she knew now had only been slumbering, this wanting that could only be assuaged by the driving energies of this one man.

Suddenly though he was releasing her, setting her back

upright again on her own side of the car. The fans were still blasting away and the air felt icy. With one swift, economical movement, Vann turned them off. The silence was almost deafening.

'So now we know, don't we?' he said, his voice as chilly as the air and, without waiting for an answer, reversed out of the space with an aggression that reflected his mood, leaving Mel shamed and stunned by the depths of her response.

Jonathan was leaning on the terrace railing, talking to Hannah and another member of his team. They were all wearing shorts and T-shirts, admiring the view. There had been a shower during the night and the air was sweet with the scent of jasmine and oleander as Mel walked over to join them.

'Have a nice time yesterday?' Jonathan asked when he saw her. His smile was cool, and Mel wondered if the other two detected that underlying edge to his voice because after their chorused, 'Good morning!' to her, they slipped unobtrusively away.

'Very constructive,' she responded, keeping her reply businesslike. He had been out when she had returned late the previous afternoon and at dinner they had been tied up with clients, after which Mel had made a hasty retreat to her room. 'In fact, he's bringing all the plans and sketches he's made of his own ideas for the new campaign today, so you'll be able to look at them if you want to. Don't worry, Jonathan.' She flashed him a brilliant, reassuring smile, honed from years of practice on anxious clients. 'He's still on the hook.'

He must have picked up on her unease because, with his eyes tugging suspiciously over the wild fire of her loose hair and her simple green cotton sun dress, he said, 'It isn't him I'm worried about. I just wonder who's trying to catch who.'

'What's that supposed to mean?' Mel asked with an oblique glance at him, wondering if he could detect something of her inner conflict.

'You spent rather a long time with him yesterday. I didn't imagine you'd be gone all day. I was hoping that perhaps we could have spent some time together. A few hours at least.' Those grey eyes continued to regard her. 'You look a bit peaky under that tan,' he remarked and, more caustically, 'Working you to the bone, is he? Getting his money's worth out of us?'

You could say that, she thought with a mental grimace. But not in the way you think. Just through the strain under which her unintentional deception had put her, even without her raging awareness of him as a man. He knew she was attracted to him, and she guessed that the sole reason for that kiss in his car yesterday had been to determine just how strongly. Which served her right, she thought, for that pompous little speech in the café about complications! And yet, after that, he hadn't referred to it or even tried to touch her again.

After leaving Amalfi, he had brought her back to Positano for a late lunch when further business was discussed and where, she discovered, he shared her own interest in good wine.

Yet as the meal had progressed he had brought the conversation round to a more personal level and she had found it increasingly difficult to evade his pointed questions. Questions about herself, her past, her family, which, coming from anyone else, would have been simply natural curiosity, but which, from him had seemed like an experiment to test her nerves! Also, behind his casual questions she had sensed a subtle yet very tangible cynicism towards her that she hadn't been aware of on the drive down, and she wondered if it all stemmed from that moment in the café in Amalfi when she had not only denied any prior knowledge of him, but had made it quite clear that she had no intention of getting involved with him. Which was probably why he had been so determined to show her she wasn't immune!

A typical male, she thought, but with a little shudder, too, because Vann Capella was far from typical. As she had warned Jonathan, the man wasn't stupid. He knew he had met her somewhere before, and all she could do was pray that she could get this week over with before he had worked out where. She was only glad she was going to be at the hotel today, and therefore would not have to be so alone with him. She didn't think her nerves or her emotions could have stood anything else.

'You are coping, are you?' She came back to the present to see Jonathan still studying her, his arms folded.

'Of course.' It took an effort but she summoned another bright smile. 'Have you ever known me not to?' And, to lead him off the track of her very personal anxieties, 'And you're right. Some time together would be nice.'

'Then I'm sorry I shall be taking her away. But you can have her back the moment I've finished with her, I promise.'

Mel's heart sank then doubled its rhythm as she swung round and met the impact of Vann's dark, brooding presence. In a white shirt and pale chinos, his hair tied in the usual way, he appeared totally in command beside the shorter, surprisingly flustered-looking MD.

'Oh, Vann. Good morning. No, that's fine,' he was saying in response to what Mel felt had been a purely superficial apology from Vann. 'Take all the time you want with her. Mel will be more than happy to accommodate you.' Jonathan's deference to their agency's top client made her skin prickle. There were times, she thought bitingly, when principles had to come before profit.

'I'll make sure I make full use of her,' Vann expressed, his lips faintly mocking in response to the look she sliced him. And, with a more than casual glance over her creamy gold shoulders, he said silkily, 'Are you ready, Mel?'

She heard the jangle of his car keys and only then realised that he was otherwise empty-handed. If he thought he was taking her off somewhere again…

In silently screaming protest she looked to Jonathan for help, and saw only pure accusation in his face.

He thinks I'm responsible for this, she realised, trying to match Vann's stride across the terrace. With her eyes boring into his broad back, she demanded, 'Where are we going?'

'I thought we'd look at the various papers back at the villa.' And when Mel, drawing level with him, shot him a glance that was purely contentious he went on, 'Don't worry. If you're concerned about your virtue I promise Quintina will protect you.' His housekeeper, she remembered from a conversation the day before.

'You're making a lot of promises this morning,' she reminded him as they walked through Reception together. The desk clerk nodded, acknowledging them. 'Do they include signing a contract with us if we satisfy all your requirements?'

'That depends.'

'On what?' she enquired, aware of the envying glances from two young women who had just stepped out of the lift, coveting the dynamic-looking man at her side.

He pulled open the swing door for her to step through, so close she could smell his cologne mingling with his more primeval masculine scent.

'I'm not easily satisfied,' he said.

His villa was a rambling, luxury residence only a short drive from Positano, with spectacular views over the sea.

Her first glimpse was of pristine white walls and meandering balconies, draped by the stark purple blooms of bougainvillaea. The grounds were steeply terraced, like most along the coast, where kitchen gardens gave on to a network of pathways and splashes of colour, through which sprawling shrubbery led on to citrus groves, and where, here and there, a classical stone statue basked in the fierce Mediterranean sun.

After the car's air-conditioning, the heat hit Mel like a furnace as Vann guided her up the wide, marble steps to the villa. It was pleasingly cool and airy inside.

Zoë would just love this, she thought, the youngster's complaints that her mother had all the fun still pricking at Mel with a little needle of self-reproach, as her eyes took in the features of the house. The beautifully carved staircase. The tasteful antiques and richly woven rugs and tapestries she could see through an archway leading to a sitting room. The flower arrangements that spilled out of baskets and jugs, which brought the freshness of the garden into the house, redeeming it from the starkly formal with their rustic simplicity.

But she had no time to dwell on any maternal remorse or the sudden uneasy speculation as to who was responsible for those obvious feminine touches, because a squat, matronly figure was crossing the hall.

Quintina, Mel assumed, which was confirmed as Vann introduced them, speaking to the woman in his fluent Italian.

'Quintina's responsible for making my house a home,' he told Mel, which went some way to explaining the flowers. A surprising degree of relief trickled through her. 'Marco, her husband, tends the gardens and makes sure we all eat healthily. But you won't see him because he's over in Sorrento, so it's just Quintina looking after us today.'

'I have big family. All...' The woman spread her hands. '...*i fratelli*.' Mel remembered Vann telling her that Quintina had been the fifth of nine siblings, all the rest male. 'I know how to care for...*un uomo*...man.'

Mel liked her. 'You've had a lot of practice,' she agreed, smiling.

Vann said something to the woman and she laughed. The feeling between them was warm and strong, Mel realised, touched. Some people in Vann's position could so easily have been condescending towards their staff.

'What did she say?' she asked, looking questioningly at Vann after Quintina, still smiling interestedly at her, uttered something rapid in her own language.

Vann said something to his housekeeper which Mel was able to gather was a request for refreshment and which, after expressing her pleasure at meeting Mel, had Quintina scuttling away.

'She said, "You're very beautiful",' Vann quoted. '"But be careful. This one has hidden depths".'

Awkwardly, Mel laughed. 'Is she clairvoyant?' Her voice held a slight tremor.

'I don't know,' he said, and his eyes never left hers. 'Is she?'

The penetration of his gaze caused a tightening in her throat. She wondered if he knew she was lying to him.

Her heart was hammering, but for reasons other than merely being found out as his gaze raked over her hectically flushed cheeks, came to rest on the soft fullness of her parted lips.

'Maybe I'm the one who'll need protection,' he remarked, the suppressed intensity of emotion with which he said it bringing her head up quickly.

For a few moments her eyes searched the cool clarity of his, wide, hungry green pools desperately seeking—yet dreading—recognition. But his lashes came down against her probing scrutiny and his mouth took on a somewhat sardonic twist.

'Let's get to work,' he said.

* * *

They spent most of the morning in his study, a room that reflected the tastefulness of the rest of the house with its classic furniture and paintings, its wall to ceiling bookcases and its wide windows, flung open on to the scented garden.

Here, in an oak and glass cabinet near the door, half-obscured by pieces of glassware and ceramics, was a mounted platinum disc. It had caught Mel's unwitting attention almost as soon as she had entered the room.

'My tribute to a spell of madness,' she heard Vann say with a hard edge to his voice, and she swung round, realising he was watching where her interest lay.

Uneasily, she moved away from the cabinet. 'Don't you miss it?' she attempted to say casually, though her tongue seemed to stick to the roof of her mouth.

'No.' His answer was cold and decisive. 'With a management which was rather more light-fingered than tempered and a partnership that was as volatile as the weather, I didn't find too much to commend it.'

He was talking about the arguments within the band that were rumoured, though never fully clarified. And Clayton. Though it had cost thousands to try and retrieve a staggering amount of lost income, it had never been recovered. Clayton had got off through some technical hitch in the law.

'Couldn't that happen in any field of business? Unscrupulous associates? Unsuitable partnerships?'

'Yes,' he accepted. 'Except that the whole experience taught me a hard lesson.'

'Which is?' curiosity made her ask.

'Control and stay in control.'

The harshness of his tone sent an unaccountable little shiver through her. Nevertheless, she felt driven to say, 'I would have thought there was no greater control than having every nubile female in the palm of your hand, having them all screaming for you.'

His face was like a granite mask. 'It palls after a while.'

He meant it, Mel thought. With all that adulation, he had just been doing a job. The leader of a partnership that had let him down in the end, because whatever he had said, he had been the driving force behind it.

'What about you?' With lazy insolence his gaze slid down over her bare shoulders and her breasts beneath the soft sundress, right the way down the length of her golden legs to her pale strappy sandals, and a sardonic smile played around his mouth as he lifted his head again. 'Did I have *you* screaming, Mel?'

His thorough examination had already heightened her senses, but that softly sensual question brought her repressed sexuality fighting for recognition. He meant as Kelly had in innocent hero-worship, but Mel's mind went winging to that raw night in the country hotel. To the blinding, mindless ecstasy of those strong, warm hands on her body, to the moment when he had pushed back the boundaries of her experience and entered her, filling her with his power, each governing thrust rocking her into a different sphere of rapture, a conflagration of need that had torn hard, guttural sobs from the depths of her soul.

She felt the swelling of her breasts and the warm moistness at the very centre of her femininity.

'As you said…' she managed to look at him levelly, hold her voice steady as she advised, ignoring his question '…let's get to work.'

It was nearly lunchtime when Vann announced, 'I need a swim.' Until then they had been discussing his sketches, working towards some innovative ideas for the new campaign. 'Did you bring something to wear? If not, I'm sure I can find a bikini somewhere that might fit you.'

'That won't be necessary,' she said, glad to reject his offer of something that probably belonged to a visiting girlfriend. 'I came prepared.' In fact, she was already wearing her bikini under her sun dress. 'I intended going down to the hotel pool some time this morning. After our meeting,' she added quickly, feeling the need to explain. She didn't want him to think she had been anticipating swimming with him.

'Strapless,' he observed softly when she emerged, a few minutes later, from the luxuriously appointed bedroom where he had said she could undress. Already in the pool, he had swum over to wait for her. On the other side, near the sun loungers, was a water feature of a stone nymph, clothed only in lichen, the water cascading through her slender hands making a silvery sound on the air.

'There's nothing more unsightly than exposing white lines in strapless dresses,' Mel stated rather self-consciously, because he was watching her progress with blatant appreciation, noting unashamedly the movement of her breasts above the brief cups of the apricot bikini, the matching scrap of fabric, fastened with strings, that barely covered the triangle of her sex.

'Yes. I do try to avoid the same problem myself,' he responded, drawing her attention willingly to the sinewy velvet of his shoulders and the deep expanse of that smooth wet chest.

He was all man. But the humour in his face was too much to resist and she started laughing, his remark defusing the situation, helping her to relax.

'If I owned all this,' Mel uttered, stopping, breathless, after covering several laps of the pool, 'nothing could tear me away!' She swam over to sit on the steps just in front of the stone nymph, admiring the luxurious white house with its balconies and bougainvillaea, the backdrop of the mountains, the cloudless blue sky. For the past few years, she remembered someone saying, he'd been living in America. 'I don't know how you can bear to leave.'

'It's the demands of everyday life in the city that make it so much sweeter to return,' he told her, swimming towards her, wet hair gleaming darkly in the sun. 'I spend a lot of my time between New York, Chicago and London, as well as other interesting but hectic capitals. Having been brought up between London and Rome, I feel as though I belong to both countries, but I always come back here when I want to unwind.' He pulled himself up on to the curved marble step beside her, water cascading off him. His thighs, like his upper torso, were powerfully muscled, like every gleaming inch of him, exercised to sinewy athleticism. A line of black hair ran from his navel below that tight waist, drawing Mel's eyes tantalisingly to where it disappeared beneath the band of his dark briefs covering the obvious protrusion of his manhood. She glanced quickly away as he dropped down beside her. 'What about you?'

Wet tendrils framed her face as she met his studied curiosity. 'What about me?'

'Where were you born? Brought up?'

Mel stiffened. She had told him yesterday that she had spent most of her adult life in London. She shrugged. 'We moved around a bit.' Well, that was true, wasn't it? she thought, deliberately avoiding mentioning the Midlands town where she had been living with Kelly. He might remember it from the press reports at the time and start putting two and two together…

He nodded, obviously satisfied, and unconsciously Mel released a deep breath.

'And your parents were divorced.' He was still watching her intently, and Mel bit her top lip. Had she told him that? When he had asked about her family yesterday, she thought, she had simply mentioned that her parents were dead. But she must have…

'Yes. My father left my mother when I was very small—too young to remember much about him.'

'So it's been a case of history repeating itself.'

It took her a moment to grasp what he was saying. Of

course. That her husband had deserted *her* in the same way. She didn't answer, tensing as the wet warmth of his arm casually brushed hers, leaving her stunned by the eroticism of the contact.

'Did you grow up fatherless?' he wanted to know. 'Or did your mother remarry?'

Holding herself rigid, too aware of him, Mel stared down at their legs dangling in the clear water. Hers were golden and smooth against the dark, hair-plastered strength of his.

'She remarried.'

'So at least you had a step-father?'

Mel caught her breath. 'Not for long.' She didn't like these questions, any more than she welcomed this disturbing and dangerous proximity to him, and suddenly she was slipping into the water with the swiftness of an alarmed seal, throwing back curtly over her shoulder, 'He left, too.'

The speed of Vann's reactions startled and surprised her. She hadn't realised he had followed her until she reached the other side. Now, letting her feet touch down, she turned round with a small, shocked gasp as his arms came up on either side of her, entrapping her against the marbled edge.

'Is that why you hate men?' His face was etched with inexorable lines. 'Or was it something else? Something that happened in your own marriage that's made you so overcautious?'

Mel's breasts rose sharply from her reckless swim across the pool, but also from his threatening nearness that was undermining all her defences, making her snap back, 'I don't hate men.'

She tried to twist away but he wouldn't let her, grasping her chin roughly between a thumb and forefinger.

'Don't you?' he challenged.

'No. That's only some weak excuse you've dreamed up just to salve your own ego.'

'You think my ego needs salving?'

The grim pull of his lips warned her she might be pushing things too far, but she retorted nevertheless, 'Doesn't it?'

'Possibly,' he conceded, 'but I still think you have a problem with men.'

'You would.' She pulled her chin out of his grasp, her features rigid from the shock of his touch. 'Just because I don't want to go to bed with you.'

'Who asked you to?'

Embarrassed heat crept up her throat. She could feel it scorching her cheeks.

'You like making me feel uncomfortable, don't you?' she accused, pressing herself hard against the side for fear of touching him because she was still imprisoned by his arms.

'On the contrary. I'd like to see you relax more, but I don't think you know how because you're afraid.'

'Afraid of what?'

'Commitment. Sex. Rejection. The driving needs of your own body.' He reached for her hand, lifting it from the water. 'This…' Turning the slim appendage, he dipped his head, pressing his mouth to the soft palm, the action so sensual and yet so tender that she found herself battling to contain an emotion that brought tears to her eyes, on top of the devastating sensations already ripping through her body. With mind-blowing sensuality his tongue strayed along her wrist, sending arrows of need piercing through her breasts and loins, keeping her as still as the stone nymph, paralysed from the fear of her own desire. And, as if he knew of her inner fight, he whispered hoarsely, 'I've no intention of doing so, Melissa, but you want me to take you to bed. You want it against all your very practical and rational decisions to the contrary, and that's what you can't—'

A sudden sound pulled them apart. They both looked up, Mel shaken, averting her gaze with embarrassment, Vann appearing no more than mildly irritated by Quintina's coughed intervention. She was saying something Mel had difficulty translating.

'Yes. *Si*, Quintina.' Vann sounded weary, impatient. He said something in Italian.

'*Grazie. Buon giorno*,' she added, addressing Mel.

'*Buon giorno*,' Mel returned, wondering how much the woman had noticed. Still, she was probably used to turning a blind eye to her employer's intimate liaisons with any women he brought here.

'Quintina has an appointment in the village and her taxi has let her down.' Already Vann was springing up out of the pool. 'Stay here and enjoy your swim. I shan't be long.'

He must have dried and dressed himself at lightning speed, because within minutes, stretched out on one of the sun loungers, letting the warm air dry her bikini, she heard the car purr into life on the other side of the house, listening until the note of its engine faded then died away altogether.

Disconcerted by what had happened, Mel turned it over in her mind, wondering how much longer she could keep up this deception. It was driving her crazy, having to be with him without saying anything. And it served her right! she thought. It was just that she would look such an idiot if he found out; no, worse than that. A cheat and a liar. And, despite the little regard he had had for her in the past, might have for her now, what he thought about her mattered. It mattered too much. She just hadn't anticipated the powerful emotional and physical effects he would have upon her. She had been a hapless teenager before, inexperienced in any deeply sexual relationships. She'd been foolish, she had always thought, when she had let her desperate need for him undermine her common sense. When drowning in the sweet oblivion of his caresses and offering pleasure and comfort with her own untutored lovemaking had seemed both natural and right. She was a woman now, she had told herself earlier in the week, and therefore capable of controlling her basic instincts, of keeping things on a strictly businesslike level. But that was before he had touched her. Before she had realised that, despite her thirty-one years and her wider experience of life, she was no more immune to him than she had been nearly fourteen years ago. In fact, his effect on her seemed to have intensified in spite of the years, because no other man had ever made her melt with just one look, with the caress of his voice, with the lift of an eyebrow. No other man had come close to stamping such a lasting mark on her in only a few short hours. And he had the nerve to suggest she had a problem with men!

She was lying face down, trying to steer her thoughts into calmer waters, when her mobile phone started to ring.

Reaching for her canvas bag on the small glass-topped table, Mel delved beneath her purse and a bottle of sunscreen lotion to answer the persistent ringing.

'What is it?' On hearing her daughter's urgent 'Mum?', Mel sat up swiftly, all her protective instincts rushing to the fore. 'Is everything all right?'

'Course, silly,' the young voice responded, unaware of the catastrophes racing through Mel's mind. 'Why wouldn't it be?'

'Because you don't usually ring like this during the day.' They had made an agreement before Zoë left for Rome. 'We said I'd ring you, unless anything happens. Unless it's urgent.'

'It *is* urgent,' Zoë announced rather impatiently. 'I've made a couple of friends. They live in the same apartment block as Karen and Simon. They're going to this pop festival on Friday and they've asked me to go with them. It's just—'

'No!' Mel sprang to her feet to give emphasis to her negation.

'Oh, Mum!'

'No, and definitely *no*!'

'But Mum…'

'No buts, Zoë. I said "no". I'm not having you going to a pop festival on your own.'

'But I won't be on my own. There are four of us going. And Gina's sixteen!'

'I don't care if she's sixty!' Mel could do nothing to temper the panic rising inside her. 'You're not going, and that's final.'

'Why not? Why can't I go?'

'Because I said so.' Roused as Mel was, her own words made her cringe. She had hated anyone saying them to her as a child and couldn't blame her daughter for objecting either as Zoë flung back,

'That isn't good enough! It's because of what happened to Kelly, isn't it?' When Mel didn't answer, sulkily Zoë tagged on, 'Karen said you wouldn't let me go.'

'Well, Karen's right. Put her on.'

'But Mum…!'

'I said, put her on!'

Listening to her daughter muttering something about forgetting what it was like to be young, Mel paced restlessly up and down, waiting for Karen to come on the line.

The high Continental sun was casting dappled rays down through the lance-shaped leaves of an oleander tree behind her, filling the air with the powdery scent of its pink flowers. Beneath her bare feet, the sun-baked terracotta tiles were almost too warm, but she scarcely noticed. Her phone's signal was breaking up and she covered her free ear against the tinkling of the fountain, trying to catch what her friend was saying.

'…when…said…wouldn't want her to…'

'You're darn right I don't! Take her shopping, Karen. Let her go to the zoo. The cinema. Anywhere! But I'm not letting my daughter go to a pop concert. For goodness' sake, Karen! See that she understands. I only—'

The line broke up altogether.

'Hello?' Mel said urgently. 'Hello?' Exasperated, she pressed the redial button, but the display was showing no signal. Letting out a heavy sigh, her features tense with worry, a movement caught her eye and she looked up to see Vann standing on the other side of the pool.

'Trouble?' he enquired crisply.

Taken aback, Mel tried to rearrange her expression into something resembling normality. She hadn't been aware of the car returning. How much had he heard?

'It was just a call from Zoë,' she attempted to explain.

The hard planes and angles of his face, bathed in refracted light from the pool, gave nothing away. 'Nothing wrong, I hope.'

'No. Just the usual headaches from a rebellious adolescent.' She glanced down at her phone, bouncing it agitatedly in her hand. 'Then the signal broke up.' She dropped the phone back into her bag, still open on the lounger.

'Why not use mine?' To her dismay, he was indicating the sitting room beyond the patio doors.

'No, that's all right. I'd finished anyway.'

'It didn't sound like it to me.' Daunting, even in those casual clothes, he was negotiating the pool, moving towards her with a slow, predatory watchfulness. 'It sounded as though you were having the devil's own job getting your point across.'

'Did it?' A nervous little laugh burst from her. She shrugged with an expansive gesture of her hands. 'Well, you know teenagers.' Mistake number one, she realised hopelessly.

His hair, loose now, shone like dark sable as he shook his head. 'I've never had any. But I've been around long enough to realise that at times they can be impossible and that sometimes it might not be easy preventing oneself from overreacting—'

'Overreacting?' Already regretting having made such a scene, her worries over Zoë, coupled with the fear of being found out and now, to crown it all, his criticism of the way she was handling things made her toss back, 'As you've already said, you haven't had any. There's nothing wrong, surely, with a mother being protective of her daughter? Anyway, I hadn't realised anyone was listening.'

'I could hardly help it. You were virtually hysterical,' he said, grimacing, stopping just a metre or so away, hands on hips, legs planted firmly apart. 'But I think we both know why…don't we…*Lissa*?'

CHAPTER SEVEN

SHOCKED, feeling utterly exposed, physically as well as emotionally, standing there in her bikini when he was fully clothed, she stammered, 'How—how did you guess? Was it just now? On the phone?'

He shook his head again. 'I suppose you could say that that just confirmed what I already knew. But I've felt something from the beginning. At the beach. When we met again at the conference. When we were dancing. And yesterday when I saw that photograph of Zoë…'

'Zoë?' Mel enquired, puzzled.

'Yes. She bore an unbelievable likeness to that angry little waif who turned up at my hotel— When was it? Thirteen? Fourteen years ago?'

'Thirteen and a half, to be precise,' she stated pointedly. So that was why his mood had suddenly changed yesterday. 'So why didn't you say something?' she asked half-accusingly.

'Why didn't *I* say something?' he uttered, looking amazed, a broad thumb turned towards his chest. 'You were the one bent on keeping your identity hidden. Why, Lissa? Or is it still Melissa? I'm afraid you'll have to enlighten me, darling. I really can't keep up.' His tone wasn't very gentle, but she supposed she couldn't expect anything else.

'It's Melissa. I just didn't like the name when I was eighteen so I shortened it to Lissa. I wasn't deliberately trying to deceive anybody.' A masculine eyebrow lifted sceptically but, ignoring it, Mel shrugged and said, 'I guess I grew up.'

The gaze that raked over the soft golden swell of her breasts, the flatness of her tummy and the slender legs—

emphasised by the high-cut of her briefs—was obviously assessing that she had—and in more ways than one. His veiled appreciation caused a disconcerting heat to steal through her.

'So why did you lie to me? Pretend you didn't know me?' His features were harsh and censuring against the wild fury of his hair, yet something like mockery touched the firm mouth as he said, 'Embarrassed, Melissa?'

'Can you blame me?' she answered, and only now could she meet his eyes levelly. 'I didn't feel particularly proud of the way I acted that night—sleeping with the man my sister had idolized—and died over because of it.' Particularly when he had never bothered to contact her again.

'But you did it anyway.'

What was he saying? Mel thought, catching the censure in his voice above the breeze that stirred the leaves of the oleander tree. Was it something to do with the note she had sent him afterwards?

'I needed…' *You*, she nearly said, but aloud, rather lamely, substituted, 'someone.' Still she could remember how desperately.

'And I was there.'

'No,' she riposted, defending her actions.

'No,' he accepted quietly, but made it sound like an accusation. 'Tell me the truth, Melissa. Didn't you come looking for me that night with the sole intention of getting me to take you to bed?'

Is that what he believed? 'No!' she stated emphatically again. 'Why would I have done that? I wasn't obsessed with you the way Kelly was. I was grieving—upset, for heaven's sake…!'

Exactly, that same raised eyebrow seemed to be saying. So what was he suggesting? That she should have known better? That they should never have made love at all? Didn't he appreciate the devastating emotions that had driven her into begging him to love her? Hadn't her feelings been apparent when she had sent him that letter? Unless, of course, he had been shocked by what she had written. Or perhaps he hadn't even received it, which would account for why he seemed to be treating her as though making love with him had been some sort of feather in her cap…

'I was angry. I just wanted to talk to you,' she said truthfully.

'But the opportunity presented itself to do a lot more than talk.'

'That isn't how—' she started, but he cut across her protest.

'It was my fault entirely—not yours. I shouldn't have let things get that far. I was older. I could have prevented it. But I was wild and headstrong and you…you were far too…gratifying…to deny.' She had a feeling he was picking his words very carefully. 'So there you have it,' he concluded. 'One ill-timed night of pleasure, instantly regretted by both.'

But I didn't regret it! she wanted to cry out, stung by his casual dismissal of something that had always remained precious to her. *I wrote to you and wanted you to contact me! But you didn't!* Because she had been just a one-night affair for him, she realised achingly now, as she had reluctantly forced herself to accept a long time ago. The only redeeming factor was that because of what he had said about her regretting it, it seemed he had never received that communication from her, and she could only be grateful for that. Perhaps Bern Clayton had never given it to him, she reflected. Or perhaps he had and it had been lost amongst the band's mountains of adoring mail. Or worse, perhaps Vann *had* received it, she thought, considering the possibility as she had done so often in the past, and he had simply chosen to pretend he hadn't, to ignore it.

Still smarting for that wounded eighteen-year-old, too embarrassed to ask, she said carelessly, 'Well, I was young and hurting. And, as you said, you happened to be there. I needed comfort. A diversion. You provided it. That was all.' But her voice cracked with the feelings she was trying to contain, the lie hanging on the silence with the silvery sound of the fountain.

Something drew a fine line between his brows, the only emotion behind an otherwise inscrutable mask. 'No,' he said quietly, moving to breach the gap between them. 'That isn't all.'

Every instinct screamed a warning as he reached out, catching a bright tendril of her hair. 'You'd like me to believe that, but you're only fooling yourself, Melissa. I think, darling,' he breathed, his voice unusually husky, 'that if I touched you I could have you writhing in my arms in exactly the same way as I did before, even though you'd like to convince yourself otherwise.'

Had he noticed the way she was holding her breath? The way the peaks of her breasts had hardened into tight thrusting buds against her insubstantial bikini top?

'Don't, please,' she protested against the hand that was now trailing lightly down the sensitive column of her neck, making her nerve endings shudder with pleasure.

'You implore me, Mel? The cool, self-assured businesswoman? The invincible female? And I thought you were immune.' His face was rigid with an emotion she couldn't define.

'Vann, don't do this,' she pleaded, held captive merely by his nearness. 'We had one night, but that was it. *Finito*.'

'Finito.' His mouth curved faintly, fleetingly. 'Believe me, my love, I haven't even begun with you yet.'

His hand was splayed across the base of her throat, resting lightly across the rapidly pulsing hollow. She swallowed, seeing the need for retribution in those glittering eyes. She had lied, deceived him, just as Bern Clayton had lied and deceived him. He didn't take kindly to being made to look a fool.

'For whatever reason you're trying to deny it, Melissa, you can't prevent this any more than I can,' he rasped, his face going out of focus as he dipped his head, claiming her mouth with his.

Her murmur of protest was lost beneath the hard persuasion of his lips, the hands that had lifted to resist him now trapped against the heated cotton of his T-shirt. The warmth of his arm across her back and the coarse fabric of his chinos against her stomach and bare thighs made her startlingly aware of how little she was wearing. Locked in his arms, she groaned her hopeless need and despair.

'You still deny it?' he challenged, lifting his head after a moment, his breathing harsh and laboured. 'When all I have to do is touch you and you turn to fire.' His lips burned kisses across her cheek, her temple, her hair. 'You're a fraud, Melissa,' he whispered hoarsely. 'And you know what happens to frauds. They get found out.'

He was still angry because she had lied, she thought hectically, that promise of sweet retribution in his voice turning her insides to liquid.

His lips moved down over the perfumed warmth of her throat and shoulders, his hands caressing the sensitive flesh of her upper arms with calculated skill.

Beneath her bikini top her breasts ached for his touch, and she knew an acute need way down inside her as her hips moved sensuously against his, met the hard, unmistakable thrust of his arousal.

Lifting his head, taking a deep breath as though to quell some inner struggle, Vann drew away just enough to unfasten her top and toss it down on to the sun lounger.

His mouth looked vulnerable, she thought, noting absently how his olive skin seemed stretched across the prominent bones of his cheeks as he gazed down on the beauty of her high, rounded breasts. When he looked up, Mel couldn't meet his eyes, knowing her own would betray the longing evoked by his caresses. But, against her will, her engorged breasts were already doing that, and she closed her eyes against the pure pleasure of his hands on their heavy, aching fullness, against his groan of satisfaction, stifling the small sounds he wrung from her as he cupped each creamy mound in turn to suckle their swollen pink aureoles.

She wanted to make love with him. She wanted it as much as she wanted life; to experience the fulfilment she knew now only this man could give her. But she didn't want to offer herself to someone who would use her again just for his own gratification. Wasn't that the word he had used? And yet what he was doing to her was so exquisite. She could feel the warmth of those smooth hands as they slid down over her body, remembering, like it was yesterday, every crease and sinew of their skilled strength, the magic they could work as they moved to massage her hips, then tug at the strings of her briefs.

Under those determined hands, the scrap of material fell away. Mel felt it skim her legs, her last protection, to land with cool disregard at her feet.

She was as naked as a nymph, feeling the warm breeze as a conspirator to arouse her, heightening her pleasure so that she closed her eyes against its sensual caress, against the heat of her own desire and what Vann was doing to her.

His lips and hands were following the same path, down over her breasts and her ribcage, over the smooth plane of her belly, down and down, his body doing their bidding, bending, stooping, kneeling now to cup the pale globes of her buttocks in his hands and taste the sweet nectar of her body.

She gave a throaty, rapturous groan, a nymph glorying in the freedom of her nakedness and the ecstasy of the man who was worshipping her. This man who had brought women to their knees, paying homage to her femininity, drawing, as though from her stone sister beside her, sustenance from the life-spring of her body.

It was exquisite agony. 'No,' she murmured, her head thrown back, praying, yet dreading that he would stop. But his hands on her buttocks tightened to draw her closer, his hair sensually erotic against her heated flesh until all at once she felt the sharp, pleasurable tingling in her thighs. Tension mounted, holding her rigid. She heard her own quickened breathing. Then suddenly with one convulsive sob, she leaned forward to clasp his head, clutching at his thick dark hair as uncontrollable spasms shuddered through her.

As ecstasy receded and normality resumed, she could hear the fountain still trickling beside the pool. The breeze still whispered through the oleander tree, and the sun was beginning to feel like a brand on her bare skin.

Her fingers still clutched the strong, masculine hair, but Vann's cheek lay against the warm plane of her abdomen, his arms tightly clasping her trembling body, giving her time to recover. She felt his lips, feather-light, brush her skin before, eventually, he got to his feet.

'Are you all right?' he enquired hoarsely. He looked flushed and tousled, a sybaritic god, satiated with the pleasure of his goddess.

Mel nodded, unable to speak. Now that it was over, she felt ashamed of her response and acutely self-conscious of her nakedness. She had left her dress in the bedroom. It was only a short step around the pool but it might have been a mile and she didn't think she could stand there and fumble with the strings of her bikini. There was, however, a towel on the sun bed.

Even as the knowledge registered, Vann was peeling off his T-shirt.

'Here,' he said softly. 'Put this on.'

Gratefully, she took it from him. It felt warm and soft and smelled of his musky scent as she pulled it over her head. She was glad it was large. Large enough to be decent, she thought, when it slid over her thighs.

'Quintina prepared some lunch for us before she left. When you're ready,' Vann advised, seemingly unaffected by what had just taken place, 'come and join me in the kitchen.'

He had to be suffering agonies of frustration, Mel thought, watching him walk away, because there was no doubt that he had been as aroused as she was, and she strongly suspected he had sacrificed his own pleasure to prove a point. That she couldn't resist him as a man, whatever the circumstances. That he could drive her wild with her need of him and still remain enough in command of himself to walk away from her afterwards. But why? Why had he been so determined to make her aware of her weakness for him? Was it because she had so rashly stated that making love with him had been no more than a distraction from her grief? Because his ego was so inflated he couldn't bear any woman claiming she was immune to him? Even as she thought it, somehow she didn't think that was true.

And what about her? she asked herself. If she could respond so uninhibitedly to a man who had devastated her life before, against her will, her common sense and her better judgement, had her reasons for making love with him the first time been as excusable as she had always believed? Had it been just sex all along when she had always believed it had been something much more than that? Had she been as besotted with him as the unfortunate Kelly while staunchly refusing to acknowledge it? Was that the subconscious motive, as he had seemed to be suggesting, that had propelled her into seeking him out under the banner of her anger and her misery? To share his bed?

She couldn't even bear to consider that that might be true

of herself and, offering up a silent apology to her sister for her shameful behaviour, she retrieved the scraps of her bikini and retreated to her room where, in the blissful privacy of the *en suite* bathroom, she attempted to scrub away the memory of his touch under the forceful jets of the shower.

They had lunch in the large, country-style kitchen, overlooking Marco's well-tended vegetable garden.

Despite everything, Mel found she was famished and tucked in gratefully to the food Quintina had left them, a simple but satisfying meal of continental cheeses and ciabatta with sun-dried tomatoes, complemented by glasses of the region's cool, clear, white wine.

'I see Harvey was right the other day when he made that rather indelicate remark about your eating habits,' Vann observed wryly, watching with something like approval as she broke off another piece of the crisp and tasty ciabatta. And softly, his words conveying a wealth of meaning, 'Got your appetite back, Mel?'

He was referring, she knew, to what had happened outside, the first time he had made any reference to it. Until then their conversation had been casual, restrained, as though they were both steering away from mentioning it.

She blushed now, bright pink, picking up her glass as a distraction, noticing the mocking twist to his lips, how relaxed he appeared, while she felt stripped of all her defences.

She was pleased when, having stacked the dishwasher to help Quintina, as well as to give herself something to do, they were making their way back to the study. They still had one or two things to sort out for the proposed new campaign.

Coming through the doorway, however, Mel stumbled over her own foot only to find herself caught by a steadying arm.

'Careful,' he warned. 'I don't think Harvey Associates

would look on me too favourably if I were to return its prize executive injured in any way.'

If only you knew! she thought, wondering how she was ever going to recover from today. It had taken her years to get over her experience with him the first time. If she had ever got over it! She had never stopped comparing him with every other man who had come after him. But not this time, she determined, gritting her teeth against his unsettling proximity, because, Heaven help her, her body was responding in the most basic way just from that casual touch.

'Your skin's a bit pink,' he remarked, causing her to stiffen from the light brush of his fingers over her left shoulder. 'We'd better put something on that.'

We?

Swallowing, she said, 'I've got some moisturiser in my bag.'

Quickly she tripped upstairs to the beautifully appointed bedroom where she had changed and showered and applied some of the smooth lotion to the sensitive area. It was a facial moisturiser, but it would have to suffice, she thought. Her back felt sore, too, but she couldn't do anything about that.

'Your back's red,' Vann commented, making her spin round to see him standing in the doorway. 'Are you sure you don't want this?' He was holding up a bottle of *Aprés Sun*.

Oh, hell.... One strap of her dress drawn down, she glanced over her shoulder to inspect herself in the dressing-table mirror.

'Swallow your pride, Mel. Let me.'

Turning round, she stood stock-still as he applied the cool cream to the reddened area, clutching her dress to her bare breasts because he needed to draw both straps down to cream almost down to her bra-line. Her bikini was still hanging over the balcony where she had placed it to finish drying before lunch. She wondered what he would say if he knew she was naked under her dress.

Oh, but his hands were so pleasurable, sliding over her tingling flesh! She closed her eyes against the heightening sensations, against the sight of his dark reflection in the mirror and all that he was doing to her. Desire tautened her bare nipples, sent a hard contraction spearing through her lower body. He had given her fulfilment in the most intimate way and yet it wasn't enough…

'I know. It's agony, isn't it?' he said huskily, shocking her eyes open to meet the tense need in his reflected features, the raw hunger in hers. Dear heaven! How could it have betrayed her? She looked wanton, wild and wet. 'I've been thoroughly guilty of self-deception,' he rasped, his hands clamping on to her upper arms. 'Any man who makes love to you and says he regrets it is a liar. I didn't regret it.' He swore almost viciously and spun her round to face him. 'I wanted you then as much as I want you now. I can't fight it any longer. I'm as worked up as you are, Mel.'

When his mouth descended on hers she was already dragging him down to her, taking as much as he was, her hands and mouth as greedy and devouring as his. It was as if a pressure valve had just exploded, a burst of boiling emotions that had no choice but to be released.

All restraint gone now, he was tugging at her dress, ripping it down while she grasped wildly at the clean T-shirt he had donned, pulling it out of the waistband of his trousers.

'God, Mel…'

He lifted her effortlessly off her feet as he had done the first time, and carried her over to the king-sized bed, coming down beside her and taking over her attempt to divest him of his clothes.

He was so wonderfully male, from the contoured muscles

of his hair-furred limbs and torso to the prominent symbol of his sex.

She was still wet from his earlier kisses, and even that was a turn on, her legs spreading like a butterfly's wings, inviting him, ready for him as he sheathed himself with a condom from the bedside cabinet and took her without the need for any foreplay, plunging deep into the cushioning warmth of her body.

'You're beautiful,' he whispered much later. 'And you make love beautifully. Just as I remember. Even at eighteen—hating me as you did—you were everything a man could wish for in his bed.'

She was lying on her side, her head on his shoulder, one arm flung carelessly across him. The bedroom door was still open, and she wondered what Quintina would say if she came back and found them.

I didn't hate you, she wanted to respond, but didn't. Instead, finding her voice, she murmured, 'That's praise indeed, coming from a man who must have had scores of women.'

'Hardly scores.'

'You had them throwing themselves at you.' And probably still do, she thought with a startling degree of jealousy. 'Night after night.'

He made a wry sound down his nostrils. 'I must admit the opportunities were there.'

'But you resisted them all like the Sir Galahad you were.'

'Not all, Mel,' he murmured softly, his arm tightening around her. 'I didn't resist you, did I?'

But he'd intended to, she thought. Even then, young as he was, he'd shown restraint at first when she'd been initiating the moves, when she had begged him not to leave her, but thankfully he wasn't reminding her of that.

'As I said, you made quite an impression. Your siren's

cries as I made love to you haunted me for a long time afterwards.'

So she hadn't been cast out of his thoughts quite as quickly as she had imagined. The knowledge gave rise to a crazy leap of hope.

'But you didn't do anything about it.' Even if he hadn't got her letter he could have found a way to contact her if he'd wanted to, she thought. Even Bern Clayton had assured her of that.

'Well, no,' Vann conceded, as though she shouldn't have expected anything else. 'I didn't actually think it was wise in the circumstances.'

Because of Kelly? Or because, having thought about it afterwards, he could see no future in any relationship between them?

Hope faded, leaving only the warm, moist lethargy of their lovemaking.

'No,' she breathed tightly, so he wouldn't know how much she had wanted him to. Yet when he turned round, rolling on top of her, she winced from the sheer pleasure of his warm, heavy body on hers.

His lips were nipping the sensitive flesh at the juncture of her neck and shoulder. Even the brush of his hair against her jaw was an unbearable turn on. She wanted him again like she had never wanted anyone. Yet all her instincts of self-preservation told her she was going to get hurt.

Those warm, slightly rough hands had already recommenced their treacherous magic, shaping the soft contours of her body. She sucked in her breath, her senses swimming from the moist heat of his tongue over her nipple, from the heady musk of their bodies, so that it took every ounce of her will to summon up the strength to say, 'Vann… Vann, I don't want an involvement.'

He inhaled sharply, and the lips that were performing their sweet torture stilled against her breast. After a moment he lifted his head to look at her. Her eyelids were heavy, her cheeks flushed with desire and her flaming hair, damp at the temples, lay tousled across his pillow.

'My dear girl, if you hadn't noticed, we *are* involved,' he murmured, a sensual smile touching his mouth, though his features were gripped by the same depth of wanting that enslaved her. 'I'm not a fatalist, but there are some things that happen just because they're meant to. This…chemistry, as you called it, has been there between us from the beginning. Even before you collapsed, sobbing and helpless in my arms. Oh, yes,' he said heavily when she looked amazed by his declaration. 'I'd never seen a girl with so much courage and spirit as I thought you had that night. I saw you and I wanted you.'

But not enough to make you want to find me again, she thought achingly.

When she didn't answer, afraid that she might say too much, he repeated, 'We are involved, Mel, for what it's worth. Deceiving yourself won't change that—won't alter the fact that you want me as much as I want you. So let's enjoy what we have. Here and now. I'm not asking for commitment.'

No, of course not, and she should be grateful that he was being honest, she thought, wanting him too much to think beyond the pleasure her murmur of acceptance would guarantee her.

Too weak to deny herself, as once again his seeking mouth found her breast, she clasped him to her with a small moan of defeat, giving herself up to the driving needs of her sexuality.

Over the next few days they saw each other every second they could spare, making love at whatever moments they could steal. At the villa. In her room. On his yacht, moored in a small, private cove, under the stars. They couldn't get enough of each other, sometimes ripping one another's clothes off as soon as they found themselves alone, a slow, leisurely ecstasy always following their first, urgent coming together.

'I never realised it could be like this,' Mel said, after one particularly adventurous session of lovemaking. 'I used to wonder why some people made so much fuss about sex.'

'Sex?' Vann queried, as though he thought the word too mild to describe their torrid, almost desperate need for each other's bodies. Then, after a moment, 'It's just as well it wasn't Harvey you decided to seduce on this trip. Somehow I don't think he would have quite come up to matching that passionate nature of yours.'

They were on Vann's yacht, having sailed around the coast that morning. It was their last day together. Now, sunbathing on deck, naked and feeling slightly bruised in places from that passion he had spoken of, listening to the waves lapping gently against the hull, she thought of what Jonathan had said to her two days before.

'You're sleeping with him, aren't you?' And when she had thrust her chin up, refusing to discuss what was, after all, none of his business, 'You must be mad!' he had thrown at her. 'You aren't kidding yourself there's any future in it, are you?'

She wasn't but she'd hated hearing Jonathan remind her of the fact, especially when he had gone on, 'He's a world-renowned entrepreneur and a multi-millionaire, for heaven's sake! People like him move in different circles from the likes of you and me. He's just having a fling with someone who's willing. I just hope you know what you're doing,' he had added condescendingly.

She did, because Vann had told her nothing but the truth. He wasn't looking for commitment. Not with her, anyway. And, as far as knowing what she was doing was concerned, well, she did, didn't she? When this week was through she would leave here, fly to Rome, and spend the following week touring Tuscany with Zoë. Bed and breakfasting. Taking it as it came. It had sounded like fun when they had planned it. And it would be, Mel determined, for Zoë's sake. After which, she would return to her normal, everyday life and pretend this madness had never happened. That this crazy affair she was conducting with Vann was enough to sustain her through her loveless existence. That she had never been in danger of actually falling in love with him…

'Do you have to go to Tuscany?' he was enquiring, as though reading her thoughts.

Lying face down on a towel, she lifted her head to look at him. He was as naked as she was, lying on his back beside her.

'Spend your extra week here. With me,' he startled her by saying.

At his villa? 'I can't…' Her throat felt dry and her heart was beating crazily. 'I've made arrangements.'

'Break them.'

'Besides, I'll have Zoë.'

'So…' He rolled over on to his side, his big body gleaming, head supported by an elbow. 'I like children. Another week together, Mel. Think of it.'

And have longer to increase the agony of parting from him?

She turned round to face him, adopting the same position. Her breasts hung tantalisingly and she felt his gaze drop to their pink buds, still erect from his kisses, incredibly sensitive.

'It wouldn't be the same,' she felt she needed to tell him, fighting the strongest desire to accept. Even as he lay, relaxed, stretched out beside her, she could see what she was doing to him. She had to stem the urge to reach for him…

'No. I appreciate that we will have to…' he lifted a hand to trace the tempting valley between her breasts '…temper our behaviour somewhat.' Even that light touch was stimulating.

'And after that?' she tried to say nonchalantly.

He seemed to hesitate before answering. 'I told you. No strings. That was what we agreed, wasn't it?'

Of course. She hoped the sudden sharp anguish inside her didn't show. 'It really isn't such a good idea.'

'Thanks, but no thanks?' His tone was surprisingly bitter. 'So what's there left to say? Have a good trip? It's been fun knowing you?' There was an almost fatalistic air about the way he said it, as though he had accepted it was pointless pursuing the relationship. She should have been glad, but her heart felt as if it were being ripped out of her.

'I've got other commitments, Vann. Bookings. Plans. I can't renege on those.'

'Of course not.' His eyes were hard, his mouth suddenly grim. 'Ever the hard-headed, self-sufficient female.'

'That's not fair!'

'Do you have any dreams, Melissa?' She wondered why he sounded so angry. 'Have you ever had a dream?'

'Yes.' She sat up, looking over his shoulder. In the distance, the dark bulk of Nureyev's island slumbered in the afternoon heat. 'I wanted that self-reliance that you're so keen to poke fun at. I wanted to be my own person and be totally successful at what I did.' And I wanted a real home, with a brother or sister for Zoë and a man to love me. But she didn't say that, uttering a small cry of protest as he suddenly reached for her, pulling her on top of him to roll her beneath him, pinning her there with his wrists and his arousing weight.

'Well, you've achieved your objective, darling, because you're definitely your own person and you're certainly successful at this!'

He kissed her then, hard and punitively, as he had kissed her in Amalfi, only this time Mel responded with a desperate anger of her own. She wanted to hurt him, as much as she was hurting inside, for his not loving her when he had made her love him, because she had to acknowledge now that she was in love with him. She always had been. He had stolen her heart that night in the country manor, which was why she had never been able to respond in quite the same way to anyone else since.

They made love like it was the last time. Because it was the last time, she thought. And if she kept telling herself she was being crazy refusing to stay, then she had to keep reminding herself that if she had accepted his offer, not only would she have become more deeply involved with him, but it would have laid her open to further, more complicated issues that she didn't want to face.

CHAPTER EIGHT

NAPLES Airport was busy, with mainly tourists making up the long queues to the check-in desks.

Battling through the crowd, Mel had a job finding the appropriate check-in point for her internal flight. Her suitcase was unwieldy, even on its castors, and the strap of her flight bag was cutting into her shoulder. After a virtually sleepless night, she wasn't feeling her best. She missed the others, too. The rest of her team had flown home yesterday, and this morning the last cases for the remaining clients had stood waiting with hers in the hotel lobby. Then they had gone, and she had been the last to depart.

The conference room had lain silent when she had checked it for the last time, the empty tables and chairs seeming to accentuate her sudden crushing isolation. Ever since she had left England she had had company. First Zoë and Karen, then Jonathan and the team, and Vann.

Vann. She tried not to think about him and the miles she had already put between them—the knowledge that she could still have been with him—as she paused for a moment amidst the maddening chaos to get her bearings, decide where she had to go.

Jostled uncomfortably by someone rushing past, she adjusted the strap that had almost been knocked off her shoulder and, seeing the sign for her airline, fought her way through a sea of bodies to join the queue for Rome.

Everyone seemed to be with someone, she noticed, having nothing better to do than scan the endless queues as she waited in line. Families with children. Couples.

She seemed to be the only one on her own, she thought

with such a strong wave of loneliness sweeping over her it had her staring down at her suitcase in an attempt to blot out the scene.

She had Zoë, didn't she? And she wasn't so much alone as footloose and fancy free. It was just this place—the crowds—that was making her feel lonely. Plus the fact that she had been with so many other people this week.

'Tickets, please.'

Relieved to see that she was next in line, Mel reached for the zipper on the side compartment of her flight bag. It was gaping open. She must have forgotten to close it when she had tipped the taxi-driver, she thought hectically, although she knew she hadn't.

Frantically, she rifled through what remained of the contents she had checked and double-checked before leaving the hotel. It wasn't possible, she thought, unable at first to comprehend the truth. But then the realisation hit her like a punch in the ribs, and to no one in particular she was exclaiming, 'My passport! My purse! Everything! It's gone!'

The check-in staff obviously weren't very impressed.

'I had everything when I came in. I know I did,' Mel stated emphatically to the exasperated-looking young Italian woman and her older male counterpart who had been summoned to help sort out what should be done.

She would have to tell the police. Get a statement from them to help with her emergency passport. Contact the British Consulate.

But all that was going to take time.

'I have to ring my daughter,' Mel told him urgently. 'I'm meeting her in Rome.' Karen and her husband were flying off to Switzerland to celebrate their second wedding anniversary as soon as Mel arrived. She had arranged to meet them all at the airport, and now there was no way she would be able to make it on time.

She reached for her mobile phone in the same compartment where her purse and document wallet had been, her arm drooping uselessly on realising that the thief had taken that as well.

'Do you have a phone I can use?' she requested, trying to remain calm. 'I've got to contact my friend.'

In the small inner office to which she was taken, however, another realisation struck Mel. She had had Karen's mobile number on a piece of paper tucked into her purse. But now her purse was gone, along with all her money, her travellers' cheques and her credit cards. As the scale of her predicament hit her, Mel found it hard even to think.

She'd have to cancel her cards, she pulled herself together sufficiently enough to realise. But the twenty-four hour emergency number had been keyed into her mobile phone book—and the thief had that! A bubble of hysterical laughter clogged her throat from the irony of it all. After a great deal of effort, however, she managed to make the man beside her understand what she wanted and, with his help, succeeded in cancelling her cards.

Next, apologising profusely to him, she quickly tapped out the number of Zoë's mobile phone, only to be told it was switched off.

Probably she had used up her credit limit—or forgotten to charge her battery, Mel thought, exasperated. But if she couldn't telephone Karen or Zoë, how was she going to let them know she wouldn't be arriving as planned? They would already have left the house, Mel realised with a swift glance at her watch, and Simon's studio would be closed now for the weekend, so there would be no chance of catching anyone there who could give her Karen's number. She was stranded here with no one to contact, no money, and therefore no hope of reaching her daughter—and that was the only thing that mattered. She didn't even care that the rest of their holiday would probably now have to be cancelled. She had to get to Zoë. But how?

Racked with worry, she dropped the phone on to its rest, her face telling its own tale. 'What am I going to do?' she asked, harrowed.

The man gave a sympathetic shrug. 'There is no one...?'

Battling against the thought that had just come into her mind, Mel shook her head. But the thought grew and flourished, goading and tormenting her. Well, there wasn't anyone else, was there?

Grabbing the phone again, Mel managed to reach the operator and waited, her heart in her mouth, for the connection to be made.

'*Buon giorno*,' Quintina answered when Mel was put through.

'It's Mel, Quintina. Mel Sheraton. Is Vann there?' He isn't, she thought desperately, following a sudden silence when she thought she had been cut off.

'Melissa?' Relief closed Mel's eyes as the deep voice came over the line, curious, strung with surprise.

'Oh, Vann! I need your help. It's Zoë.'

'Zoë?' Surprise gave way to concern. 'What's happened to her?'

'Nothing,' Mel quickly assured him. 'But I can't get to her. She'll be waiting in Rome and I've missed my flight because I've been robbed! They've taken everything!'

'Whoa! Whoa! Take it easy.' Through the loud announcement of a plane being ready to board and the sudden rush of activity in the passenger terminal outside, Vann's voice was soothing and calm. 'Now, tell me again, slowly.'

So she did, and when she had finished he said without any further ado, 'Stay exactly where you are. I'm coming to get you.'

'But what about Zoë? She'll be waiting at the airport. Karen and Simon will have to cancel their trip because of me. And I've imposed upon them enough. I don't think they'll leave her, but she might try and persuade them to. She's so strong-willed and determined. I'll never forgive myself if anything happens to her.'

'Nothing's going to happen to her,' he stressed phlegmatically, taking control. 'I've got contacts in Rome. I'll send a car for her and leave a message at Arrivals in case you can't contact her before she gets there. Don't worry. Everything's going to be all right.'

Mel's lashes came down as she took a deep breath to steady herself. He was right. Of course he was. 'I don't want to put you to all this trouble,' she said apologetically. 'Just as long as Zoë's all right. You don't have to worry about me.'

An almost amused chuckle came over the line. 'And why would I worry about Zoë and then leave her mother stranded at Naples Airport?'

Because she's young and vulnerable. Because she's only twelve. *And because she's your daughter, too!*

For a moment Mel thought she had screamed it aloud. It was only when Vann said calmly, 'Do as you're told. I'm coming to get you,' that she realised she hadn't.

He was with her in such a relatively short time that Mel didn't dwell on how fast he must have driven to cut the nearly two-hour journey by as much as he had. But waiting in the airport lounge, having been interviewed by police and kept supplied with coffee by a generous member of staff, Mel felt herself weakening with joy as she saw him striding towards her.

'Vann.' The next moment she was being embraced by his warm strength, her arms around him, her head against the coarse fabric of his shirt. 'Thank you for coming.' It seemed an inadequate thing to whisper, especially after the way she had shunned his suggestion of spending her holiday with him.

'My pleasure,' he whispered hoarsely. 'What are friends for?'

Crazily, that simple remark brought tears to her eyes. She hadn't realised he'd ever consider her a friend.

It was a relaxed, easy journey back to the villa. Sitting there, between the jagged coast and the towering reaches of the mountains, Mel thought how all the gods had to be working for Vann because he had got his own way, hadn't he? He hadn't wanted her to leave. And fate, it seemed, had stepped in to help him.

'It seems to be becoming a habit—rescuing Sheraton women,' he commented dryly, unaware of how that simple remark touched something deep down in Mel.

Because, of course, he had saved Zoë's life that day without even realising he was already responsible for that life…

Through suddenly blurred vision, she looked at him steering the car with his usual competence, a glance at his dark profile making her whole being ache with the need to tell him. But all she said lightly, with her eyes guarded, was, 'You must be feeling pretty smug.'

Flicking a switch to block out the fumes from an ancient truck they were following, he said, glancing in her direction, 'Why should I feel smug? In a minute you'll be saying I engineered the whole thing just to bring you back here. I might have, if I'd thought of it,' he added rather dryly, 'but I didn't. You've suffered a trauma,' he went on. 'You've lost all your valuables and you've been at your wits' end over Zoë. Of course I don't feel smug. Oh, I admit I'm glad you're still here. And I'd be lying to say that I wasn't more than happy to be taking you home with me. But smug I definitely am not!'

So that was her suitably chastened, Mel thought, grateful, in spite of what he had said, that he had taken control. Grateful, too, for the message he had left at Rome Airport for Karen to ring him on his mobile, for getting Karen to contact her while she had been waiting at Naples. She had even managed to speak to Zoë.

Now, sitting beside the man she loved, with Zoë on her way to join them, Mel tried not to dwell on the inevitable complications that lay ahead.

'I can't get over this place!' Zoë enthused, coming down the villa's sweeping staircase.

She had been expressing as much ever since she had arrived, with far more bags than she had left with, bursting with excitement about the drive down from Rome, the humorous Italian chauffeur who had teased and joked with her for most of the journey, the stupendous car.

'It even had a video screen fitted into the back of the seat in front and a whole load of videos!'

If Mel had been concerned about her daughter being bored on such a long drive alone then she needn't have been, she'd thought wryly, remembering to thank Vann later for selecting that particular car and driver.

'Did you think I'd forgotten what it was like to be young?' he had said with a crooked smile, pulling her against him as she got up from one of the deeply cushioned sofas to go to bed. She had left Zoë luxuriating in bubbles in her own personal *en suite* bathroom earlier, singing her head off. Quintina and Marco had already retired to their private rooms. 'I might not have kids of my own, but I am aware that their boredom threshold can sometimes use a little bolstering. And I think the least you can do is thank me properly.'

Before she had known what was happening, he had covered her mouth with his, evoking a wild response from her with his hard virility. She had moaned against his mouth, ignoring the goading little voice inside her that screamed she should be telling him the truth, not leading him on like this without his knowing the facts. And she would, she told herself, but not now. Not yet.

But he hadn't let their hunger for each other get out of hand, exercising immense self-control, although he was flushed and breathing heavily as he lifted his head.

'I promised you restraint,' he said, which he had, on the journey down. 'So I think you'd better go to bed before I completely abandon that promise and take you here and now.'

If only you would, she had thought, remembering he had insisted on separate bedrooms as well. She thought it was because of Zoë, but then couldn't help the nagging suspicion that it might be because of his staff. The previous week he had been discretion itself, only making love with her at the villa if no one else was around. But if the two of them shared a room, leaving no doubt in anyone's mind that they were lovers, perhaps he was worried that the relationship might become public…

Frustrated, troubled by doubts and her own conscience, she had fled.

That had been two days ago and now, in the brightness of the sunny morning, Mel tried to shake off her worries, share some of Zoë's delight in her surroundings and this unexpected turn of events that had meant discarding their original plans and coming here instead. But she couldn't. Now that Zoë was here there was every chance that the child might say something to Vann that would make him realise her mother hadn't been straight with him. Not that she had actually lied, Mel deliberated, thinking back. Just that she hadn't actually corrected him when he'd made such blatantly inaccurate assumptions. She had let him go on believing something that wasn't true, and now there was no easy solution to putting things right. Anyway, what was she supposed to do? Come right out and say it?

Oh, by the way, she's your daughter. Mel caught her

breath from just thinking about what his reaction might be, and felt that gnawing anxiety that always surfaced every time she thought about telling him.

'I'm going for a swim,' Zoë announced, stepping lithely off the bottom stair. She had tied a large coloured scarf, sarong-style, around her small, developing figure. 'Vann said he'd help me with my butterfly stroke. Are you coming, too?'

Through the archway, beyond the sitting room and the open patio doors, the pool looked temptingly blue and still.

Mel shook her head. 'No. You run along,' she advised. All her tensions over being robbed, coupled with finding herself in this situation which she had been so keen to avoid, seemed to have come to the fore this morning, causing the familiar dull pain above one eye. Besides, just thinking about the shocking intimacy she and Vann had shared by the pool on that first occasion only made her blush to her roots and her temple throb. 'I've got a threatening headache,' she enlarged.

Zoë's nose wrinkled as she groaned a protest. 'You always say that when you want to get out of doing something.'

'I do not!' Mel replied a little too sharply. She knew she had misled Vann, but she certainly wasn't guilty of ever lying to her daughter. 'That's unfair and you know it is.'

'And what are you accusing your mother of trying to get out of?'

They both looked up as Vann came down the stairs, wearing dark swimming shorts, a blue towel slung over one shoulder. His body was beautiful, lean and tanned and fit, and Mel was startled to realise how much her fingers ached to touch him.

'Having a swim with us,' Zoë told him, looking rather sheepish suddenly. 'She says she's got a headache.'

'Then you must accept what she says.' Those blue eyes

clashing with Mel's made her pulse beat ridiculously fast. 'I think she deserves an apology, don't you?'

Zoë looked shocked at what he was suggesting. His gaze, however, was fixed so penetratingly on her that the girl backed down, looking at her sandalled feet as she murmured, 'Sorry, Mum.'

Over her head, Mel and Vann exchanged glances. 'Run along,' he said to Zoë. 'I'll join you in a minute.' Not needing to be told twice, the child obeyed, her eager footsteps echoing over the marbled tiles.

'A bit of air and relaxation might do your headache some good,' he suggested softly, with a look that said he knew why she was so reluctant to join them outside. Perhaps that was why he was so insistent on keeping their affair under wraps, she thought suddenly. Simply for her sake, although she doubted it. She hadn't realised, though, that being without a man for so long had made her so shy. 'How about it, Mel?'

Why did she find it so easy to be persuaded by him? she wondered when, having substituted her apricot bikini for her shorts and sun top, she was floating on the blue water some minutes later. But he was right. Her headache had eased, she realised, listening to her daughter's giggling attempts to follow Vann's patient instructions, her ears attuned to his deep, companionable laughter, his every casual word, the sheer addiction to his nearness driving any other unwanted thoughts from her mind.

Lying, face upturned to the sun, using only the gentlest movement of her hands and feet to keep her buoyant, Mel thought how great he was with Zoë. He had taken them both water-skiing the previous day, and then during the afternoon had arranged a trip for the child with the gentle, moustached Marco and his ten-year-old grandson to a local farm where they were both able to ride.

As far as her own problems went, he had been helpful in

the extreme. She marvelled at the dexterity and speed with which he had helped sort things out for her—transfers of money, getting her new passport processed, translating in his fluent Italian where necessary.

'Watch that beautiful skin,' he whispered, his head suddenly coming up out of the water right beside her. 'Or I shall be left with the not altogether punishing task of having to rub sun cream all over you, and you know what happened last time.'

A lick of desire passed through her, so intense she lost her balance and would have gone underwater if he hadn't caught her. But the brush of his flesh against hers was too erotic for comfort, especially after their sustained abstinence, and with a sudden wrench she was striking out for the edge of the pool, his laughter following her with the tinkling sound of the fountain.

Zoë pulled a knowing face as she swam up alongside Mel.

'Just think. If you married *him*—he'd be my dad,' she breathed, clearly relishing the idea, but Mel's insides knotted up.

She'd have to tell her—tell them both, she thought but weighed down by her anxieties all she could manage at that moment was, 'Just think again.'

A sudden splash made them turn. Vann had swum right up behind them.

'You heard her, Zoë.' He was reaching for the edge, hauling himself up out of the water. 'There's definitely no chance that your mother and I will ever be getting married.'

Heart sinking, Mel watched him stoop to grab his towel from one of the loungers and stride off across the patio into the house.

Had he heard her? Was that why he had said that? she wondered, mortified. Or was he simply making it clear to *her* that their relationship was definitely a no-strings attached affair? Convinced of the latter, she turned and plunged forcibly under the blue water, striking out against the screaming anguish in her heart.

The following day, Vann drove Quintina into Positano to do some shopping, and Zoë leapt at the chance to go with her when Quintina suggested it.

It was agreed that Marco would pick them up on his way back from a neighbouring vineyard later in the morning, which meant that Vann would be free to return to the villa as soon as his own business was done.

Mel's heart leapt like a gazelle when she heard him discussing the arrangements with them in their own language and grasped that, with Marco gone as well, she and Vann were going to be entirely alone.

Minutes later, seeing them off, watching Vann's indulgence with Zoë, noticing the way he teased her, ruffling her hair as she tripped, giggling, ahead of him out of the villa, made Mel's heart contract painfully.

They should *know*, she thought. And promised herself again that she would tell them…soon. She just hoped Zoë didn't say anything that might start Vann thinking. It was a risk she took every time the two of them were together, she thought, which meant her nerves were strained to breaking point for a lot of the time. Still, Zoë was going to be with Quintina for most of the morning, and Vann was coming back on his own. His departing, 'I'll be back shortly,' caused her insides to quiver with traitorous anticipation, making her wonder if she had imagined that meaningful glitter in his eyes.

Aching for nothing now but his return, Mel raced upstairs, changing the shorts and T-shirt she had pulled on after she had showered for the floaty, feminine skirt she had purchased the previous week. The flame and ochre colours reflected the highlights in her loose and riotous hair, she noted, teaming it with a plunging V-necked lemon top which, as she was braless, showed off the tantalising fullness of her breasts. Low, strappy gold sandals accentuated her tanned feet. Some mascara, a little lipstick, and a spray of perfume. There, she thought, catching sight of her flushed features and her wide, dilated pupils in the mirror. She looked like a sex slave, eagerly awaiting initiation by her master.

She gasped as the phone rang, like some criminal caught in the act of doing something she shouldn't.

It was the police in Naples. Amazingly, they had found her passport and her purse, emptied save for a book of stamps and a photograph. The man spoke good English and said she could collect them on production of some identification.

'Thanks,' she uttered breathlessly, ringing off.

She should start packing, she chided herself, hearing Marco's car start up outside. Not titivating herself to try and seduce a man who didn't really want her. Because that was all she was doing, she realised.

Five minutes after the sound of Marco's car died away she heard the low growl of Vann's, and reached the foot of the stairs just as he was mounting the steps. The front door was open, spilling sunlight into the wide hall with the lucid note of a bird on the scented air. But Mel was senseless to everything but the man.

In a long-sleeved white shirt and dark trousers, he was looking down at the steps and didn't see her at first, and her heart gave a painful lurch.

He'd want to make love to her. He had to want it as much as she did, she thought desperately, feeling every feminine cell leap towards his hard masculinity.

Then, as he came in, he looked up and saw her, and the blood suddenly drained from her face.

'What's wrong? What is it?' she murmured. His face, too, seemed bloodless, and there was a cold severity to his mouth that almost frightened her.

'Well, well,' he said, shutting out the scented garden with one forceful thrust of his hand. 'Are you wearing anything under that, Mel? Or do I have to wait until I rip it off you to find out?'

'Vann…' What is it? she had been going to ask, but that hard edge to his voice stopped her.

'Isn't that what you want me to do, Mel?'

'No…' She did, but she couldn't understand why he was being like this.

'Oh yes, Melissa, I think it is.' He was moving in that dark predatory way of his towards her, and unconsciously she grabbed the carved newel post just behind her for support. 'But then you've always found difficulty telling the truth, haven't you?'

Oh *no*!

'Oh yes,' he breathed again, seeing her dismay. 'Fortunately, Zoë doesn't seem to have followed in the same footsteps as her mother.'

Mel didn't need to ask him what he meant. So this was it, she thought, what she had dreaded all along, and steeled herself for his tirade, his inevitable anger.

'There's a whole year's difference between only just twelve and thirteen in two weeks!' he tossed at her. 'I wouldn't have known if I hadn't heard her innocently telling Quintina. That means she was born around seven months after we…' He broke off, looking wounded, baffled, as though he were trying to comprehend. 'Unless you were already pregnant when we made love that night…' His breath seemed to shudder through the hard cavity of his chest. 'She's mine, isn't she?' His hands were on her shoulders, hard against her smooth skin. 'Isn't she?' he demanded heavily.

Mel's Adam's apple worked nervously, an irrational fear gripping her. She could have denied it, told him she had already been pregnant, as he had just so lightly suggested.

At least that could have excused her so carelessly having sex with him without any precautions. But there had been enough deception, she thought, and with a small sigh of defeat, shoulders slumping, she said, 'I was going to tell you, but the time just never seemed right. She was born two months premature, and I nearly lost her. It was touch and go—whether she'd survive—all the way through.' The doctors had said it was because of losing Kelly and her mother so close together, but that fact alone made her baby the only thing to hang on to—made Zoë all the more precious to her when she had survived.

'Why didn't you tell me? Straight away? As soon as you found out?' He was shaking his head, still trying to understand.

'I didn't think you'd want to know. Especially as I'd already written.'

'Yes, well…'

He wasn't questioning that? Did that mean he'd received her letter?

'You got my note?' she uttered incredulously.

'Yes,' he said grimly, his hands falling away from her. So why did he look—sound—so forbidding? 'You really didn't believe in holding anything back, did you?'

His words cut her to the quick. She'd always known she'd been a fool to write it. A total fool, she thought achingly as, angry and clearly upset at having been denied his parental right, he roughly went on, 'What did you decide when you found out you were pregnant? That you'd burnt all your bridges? Or wouldn't your pride let you contact me?'

Because he hadn't replied?

'You missed your chance there, Melissa.' His laugh was harsh and mirthless. 'You could have whacked a nice fat paternity suit on me!'

Her eyes were dark with bewilderment. 'Why would I have wanted to have done that?' And, when he didn't answer, 'Did you think I was just after your money?' she whispered, having never considered that possibility.

Letting out a huge sigh, rather wearily he said, 'No,' shaking his head. 'However else I reacted at the time, I didn't seriously think there'd be any more repercussions from tumbling into bed with Lissa Ratcliffe. I knew you weren't a gold-digger.'

Well, thank heaven for that! Mel thought, stung nevertheless by the way he had referred to their lovemaking.

'Sheraton,' she said then, coming clean.

He frowned. 'What?'

'Kelly and I had different fathers. Kelly's name was Ratcliffe. Mine was Sheraton.'

A host of conflicting emotions chased across his face. 'So…there wasn't any husband, either?'

Contritely, she shook her head.

'Yet you let me think there was. Lied to me. About everything,' he said hoarsely. 'About who you were. About Zoë.' Anger surfaced, darkening those glittering irises. 'About her age.'

'No!' He was looking at her as though he didn't know who she was any more and she couldn't bear it. She hadn't wilfully set out to deceive anyone, beyond keeping him from guessing who she was, and only then because she was so embarrassed at meeting him again. 'OK, I lied about having met you before,' she admitted with heartfelt remorse, 'but I felt so dreadful.' How was I supposed to feel? she thought. I sent you a letter but you hadn't bothered to reply. Not that I ever really expected you would, but I wanted you to. So much! 'But I didn't blatantly lie about anything else. When you asked how old Zoë was and I said…' She thought back, trying to remember. 'I don't know exactly what I said, but I only meant she wouldn't be twelve for much longer, but you assumed the opposite. You assumed everything! I didn't actually tell you I'd been married. You assumed it.

Just like you assumed everything else. It was what you wanted to believe!'

'And you let me. Misled me all the way through. Even about my own daughter.' Bare emotion slashed harsh lines across his face. 'Didn't you think I had a right to know?' She glanced away, looked down at his dark slip-on shoes, unable to bear the tortured accusation in his eyes. He grasped her roughly, forcing her to face him. 'Didn't you think Zoë had a right to know?'

'Stop it!' He had hurt her where it hurt most, at the very core of her maternal pride, and she tried to pull away, but he wouldn't let her, his fingers bruising the tender flesh of her upper arms.

'What do you say to her, Mel? What do you tell her when she asks? That you don't know who her father is? Or do you spin her some cock-and-bull story to try and deceive her, too?'

'No!' Now her own anger gave her the strength to twist out of his grasp. 'I've never deceived her! How dare you even accuse me of doing that? If you must know, she knows her father was someone I met very briefly, even if she doesn't know the circumstances, or exactly who you are. But I've always told Zoë her father was someone very special—and that he'd be proud of her.' And, on a more wistful note, 'I couldn't guarantee that,' she added, 'but at least I hoped it would be true.'

'Oh, Mel…' One swift stride brought him to her again, his arms going round her. 'Why didn't you let me know?' Beneath her hands, his shoulders were like twin rocks. Strong, sturdy, immovable. She laid her head against one.

'I wasn't in any fit state,' she murmured, wishing she could believe that that raw edge to his voice wasn't just because of finding out he had a daughter. 'My mother died two weeks after Kelly.'

'What?' He drew back, looking down into her anguished face, his expression disbelieving, horrified.

'It made all the papers. The story was too new not to.'

'I didn't realise. No one told me. I was in Australia.' He sounded as though he should have known.

'After she died, my own father materialised from out of the blue and insisted I went and stayed with him. I was like an automaton. I could only do whatever he suggested,' she continued, reliving the misery of that time. 'So I stayed with him for a few weeks until I found out all he wanted was the proceeds of the house. It didn't work out anyway, and as soon as I could I moved out. My mother had willed the house to Kelly and me. I gave him some of the money and got myself a small flat with the rest. He would have gambled it all away anyway. I think he went abroad because I never saw him again. But at least I was able to provide some sort of home for my child.'

'Our child,' Vann corrected, his regard hard and analytical. 'Yet you would still have kept it from me. Why, Mel? After how intimate we've been together, you still didn't want me to know.'

'I don't know,' she uttered quickly, avoiding his eyes, because she couldn't tell him. She wasn't sure she even knew herself. 'Anyway, what would you have done? If I'd written and told you I was going to have your baby?'

'Then?' He lifted his head, staring over her shoulder as though at some point in the past. 'What do you think?' he said, his attention returning to her. 'As I told you before—I believe a child should have two parents.'

So he would have honoured his commitments. Married her and provided a home for their baby even though he didn't love her. She wasn't sure whether she could have borne that.

'And what if I'd objected?'

'Then I would have thought it a fitting punishment to drag

you screaming to the altar. The child would have come first.'

Of course. Family ties would mean everything to him because of his childhood, because of how resented he had been made to feel by his own parents.

'And now?' Mel ventured tentatively.

'I want to get to know my daughter,' he asserted, suddenly releasing her. 'Which means that when you go home I want her to stay on here until the school holidays end.'

'No!' A hot emotion seized her, jealously possessive. Still, she should have expected it, she thought. They had come a long way in fourteen years. They had both matured, particularly her, because she had needed to, emotionally at any rate. No longer a lonely adolescent, frightened for the future, she was her own person, independent, successful, her baby nearly a woman. He need make no commitment now to the mother of his child.

'Yes, Melissa,' he countered in response to her firm denial. He only called her that, she realised distractedly, when he was angry with her—or making love… 'You're going to grant me some share in my child's life and give Zoë the chance of a father—a little late in the day but, as I'm sure you'll agree, better late than never—and you'll start by telling her exactly who I am.'

'No!' She could feel the fear like a dark chasm opening up before her.

'If you don't,' he threatened, those strong features grim, uncompromising, 'then I will.'

'All right.' She put up her hands as though to stave off something abhorrent, her eyes tormented, appealing to him. 'But you've got to let me do it my way. In my own time.'

The phone shrilling loudly in the sitting room almost made her jump, her gaze following his towards the sound echoing through the empty villa.

'The time is now, Melissa,' he told her, striding away.

CHAPTER NINE

'WHY didn't you ever *tell* me?' Zoë remonstrated with oh, so Vann-like censure after Mel had told her everything, holding nothing back, later that afternoon. 'Why didn't you let me *know*?'

First there had been shocked disbelief from the teenager, then tears of joy—excitement—and now this rebuke.

'There was only ever that one meeting,' Mel tried explaining gently. 'I didn't think he'd want to know—that he'd want to see us.' And I didn't want you to know what it was like to be rejected, she thought achingly, wanting only to protect her daughter from anything that threatened her happiness—the rejection by her own father and then her stepfather still having the power to hurt.

'You should have told me,' the girl berated her. They were walking in the garden, having picked peppers and courgettes for Marco. From some distance away, behind a pergola of sweet scented jasmine, came the occasional scrape of his hoe on the baked earth. 'Did you love him?'

'Zoë, I was eighteen!' Mel emphasised, uncertain how to answer. 'Just a few years older than you are now.'

'But you must have loved him to have gone to bed with him.' Coming from a twelve-year-old, this was disconcerting, to say the least.

'Yes, I loved him.' Mel sighed. After all, it was true, wasn't it?

'Do you love him now?'

Mel held her breath, unable to meet those enquiring blue eyes beneath the thickly shaped brows. 'It was a long time ago,' she murmured. 'People change.'

'But when you fall in love with someone, I thought it was supposed to be for keeps,' Zoë retorted, kicking at the sandy path with one petulant, sandalled foot. 'That's what you always keep telling me.'

'Not exactly,' Mel countered, deciding her daughter was mixing up romantic love with her views on marriage and commitment. 'It's nice if it can be, but life isn't always like that. Besides, it has to be two-way.'

A frown wrinkled the young forehead. 'You're going out with him,' she stated after some consideration. 'And he's letting us stay here. I thought...'

Dear Zoë. She couldn't yet comprehend the complexities of adult relationships.

'We're just his guests, Zoë. Don't put any more significance on it than that.'

'But he's bound to like you more than any of his last girlfriends.' It was an innocent enough statement, but it sent a shaft of pain spearing through Mel.

'Why?'

'Because of me.'

Putting an arm around the small, bony shoulders, Mel couldn't help giving a cynical chuckle at her daughter's naïvety. If only it were that simple, she thought.

'He said he wants to get to know you. He's asked me to let you stay...' it took an immense effort on Mel's part to put it into words '...after I've gone.'

'What?' Zoë's face lit up. 'Just me on my own?'

Mel wished she could share her daughter's delight, feel great about the fact that her daughter had finally found her father. And she did. Of course she did. But she couldn't help this gnawing anxiety.

'He suggested you stay until the end of the holidays, but I want you home before that.'

'Why?' Zoë asked, pulling away from Mel. She looked defiant, rebellious.

Why? Mel thought quickly. 'Because you have to prepare for school.'

'Ugh! That will take a day! You just want me to go home early because *you* have to,' the girl accused unfairly. 'He's my father and if he wants me to stay longer, I'm staying,' she delivered with her arms folded, an obstinate pout to her mouth.

'And I'm still your legal guardian,' Mel emphasised strongly, wishing she could have avoided this set-to with her daughter. Already she could feel the division, the threat… 'And when I say you're coming home, you're coming home.'

In fact, in the end, what Mel wanted didn't come into the equation. Vann stayed firm, with Zoë only too willing to back him up, so that Mel was left with no choice but to give in.

'Is that child of yours still in Italy?' Jonathan enquired one morning towards the end of August, coming into Mel's office as she was watering a plant on top of her filing cabinet. Though he hadn't actually asked, he seemed to think Zoë was still with Karen, and Mel hadn't been able to bring herself to enlighten him. Nor had she told him, since the need hadn't arisen, that she had spent her second week in Italy at Vann's villa.

'Yes, she's still there,' she responded, relieved to be able to tag on, 'but she's flying home tomorrow.' She was meeting Zoë at the airport around lunchtime and was counting every second. It was the first time Zoë had ever spent a birthday away from her and Mel had missed her unbelievably—not just on her birthday, but over the whole lonely month.

'In that case, why don't we both go out and celebrate tonight?'

'Celebrate?' Mel echoed, eyeing him curiously. He in

turn was eyeing the cheese and tomato sandwich lying, half-eaten, on a paper napkin on her desk.

'I see you're lunching early today.' He grinned, making a great show of consulting his wrist-watch, glinting gold against the golden hairs. It was only ten-forty and he knew she would already have had a light breakfast. 'Must be one of your hungry days. It's just as well then that I've got somewhere special lined up for dinner.'

'Have you?' The thought of Zoë coming home lent added warmth to her smile. 'And what are we celebrating?' she enquired brightly.

'Winning Vann over on to our side. We had the go-ahead to handle all Heywood's new advertising today.' Admiring grey eyes ran over the dark tailored jacket and skirt she wore so well. 'I know we had a few cross words while we were in Italy, but I understand perfectly how a guy like that could turn any woman's head.' Did he? 'After all, I did practically throw the two of you together.' He looked spruce in his dark grey suit, blue shirt and grey and blue striped tie as he placed a file down on her desk. He seemed happy, friendlier towards her, too, than since before the conference. She realised it was because he thought Vann was out of the picture again. 'I'd just like to say, good work, Mel.'

She tried not to let any feelings show beyond those of a professional nature as calmly she accepted the news of the Heywood contract along with Jonathan's praise and his invitation to dinner.

Well, why shouldn't she accept? she thought, after he had gone. Staying in at night, thinking about Vann, was only a recipe for disaster, and that was what she had been doing most evenings since she had come back.

During those last few days in Italy he had been courtesy—even kindness—itself, throwing himself into his new found role of fatherhood with a joy and enthusiasm that had been no less than genuine. One evening he had taken them both to a concert in Ravello, a village situated way up on the rocky mountainside, where they had listened to classical music in the roof-garden of a Norman-Arabian villa.

They had spent hours on his yacht, when he had shown both Zoë and Mel the basics of sailing. Another day they had taken a picnic to a private beach and thrown pebbles into the sea, seeing who could throw the farthest, like a normal, everyday family doing normal, everyday things together. But the uninhibited lover of the previous week had stayed well and truly in the wings, held by a rigid self-discipline that had both frustrated and tortured Mel.

Whether he had wanted to or not, he hadn't touched her, or allowed himself even to be alone with her for any length of time, as if he'd feared that, in doing so, he might be stretching that iron-hard restraint too far. And when the day had come for her to leave, he had let her, driving her to the airport, alone, since Zoë had chosen to stay and help Marco and Quintina harvest the olives. Their conversation had been non-committal on the journey to Naples, their relationship too tenuous to risk anything else. It was when it had been time for her to go through into the departure lounge, before she had even realised what was happening, that he had swept her into his arms, kissing her with a hard finality that had only assured her of what she already knew. That this was goodbye. His breathing had been laboured when he'd released her, as though he had put all his pent-up frustrations over the past week into that one kiss. So why had he been so determined to deny them both?

Tearing into the rest of her sandwich with wounded aggression, Mel forced herself to carry on working, as though she didn't feel this great gaping emptiness inside.

She was the same self-reliant, self-assured woman she had been before she had gone to Positano, she told herself firmly, but knew she couldn't fool herself, even if she managed to fool the rest of the world. Seeing Vann Capella again had changed her.

She didn't feel like going out with Jonathan that evening and it took every ounce of will-power she possessed to get herself ready.

She was in her bathrobe, make-up fixed, hair still loosely swept up from her shower, when the doorbell rang at seven.

Darn it! she thought, wondering why he had to be so early, but when she opened the front door it was with a cry of surprised pleasure.

'Zoë! What are you—?' The girl's arms were around her, her thin jacket wet from the rain that had started as Mel was driving home from work. But it was to the familiar figure of the man standing behind her daughter that Mel's disbelieving eyes flew. 'Vann!'

'Hello, Mel,' he greeted simply, a warm curve to his mouth as he followed the teenager inside.

'What—what are you doing here?' she found she was stammering as Zoë released her, heading straight for the kitchen as she always did, leaving Mel staring up into those formidably attractive features.

'I had to come to London,' he said. 'You didn't think I'd let our daughter come back on her own, did you? It just meant her coming home a day earlier than expected, that's all. I take it that's all right.'

She couldn't remember him closing the front door, but he had. Inside her home for the first time, he was looking curiously past her, along the wide and tastefully decorated hall with its high Victorian ceiling and silk paintwork, to the small mahogany table and her figurine lamp which was casting a pink glow over the walls.

'Yes,' Mel breathed, not thinking straight, because to have him actually standing there in her hallway filled her with an acute longing to throw herself into his arms, bury her face against his broad chest and sob out how much she had missed him. And because even though there were raindrops glistening on his loose hair and dark splashes on his light, casual jacket, the dreary English weather couldn't detract from his tanned magnificence. It was there in the hard vitality of his face, in the dark strength of his throat above the open-necked white shirt he was wearing with light, fitted trousers, so that he seemed almost to have brought a little piece of Italy with him.

'You look beautiful,' he whispered.

So do you, Mel thought, entranced, shaken out of it only by the disappointed young voice calling from the kitchen, 'Mum! There's nothing in the fridge!'

Those steel-hard eyes were watching her solicitously. 'Have you not been eating properly, Mel?'

'In the cupboard!' she shot back over her shoulder. It was where she kept a stock of Zoë's favourite cereal bars. 'I was planning to go shopping tomorrow, on the way back from the airport,' she explained, turning back to Vann. 'I had breakfast, elevenses and lunch. And someone brought in cakes this afternoon.' What did he imagine, that she was pining for him? 'Anyway, I'm going ou—'

She broke off abruptly. Jonathan!

'Yes?' Vann prompted meaningfully.

A cupboard door banged closed, followed by the impatient rustling of paper wrapping.

'I was going out to dinner,' she enlightened him, aware of that shrewd regard on her lightly made-up green eyes, on her smooth complexion, flawless even without the foundation cream she had only just finished applying. Now there was no question of doing anything else but cancelling her arrangements. She couldn't—wouldn't—dream of going anywhere—now that Zoë was home.

'A date?' Vann was behind her as she crossed over to the telephone on the table.

'It's mainly business,' she said.

'Not the obsequious Harvey!'

'He's not obsequious!' Mel snapped, swinging to face Vann, her stomach doing a triple somersault just from looking up into those dark, brooding features. Jonathan might come over as the far too dedicated company man, but that didn't mean she was going to stand for insults on his behalf which, after all, reflected badly on her.

'So it is him!'

God! Why was he always so smug?

'Yes, it's Jonathan,' she took some degree of satisfaction from saying. 'If you must know, he's coming round at seven-thirty.'

'Then you're obviously going to have to put him off,' he advised, a grim determination belying the silky tones. 'And, as you've nothing in the cupboard to feed either yourself or your daughter, you're both going to have to have dinner with me.'

'I can't...' Mel started to protest. Spending any time in his company now, loving him as she did, when it was all so pointless would tear her into little pieces, she thought, before another petulant groan came from the kitchen.

'Mum, is this all there is? I'm starving!'

Lifting the receiver from its cradle, Vann handed it to her. 'Better phone him, Mel,' he said.

Jonathan didn't take very kindly to Vann turning up and ruining his evening. He was already on his way to pick Mel up when he answered his phone.

'What do you mean? Capella's turned up with Zoë? I don't get it. I thought she wasn't coming back until tomorrow. And what's Vann got to do with it?' A car horn blared. It sounded as though Jonathan had just driven into a tunnel.

'I don't want to talk about it now,' Mel responded. She didn't want to talk at all with Vann standing there, coolly watching her. She also didn't think it was a particularly good idea to break the news about Vann and her daughter to Jonathan while he was on the road.

'You've just called off our date and I want to know why and I want to know now!' the MD's voice persisted from somewhere in the dusky suburbs.

Mel's mouth compressed, her eyes making a very expressive attempt at moving Vann into the sitting room. Fortunately, he took heed of her need for privacy and left her to it.

'I thought it was over between you and that guy,' Jonathan pursued as she watched Vann's dominating figure disappearing down the hall. His shoulders seemed to fill the doorway into her sitting room. 'I thought it was just something you had going in Italy. Don't lead him on, Mel. You don't stand a chance of pinning down a guy like that. So why are you letting yourself get so involved with him? And Zoë?'

You asked for it, Mel thought, turning her back on the now empty hall to say simply, 'He's her father, Jonathan.'

'What?' An invective came down the line as though Jonathan had had to make some sudden, swift manoeuvre. Another horn blared. 'You could have told me,' he grumbled after she had answered his further shocked questions with succinct openness.

'I just did,' she snapped, rather unfairly, she thought after she had put down the phone. Jonathan deserved better than that. But she was too keyed up by Vann's unexpected arrival to be her amiable best, especially when he could hear every word she was saying and might try to make something of her conversation with the other man. She could hear him talking to Zoë who had obviously joined him in the living room. They sounded relaxed, intimate, clearly at ease with one another.

'Disappointed, was he?' Vann said dryly when Mel joined him. He was sitting comfortably, long legs crossed at the ankles, one arm flung carelessly across the back of her settee.

'Not unduly,' she lied, glad that Zoë had gone through into her bedroom. 'We had a few things to discuss, but they can wait.'

'I'll bet they can.' He still looked grim but she ignored his innuendo that there was more to her relationship with her boss than there actually was.

Let him think so if he wanted to, she thought through a crushing desire to tell him that Jonathan meant nothing to her, that there was only one man who had ever made her feel a complete woman and that was him. But she kept silent on that score, graciously giving in to Vann's insistence on taking her and Zoë to dinner, although when it came to paying the bill in the small Greek restaurant where he had taken them Mel tried to insist on an equal contribution.

'Scared that letting me pay the bill will constitute surrendering your independence, Mel?' he enquired almost derisively, glancing after Zoë who was heading in the direction of the Ladies. 'This isn't one of your PR dinners. And tonight I'm not one of your clients. This is called sharing a pleasant evening with my daughter and the mother of my child. You denied me any right to do anything for her all the time she was growing up. Don't deny me this.'

She would have protested further, but something in his tone tugged at her heart, making her accept his generosity without any further fuss.

He stayed four days in all, booking into the West End hotel where he was negotiating a deal with some Japanese clients.

'Why isn't he staying with us?' Zoë enquired, getting up the morning after Vann had brought her back, only to find her father had left shortly after she had gone to bed.

'Because he has to be near the people he's involved with,' Mel answered, unable to tell her daughter the truth. That she hadn't invited him to, especially since he had shown no inclination to stay.

Apart from when she had left Naples that day when he had sent her off with that devastating parting kiss, he had shown her nothing but that same cool restraint. All he saw fit to bestow upon her on leaving each evening was a light peck on the cheek, as though his fierce passion for her had burned itself out in the heat of the Neapolitan sun. The only thing binding them together now was Zoë, she accepted painfully, with whom he spent every available moment when he wasn't working.

The evenings, though, were bitter-sweet for Mel. Whether they went out or stayed in, when she cooked dinner for the three of them, as she insisted on doing that last evening of Vann's visit, neither their fascinating discussions on books, music or current affairs after Zoë had gone to bed, nor even their shared humour, could break through the impenetrable barrier that seemed to have sprung up between them.

For Mel it was a strain, and sometimes, particularly during that last evening, she noticed the tense lines about his face and realised that he was finding it a strain, too. Obviously, any sexual involvement with her now that he knew she wasn't just a willing female but the mother of his child, could cause complications he definitely didn't want. Being with her, therefore, had to be taxing his red-blooded urges to the limit, just as being with him and remembering the shameless passion they had shared, was taxing hers. She was only glad that at least Zoë was happy. After all, she tried convincing herself, that was really all that mattered.

The following day was the start of the new school term and Mel would normally have driven Zoë to school on her first morning. But, waking with one of her blinding headaches, Mel was only able to phone for a taxi for the teenager before taking a couple of pain-killers and going straight back to bed.

The doorbell woke her, ringing persistently through the flat.

Her headache was gone, leaving only the usual grogginess, Mel was relieved to discover as she padded, barefoot, down the hallway to the front door.

'Vann!'

'Are you all right?' he asked, his concerned eyes straying briefly down over her short white cotton robe. 'I rang your office. Hannah told me you were off sick.'

She nodded, pulling the door wider to admit him. What was he doing here? Wasn't he supposed to be flying somewhere this morning?

'Yes,' she said, explaining, but not that she had been awake all night wondering how he could leave her with only the usual emotionless kiss, without making any plans to see her again.

It was only then that she realised how awful she must look with no make-up on and her hair falling wildly about her shoulders.

'You've never looked sexier.' He grinned, aware of why her hand had suddenly flown to her face, while her heart seemed to clamour.

In an immaculate dark suit and white shirt, this was one rare occasion when he was sporting a tie, an image which, from his constrained black hair to his gleaming black shoes, was no less than awesome.

With a composure she was far from feeling, she asked, 'Why did you ring the office?'

'I wanted to talk to you. Alone. There are things we need to discuss.'

'Like what?' she queried.

'I don't suppose you've seen this?'

He was unfolding one of the more gossipy tabloid newspapers. It had been folded over at a certain page. There, taken in the busy restaurant where she had met Vann and

Zoë during her lunch-break two days before, was a picture of Mel looking besotted by the dark man sitting across the table from her. Inset, there was a separate picture of Zoë.

'That man with the camera!' she said, aghast. There had been a hen-party or something going on behind them, and she had thought he had been photographing that.

Quickly, Mel took the newspaper from him and read the short article beneath the picture with growing disbelief.

It was all there. Who *she* was. The double tragedy fourteen years ago. Speculation about Zoë. It left nothing to the imagination but that Vann had fathered the child.

'I don't believe this!' Mel breathed, utterly dismayed. Someone had done their homework on her and done it well. 'Why would anyone have wanted to have done this?' she agonised, and knew the answer even before Vann replied.

'Sensationalism. That's all it is. It'll simmer down when there's something more newsworthy to print.'

'Simmer down!' Mel breathed, flabbergasted. 'And what about Zoë? It's her first day back at school. She'll suffer agonies over this when her peers find out.'

'I don't think so,' he said, calmly removing the newspaper from Mel's trembling fingers. 'Unlike you, she hasn't wanted to keep it hidden that I'm her father. She's been telling practically everybody we've bumped into—here and in Italy—so it's hardly surprising someone got hold of the story. Unlike you, my sweet, she seems very proud of the fact.' His tone wasn't very gentle, neither was his endearment. 'I suppose it was bound to become public sooner or later.'

'But it makes it seem as though I…I went to bed with you even though Kelly died. Regardless…' She was shaking her head, unable to bear it. Now everyone would read her shaming secret. Colour suffused her cheeks just thinking about it.

'The truth is, Mel…' the paper rustled as he folded it

again, tossed it down on to her little mahogany table '…you did.'

That wry comment didn't help to make her feel any better. It was all right for him, she thought waspishly. He was used to publicity!

'It wasn't quite like that, and you know it,' she tossed back in defence of her actions. 'But no one's going to know that. People are going to think—'

'To hell with what people think!'

She flinched from his raw anger. 'People believe what they read,' she told him abrasively.

'Yes,' he accepted after a moment, and she wondered if it was remembering how she had been so ready to—and about him—that made his lips compress, made him drag in his breath as though for steadying air.

'I think we should get married,' he said.

'What?' She looked at him incredulously, not sure she had heard him correctly. And when he repeated the statement, 'Why?' she challenged, her heart beating like a bat's wings in her ears. 'Because of that article?'

'Don't be ridiculous,' he said. 'My skin's thick enough to be able to withstand journalistic dross like that. I was going to suggest it even before I saw that paper.'

Was he? She was going weak at the knees.

'Why then?' He couldn't possibly want to, not just for herself, not after the way he could so easily call a halt to any relationship with her even if, for some reason, he was changing his mind about it now. 'Because of Zoë?'

The battle she was having to keep her emotions reined in made her sound as though she were almost jeering his proposal and, from his hard assessment of her, he thought so, too.

'Isn't that a good enough reason?' he asked, his tone devoid of emotion.

No, I want the man I marry to love me! I want you to

love me! But she merely looked at him askance, hurting as she said bitterly, 'To make it legal and above board?'

A nerve twitched on one side of that clean-shaven jaw. 'I don't give a damn about legality or how things look,' he breathed. 'What I do care about is dragging my daughter backwards and forwards between where you are and wherever I might be, because, believe it or not, I want to spend as much time with her as I can. I missed her childhood, but I'm sure as hell not going to miss out on her adolescence. I'm going to be there for her—whenever she wants me—with or without her mother—but, unless you're prepared to be totally selfish, I'm sure you'll agree that I'm making some sense, and say "yes". The kid needs two parents. Living and working together. At least while she's still growing up. When she's an adult—got a stable life of her own—that's different. You can do what you like. Divorce me if you want to.'

Just like that. He was proposing to her like it was some business deal, Mel thought torturedly. A contract that could be terminated as soon as it had been deemed to have served its use.

For a moment she closed her eyes, trying to blot out the sight and sound and scent of him, that subtle spice he used that, without all his other assets and attributes, was working on her senses to try and lure her into accepting one glorious chance to be with him.

But he hadn't said he loved her. How could he, when he didn't? When his world hadn't been knocked off its axis as hers had been? He was only motivated by the misery of his own childhood. That was what was making him insist on marrying her. But, even for Zoë's sake, she couldn't do what he was suggesting. If she did, she would only end up with a heart torn in more pieces, if it were possible, than it was now.

'But I don't love you.' It was agony to say it, but somehow she managed it, and saw his lashes come down, veil any emotion her declaration might have produced.

'I'm not asking you to,' he said, sounding cold and unperturbed. 'Only that you help me provide a loving, secure home for our daughter. We like each other, don't we? Intellectually, we're well suited. And even you can't dispute that we're pretty darn good in bed.'

She wished he hadn't mentioned that. Just the thought of their wild, uninhibited lovemaking while they had been in Italy was making every erogenous zone work overtime. She had to stay strong.

'It was good. But not that good,' she tossed back crazily in a desperate attempt to stave off the temptation of all he was suggesting.

And knew it was a mistake when he said sardonically, 'No? Then perhaps you need reminding.'

'No, Vann!' As he reached for her, Mel's hands flew up to resist him, and met a wall of steel beneath the impeccable suit. But her own body was his ally, an addict for the pleasure that only this man could give her and, even before he swept her up into his arms, she knew it was already too late.

CHAPTER TEN

SHE had been prepared for brutality, a swift, angry pleasure she would nonetheless have welcomed, heightened by enforced abstinence and their weeks apart.

It was therefore a shock to realise that those masculine energies were still governed by an iron control, held in check even when she made him gasp with the most intimate caress of her mouth, even when she lay there, begging him to love her. He seemed determined to take his time and he did, opening her body to his with the prolonged and torturous rapture of his tenderness.

She cried out his name as he took her, and was sobbing as the shuddering spasms of their mutual orgasm ebbed away.

Without a word, Vann eased himself away from her, got up and went into the adjoining bathroom, turning on the shower. Within minutes he had returned, one of her peach bath towels slung around his hips, as he stood with his gaze raking over her tear-stained cheeks, over her mouth, soft and swollen from his kisses.

'Do I take it then that this is your answer?'

Oh, how could he? Mel thought, wanting to tell him that it was because it had been so wonderful that she was crying. Because it had moved her so much that until he had looked at her in that cold, unsympathetic way she had been all for surrendering her very future to him. But how could she? she thought wretchedly, when the reality was that he didn't love her? When he could make any woman feel as though she had died and gone to heaven, simply by taking her to bed, while he remained unaffected and immune?

'Vann, I...' What could she say? Not the truth. Anything but that. It was humiliating enough his knowing that she couldn't resist him sexually. But if he knew of her emotional vulnerability as well, he would use every ounce of persuasion he had to get her to marry him. And it wouldn't take much... 'I can't. It's much too soon. I can't do it. Even for Zoë,' she added to strengthen her argument. It was easier than saying, I want you and need you, and I would never be able to bear it if you decided to leave me. 'And I've got my career...'

'And nothing in the world should be allowed to stand in the way of that!'

'That isn't fair!'

'Isn't it?' he rasped.

'No!' She was sitting up now, holding the duvet to her nakedness, watching from under her spiky lashes as he shrugged back into his clothes.

'It's not just your career, is it, Mel? The reason you won't consent to marry me. I think it goes much, much deeper than that. You're nursing a grievance and it's going to swallow you up, Mel, unless you come to your senses and do something about it before it ruins your life.'

What did he mean? she wondered, aware of him slipping on his shoes, stuffing the tie he'd been wearing unceremoniously into the pocket of his jacket. Was he saying she still had some grudge against men as he'd come right out and accused her of having that day at the villa? Or was it simply because she'd made a fuss the other day when he'd bought Zoë some shoes? Because he'd resented being told that she was responsible for her daughter's clothes? 'When you've sorted yourself out,' he went on, moving away from the bed before she had a chance to challenge him about it, 'perhaps you'll let me know. *If* that day ever comes.'

With that he walked out of the room and a few moments later she heard the front door close firmly behind him.

* * *

The next few weeks passed in a blur of misery for Mel. The only time she saw Vann was during his brief visits to collect or return Zoë, on top of which she couldn't help noticing a gradual change in her daughter.

'She's so uncommunicative these days,' Mel confided to Karen over tea at the Ritz during one of the model's regular shopping trips to London. 'Unless she's talking about Vann,' she appended, piqued. 'She can't wait to spend her weekends with him when he comes to London, but she never tells me anything about what she's been doing. I know I'm probably being silly, but I feel I'm losing her, Karen.'

'She's only doing what all normal teenagers do, Mel,' the brunette told her reassuringly, looking willowy in a dark blue blouse and fluid trousers as she poured tea into two delicately patterned cups. 'As for Vann, he asked you to marry him and you refused, so now he's just getting his own back, probably by trying to show you what you're missing. Reading between the lines, I'd say the man was crazy about you,' she concluded laughingly.

With a sudden quickening of her heart, Mel took the steaming cup her friend handed her, but she wasn't convinced. OK, Karen *was* shrewd, she thought. After all, the woman had shown a distinct lack of surprise the last time they had met up, just after Karen had come back from Switzerland, and Mel had told her about her past relationship with Vann.

'I guessed there was more to it than you were letting on,' the ex-model had amazed her by saying, adding with discomfiting canniness, 'And I think there still is.'

But Karen didn't know Vann, Mel told herself, spreading her second scone with a good dollop of strawberry jam. Or the way his childhood had affected him. No, he just thought she was being selfish for not giving in to his demands to—as he thought—put Zoë first. That was why he was getting his own back, she decided. Not for the romantic reason Karen seemed to think.

The half-term holiday came, and with it Vann to take Zoë off to Italy.

'I don't know why you have to keep her the whole week,' Mel complained, folding clothes into the open suitcase on the teenager's bed while Zoë sorted out her toiletries in the bathroom. 'Don't you think that sometimes it would be nice if she could spend some of her free time with her mother?'

'Have you asked her to?'

'What do you think?' Mel looked accusingly up at him standing there on the other side of the single divan. A collection of posters of Zoë's favourite pop idols filled the wall behind him. 'She'd rather spend her time in Campania.' Her tone was clipped, her actions reflecting it as she tossed a light sweater unceremoniously into the suitcase, concluding, 'Much more fun!'

'You can come, too.'

She looked at him quickly, the cool penetration of his eyes on top of that softly delivered statement making her turn away, flummoxed.

'You know I can't.' She had to work, for one thing. For another, he wasn't getting round her like that!

'You could join us, you know, later in the week.' He had already told her that they would be flying back and spending two or three days in Surrey where he had business to attend to. 'I'm sure we'd both appreciate it if you did.'

She knew she could easily have done as he was suggesting and still get to the office, wondering if he thought he could tempt her with the prospect of being waited on for a few days in one of his usual five-star hotels. Because she was tempted, and not just by that. But even his invitation seemed to bracket him and Zoë together, leaving her, Mel, on the outside, and so, shaking her head, she said, 'It's too unsettling, racing off all over the place when I've got so much paperwork to take care of here,' knowing she was only depriving herself by refusing, but she couldn't help it.

'The offer's still open,' he said.

He meant his offer of marriage.

Mel held her breath, every molecule screaming in defiance of her decision not to give in. Just one word. That was all it would take…

'If I remember correctly,' she said, coming round the bed and having to pass him to reach Zoë's small chest of drawers, 'it wasn't exactly the proposal of the century.' Her voice was shaky, body still trembling from the accidental brush of her arm against his shirt sleeve as she selected the skimpy tops that Zoë wanted to take with her.

'With a woman as obstinate as you, Mel, the hearts and flowers didn't somehow seem appropriate.'

She elbowed her way past him. 'So you thought you'd try and bully me into it instead.'

'Is that what you thought I was doing? Bullying you?'

'Wasn't it?' Back on the other side of the bed, she threw the tops down into the case on top of the sweater. 'No woman likes to be told she's only wanted for her child's sake!'

'Well, of course I didn't just mean that.' He glanced over his shoulder, satisfying himself from the clunk of jars and bottles coming from the bathroom that Zoë was still in there. 'I've never been much good with this sentimental stuff, but supposing I told you that…that I want you to marry me because I want *you*. And not just for Zoë's sake, but for mine as well. Because seeing you and not being able to have you is driving me nigh on insane.'

An answering response pierced Mel's loins as she met his darkly intense features across the bed. Dear Heaven! she wanted to believe him. Unwittingly, her gaze fell to the evidence of his hardening arousal and unconsciously she touched her tongue to her top lip, aching for the driving power of his body.

So that was it. Sex. And he knew just how much she craved it with him, she thought, forcing her reckless, shaming need for him under control, realising with a crushing disenchantment the little game he was playing.

'I think,' she said, fixing him with faltering green eyes, 'that you'd say anything to get your own way. After all…' she shrugged '…what have you got to lose?'

'My self-respect,' he said. 'I'm not going to beg, Mel. It wouldn't matter what I said, would it?' He grabbed the handle of the case she had just thrown closed, swinging it off the bed. 'The truth is, you wouldn't believe me if I wrote it in blood!'

Ten minutes later he pulled out of the communal driveway with an excited Zoë, leaving Mel with the cool touch of his lips still lingering on her cheek and the feeling that it was more than just Zoë's company he was taking from her, and she didn't like it.

Throughout that week she kept herself fully occupied, working late or meeting colleagues for dinner to avoid going home to an empty flat. She even enrolled in a yoga class with Hannah, who didn't stop talking about Jack. Only that week, it became apparent to Mel, he had put Hannah out of her misery by finally overcoming his shyness and asking her out. But nothing, especially the younger girl's starry-eyed chatter, could stop Mel thinking about Vann and the life she could be enjoying with him if only she could let herself go and accept him on his terms. After all, because of her mother's two disastrous marriages she was under no illusion about romantic love. And, if she were honest with herself, wouldn't she really have him on any terms rather than suffer this agony of loneliness she was suffering now? So what was stopping her? she wondered, and couldn't really give herself an answer. And, if that wasn't bad enough, Zoë had scarcely spoken to her since she had been away.

It wasn't like the teenager not to keep constantly in touch. Normally she was on the phone at every available opportunity. But obviously Vann was keeping her so amused she didn't feel the need to keep calling her mother, Mel decided, sitting there in her office on Thursday morning, peeved and unhappy. It was just another example of her daughter growing away from her.

But they would be in Surrey now, she reflected, having spoken to Vann and then Zoë even more briefly after their plane had touched down yesterday morning, and telling herself she could have been with them if she hadn't been so stubborn didn't help. She also knew she could have phoned the teenager herself, but she hadn't wanted to appear like the possessive mother. But out of sight was clearly out of mind! And it was all Vann's influence, she told herself bitterly, with hot tears of resentment burning her eyes. He was responsible for taking everyone she had ever loved away from her. Kelly. Her mother. And now Zoë.

She sniffed back her tears, wiping her nose with the back of her hand like some angry adolescent, remembering feeling this loss—this sense of devastation before—and because of this one man. But it wasn't then. It was now.

Reaching for a tissue in her bag and blowing her nose, she told herself to be sensible, to pull herself together. After all, she wasn't an adolescent, she was a grown woman, she reminded herself, and surely able to handle things without falling apart like this!

But at last she was having to face the truth. Perhaps this was what Vann had meant when he had said her career wasn't her only problem. Perhaps this was the grudge he had referred to, this possessive jealousy and resentment that he had been aware of, even when she hadn't. But was she really allowing this deep, psychological hurt to control her life to such a degree?

Perhaps she was, she thought. But that didn't alter the fact that he was doing his level best to come between her and Zoë. And there was no way he was going to get away with that!

Trying to pull his number out of her fuddled brain, she started as the phone in her handbag suddenly began to ring.

Mel knew, the instant she heard Zoë's voice, that something was wrong.

'It's Dad! He's had an accident! I've sent for an ambulance! Oh, Mum, it's awful! You've got to come!' The teenager's words were punctuated by broken sobs.

Oh, God! Quickly Mel sat forward. Her blood felt as if it were leaving her. 'What sort of an accident? Zoë, answer me!' she demanded fearfully, because the youngster was sobbing too much to respond.

'I'm here,' Zoë said at last. 'He was checking something in the loft after the workmen left. They said…they said everything was safe, but the staircase collapsed! Oh, Mum! He isn't moving or anything!'

Wasn't *moving*… Fingers of ice clutched Mel's heart, her brain trying to assimilate what Zoë meant about him checking the loft. What loft?

'Zoë, where are you?'

Trying to stay calm for her daughter's sake, Mel quickly scribbled down the address Zoë gave her.

'So you…you aren't at a hotel,' she observed uncertainly.

'No, it's Dad's house.'

His *house*?

'Oh, Mum, hurry. Please hurry.'

'Are you all alone?'

She wasn't. A neighbour, it seemed, had called only seconds after the accident had happened, had offered to stay until the ambulance arrived.

'I'm on my way,' Mel said simply, before ringing off.

It was a horrendous journey out of London. The traffic was heavy and Mel's patience would have been strained without the added worry of how she might find Vann as well.

Zoë had said he was unconscious. That he'd fallen goodness knew how many feet. But what if he was terribly injured? What if he died? she thought torturedly, the sign for some roadworks blurring before her eyes from the tears she couldn't contain. She loved him and, if he weren't around, nothing in her life, with the exception of Zoë, would have any meaning. She had to find out how he was. She had to!

Stopping at some temporary traffic lights, unable to wait for a more convenient place to pull in, she dived into her bag on the passenger seat for her phone, only to discover that it wasn't there. It was always there, she thought, dismayed, checking pockets she had already checked, until she remembered. She had come out in such a rush she had left it in the office!

She thought of Jonathan and how put out he had seemed when she had said she had to leave at such short notice, and she guessed it wasn't so much the time off as her rushing out to see Vann that he objected to. He hadn't even asked about Zoë, though he'd been interested enough in the client Hannah had shown in just as Mel was leaving his office.

Vann was right about Jonathan, she thought. His interests were only ever self-motivated, his sincerity superficial. Whereas, though Vann might say what he thought, and not necessarily what one wanted to hear, at least he was always truthful. He made no false pretence. At friendship. At being anything he wasn't. At loving…

For what it was worth, he had asked her to marry him—asked her twice, she thought, pulling away from the lights, and both times, like a fool she had refused, flatly and ungraciously, only to realise too late that she wanted to accept—and on any terms—and that the only thing stopping her had been her own petty jealousies and resentments. Too late because she knew, after their last meeting, that he would never ask her again.

Zoë had said she was at his house, she reflected painfully. But Mel hadn't even known he had a house here in England besides the bachelor penthouse pad he used in town. Had he even told her? She racked her brain, realising he could have said he was staying on Mars for all the interest she had taken last weekend when he'd invited her to join him. She'd been too busy thinking up reasons why she shouldn't. And now…

She had left the city behind for the rural suburbs, hardly noticing the autumn landscape, the cattle in the verdant fields. Hardly noticing that the forest through which she had just driven was splashed with flame and gold, merely aware from Zoë's instructions and the dip of the hill, as the road opened out again, that she was almost there.

Mel steered, braked, changed down the gears and, coming out of the bend, gasped as she caught her first view of Vann's house.

Nestling in its own valley, at the end of a long, descending drive, it was a period, stone-built manor. Large enough for one to be able to breathe, but not so large as to be ostentatious, Mel decided, the adjoining woodlands beyond the rambling gardens and the quiet lake marking it out as a hideaway for the wealthy.

It was with trepidation that she knocked on the front door a few moments later. What would Zoë tell her? she wondered with her stomach muscles knotting. Or would she have gone to the hospital and left the neighbour to break the news?

How she got through the next few moments she wasn't sure, but she thought her legs would buckle in suspense when the door opened and a relieved-looking Zoë said, 'Mum! I've been trying to ring you! I've been trying and trying but all I kept getting was voice-mail—'

'Why? What's happened?' She was over the threshold, her hands fearful, gripping on the girl's slender shoulders. 'Oh, Zoë, how is he? Tell me!'

CHAPTER ELEVEN

'IT'S all right,' Zoë said. 'Mum! It's all right! That's why I've been trying to reach you. He's—' A sudden movement made the teenager turn, and Mel looked up.

'Vann!'

In blue denim from head to foot, his hair unusually tousled, he looked, as he emerged from one of the rooms off the spacious hall, big and strong and incredibly sexy. Not like an invalid lying injured somewhere. Not dying, as she'd let her imagination convince her he was, but very much alive!

Her throat clogging with emotion, she watched his measured approach, feeling his hard assessment of her grey trouser-suit, her pale and probably, she realised, very blotchy face, but she was too overwhelmed even to care.

'Tears, Mel?' They were welling into her eyes even as he said it. 'Over me? Surely not?'

'I thought…' She stopped, unable to go on and saw his chin lift in the subtlest gesture towards Zoë.

'Oh, well… I'll leave you two guys to it,' the girl announced, as though making up her own mind. 'Dad's bought me this fantastic pop video. It's really, really cool!' She made to run off, but then stopped, hair flying as she pivoted round and, with her young features turning more serious, said, 'I'm glad you came, Mum.' She shot a kind of triumphant look towards her father. 'I'm really glad you're here.'

Through misty eyes, Mel watched her daughter's swift retreat up the wide mahogany staircase. The whole place smelled of new wood, fresh plaster and paint.

She turned back to Vann, her eyes guarded, questioning. 'Zoë said you were injured.'

He was reaching around her. 'Zoë overreacted.' His achingly familiar scent, as he pushed the door closed, seemed to erase all the others. But, glancing over her shoulder, Mel noticed the pain that even that simple action had caused him.

'You *are* hurt!' Without a thought, her hands flew to help him. 'Why aren't you in hospital? Zoë said—'

'I'm all right,' he told her, but didn't resist the tentative arm she put out to assist him through the nearest doorway into the large yet comfortable sitting room, his hand clutching his ribs. 'I—don't need a—hospital.' Wincing between words, he dropped heavily down on to the rich burgundy settee that matched the thick brocade curtains and a large standard lampshade behind one of the easy chairs. 'Zoë just panicked.'

'But she said you were knocked out…'

'I've been knocked out by a lot of things in my time, but I always recover.' Cynicism hardened his voice, the painful twist of his smile.

'Vann, don't,' she whispered.

'Why not? You're not going all sentimental on me, are you? That's not like you at all.'

The pained lines etching his face made him look harder, more formidable than ever and, ignoring the gibe, she glanced away, absently absorbing his impeccable taste in the surrounding décor and furnishings. If she'd had a free hand with this room she might have chosen the same things herself, she appreciated distractedly. That painting over the fireplace. The warm colours. The style of that chair…

'Of course you'll want to take Zoë home.'

She looked at him quickly. 'Why do you say that?'

'Isn't that the main reason you're here?'

'No.' I want to stay and look after you, she nearly said, but checked herself. She didn't want to tell him while he was in this mood. 'She said she'd sent for an ambulance. What did you do? Make her cancel it?'

'You're darn right I did!' he said, ignoring the small reproof in her voice. 'She didn't want to, but I insisted.'

She could see Zoë protesting over the ambulance, imagine the battle of wills that would probably have ensued. But, unlike with her, Mel thought, when sometimes she had to yield to her daughter's intractable spirit, Vann would have got his way.

'I was going to bring her back early tomorrow in any case.' Pain furrowed his brow as he shifted his position slightly. 'Something's come up that means my going away—indefinitely. Or it will, as soon as these infernal bruises heal. I'll send for her sometimes. I don't intend losing touch with my daughter. But you were right. It was wrong of me to try and force you into marrying me—to try and put something there that wasn't. Wrong of me even to pursue you when you so clearly didn't want to get involved. God!' He laughed harshly at the air, wincing from the sudden movement. 'You told me enough times! It was my own fault for being conceited enough to think I could ever change your mind—that you might have changed your mind about me. But you've never really forgiven me, have you, Mel?'

She dropped down on to the settee. 'For what?' she whispered.

And realised, even before he said, 'For your mother—your sister. But I thought you'd had your pound of flesh fourteen years ago—over Kelly, at least. After that note you sent I could only deduce that that was your reason for sleeping with me. I told myself you were young and hurting. That it was understandable if you wanted to lash out at me…'

'Lash out at you? What do you mean?' She couldn't understand what he was saying.

'What else could I take it to mean? After the experience we shared. How close we got. Letting you know I wanted to see you again. Those four little words said it all—really gave me my comeuppance. *Thanks but no thanks*!'

'What are you talking about?' she queried, baffled.

'Your note. The one you wrote to me after our first night together.'

'But I never wrote anything like that,' she breathed. 'I sent you my number like you asked me to—and I said one or two other things, but it wasn't that. I'd never have said that.' How could he have believed that about her?

'Oh, come on, darling. It might have been in the heat of the moment—'

'It wasn't. I *didn't* write it.' Mel's teeth were almost clenched with the effort of trying to convince him. But she had to tell him. She loved him too much for him to go on thinking the worst about her and, steeling herself, she said, 'I'd never been with anyone before—not like that—and I wanted to tell you.' And she had, scribbling it down so joyously on the hotel's headed notepaper, convinced in her girlish innocence that he'd be flattered. 'I only intended to jot down my number, like you asked, but when I started writing I couldn't stop. I told you that it was my first time—that I'd been a virgin—and how what we had done was so special, had meant so much to me. I said how sorry I was about all you'd had to go through in your life and how much I was looking forward to hearing from you again. I thought, when you didn't reply, that I'd scared you off. That I'd sounded like a love-struck kid instead of the experienced type of girl you probably thought I was. But that's what I wrote. Not anything so vindictive and nasty as you're suggesting.'

Something besides incredulity lit the steely blue eyes. 'Then…' His face was lined now with puzzlement rather than pain. 'If it wasn't you, who…?'

'I don't know. I left it for Bern Clayton to give to you when—'

'Clayton.' Contempt was suddenly giving way to a hard, dawning clarity. 'So that's how he…' His sentence tailed off, his voice almost cracking. 'We'd had a row about my wanting to leave—give up the whole music scene. He would have been prepared to do anything to keep me on the road—lining his pockets. That sheet of paper was torn—over half of it missing…' he reflected aloud. 'Just those words under your reminder that I'd asked you to contact me. If you didn't write them, then I suppose he could have doctored your letter—added that vengeful little comment to make me think…to remove any reason for my wanting to stay in England…'

'What do you mean? He substituted what I'd said—and you believed it for all these years? Thought I'd written something so horrible?' she stressed, unable to comprehend herself how anyone could do anything so cruel. And when his eyes narrowed, as though he still couldn't quite come to terms with what she was saying: 'You were the one who told me not to believe everything I read, and you've done just that,' she pointed out. 'Been guilty of the very thing you accused me of in the beginning. For all this time…' Not surprising then that he had thought she had slept with him just to get her own back. To bruise his ego in the most basic way because of what had happened to Kelly. 'No wonder you didn't bother to contact me. And I thought—'

'Oh, but I did.'

'You did?' Her head came up in a blaze of fire. 'When?'

He shrugged. 'Oh, some months later. When I came back from Australia, although I must admit it was a rather half-hearted attempt after what you…what I thought you'd written. After all the publicity over…well, you know… I found the address where Kelly had lived—even contacted it—but there were new people there and no one had heard of Lissa

Ratcliffe. I didn't realise then that Kelly had been your half-sister and that Lissa wasn't even your real name.'

So he had come looking for her. Had wanted to find her again. How different life would have been if he had! she thought with a flash of pain.

'Is that why you tried to keep me at a distance when we met again in Italy? Because you thought I'd ignored your letter?' he asked wonderingly as the truth sank in. 'Do you really think I'd have ignored it if I'd received something from you like that?'

'Wouldn't you?'

'You really believe that?' He swore viciously, all his vehemence directed towards his old manager.

'You're in pain,' she murmured, her eyes anxious, when the sudden effort of moving made him wince again.

'Too hell with that!' He was reaching for her, and warmth and need and excitement ran through her as he sank back against the sofa, dragging her with him across his chest. 'Oh, my poor love.' He was stroking her hair, his hand strong and warm against her temple. 'What must you have thought of me? Don't you know I'm crazy about you? That I've always been crazy about you?'

'Oh, Vann.' She couldn't believe what she was hearing, her senses already spinning from the warm, hard contact of his body. Even injured, she could feel its latent power, and he smelt nice, too, so fantastically masculine.

'I just couldn't seem to find a way to show you. Or to make you see that what we had together wasn't just sex. That it was more than that. On both our parts. Because you do love me, don't you?' One strong hand crushed the wild flame of her hair at the nape of her neck, pulling her head back. 'Don't you?' He spoke with a raw emotion that threatened devastation to himself—and her—if she denied it.

'Yes.'

'Then let me hear you say it.'

'I love you. I love you! I love you!'

He exhaled sharply, burying his face against the perfumed column of her throat. 'Then why have you been so determined to keep us apart?' The pain was there in his voice. Not physical pain this time, but something deep and raw and impassioned.

'I don't know,' she admitted meekly. 'I was afraid.'

He lifted his head, eyes uncomprehending. 'Of what?'

'I don't know.' She tried to think, her expression as tortured as his. 'Lots of things. You didn't ever commit yourself, for one thing.'

'How could I?' His tone was disbelieving. 'You wouldn't ever give me the chance.'

'Only because I thought you only wanted to marry me to make it right for Zoë.'

'Only to—' He sighed heavily, shaking his head. 'I asked you to marry me, quite simply, because I love you, Mel. Surely you must have realised that?'

'But that week at the villa—you didn't want to sleep with me. You didn't even want to touch me!'

He gave an almost derisive chuckle at that. 'Didn't want to sleep with you? Not want to touch you?' He looked staggered that she could think so. 'Do you realise the battle I had keeping my hands to myself every time I looked at you? But I only insisted on separate rooms—tried to keep our relationship so low-key—because I wanted to prove to you that I was serious about more than just your body. I also wanted to prove it to myself because I was so wild for you all the time. I've never met a woman I've wanted so much, and I wanted to be sure it wasn't just some deranged state of infatuation that would fade if it were denied its most fundamental force. And you must admit, darling, it's one hell of a force between us. As for anything else, do you really think I'd marry someone I didn't love—who didn't love me—and make two—no, three—people's lives miserable simply to make things legal? I know I've got some old-fashioned values, but they aren't quite that archaic!'

'But you said I could divorce you as soon as Zoë was grown up…'

Momentarily, a cleft appeared between his brows. But then he laughed for the first time, showing his strong white teeth.

'Oh, you little fool!' he said with a smile. 'That was only because I was at my wits' end over how I was going to get you to marry me. I thought you'd be more inclined to if you felt you weren't making a lifelong commitment—that you wouldn't feel so tied. But that was simply desperate measures for a desperate man.'

'I wouldn't have refused,' Mel admitted then, 'if I'd known how you felt.'

'Do you believe me now?'

For answer she reached up and, slipping a hand behind his head, tilted her lips to meet his. 'You'll just have to keep telling me,' she whispered.

Those arms around her tightened and he said, 'I love you, Mel. With my heart. With my mind. With my body. I think I fell in love with you that first night when you came to my hotel, although I didn't know it then, not until afterwards when I received that terrible note I thought you'd written. But that night you gave me something to believe in. You seemed so lost and yet at the same time so courageous. I'd never met anyone who seemed so totally trusting—so sincere. When we made love, you gave of yourself as though I mattered. As though I were a real human being and not just some craved idol you were acting out a fantasy with.' As must have happened, she thought, with some of the girls he'd been involved with then. 'That's why I wanted to see you again, not only to know you were all right but because I think, even then, I recognised your capacity for loving. I wanted a share in it. I thought I could qualify. That's why it seemed like such a comeuppance to be sent that note.

'When I saw you again, that day at the beach, even though I didn't recognise you, I sensed something so profound between us I knew I had to pursue it, whatever the cost. Afterwards, when I found out about Zoë, I couldn't have been more pleased, but I was angry too because you hadn't told me she was mine. I thought it was because you really didn't like me very much—you seemed so adamant about not getting involved with me. I've tried telling myself that you wouldn't have responded to me in the way you did if you didn't care anything for me—yet…'

From what he left unsaid she recalled her unspeakable behaviour towards him.

'I've just been so scared,' she admitted quietly. 'Scared of making a commitment. Scared of losing Zoë. Oh, Vann! I've been so mixed up.'

'You're telling me, my love,' he murmured indulgently against her ear, cradling her in his arms, his lean hardness evoking those primal feelings in her. She didn't feel insecure any more. 'That's why I came over so heavy-handed at times, because I knew someone had to take charge of your life. For a company director you were making a pretty good hash of it. And I've never wanted to take Zoë away from you—only to share her with you. That's why I bought this place when it came on the market recently. I was hoping that eventually I could make it a home for all of us. Some parts of it were in a bad state of repair—' he grimaced '—the back staircase being one of them. But I've had work done—and not always satisfactorily,' he said, reminding her of how he might have been killed through someone else's negligence, 'for the past few weeks. I knew it wouldn't be too far for you to commute and I wanted so much for you to share it. I wanted to surprise you. I must admit on that score I had a good team. I couldn't have done it without Zoë.'

Mel's glance swept over the room—so pleasing to her taste, her mind going back over the past few weeks to her daughter's secretiveness, her eagerness to be with her father. She had thought the girl just didn't want to be with her. And all the time…

'Just wait until I see her,' she threatened jokingly, her eyes shining with joy. 'And the job be hanged!' Until today, she hadn't realised how little it meant to her. 'I'll go anywhere where you are. To the moon if you want me to. Stay here and make a home for you, if that's what you want.'

He put up his hands, laughed, and said. 'Hey, steady on! Is this Ms Sheraton speaking? No, I wouldn't demand that of you. You wouldn't be happy unless you were out there tackling new innovations. Clinching deals. The only stipulation in this relationship will be that you keep the master's bed warm and give some consideration to letting him make you the mother of all his children.'

'Is that all?' A kick of desire made itself felt deep in her lower body. She wanted him so much. 'A pity we can't start now.' Her hands were already moving inside his shirt.

'You're sure you want that?' He sounded uncertain.

'I'd like nothing better than to have another baby with you, but to watch it grow up together this time. And I know Zoë will be thrilled. Only…'

'Only what?' he queried, seeing her frown.

'You said you were going away.' A little cloud settled on her sunny horizon.

'Only on our honeymoon.'

'But you said…'

'What I said was that something urgent had come up—which it has in one of my European companies—and that I might be going away indefinitely, which I was prepared to do until you came here and I realised how much you cared.

I didn't think I could stay here any longer, needing you so much and thinking I could never have you. I would have kept in constant touch with Zoë, but, my dearest, I just couldn't bear it, thinking I was driving a wedge between you. And another rejection from you would have been too much to take. As it is…'

'As it is?' she queried, catching the sensual note in his voice.

'As it is,' he said, 'I'm quite happy to delegate responsibility to one of my senior management. I think, darling, you'll have to help me upstairs, because something far more pressing has come up here.'

'You're injured!' She laughed, heart leaping from his innuendo. But she could see what he meant.

'I've still got hands, haven't I?' His smile was wicked. 'So have you.' His gaze dropped, assessed, appreciated. 'A beautiful mouth, too. Besides, that pop video's going to last for at least another hour.'

And suddenly she was lying fully across his lap, locked in his arms, any sign of the pain he was suffering lost in his groan of satisfaction as his tongue penetrated the soft mouth that parted so willingly beneath his. 'Mel. My beautiful Lissa. Melissa.' In his whispered words there was sensuality and torture and awe. 'I'm not presuming too much, am I? You really do want to marry me?'

With his hands sliding down her body it was difficult to respond to anything but the raw pleasure of the moment. She was drowning in the rapture of their mutual love and need and desire. But she thought of the years that had been wasted. That cruel note from his rogue of a manager that must have torn him apart—torn both of them apart, until now. And, in response to his proposal, and the sudden thrill of his fingers on her bare midriff sliding upwards again, searching, teasing, creating ecstasy, she murmured, 'Yes, oh, yes. Yes, please…'

A LATIN PASSION

by

Kathryn Ross

Kathryn Ross was born in Zambia where her parents happened to live at that time. Educated in Ireland and England, she now lives in a village near Blackpool, Lancashire. Kathryn is a professional beauty therapist, but writing is her first love. As a child she wrote adventure stories and at thirteen was editor of her school magazine. Happily, ten writing years later *Designed with Love* was accepted by Mills & Boon. A romantic Sagittarian, she loves travelling to exotic locations.

[illegible]

Don't miss Kathryn Lasky's exciting new novel [illegible]

[illegible] from the cold [illegible] thought of [illegible] her [illegible] would [illegible]

[illegible]

But [illegible] had [illegible]

[illegible] with and the [illegible] Maybe [illegible] better [illegible]

[illegible] of a beauty [illegible] and one of the world's [illegible] greatest tax-

CHAPTER ONE

WHAT was that old proverb…? Something about keeping your friends close but your enemies even closer…Penny mused as she walked into the head offices of Lucas Shipping. Well, this was her first step into the rival camp and it felt strangely liberating. At least she was doing something constructive, not just sitting waiting for the axe to fall, as her father seemed intent on doing.

A blast of cold air washed over her skin as she went from the tropical Caribbean heat into the air-conditioned foyer, and a shiver ran through her…but whether it was from the cold or the thought of what her father would say if he knew she was here, she didn't know. A few weeks ago, when she had phoned him and voiced the idea of approaching Lucas personally, appealing for more time to pay what was owed, her father had gone almost apoplectic with rage. 'Lucas is the devil incarnate,' he had bellowed.

'But, Dad, you don't really know that,' Penny had insisted softly. 'It was Lucas's father that you had trouble with, and he's dead now. Maybe his son will be better.'

'You can be very naïve sometimes, Penny,' her father had grated angrily. 'Lucas Darien is just like his father, and I'll tell you this: I'd rather go under than ask a member of that family for any favours.'

Penny could just have left things. After all, it was really nothing to do with her; this was her father's business. She had her own career to think about, and as manageress of a beauty spa on board one of the world's biggest luxury cruise liners she was too far away to do anything anyway. However, a few phone calls later she had heard her father's anger turn to depression and she had known that she cared too much about him not to try to step into the breach. If she'd had enough money she would have tried to bail him out herself, but the next best thing had been to ask for leave from work and fly out to Lucas Darien's head office in Puerto Rico. Maybe her father was too proud to ask for help, but Penny wasn't.

Okay, maybe the estate had to go…maybe it was time her father retired. The sugar industry had been going through a bad patch, and he had been struggling for a long time to make the estate pay, but surely he didn't have to lose their family home as well as all their land? That house had been handed down through three generations of their family…it was far too precious to let go without a fight…even if that did mean humbling herself before the enemy.

'Can I help you?' The receptionist looked up enquiringly as she approached. She was a young woman in her early twenties, with ash-blonde hair and a slightly harassed expression in her blue eyes.

'I'm here to see Lucas Darien,' Penny said with brisk confidence, as if she had every right to see the man straight away, sidestepping the little fact that she had no appointment and knew that the man's time was like gold dust.

'Oh, you must be Mildred Bancroft, Mr Darien's new PA.' The woman's whole demeanour suddenly seemed to lighten, and she smiled at Penny warmly. 'Gosh, am I glad to see you…' Before Penny could say anything the phone next to them rang and the woman turned away to pick it up. 'Excuse me a moment…'

Penny was left in a quandary. If she owned up straight

away to the fact that she wasn't Mildred, the new PA, she probably wouldn't get past the reception and wouldn't see Lucas Darien today. She had already phoned twice, trying to make an appointment, and had been told she'd have to wait until the end of the month. Her father didn't have that much time to spare. He had already been warned that an eviction order for the twenty-fifth of this month was likely.

'Oh, hi.' The receptionist giggled at whatever was being said to her at the other end of the line. 'No, things are getting better around here now; the cavalry has finally arrived in the shape of the new PA, so that should take some of the pressure off me…thank God. Yes, I can make dinner tonight—'

'Shauna.' A deep voice boomed from the inner office…a voice that was unquestionably disgruntled. 'Will you please get me the files I asked for half an hour ago?'

'Got to go, Paul.' Shauna hurriedly put the phone down and grimaced at Penny. 'That's the boss,' she hissed. 'But don't worry, his bark is worse than his bite…he's quite nice, really.'

'I'd like them today, Shauna, if that wouldn't be too much trouble,' the voice continued in an even fiercer tone.

'Coming, Mr Darien.' Shauna flushed bright pink. 'He's not in a very good mood recently,' she whispered to Penny as she searched through a pile of papers that were sitting next to her in an untidy heap. 'His girlfriend broke up with him a few weeks ago, then his PA left to get married, and he's been snowed under with work…what with trying to organise things here and sort through his late father's business affairs. I'm having to do more and more…'

'Really?' Penny murmured. It was good to know that

the enemy was having his fair share of problems, and she couldn't help hoping the guy was absolutely miserable. He deserved it after the way he and his family had treated her father. She watched as Shauna started to rummage through the papers with increasingly nervous fingers.

'Where the heck did I put those files?' she wailed under her breath. 'I had them a moment ago. You can't see them, can you? They're in a green folder.'

Penny couldn't help liking this girl, with her dizzy manner and careless chatter. 'Is that them over there?' She pointed to a shelf behind, where two green folders sat next to a cup and saucer on a silver tray.

'Thank heavens for that!' Shauna exclaimed. 'Whoops…I forgot his coffee and it's cold now…another bad mark for me…'

'Well, you can't do everything,' Penny said sympathetically.

'No…' The woman smiled at her gratefully. 'I'm so glad you are here.'

The words were said in such a heartfelt fashion that Penny started to feel a bit guilty that she was not Mildred, the perfect new PA.

'Shauna, what is taking you so long?' Lucas Darien appeared in the doorway, one expensively shod foot tapping impatiently.

Penny's gaze went from that black shiny shoe up over the dark business suit. He was very tall and lean, and yet he had a powerful breadth to his shoulders. Her gaze locked with the dark intensity of his eyes and a frisson of shock surged through her. Lucas Darien was not at all what she had been expecting. The man was absolutely gorgeous. He was probably about thirty-six, he had melting dark eyes and a ruggedly handsome face; his jaw was firm and square, giving the impression of strength and determination, yet his lips had a sensual curve. She wondered what it would be like to be kissed by those lips…

The though sent further shock waves through her and she mentally pulled herself up. Okay, he was attractive…so attractive that he probably wouldn't be out of place playing some macho romantic lead in a movie. But she couldn't let herself forget exactly why she was here. This was Lucas Darien, her father's enemy, not some heart-throb off a movie set.

'This is Mildred Bancroft, Mr Darien,' Shauna said quickly. 'Your new PA.'

'Really?' Surprise registered in his dark eyes. 'You're not what I was expecting.' His gaze swept over her in an almost brutally assessing way that made heat run rampantly through her. How dared he look at her like that? And what did he mean by that statement?

'You are not what I was expecting either,' she murmured, tipping her chin up defiantly.

'What were you expecting?' he asked immediately.

The question took her by surprise, as did the sudden softening of his tone, the smile that played around the dark eyes.

'Well…' She shrugged. In truth she had been expecting him to look more like his father. She had met Lucas's father twice. He had been tall and handsome, but that was where the similarity ended. Lawrence Darien had possessed cool English looks: pale blond hair, pale blue eyes and an aristocratic nose down which he had seemed to peer rather contemptuously. No, Lucas was nothing like his cold, autocratic father…obviously he took after his Spanish mother. Maybe there was some hope that he would be more compassionate than his father…

'Well?' Lucas prompted her, and she realised he was still waiting for an answer.

'You're younger than I expected,' Penny improvised hastily. If she told him who she was before she got into his office, she ran the risk of being shown the door before she could have her say.

'Strange, I was going to say exactly the same thing to you.' Lucas smiled. 'From the CV that the agency sent me, I expected you to be at least fifty.'

Penny felt herself blushing wildly. Obviously he knew she wasn't Mildred Bancroft. 'Eh…well…I can explain…'

'Shauna, bring us through a coffee when you have a minute.' Lucas cut across her to instruct his receptionist, who seemed mesmerised by their exchange.

'Come through into my office.' He stood back and waved Penny through to the inner sanctum.

This was very promising, Penny thought with a smile. He knew she wasn't his PA, but he was still going to give her some of his time.

'Thank you.' She gave him the benefit of her sweetest smile as she passed him in the doorway. He didn't respond, which was somewhat unusual.

Penny was an attractive woman, twenty-eight, with long golden blonde hair, wide green eyes, and a petite figure that curved in all the right places. She was used to men smiling back at her. Persuading this man to treat her father leniently was not going to be easy, she acknowledged grimly.

The office was dark after the brightness of the outer reception. It took a moment for her eyes to adjust to the gloom. The walls were lined with bookshelves. The central desk was awash with files, and behind that were filing cabinets, their drawers wide open as if someone had been searching for something. Another desk in the far corner was covered in boxes that were filled with books and files. It looked as if Lucas Darien had recently disturbed a robbery in progress…either that or he was desperately in need of clerical help.

He motioned her towards the leather chair opposite his and watched as she sat. It wasn't lost on her that there was a brief flicker of interest in his dark eyes as she crossed long shapely legs. At least he wasn't completely immune to her. She had selected her pale green dress very carefully this morning, with the knowledge that it emphasised her curvy figure and had a small split at the front that was teasingly provocative. Penny had figured that if she was going to throw herself on the mercy of her father's enemy she needed all the help she could get.

'Obviously your CV isn't entirely accurate…Ms Bancroft.' He sat down behind the desk and leaned back in his chair to survey her through slightly narrowed eyes.

The statement took Penny by surprise; she had thought he had already figured out that she wasn't Mildred Bancroft. Before she could formulate her reply he was proceeding briskly.

'Let's see…there was ten years at Danovate…five years as PA to Sir Gordon Marsden…then your last job, three years as PA to Lieutenant Colonel Montgomery Cliff in Barbados?' One dark eyebrow rose. 'Unless you started work at the age of ten, I'd say something doesn't add up, Ms Bancroft.'

The sarcasm in his tone grated on her sensitive nerves. 'Or may I call you Mildred?' He leaned forwards suddenly, as if intently interested in hearing her answer.

There was something about his manner, or maybe it was the way his eyes seemed to linger on the softness of her lips, that made her nerves drop into freefall. 'Eh…well, you see, the thing is… You can call me Mildred if you like, but really…my name…' She was starting to sound as if she suffered from a bad speech impediment. Pull yourself together, Pen, she told herself crossly. Tell him who you are and how worried you are about your father. Damn it, cry if you have to…

'Good.' He didn't give her the chance to finish her sentence, just sat back with a satisfied smile. 'Mildred it is, then.' He drummed his fingers on the walnut desk. To Penny's overwrought nerves the noise sounded like a drum roll prior to an execution. She really needed to tell Lucas the truth now. Prolonging this misapprehension was just getting in the way of her reason for being here.

'You see, the thing is, Mildred, as long as you are up to the job here I'm prepared to overlook a slight exaggeration with your qualifications.' The drum roll seemed to be getting louder. 'As you can probably tell, I'm desperately short of staff here. So we'll give it a two-week trial, shall we?'

'Actually, Lucas, we are at cross purposes here,' Penny plunged in. 'I feel I must tell you—'

'Really, Mildred, I don't want or need to know your explanation about the CV. You obviously impressed the agency, because they have said you are worth waiting for, and they have a terrific reputation, so that is good enough for me. If you could just start as soon as possible that would be great.'

Shauna shouldered her way in with a tray of coffee. 'We really need an extra pair of hands around here, don't we, Shauna?' Lucas said jovially.

'Oh, yes.' Shauna nodded and smiled at Penny. 'Helen…that's Mr Darien's last PA…well, she left without giving proper notice. And things have been crazy around here.' She nodded towards the desk behind her. 'All those boxes need sorting out and I can't do everything—'.

'Yes, okay, Shauna.' Lucas hastily cleared a space on his desk and then reached to take the tray from her. 'Better get back to your desk now, and hold my calls for a while until I'm finished talking to Mildred.'

As the door closed behind the woman Lucas smiled wryly. 'Poor Shauna has been struggling to cope.'

'Yes, so I noticed.'

'This office is always busy; we deal with major businesses in the West Indies, and ship imports and exports from different islands. On top of that we now have my father's business to sort out, as he died six months ago and his affairs were not quite in order.'

'I'm sorry,' Penny murmured, for some reason feeling obliged to offer her condolences.

'My father was a property developer,' Lucas swept on, as if she hadn't spoken. 'And he had a large portfolio of investment properties which have all been passed down to me.'

'Lucky you.' Penny tried to keep the edge out of her voice. His father had been a charlatan.

'Mmm…but it's not as straightforward as it sounds. I've recently had to dispense with the services of my late father's solicitor—due to the fact that he was acting like a used-car salesman crossed with a Rottweiler. So, the boxes you see on that table, plus the cabinets behind me…along with two other rooms full of documentation at my home…have all been transferred from my father's office, and I'm trying to sort through the chaos myself. Which is where you come in. I'd like you to sort through the debris, filing and organising—'

'Lucas, I feel we have got off on the wrong foot here,' Penny cut across him impatiently. 'You see, Shauna misunderstood the situation when I came into the office. I really came—'

'Do you take milk and sugar?' Lucas asked her smoothly.

'Just milk,' Penny answered distractedly. Why wouldn't he listen to her? she wondered angrily.

'You see, the thing is that a number of my father's documents have gone astray—some very important ones at that. Deeds and other documentation for an old plantation house on Arbuda… You probably haven't heard of the island. It's tiny—just south of the British Virgin Islands.'

'Yes, I've heard of it.' Penny felt a tingle of uneasiness; of course she had heard of Arbuda, it was the island where she had grown up, and it sounded as if he was talking about her father's estate. 'You've lost the deeds to a plantation house?' she ventured cautiously.

'Well, they are not lost, exactly. They are somewhere amidst the chaos.' He waved a hand expansively to indicate the boxes and the cabinets behind him. 'But I need to find them pretty quickly. My father was in the process of repossessing the estate when he died. He had been holding the deeds as collateral because the old guy who lives there, William Kennedy, had owed him money for years. They used to be business partners, but my father had problems with the guy and dissolved the partnership. He told me that out of sentiment he let the debt ride for longer than he should. Kennedy is a bit of a no-hoper, by all accounts. Better that he leaves the place before he gets any further into debt.'

'Really?' Penny could hear her tone hardening. How dared he talk about her father like that? A no-hoper, indeed! Who the hell did Lucas Darien think he was? Her father had worked hard all his life…he was a decent, honest man…unlike his father. Lawrence Darien had been nothing more than a pirate…luring her father onto the rocks of bankruptcy and then trying to steal his land. The worst thing her father had ever done was to go into partnership with that man. It had ruined him financially and spiritually.

'Unfortunately I can't proceed with the repossession order until I find some of the relevant documentation,' Lucas continued, totally oblivious to the fact that Penny was rigid with fury. 'And if I don't find the documentation within the next two or three weeks my father's plans for the place are down the tubes.'

'What were your father's plans for the place?' Penny asked, trying not to sound too interested.

'He owned the neighbouring beachfront property, and there are plans for one hundred houses to go up there. William Kennedy's estate would provide vital access from the main road out to the beachfront development.'

They were going to build one hundred houses along that unspoilt coastline! Penny felt as if her heart had jumped into her mouth. She felt totally sick. All right, she no longer lived in Arbuda. Most of her time was spent at sea. But when she was given leave she always went home…loved her weeks of solitude, just walking and lapping up the scenery. The countryside around her family home was among some of the most unspoilt and beautiful in the Caribbean. It was a natural habitat for rare species of flora and fauna. How the hell had Lawrence Darien managed to get planning permission for one hundred houses?

'Unfortunately the building permission for the land runs out in a month's time, so if we don't make a start before then permission will be revoked due to a change of administration in the planning department in Arbuda.'

'You mean your father greased somebody's palm in

the planning office but that person is no longer there?' Penny murmured in a brittle tone.

'Probably.' Lucas shrugged. 'Anyway, we can't start the building work without the access through Kennedy's land, and if we don't get that within the next few weeks the whole idea is out the window.'

'What a shame.' Penny's tone was dry.

'Yes…isn't it?' Lucas took a sip of his coffee and regarded her steadily over the rim of the cup. 'So, you see, the sooner you can start sifting through the files and boxes the more chance I have of finishing my father's last project.'

Penny didn't say anything to that—her mind was working overtime. If those documents weren't found before the end of the month then the building wouldn't go ahead…plus it would stall her father's eviction from the land.

Could she continue with this pretence of being Mildred Bancroft, find the documents and then misappropriate them? All she would have to do was hide them somewhere, giving her father a few weeks' leeway until the danger had passed. The idea slipped surreptitiously into her mind.

But that would be dishonest, a little voice argued sharply, and she was not a dishonest person. Plus the real Mildred could turn up at any moment, exposing her as a fraud.

Then again, Lucas's father had been dishonest in his dealings with her father—plus he had obtained building permission fraudulently. She would only be helping to put that right.

In fact, if she misappropriated the documents for her father's property she would be helping to conserve an area of outstanding natural beauty, as well as buying time for her father. In a few weeks he would be harvesting the sugar cane and he would have enough money to make an interim payment towards clearing his debt. Okay, it was just prolonging his time on the estate, but it was better than giving up.

'So, when do you think you can start?' Lucas asked her suddenly.

Penny took a deep breath. She could probably manage to fake a few days as a PA. She had secretarial skills, and the management course she had taken before taking over the running of the beauty spa would stand her in good stead. 'How about straight away?' she answered quickly, before she could change her mind.

CHAPTER TWO

THEY said that night was the mother of council, and it was probably true—because all that night Penny tossed and turned and regretted the wild impulse that had made her pretend to be Lucas Darien's PA.

It had been a crazy thing to do. Mildred Bancroft could turn up tomorrow, and then she would be in deep trouble. Lucas could call the police; she could be prosecuted for fraud. Penny stared up at the fan that whirled around on the ceiling of her hotel bedroom and felt sick with apprehension.

All her life she had played by the rules… And now, due to one moment of insanity, she could be in deep trouble. But she had just been so incensed by Lucas's cavalier remarks about her father…a no-hoper, indeed! Her father had been a successful businessman before getting involved with Lawrence Darien. And as for Lawrence going easy on her father out of sentiment because they had once been partners…well, frankly there was more truth in one of the brothers Grimm fairytales than there was in that!

Lawrence had been out to ruin her father. The feud between the men went back years, to a time when they had been successful business partners. And the reason they had first fallen out was not over money, but over the love of a woman…and the woman had been Penny's mother.

Before she had married Penny's father, Clara had dated Lawrence Darien—had been head over heels in love with him, by all accounts. Then she had discovered he already had a wife in Puerto Rico, and a son! Clara had been devastated and had sought solace in the arms of William Kennedy. Two months later they had married.

Lawrence had been furious and had disappeared back to Puerto Rico, vowing revenge and leaving their business dealings unfinished.

Her father had gone back to running his estate and had tried to put Lawrence Darien out of his mind. Penny had been born twelve months later and the couple had seemed very happy. Penny had enjoyed an idyllic childhood, and if Lawrence Darien was mentioned it had only been briefly in passing. Yet Penny suspected that her father had never been completely sure of his wife's love for him, that there had always been that knowledge that he had captured the beautiful Clara by default, that she had really only married him on the rebound.

Then, when she was sixteen, Penny's mother had died and everything had changed.

Lawrence Darien had turned up at the funeral. He had offered his profuse condolences to her father and the two men had seemed to rekindle their friendship…and later their old business ties. Their partnership had never been legally terminated, so it had been easy to pick up where they had left off. And her father had found himself investing in land and dealing in property that sometimes he hadn't even seen.

Penny had been uneasy about the reunion. She remembered the two men sitting out on the porch until late at night drinking… She remembered the hard glint in Lawrence's eyes whenever her mother's name was mentioned. When she had pointed this out to her father he had waved it away as her imagination. But it hadn't been her imagination. Lawrence had systematically and ruthlessly set out to ruin her father. And by the time William had realised the fact it was too late.

Her father's judgement had been flawed not because he was a no-hoper or stupid, but because he had been in a state of grief. And Lawrence had taken advantage of that. Had even managed to get hold of the deeds of their estate. Now, almost thirteen years down the line, even after death he was about to exact his last and terrible revenge. The loss of the estate would kill her father; she felt sure of that.

Penny tossed and turned in her bed. If there was an opportunity to even the score wasn't she right to take it?

She stared up at the fan on the ceiling. She remembered the last time she had seen Lawrence Darien. She remembered asking him why he had treated her father so ruthlessly. He had smiled at her with cold contempt. 'I always settle old scores,' he had murmured, before turning his back on her.

Well, wasn't it her turn to settle the score once and for all? she asked herself angrily. For her mother, who had been badly hurt at that man's hands, as well as her father…

Finally, as dawn broke outside, Penny drifted into sleep. But her slumber was beleaguered by wild, terrifying dreams. Lawrence Darien was pursuing her through dark corridors. 'If you think you can fool a member of my family then you are wrong,' he told her when finally he caught up with her.

The touch of his hand on her shoulder made her blood curdle, but as he swung her around to face him something happened. The cold, angry face didn't belong to Lawrence—it was Lucas who was holding her.

'There is a price to pay for deception,' he murmured, his eyes on her lips. And suddenly the feeling of the dream changed from deeply troubled to intensely sensual. 'I hope you can afford to pay…'

'What is your price?' she asked huskily.

Then he leaned towards her and his lips crushed against hers in a kiss that was so incredibly passionate it was mind-blowing. Her senses reeled, as if she had just been pushed out of a plane at thirty thousand feet. She kissed him back, wanting so much more, wanting his hands on her body…

The shrill ring of the alarm made her sit upright. Her heart was thundering…and she felt incredibly turned on. That was the weirdest dream she had ever had. Even now the erotic intensity of it was deeply disturbing…so real it seemed to mock her somehow.

She pushed the covers of the bed back and went through to the bathroom to run a shower. Obviously she had eaten too late last night…or maybe it was the heat of this room. The air-conditioning didn't seem to be working properly and the fan was ineffectual.

If she was going to stay here for another night she should report it at the reception desk. Should she stay another night? Should she go through with this deception? Or should she fly home and comfort her father…help him pack up a lifetime of belongings, ready to move. Her company had told her she could take up to five weeks' leave, so she had time to organise the move.

The thought made a shiver of anger run through her. Why should her father move from his home? It was outrageous. Why should Lawrence Darien get away with what he had done? No, she would stay here and risk playing the part of Mildred Bancroft for today at least…

Maybe she would be lucky and find the papers straight away…put them somewhere Lucas would never think of looking and then fly back to Miami to join her ship.

Lucas Darien might never connect her with the missing papers…might never find out who she really was. And, even if he did, mislaying papers was hardly major fraud.

'Mildred…? Mildred…? Mildred, are you deaf?'

Penny looked up as she suddenly realised that Lucas was talking to her. 'Oh, sorry! I was miles away.'

'What on earth were you thinking about?' Lucas perched on the edge of her desk and grinned at her.

His closeness was deeply unsettling, as was the way his eyes crinkled at the edges when he smiled at her. 'I was thinking…'

Her mind groped for an excuse. She could hardly tell him that she hadn't recognised her own name! Or that she had been thinking that expecting to find the missing papers in one working day had been wildly optimistic. She had been in this office since nine, hadn't even bothered taking a lunch break and it was now time to go home…and there was no sign of the missing papers and depressingly she had only cleared two filing cabinets.

'I was just thinking that it must be nearly dinner time…my stomach is starting to feel like my throat's been cut,' she improvised.

'I'm not surprised. You've had no lunch and you've been working very hard.' Lucas looked with approval at the way she had neatly and methodically catalogued everything she had taken from the cabinets. 'You are very thorough.'

Penny shrugged. She was meticulous and organised in her running of the spa; she did accounts, kept track of stock, dealt with clients and staff. Putting Lucas's office in order was relatively simple, if somewhat time-consuming.

'You better call it a day now, though,' Lucas said as he glanced at his watch. 'Shauna left half an hour ago.'

'Did she?' Penny was surprised she hadn't heard the other woman leave. 'I didn't realise it was that late.'

Lucas grinned. 'She had a hot date, and I didn't have the heart to tell her she was actually leaving early…she has put in a lot of overtime these last few days.'

Lucas could be very nice, Penny thought hazily as her eyes drifted over him, and he looked extremely handsome in that dark suit. She wondered if he worked out to get that superbly fit physique, or if it just came naturally to him. Her gaze moved towards the penetrating intensity of his dark eyes, to the soft curve of his lips, and suddenly she found herself remembering her dream this morning…the sensual way he had kissed her. Heat licked its way through her entire body at the memory.

Hastily she pulled her gaze away from his face. That dream had been absurd, she told herself as she transferred her attention to the last pile of papers on her desk. Being attracted to Lucas Darien would be asking for trouble. Behind all that charm he was probably just like his father…he was probably married as well… Although hadn't Shauna said something about him not being in a good mood due to his relationship with his girlfriend ending? So maybe he wasn't married? Not that she cared.

'By the way, Mildred, I need some details from you so I can put you in the system—you know, the usual kind of thing…your bank account number so I can organise your salary payments direct to your bank account, and—'

'If you don't mind I'd like to wait until my two-week trial period is over before you put me into the system,' Penny cut across him swiftly. She was amazed at how coolly self-assured she sounded, when in reality her heart was starting to beat with fear and dread.

Lucas regarded her steadily, his dark eyes never wavering from her face. 'Why is that, then? Are you thinking you might not want to stay?'

'No…' Penny tried to smile. She had to play this very carefully, because if Lucas found out she was an impostor things could turn very nasty, very quickly. 'I'd just like to keep things on a casual footing until we decide to make my job permanent.'

'You mean our trial period is a two-way street?' Lucas shrugged. 'That's fair enough…' He grinned. 'I'd better be on my best behaviour, then, if I want to keep you.'

Penny was intensely tempted to relax and grin back at him, make an equally jesting remark. It would be all too easy to be taken in by his amiable manner, she thought hazily as she looked into the warmth of his eyes…all too easy to respond to him and relax her guard, and then…then he'd discover she wasn't really Mildred Bancroft and all hell would break loose. So instead she just nodded her head. 'Yes, good idea,' she remarked, and smiled lightly before turning away from him to continue going through the remainder of the papers in front of her.

'So how about if I start by offering you a lift home?' Lucas continued.

'That really isn't necessary…but thank you anyway.' Once again she gave him a very brief, cool smile before continuing on with her work.

But she was only pretending to be deeply engrossed in what she was doing; in reality she was intensely aware of his close proximity and she wished he would move away.

'I know it's not necessary, but I'm offering anyway.' Lucas seemed completely undeterred by her frosty responses. 'Whereabouts are you living, Mildred?'

The casual question caused a deep ripple of anxiety inside Penny. She wished she knew something about her namesake. Where was Mildred from? What information did Lucas already possess? She looked up at him, consternation clear in her green eyes. She hated this...she was no good at lying...she was going to be found out. Panic clouded her mind.

Then suddenly the fog lifted and she remembered something Lucas had said when he was interviewing her. Mildred's last job had been three years as PA to Lieutenant Colonel Montgomery Cliff in Barbados. She latched on to the memory in grateful desperation.

'Since leaving Barbados I've been in a state of flux, really. A lot of my possessions are still in storage, so at the moment I'm staying in a hotel here in San Juan.' Considering the only part of the statement that was true was the end bit, it sounded remarkably convincing. Penny found herself marvelling at her own ingenuity.

'So I take it it's not just Lucas Shipping that's on trial? It's Puerto Rico as well?' Lucas hazarded a guess. 'You're not sure you want to stay here?'

Penny nodded, willing to go with that theory and praying he would call a halt to the questions now.

'Well, I don't think you will regret coming to Puerto Rico. It's a truly beautiful island—very exotic, mile after mile of stunning beaches, a rainforest and mountain scenery that is quite breathtaking...plus its people are amongst some of the warmest and most hospitable of the Caribbean.' He grinned, a boyishly teasing grin. 'However, speaking as someone who has lived here most of his life, I'm obviously biased...'

She smiled back at him. 'Obviously.'

'So where are you from originally?'

The follow-up question was unexpected. 'Well, I...' Penny coughed to clear her throat. If she told him she was from Arbuda he was going to put two and two together before very long. 'I'm originally from Barbados.' She stuck to the same island that she was supposed to have worked on...in the hope that it might simplify things and she might remember what she had told him.

'Nice island. It must have been a wonderful place to grow up.'

'Yes...wonderful...' Penny could feel herself growing very hot and uncomfortable.

'Do you still have family in Barbados?'

'Eh...' She coughed again, and caught her breath.

'You okay?' He reached and slapped her on the back as she struggled to regain a lungful of air.

'Fine...thank you...' she wheezed.

He stood up and went to get her a glass of water from the drinking tap just outside the office door. Penny watched him surreptitiously from beneath her eyelashes. Did he have suspicions about her? she wondered. He seemed to be asking a lot of questions.

She had managed to compose herself by the time he returned, but she pretended that she was still short of breath just in case he started to resume his questions. But Lucas didn't pick up where he had left off; he just watched as she sipped the ice-cool water.

'Thank you,' she whispered hoarsely as she put the cup down.

'You're welcome.' He smiled, and then stretched over to switch off the desk lamp beside her. 'Come on, let's get out of here. I think we've both worked hard enough for one day.'

Penny reached for her bag, glad to push her chair back

and stand up. She desperately wanted to get away from him in case more questions were suddenly fired at her.

'Right, well, I'll see you tomorrow morning,' she said briskly.

He glanced over at her with a raised eyebrow. 'It's Saturday tomorrow, Mildred.'

'Is it?' Penny's heart sank. The weekend was the last thing she needed right now. It was vital she found those files before Mildred turned up and blew her cover...a two-day break could be disastrous. 'I'd lost track of time,' she murmured.

'Actually, I was going to ask you if you wouldn't mind doing some overtime this weekend?' Lucas asked as he switched off the overhead light and then held the door for her to precede him out of the office. 'The thing is that I really need to find those missing documents, and time is not on my side.'

'Yes, I quite understand.' Penny grabbed the straw gratefully. 'I don't mind doing a bit of overtime at all, Lucas. I've got nothing planned this weekend anyway.'

'Great.' Lucas smiled across at her. 'I'll make it worth your while financially, of course.'

Penny found herself waving a hand in airy dismissal. She couldn't have cared less what Lucas was planning to pay her because she didn't plan on sticking around to take any of his money. 'We'll sort that out at a later date, once I've decided to stay. Or you've decided you *want* me to stay...' she added hastily, not wishing to sound too sure of herself.

'I get the feeling that it's a rare occurrence for employers not to want you to stick around,' Lucas said with a grin as he opened the outer door for her.

'Modesty prevents me from answering that question.' Penny couldn't resist smiling back at him. It sounded as if he didn't have any suspicions about her at all…that had just been her guilty conscience. He'd probably just been making polite conversation when he'd asked her a few questions about herself. She was going to have to stop being so edgy around him otherwise he was bound to suss her out.

'So, where can I drop you?' Lucas asked as he locked the office door. 'My car is just down the road.'

'I'm going to get the bus, Lucas—'

'Don't be silly.' He strode away from her towards the entrance to a car park, leaving Penny little option but to follow.

In one way she was glad to get a lift back; she was tired and hot… On the other hand Lucas would know where she was now…would be able to go into the hotel and enquire about her.

Lucas unlocked a silver-grey Mercedes and she slipped into the passenger seat. Although it was nearly six, and the sun was starting to set in a blaze of orange and pink light, the heat of the day was still intense. The cool air from the conditioning unit in the car was blissful.

'So, where to?' Lucas asked as he pulled the car out of the side street and into the busy flow of traffic on a one-way street.

'I'm staying in the old quarter of San Juan.'

'Picturesque down there, isn't it?' Lucas remarked as he waited for the traffic to move.

'Yes, it's lovely.'

'Which hotel?'

'Casa del Clarinda. It's only a small hotel. It's on—'

'Yes, I know exactly where it is.'

'Oh…' Penny fell silent. She wished he hadn't said that, because for some reason it made her feel even more vulnerable. Now she was wondering if he knew the owners… After all it *was* a small hotel, and it was strange he knew 'exactly' where it was. She imagined him bumping into them in some bar somewhere and saying, *You have my PA Mildred Bancroft staying with you.* And the puzzled looks on their faces.

Then he'd start to describe her. *Long blonde hair, about twenty-eight, green eyes, five foot six….*

Oh, that sounds like Penny Kennedy.

A cold shiver ran through her.

'Is the air-conditioning a bit fierce?' Lucas glanced across at her.

'No, I'm fine.'

'You're shivering. Wind down the window and let some warm air in if you want.'

'Thanks.' Lucas Darien didn't miss much, she thought warily.

The car picked up a bit of speed as the traffic thinned out, and warm air flowed in, brushing the heavy weight of her hair back from her face. 'How come you know where my hotel is?' she asked, trying to sound nonchalant.

'It's got a very good reputation. Everyone knows it.'

It didn't sound as if he knew the owners…relief was immense.

'I was thinking that tomorrow you should work up at my house,' Lucas continued casually. 'I have two whole rooms full of my father's files up there, so the sooner you can make a start the better.'

Two rooms! It had taken her a whole day to get through two filing cabinets, so how long would it take her to get through that lot? she wondered distractedly. By the sounds of things she would be extremely lucky if she found those missing files before Mildred Bancroft arrived.

'But don't worry—I'll give you a hand to sort through them,' Lucas continued when she didn't say anything. 'I've got time tomorrow.'

'Oh, really, there is no need,' Penny assured him hastily. The last thing she needed was Lucas watching her every move; it had been bad enough having to share an office with him today.

'We'll get through them quicker with two of us working.'

'I suppose you're right.' There was little else she could say. Penny's heart sank. If he found the documents all this could be for nothing.

Lucas turned left, and the car bumped over the cobbled road as they entered the old quarter of San Juan. Penny knew this area quite well as her ship often pulled into port here. It was an area that was over five hundred years old and had been designated as a world heritage site. Buildings that were Spanish in character flanked the quaint narrow streets; they were painted cool pastel shades and had wrought-iron balustrades, some filled with a profusion of flowers.

'You can drop me here, if you like,' she said as they approached the crossroads that led down to her hotel.

'I'll drop you at the door; it's no problem,' Lucas answered in a tone that brooked no argument. 'What made you decide to come to Puerto Rico, Mildred?' he asked idly as he turned slowly down her road.

'Well…the agency offered me this job and I thought it sounded interesting…' She felt slightly breathless. 'I like to move around…see different places…'

'You're a bit of a free spirit, I take it?' He glanced over at her speculatively.

'Yes, I suppose I am.' At least that was the truth. She

did like travelling—it had been one of the reasons she had applied for a job on a cruise liner.

'That's something we have in common, then.' He pulled up outside her hotel. 'One of the reasons I started a shipping company was my fascination with faraway shores.'

'Did your father help you build up your business?' she asked curiously.

'No, he was never interested in trade on the high seas…just on dry land.'

'And were you involved in his property deals?' She didn't know why she asked him that; curiosity, she supposed. There was a part of her that couldn't help wondering how close he had been to his father and if he knew just how shady the man had been.

'No, I was always too busy with my own business. Why do you ask?'

'I just wondered if you had any idea where we should start looking in those files tomorrow,' she improvised wildly, and was suddenly glad that it was dark and he couldn't see how red her skin had become. She shouldn't have asked that question; it wasn't a good idea to sound too interested in his affairs.

'No…unfortunately I don't.'

'Never mind. I'm sure between us we'll find them tomorrow.' She spoke positively.

'Let's hope so.'

And let's hope I find them first, she added silently as she reached to open the car door. To her surprise Lucas got out and came around to open the door for her. Such old-fashioned courtesy took her aback.

She accepted the hand he offered and stepped out onto the pavement. The touch of his skin against hers sent a strange sensation of intense awareness shooting through her. Abruptly she let go of him.

'Thank you for the lift.' Her voice was primly polite.

'You're welcome.' He grinned. 'It's the least I could do after you've worked so hard, and through your lunch hour.'

The evening air was warm, perfumed by the bougainvillaea and jasmine that cascaded from the balcony of the hotel.

For a moment she stood staring up at him. Lucas Darien was incredibly handsome, she thought hazily. Tall and lean, yet there was that air of latent power about him. Maybe it was the breadth of his shoulders that gave him such a commanding presence, or maybe it was the way he met her eyes with such calm self-assurance. Whatever it was, he seemed to just exude sex appeal.

'I'll pick you up tomorrow morning, about eight-forty-five,' he said quietly.

She was so mesmerised, looking up into the darkness of his eyes, that it took a moment for her to register that him picking her up might not be a good idea. If he was to walk into the hotel and ask for Ms Mildred Bancroft she'd be in deep water.

'It's okay,' she said hastily. 'If you give me your address I'll take a taxi.'

'You like to be independent, don't you?' He smiled. 'But it's no problem. I have to come down to the dockside in the morning anyway. I have some business to take care of.'

'Oh…but—'

'If I'm running late I'll phone you. What's your room number?'

'Em…I…I can't remember. But, listen, it's just as easy for me to catch a cab and—'

Lucas reached out and tipped her chin upward, so that she was forced to look directly into his eyes again. The contact was brief and light, yet the sensation sent shivers of pandemonium racing through her from nowhere.

'I'll pick you up,' he said firmly. 'Don't worry about your room number—I'm sure the Casa del Clarinda has only one Mildred Bancroft in residence.'

That's what he thinks, Penny reflected in alarm as she watched him walk away from her.

'See you tomorrow, Mildred.'

'Yes…tomorrow…'

Lucas got back into his car, but he didn't drive away immediately. Instead he waited and watched as she turned to walk into the hotel. For a moment she was silhouetted against the light from the foyer. He noticed the shapely curve of her figure in the pale blue dress, the way her hair shone like spun gold. He remembered the way she had looked up at him a moment ago, the way her eyes had been flecked with some deep emotion… She had looked at him like that several times today. It was as if one moment she was deeply distrustful of him…ready to do battle with him…and the next she relaxed and gave him a most breathtakingly beautiful smile.

He would give anything to know exactly what was going on in her mind…

Lucas put the car into gear and pulled away from the sidewalk. The delicate scent of her perfume still lingered in the car, just as the memory of her wide clear green eyes lingered in his mind. There was something about the delectable Ms Bancroft that intrigued him, an air of mystery that needed further investigation…

CHAPTER THREE

PENNY woke at first light and quickly showered and dressed in a lightweight trouser suit that was a pale shade of oyster-pink. She applied a little make-up, to disguise the fact that she hadn't slept very well again, swept her hair back from her face with a clip and then went downstairs to the reception, to see if she could solve the little problem of what would happen when Lucas asked for Ms Bancroft.

Penny's heart sank as she noticed that the woman receptionist who was normally on duty wasn't there. Instead it was the man who had checked her in on her arrival. He was in his early thirties, and had a swarthy complexion and eyes that were boldly assessing. Penny hadn't particularly liked him—had thought he was just a little too interested in her.

'Morning, Ms Kennedy,' he greeted her with a smile as she approached the counter. 'You're up bright and early.'

Penny tried not to notice the male interest in his eyes as they swept over her figure in a rather blatant way, and instead smiled back at him. 'Thought I'd take a stroll before the heat of the day got too intense.'

'Good idea. Have you any special plans for the rest of the day?'

'Actually, I'm going out for the day…with a friend.' She kept her smile in place with great difficulty. Why couldn't the nice woman from last night have been on duty? she wondered with an inner sigh. She wouldn't have asked anything. 'In fact, he should be picking me up in a couple of hours.' She kept her voice light. 'Will you still be on duty?'

'Yes, I'm here until ten.'

'If you'd ring me when he arrives that would be great.' She fixed him with her most winning smile. 'Oh…and I almost forgot,' she said as she made to turn away. 'He'll probably ask for me by the name of Mildred Bancroft. That's my professional name.'

'What profession is that, then?' the man asked immediately, the light of interest rekindled.

'Oh, I do a bit of writing in my spare time, under the name of Mildred Bancroft. That's why I'm in Puerto Rico, actually, to do a spot of research for a book. Perhaps you'd be kind enough to tell the other receptionists, so that if a call comes for Mildred Bancroft they will put it through to my room, or take a message for me? I don't want to miss any important calls from my publisher.'

The receptionist opened his mouth, probably to ask her what she wrote, but Penny wasn't about to start embroidering her tale any further. She'd had enough lies for one day. 'Anyway, I'd better dash,' she said quickly, and pretended to look at her watch. 'The day is flying by, and I won't get my walk if I don't hurry.'

Her heart was thudding unevenly as she stepped outside into the bright sunlight. She hated all these lies. Had the man been convinced? she wondered. In case he hadn't she intended to find a shady spot to wait for Lucas's arrival, waylay him before he had a chance to go into the hotel.

Finding a shady place to sit and wait turned out to be easier than expected. There was a square directly opposite the hotel, and as luck would have it a tiny coffee bar was open. She took a seat in the window, so she could watch for Lucas's car in case he arrived early, and then ordered a cappuccino.

Hopefully she would find the missing files today. Then she would get a flight out of here and put this unpleasant business behind her. Her father need never know that she had meddled in his affairs…it would just be a pleasant surprise for him when the eviction order didn't come through on the twenty-fifth. That was presuming she was successful in finding the documents, and that Mildred Bancroft didn't turn up and ruin everything.

She was on her second cup of coffee when she saw Lucas's car pull up outside the hotel. Hurriedly she put some dollar bills on the table and rushed out without waiting for her change.

'Good morning, Lucas.' She called to him from across the road as he locked his car door. For a moment she thought he hadn't heard her. Then he turned around.

'Morning.' He leaned back against the bonnet of the car and watched as she made her way across towards him.

A warm breeze blew her jacket back, giving a glimpse of a black lacy top that fitted her svelte figure like a second skin. His eyes swept over her, noticing the long length of her legs in the elegant trouser suit and the fact that she was wearing very high heels that were impeding her progress across the cobbled street.

'You're out and about very early this morning.' He grinned at her as she reached his side.

'Thought I'd get a bit of fresh air before the heat of the day closes in.'

'Good idea.' He smiled at her; it was a warm, inviting smile and it made her feel a bit breathless. There was something about Lucas Darien that seemed to set her pulses racing. She tried to tell herself it was just nervous tension, because of all these lies that she was telling, but deep down she knew there was more to it than that. The thing was that she found him dangerously attractive. She knew she shouldn't be drawn to him, that it was a bit like the fascination that a moth felt towards a flame, but she couldn't seem to help herself.

'I always think that the morning is the best part of the day,' Lucas said as he went around to open the passenger door for her.

'Especially when the rest of the time is going to be spent in an office,' she agreed, trying to concentrate on the conversation and not on him.

'Are you wishing you hadn't agreed to overtime this weekend, by any chance?' He grinned.

'No, I don't mind.'

'Well, I promise not to work you too hard today. We'll stop about midday and have a leisurely lunch—how's that?'

'Let's see how far we get through those files before we decide how much time off we can have,' Penny said non-committally.

'If you are trying to impress me with your commitment to work then you are succeeding, Mildred Bancroft,' he said, a glint of humour in his dark eyes. 'Are you always so focused?'

'I try to be.' She got into the car and watched as he walked around to join her. It was true she usually had no problem concentrating on what was important. Trouble was, she seemed to be focusing on the wrong things when she was around him. He was very distracting. And the way he was dressed this morning was even more of a distraction. He was wearing casual clothes today, faded blue jeans and a pale blue T-shirt that seemed to emphasise the wide expanse of his chest and the taut flatness of his stomach. She was willing to bet that beneath that T-shirt there was a toned six-pack.

Swiftly she averted her eyes from him. Don't think about things like that, Penny, she told herself crossly. Keep focused on the reason you're here. Lucas Darien is the enemy.

He got into the car and smiled across at her. She smiled back at him. He had the sexiest eyes, she thought hazily.

'Don't forget your seatbelt,' he said.

'No, of course not.' Hastily she snapped out of her reverie and reached to put it on. Strange thing was, she hadn't felt this strongly attracted to a man in years… The last person who had interested her like this was Nick, and that had ended in total disaster. He had been the reason she had left Arbuda and gone to work at sea.

She had been deeply in love with Nick. They had lived together for over a year and she had been committed to the relationship, had thought he was too. It had come as a hell of a shock to discover he had been seeing someone else behind her back. That all the nights he had said he was working overtime because they were saving up to get married he had in fact been wining and dining another woman. The betrayal had hurt; Penny had sworn nobody would ever get under her skin like that again…ever.

Even though her break-up with Nick had been two years ago it still pained her to think about it. Firmly she switched her attention to the scenery outside. They had left the town behind now, and the powerful car was climbing easily up narrow mountain roads. The countryside was green and tropical—they passed plantations of banana and grapefruit—and the view down over the tumbling greenery towards the turquoise of the sea was spectacular.

Lucas turned the car through a narrow driveway that twisted up through manicured gardens lined with palm trees, before coming to a standstill outside a large colonial-style house. Steps led up to a wide porch, which wrapped around the building and was furnished with wicker furniture and a swing chair that was positioned to give the best view through the trees towards the sea.

The first thing that struck Penny as she climbed out of the car was the silence of the surroundings. All she could hear was the rustle of the warm breeze in the palm trees and the sound of the birds. It reminded her of her father's house in Arbuda.

'You've got a lovely place here,' Penny said as she walked up the steps with him to the veranda.

'It used to be an old coffee plantation house, but previous owners sold it separately from the land many years ago. It had fallen into a bad state of disrepair when I bought it, and needed a lot of work to restore it back to its former beauty, but I think we got there in the end.' He held open the screened door for her and allowed her to precede him into a large hallway.

Penny could see at once that no expense had been spared in restoring the beauty of the place. It had solid wooden floors covered by a Persian rug, and a wide sweeping staircase where a magnificent grandfather clock stood on the turn of the landing. She had a glimpse of a drawing room to the right, with gold and blue furnishings, and to the left a formal dining room with a long polished mahogany table. The house had a comfortable elegance that spoke of bygone days.

'My study is at the back of the house—' Lucas broke off as a door was flung open and a little girl raced down the corridor, closely followed by a black Labrador who barked excitedly.

'Guess what's happened this morning,' the child said eagerly, reaching up so that Lucas would pick her up.

'What's happened?' He obligingly scooped her up into his arms and then glanced over at the dog. 'Be quiet, Flint,' he said sternly, and the animal immediately fell silent, but stood wagging his tail and looking up at his master expectantly. 'So what's all the excitement about?' Lucas asked the child.

'Mrs Gordon was baking a cake and it burnt and black smoke came out of the oven and the smoke alarm rang and she shouted a lot.'

'Sounds like a morning of high excitement.' Lucas grinned over at Penny. 'We never have a dull moment here. Mildred, this is my daughter, Isobel.'

Lucas had a child… Penny was completely taken aback by the discovery. Did that mean he also had a wife? Since Shauna had mentioned his break-up with his girlfriend she had more or less decided he must be single. But she should have known better. He was probably a womaniser, just like his father.

She was aware that the knowledge sent a curious pang of disappointment flooding through her.

The little girl looked over at her with wide, serious eyes. She only looked about six years of age, and she was adorable, with a cute heart-shaped face, straight shiny black hair and eyes that were so dark they looked almost jet-black.

'Hello, Isobel.' Penny smiled at her.

'Hello.' She smiled back.

A woman appeared in the corridor behind them, one hand on her ample hips and a frown marring her rounded face. 'Isobel, come and clear up this mess you've made in the pantry, please.'

'Yes, Mrs Gordon.' Isobel didn't look in the slightest

bit chastened. In fact her eyes danced with mischief and merriment as she slipped down from her father's arms and dutifully headed back towards the other woman.

'I believe you've had a bit of an exciting morning in the kitchen, Mrs Gordon,' Lucas said jovially.

'The thermostat on the oven must be faulty,' the woman said with a shake of her head. 'I've never had such a disaster.' She glared at the black Labrador as he tried to sneak past her to follow Isobel through the door. 'And I've told you that the kitchen is no place for a dog,' she said sternly, pointing a finger at him. 'Out with you.'

Flint backed away and then stood staring at the door dejectedly as it banged closed behind the woman and child.

'And that was Mrs Gordon, my housekeeper…cum nanny,' Lucas said with a smile as he turned to lead the way down a side corridor. 'Don't be misled by her grumpy exterior; the woman is a treasure. Runs the house with smooth efficiency… Well, she usually does.' Lucas grinned. 'I've never known her burn anything before.'

'We all have our off days,' Penny murmured. 'Your wife must be grateful for her help. This is a big house to keep in order.'

'Unfortunately my wife died four years ago.'

'I'm so sorry.' Penny looked over at him in consternation. She felt guilty now, for thinking he was a womaniser like his father.

Lucas opened a door into what would have been a large airy study, but filing cabinets and boxes took up all the available space and practically obscured the French windows that lined one side of the room.

'Told you there was a lot of sorting out to do,' Lucas said as he glanced over and saw the expression on her face.

But Penny wasn't thinking about the files and the amount of work; she was thinking how wrong it felt to be deceiving this man. Guilt was eating through her in waves. Maybe Lucas was nothing like his father…maybe she should come clean and admit exactly who she was?

Before she could say anything the phone on the desk rang and Lucas strode across to pick it up. 'Hi… No, I haven't found them yet. Hopefully they'll turn up today, and we can have William Kennedy out promptly at the end of the month. Then the bulldozers can move in.'

Penny felt herself stiffen as she heard her father's name mentioned in such a cold way.

'I'll ring you and keep you up to date, Salvador. Yes…no problem. How's Maria? Well, give her my love.' Lucas put the phone down and glanced over at her. 'Are you okay?' he asked, and she realised she was standing inside the open door just staring at him.

'Yes…fine.' Hastily she moved away from the door and closed it behind her.

'That was Salvador. He's a family friend as well as my solicitor. His wife is expecting their first child any day now, so it's all excitement over there.'

'I'm surprised he has the time to think about work on a Saturday,' Penny said as she crossed towards the desk.

'Yes, he's a good man. I'm grateful to him for agreeing to take over from my late father's solicitor. That guy was very shifty indeed. I didn't trust him at all.'

Which was probably why his father had employed him, Penny thought wryly. He'd probably deliberately sought the services of a less than scrupulous solicitor.

'So your friend is going to oversee the eviction order on Mr Kennedy?'

'If I can find the relevant documents.'

Penny pretended to be engrossed in clearing a space

on the office desk so that she could begin work. 'Do you have any misgivings about this?' she asked lightly.

'About what?'

'Evicting an old man from his property?' She tried to keep her tone as casual as possible.

Lucas didn't reply immediately, and she glanced over at him, suddenly realising how much she wanted him to say yes. Maybe he didn't know how corrupt his father had been…maybe there were other things besides the dodgy solicitor that were concerning him. And if he admitted that to her she could tell him the truth. They could sit down and talk about this situation in a civilised manner and come to some arrangement that would save her father's house.

He gave a wry smile. 'That's a strange question.'

'Is it?' Panic raced through her as she wondered if she had overstepped the line.

'Yes.' Lucas leaned back against the filing cabinet behind him and fixed her with a look that was deeply probing. 'Why are asking that?'

'I…I just remembered you saying that the man used to be your father's business partner, and I wondered if there was a part of you that regretted having to take such a drastic course of action, that's all.'

'Well, you know what they say, Mildred…there can be no sentiment in business.'

It was the kind of cold, hard answer his father would have given, and Penny felt a wave of disappointment. She wanted to tell him that this wasn't business, that this was a vendetta against an elderly, frail man—a vendetta that his cold-hearted father seemed determined to pursue even after death. But to say as much would be to reveal her hand, and she wasn't sure that was the right thing to do…not after hearing him in action, speaking to his solicitor.

Lucas seemed keen to evict her father, probably because there was a hell of a lot of money riding on this property development. And, as he had just said, there was no sentiment when it came to business. There also seemed very little in the way of ethics or morality either, when it came to the Darien way of doing things.

'Well, I suppose we ought to get started,' she said instead as she took off her jacket and reached for one of the files. To hell with it anyway, she thought as she emptied it out onto her desk and ruthlessly started to rake through the contents, searching for her father's deeds. Modern-day life seemed to be dog eat dog…she might as well just get in amongst the pack and make the most of this opportunity. It might be the only chance her father had of surviving.

The hours seemed to fly by after that. File followed file, and still there was no sign of the missing papers. When Lucas suggested breaking for lunch Penny shook her head. 'We need to get on. Time is against us as it is,' she murmured.

'Well, I'll tell you what—we'll have a working lunch, but on one condition only.'

'What's that?' She glanced across at him.

He smiled. 'That you stay and have dinner with me tonight.'

There was something about the way he issued the invitation that made her heart miss several beats. 'I really don't think I can,' she said hurriedly.

'Why not?'

'It's very kind of you…but I wouldn't want to intrude—'

'You're not intruding. I want you to stay.'

And the awful thing was that she wanted to stay, even though she knew she should be keeping her distance. 'Well, I suppose it would mean that we could do some more work later, after dinner.' She tried to justify the acceptance to herself.

'Are you for real?' Lucas fixed her with a teasing look.

The question and the way he looked at her made her skin flare with colour. 'Well...I'm just trying to be sensible. Time is imperative—'

'I think we will have done quite enough work by dinnertime,' he said firmly, and then pushed his chair back from the other side of the desk. 'Now, if you'll excuse me, I'll go through and see if Mrs Gordon will make us something to eat to tide us over until then.'

Penny sat back in her chair with a sigh as he left the room. If only he was cold and nasty this would be a lot easier. She glanced across to the other side of the desk and the files that he was working on and wondered if she should have a quick look through them before he got back. It would be just her luck if he found the papers. Then all this would be for nothing.

Hurriedly she got up and went around to try and scan through the remainder of his file. It would be a lot easier if she knew what the documents in question looked like, she thought.

Penny was leafing through a stack of letters when she came across some correspondence from her father that was dated last year. In excitement she started to delve deeper into the file. If there was one bit of information pertaining to her father in the box, then maybe the elusive documentation for his house would also be there.

She hadn't got very far when she heard Lucas's footsteps returning along the corridor outside.

Hastily Penny reached over and swapped his file with

the one she had been working on. Then returned to her seat.

'How's it going?' Lucas strode in just as she sat down.

'Fine.' She smiled up at him.

'Found anything?' He put a china mug of coffee down beside her.

'Not yet…'

'Maybe I'll be lucky with this file,' he said casually as he sat back down across the desk from her and reached for the box next to him. 'I noticed there was a few letters from William Kennedy in here, so maybe the documents for the house are here as well.'

'That does sound hopeful.' Penny could feel her stomach starting to tie into knots. She hadn't realised he'd already looked in the box. He was going to know that she had swapped them around!

'Strange…they don't seem to be here,' he murmured as he delved into the file.

'You mustn't be looking in the right box.' Penny got up and crossed to one of the filing cabinets behind him, busying herself putting away the papers she had already sorted. She couldn't bear to sit opposite him, because if he looked over at her directly and asked her if she had touched the file she was sure she would go bright red with guilt.

The door of the office opened and Mrs Gordon came in with some sandwiches. Isobel stood in the open doorway behind her.

'Daddy, you won't forget that you said you'd swim with me this afternoon,' she said shyly.

Lucas glanced over at his daughter and grinned. 'No, I won't forget, honey.'

The child smiled back and then ran into the office to climb up on his knee. 'How long will you be, Daddy?'

'Give me one hour and then I'll be all yours.' Lucas stroked her dark hair back from her face tenderly. 'Have you had some lunch?'

Isobel nodded. 'I had pizza.'

'Did you eat some salad with it?' Lucas asked with a raised eyebrow.

Isobel wrinkled her nose.

'You know you should eat something green, Issy…' Lucas said gently. 'We've talked about this before…remember?'

'There is green jelly for afterwards,' the little girl said solemnly. 'I'm going to eat that.'

'That doesn't count.' Lucas tickled her and she giggled breathlessly. 'You'd better eat some salad, young lady, or you are going to be in big trouble.'

'Okay…okay…' The child squealed with laughter as he tickled her some more.

'Good girl.' He kissed her on the forehead. 'Now, run along and let Daddy get back to work. I'll see you for a swim a little later.'

The child wrapped her arms around his neck and kissed him back. 'I love you, Daddy.'

'I love you too.'

Isobel raced over to where Mrs Gordon was waiting for her by the door.

'Sorry about that,' Lucas said distractedly as he turned his attention back to his work. 'As you probably deduced, I'm going to have to leave you to it for a few hours and spend some time with my daughter.'

'That's okay.' Penny returned to her seat. The tender exchange between father and daughter had touched her. Lucas was obviously a devoted dad, and it made her like him even more. 'It must be difficult, running a business and being a single father.'

'It's not easy,' he admitted with a nod. 'And I hate it when I have to put in overtime. But Mrs Gordon is reliable, and Isobel adores her, so that takes a lot of the strain out of things.' He reached for the file in front of him.

Penny waited for him to comment again about the missing letters, but he said nothing further about them.

She glanced over at him. He was reading a document and seemed deep in thought. Uneasily she went back to the pile of papers in front of her. She didn't dare risk looking through the file with the letters in it, deciding that could wait until he'd left the room.

Silence descended between them, broken only by the rustling of paper and the occasional scribble of her pen as she labelled and reorganised.

'There's a stack of papers here that I think can be thrown away,' she murmured after a while. 'They seem to be mainly advertising bumph, but maybe you'd better look through them first, in case there is anything important there.'

'Fine—just put them to one side for me.' He barely looked up.

What was he so engrossed in? she wondered.

Silence resumed. Flint wandered in and sat down next to Lucas's chair. He leaned his head against his master's knee and Lucas stroked his head absently. The dog's breathing seemed loud, and the occasional thump of his tail on the polished floor distracted Penny.

'Well, that's all very interesting,' Lucas remarked suddenly.

'What is?'

'I've found some paperwork regarding the business partnership between my father and Kennedy.'

'Oh?'

'And I've found the deeds to the Kennedy property.' He held up some yellowing documents and smiled across at her.

Penny's eyes widened. She couldn't believe it; the damn papers had been in her file all along. If she hadn't swapped them over she would have found them. This was just her damn luck! 'Oh...great!' From somewhere she tried to insert enthusiasm into her voice. 'Does that mean you'll be able to proceed with the eviction straight away?'

'According to Salvador there are a few more papers I could do with—copies of earlier warning notices that have been sent to Kennedy, that kind of thing. But having the deeds strengthens my hand considerably.' Lucas pushed his chair back from the desk. 'I'll put them somewhere safe and take them to Salvador on Monday morning...or maybe tomorrow if he is free.'

Penny watched as he walked across and put them in the top drawer of a filing cabinet, then locked the file and put the key in his jeans pocket.

'I'm going to spend a little time with my daughter,' Lucas said easily. 'So, can I leave you to carry on sorting through the files and looking for those notices...?'

'Of course.' Her smile was somewhat strained.

She watched as he left the room, closely followed by Flint. Then she leaned back in her chair and groaned. If only she hadn't swapped that file...!

She supposed her only chance now was to find some of the other papers. Her eyes moved around the room, taking in the various boxes and metal cabinets. Suddenly her task seemed even more daunting than before. Apart from everything else, she had the horrible feeling that the real Mildred was going to turn up sooner than those papers were.

CHAPTER FOUR

PENNY worked solidly for the rest of the afternoon, but there was no sign of the missing papers. Her glance kept going over to the filing cabinet where the deeds to her father's house were. Knowing they were there and yet being unable to reach them was extremely frustrating. She wondered for the hundredth time why Lucas had locked them away.

The sound of a child's laughter drifted in from outside and Penny got up to look out of the window. She could just see the edge of a swimming pool and a long terrace, where a table and chairs were placed invitingly under the shade of a large parasol. As she watched Lucas swam into view, and then Isobel also appeared as she ran around the side of the pool dressed in a red swimming costume.

Lucas stood in the water and held his arms up for her. With a shriek of pleasure the child jumped in and then Lucas lifted her onto his shoulders.

'Again…again…' Her voice drifted in to Penny, as did her chuckles of delight as Lucas spun her around before helping her to get out so that the whole performance could be repeated.

He had infinite patience with her, Penny thought with a smile as she watched the game. Isobel clearly adored him. Water glistened on the powerful breadth of his shoulders and arms as he hoisted himself up out of the pool with athletic ease. And suddenly Penny found her mind drifting from how good a dad he was to what a fabulous body he had. His torso was strong and toned and incredibly powerful. She found herself wondering what it would feel like to be cradled in those arms… The very idea made her stomach muscles contract sharply with a thrust of pure desire.

Angrily she turned away from the window and returned to her work. She needed to stop thinking about Lucas in any other terms than those of the enemy. Anything else was pure folly. She was so annoyed with herself that it gave her the impetus to push on with even more speed through the next box of papers. But it didn't do her much good. The papers were nowhere in sight.

By the time Lucas returned to the office an hour later she had worked her way through several more boxes to no avail, and was feeling very dispirited.

'You've done well,' Lucas said with approval as he noticed the space she had cleared in the room. 'Any luck with those papers?'

She shook her head.

'Never mind. They are not so crucial now that I have the deeds. Maybe we'll find them tomorrow…' He smiled at her. 'In the meantime, why don't you join me in a pre-dinner drink out on the porch?'

Penny leaned back in her chair and looked up at him. He'd changed, she noticed, into black jeans and a black short-sleeved shirt. His hair was sleeked back from his face and was still damp from a shower.

It was a pity she found him so attractive, she thought hazily. It made the situation so much more perilous.

'What do you say?' He fixed her with a look that was slightly teasing. 'Shall we watch the sun go down over an ice-cold gin and tonic?'

The offer sounded incredibly tempting. Frankly, she'd had enough of being cooped up in here for one day.

Maybe a drink was just what she needed. 'That would be very nice.' Leaving her jacket hanging over the back of the chair, she stood up and followed him out of the office.

Although the air was warm outside there was a delicious breeze that soothed the senses. Penny leaned against the wooden rail of the veranda and stared out across the garden through the tracery of trees towards the sea. The sun was starting to go down in a brilliant blaze of blood orange that streaked the sky and lit the sea with incandescent splashes of fire.

Lucas joined her and handed across her drink.

'Thanks.' She smiled at him as she took it. 'You have a fabulous view from up here.'

'Yes, I do.'

For a moment there was silence as they both contemplated the sunset. She supposed she should have insisted on going back to her hotel, but it was very pleasant standing here with him. She turned slightly and looked over at him, only to find that his eyes were on her. Was it her imagination or was he watching her very closely?

'I suppose coming from Barbados you are used to stunning views?' he remarked.

It was a casual enough statement, yet it instantly set Penny on guard. 'Barbados is a beautiful island,' she agreed, her tone carefully neutral.

'Where did you used to live? The Caribbean side of the island or the Atlantic?'

'The Atlantic.' It wasn't a lie exactly; she had lived on the Atlantic coast of Arbuda.

'The views are spectacular there,' he said. 'Especially along the east coast road towards Bethsheba.'

'I take it you have visited Barbados?' She tried to change the slant of the conversation so that it was focused on him. These lies were making her far too uncomfortable.

'I go over on business a lot. But I also spent my honeymoon there.'

'That's a romantic place for a honeymoon,' she said softly.

'Yes…' Lucas paused for a moment, and Penny thought she glimpsed some raw emotion that was almost verging on anger in the darkness of his eyes, but it was hard to see him clearly. The sun was sinking fast now, and deep purple clouds of darkness were stealing over the landscape, shadows lengthening across the gardens and the porch.

'You must miss her a lot,' Penny said.

He inclined his head. 'It's been hard these last few years.'

Night dropped like a blanket over everything, and the sound of insects filled the heat of the air with a heavy cacophony.

'Do you mind my asking what happened to her? Or is that too personal a question?'

'No, I don't mind you asking.' He shrugged. 'She died trying to save a man from drowning. He shouldn't even have been in the water. Not only had he had too much to drink, but also they had issued storm warnings that day. The beach had red flags flying but he chose to ignore them. The really ironic thing was that the guy was okay. He managed to get back to shore, and Kay, who was a strong swimmer and taught physical education, didn't…'

Penny was horrified. 'Were you there when it happened?'

Lucas shook his head. 'No. I was at work. The first I

knew of it was when the police turned up at the office to give me the news.'

'I'm so sorry, Lucas. You must have been devastated.'

'It took me a while to come to terms with it, that's for sure.' Lucas took a sip of his drink. 'Anyway, that's enough of that depressing subject. Tell me about you.'

'Me? Well, there's not much to tell.' The swift change of subject caught her unawares.

'I don't believe that for one moment.' He grinned at her. 'I bet there are a lot of intriguing things you could tell me.'

'Depends what you call intriguing.' Penny was distinctly uncomfortable now.

'Well, for one thing how come your CV is less than accurate?'

'Is it?' Penny felt colour starting to seep into her face.

'You know it is. By all accounts, according to the paperwork the agency sent me, you should be fifty-five.' He grinned. 'How old are you anyway?'

'You know it's not gentlemanly to ask a lady her age,' Penny hedged.

'Well, I've never laid claim to being a gentleman,' he said with a spark of humour in his eye. 'I reckon you're twenty-six.'

'Twenty-eight,' she corrected him.

'So I rest my case. Something doesn't add up.'

'I've just found that employers tend to favour having an older woman as their PA, so I've used a little artistic licence on the forms, that's all.' She kept her voice airily light with intense difficulty. 'Once I'm in employment nobody has ever complained about my work.'

'And I'm not complaining either…at least not yet.' He grinned at her. 'So, apart from using artistic licence on forms, what else are you up to?'

'I beg your pardon?' Her heart bounced unevenly in her chest.

'What do you do in your spare time?' He clarified the question.

'Oh…I see.' She smiled and relaxed. 'Well, I like to read, listen to music, and do yoga for relaxation. And I learnt to sail when I lived in Ar…Barbados….' She trailed off in consternation. She had very nearly said Arbuda, had nearly blown her whole cover. Her heart raced against her chest. She was lousy at lying and she hated it. She especially hated lying to him—he seemed so…likeable.

His eyes flicked over her with a slow, assessing thoroughness. 'I like sailing too, when I get time. I have a yacht moored not far from here.'

At least he hadn't noticed her slip of the tongue, but she was going to have to be very careful.

'Maybe you'd like to accompany me one weekend?' he invited smoothly. 'As a thank-you for all your hard work.'

'That sounds wonderful.' She smiled. As she looked up into the darkness of his eyes she realised that it did indeed sound wonderful. She would have liked to spend more time with him. Get to know him better…

Hastily she looked away from him and sipped her drink. It wasn't going to happen. She was here for one reason only. He was her father's enemy and that was all she needed to know about him. Even thinking he was nice was a gross disloyalty.

'Maybe we could go next weekend,' he continued. 'I've got a feeling that we should have all this paperwork under control by then.'

'Let's hope so,' she said lightly.

'Well, if I haven't found the necessary papers by then

I may as well kiss goodbye to the whole Arbuda deal, because the planning permission runs out soon.' Lucas took a long swallow of his drink. 'Which means I'll probably lose my buyer for the project too.'

Penny looked up at him questioningly.

'A builder has offered me a good price for the Kennedy estate plus the beachfront land, and I have accepted it because I have no intention of developing the project myself. Only snag is that if we can't finalise by the end of this month the deal is off.'

'Shame.' Penny's voice was dry.

'Well, hopefully now I've found the deeds the other papers won't be far behind and we can get things moving.'

Not if I can help it, Penny thought glumly. The nerve of the guy! He had already found a buyer for her father's house and it didn't even belong to him yet! She wished for the millionth time that she had found the deeds first and buried them deep at the bottom of some drawer, where Lucas wouldn't find them for months. It would have served him right for heartlessly wanting to throw an old man out onto the streets.

The housekeeper came out of the doorway behind them. 'Dinner is served.'

'Thank you, Mrs Gordon.' Lucas smiled at Penny. 'Anyway, let's not talk any more about business for one night,' he said.

'No, let's not,' she agreed lightly. 'I think I'll be seeing business papers and box files in my dreams tonight.'

Lucas laughed. 'Sounds like a nightmare.'

In more ways than one, she thought as she followed him into the house.

The dining room was set with two places facing each other across the long table. Candlelight reflected and danced over the polished mahogany surface and silver cutlery. White lilies graced the sideboard next to them, scenting the room with their exotic fragrance.

'These are my favourite flowers,' Penny remarked as she stopped next to them to admire the display.

'Mrs Darien always liked the house to be filled with fresh flowers.' Mrs Gordon bustled past her to put some wine on the table. 'Lilies were her favourite too.'

'Mrs Gordon was devoted to my wife,' Lucas told Penny when they were left alone again. 'She looked after Kay when she was a little girl and she was the first person Kay thought of when we were looking for a house-keeper.'

Penny took her seat at the table. 'It must be a weight off your mind, knowing you have someone for Isobel that your wife approved of.'

'Yes, it is.'

'Daddy…' A small voice from the doorway made them both look round.

Isobel was standing just inside the room. She was dressed in a pair of white satin pyjamas, a teddy bear under her arm. 'Mrs Gordon says I've got to say good-night. But can't I stay up a bit longer…? There's no school tomorrow…'

'I don't think so, pumpkin, you've got an early start tomorrow… Grandma says she wants to pick you up at seven-thirty.'

Isobel padded further into the room. 'But I'm not tired.'

'You will be in the morning if you don't get a good night's sleep.' Lucas reached out an arm and lifted her up onto his knee. She giggled happily and looked across at Penny with wide, sparkling dark eyes.

'Are you Daddy's new girlfriend?'

For some reason the question made Penny self-consciously aware of Lucas's eyes resting on her. 'No, Isobel. I work for your daddy. I'm helping him tidy up all those files in the office.'

Isobel nodded. 'I'm going to be a fairy princess in the school play,' she told Penny seriously.

'I'm sure you will make a very beautiful fairy princess,' Penny said. 'What will you be wearing?'

Isobel frowned. 'I don't know.'

'Well, a fairy princess usually has a wand, with a star on the top, and sometimes she wears a crown on her head and has a long white dress. Do you think you'll be wearing something like that?'

'Maybe…' Isobel grinned, and Penny noticed she had a gap between her front teeth. 'Mrs Gordon is going to take me shopping.'

The housekeeper came in at that moment. 'I won't take you shopping if you aren't in bed in five minutes, young lady.'

Isobel squealed dramatically and then kissed her dad on the cheek. 'Night, Daddy.'

'Night, pumpkin. I'll be along soon to tuck you in.'

The child slipped down from his lap and then to Penny's surprise came around and reached up to kiss her goodnight as well. She smelt of baby lotion and talcum powder, and her hair was glossily soft next to Penny's skin for a moment before she drew back. 'Do you think I'll need wings to be a fairy princess?' she asked, looking up at her with intently serious eyes.

'Most definitely,' Penny said solemnly. 'All fairy princess have wings.'

Isobel smiled. 'I can't wait,' she said happily. Then with a little wave in her father's direction she left the room.

'She's been talking about nothing but this school play for the last week,' Mrs Gordon said with an amused smile as she put their appetisers on the table in front of them. 'I think maybe she's going to go on the stage when she grows up. She's a real little actress.'

'Adorable with it,' Penny said instantly.

'Yes, she is.' The housekeeper smiled at her. 'Anyway, I'll leave you to enjoy your meal.'

As the woman left the room Lucas reached to pour some wine in Penny's glass. 'How are you finding things at the hotel, Mildred?' he asked casually.

'It's very comfortable.' She still found it strange answering to that name.

'I suppose you'll be looking around for an apartment soon? That's if you decide to stay on here, of course.'

'I suppose so. I haven't really thought about it yet.' She pretended to be interested in the prawn and avocado starter before her. 'This looks delicious,' she said, hoping to change the subject away from her plans for the future.

'Yes, Mrs Gordon is very skilled in the kitchen,' Lucas agreed, before continuing right back with the conversation. 'There are some new apartment buildings not far from the office, and I've heard good reports about them. Apparently they're well designed. It wouldn't hurt to go and look at them.'

'I'll bear that in mind, Lucas,' she said off-handedly.

'They are rental apartments, so it wouldn't be too big a commitment.' He smiled at her. 'Bearing in mind that you're a free spirit.'

She reached for her wine and took a sip. 'Maybe I'll go and take a look next week…if I've got time.'

'I'll give you an extra long lunch on Monday.'

'Are you on commission for these apartments?' she

asked him, her eyes sparkling with amusement. 'You seem very keen for me to look at them.'

'Just trying to be helpful,' he said easily. 'I know it must be difficult for you, settling in to a new job and looking for somewhere to live all at the same time. I think looking around at the accommodation available will give you a better idea of whether you want to stay on here or not.'

His thoughtfulness touched her, made her wish for a moment that she really was intending to stay on as his PA. 'Thanks, Lucas, I appreciate that.' She felt so guilty that she couldn't quite meet his eye as she spoke.

Penny was glad when Mrs Gordon bustled in to clear the table.

'If you'll excuse me for a moment, Mildred.' Lucas pushed his chair back from the table. 'I'll just go tuck Isobel in and wish her goodnight.'

'Yes, of course.' For a little while Penny was left alone in the room. She toyed with her wine glass, watching the way the candlelight twinkled over the crystal. Her surroundings were so tranquil that it added to the sense of unreality inside her. She shouldn't be here; she shouldn't be doing this, a small voice told her sharply.

Maybe she should leave now, just walk away while there was no real harm done. She had merely helped Lucas to tidy his office. Even if she wasn't the real Mildred, how annoyed could he be about a little unpaid clerical assistance when he was so clearly desperate for staff?

As she made to push her chair away from the table Mrs Gordon came back into the room with their main course. 'There you are, dear,' she said, as she placed a plate in front of her with succulent slices of roast beef on it. 'Lucas will be along in a moment; Isobel is always asleep within two minutes once he's tucked her up.'

'Thank you.' Penny smiled at the woman and realised that walking out wasn't really an option. It would be incredibly rude after Mrs Gordon had gone to so much trouble. Maybe she should feign illness once Lucas got back to the table? She could have a sudden migraine attack and get him to drop her back at the hotel. At least once she was there she could think a little more clearly about all this. Sitting here accepting Lucas's hospitality just didn't feel right.

The housekeeper put down a serving dish of potatoes and vegetables. 'If you don't mind my saying so, you remind me somewhat of Lucas's late wife,' she said suddenly as she glanced across at her. 'Kay had the same beautiful blonde hair and green eyes.'

'Did she?' Penny was taken aback by the observation. 'Isobel has such dark hair I would have thought Kay would have been dark also.'

Mrs Gordon shook her head. 'Isobel is like her father; she has his Spanish blood. And of course Lucas takes after his mother...Isabella. She was a most beautiful woman.'

'Getting the family history, I hear,' Lucas said with a grin as he returned to the room.

'I'm just saying how beautiful your mother was,' Mrs Gordon continued unabashed. 'How is Isobel?'

'Fast asleep, thanks, Mrs Gordon.'

With a satisfied nod the housekeeper left the room.

'Mrs Gordon could sit an exam on my family and pass with honours,' Lucas said with a grin as the door closed behind her.

The woman was certainly right about one thing, Penny

thought as she glanced across at him. Lucas looked nothing like his father…and maybe he was nothing like him in character either.

'Would you like more wine?' Lucas asked, and lifted the bottle towards her glass.

'No, thank you.' Hurriedly she declined, and noticed that he put the bottle down without refilling his own glass.

'I'll keep a clear head for later,' he said when he caught her eye.

'Later?' She wondered if it was her imagination—or did his voice hold the husky promise of invitation…?

'Driving you home.'

'Oh, I see.' For some reason she found herself blushing. 'I can take a taxi, Lucas.'

'I wouldn't hear of it.' Lucas waved the offer aside dismissively. 'I'd like to see you home.' There was a certain warmth about his tone and in his eyes that sent little darts of awareness rushing through her.

'So tell me a little more about yourself…Milly. May I call you Milly? It seems somehow to suit you more than Mildred.'

'Does it?' She moistened her lips nervously.

'Yes, it does.' He smiled.

Their eyes met and held across the table and she felt her heart give a crazy kind of skip.

She wondered what would happen if she told him the truth right now. Would he hate her and throw her out without waiting for an explanation? Or would he patiently listen to what she had to say?

The thought of him hating her was appalling.

'Tell me what it was like growing up in Barbados,' Lucas invited lazily.

Hastily she pulled herself together. 'Much the same as growing up here, I would imagine.'

'I went to boarding school in England for a good many years,' Lucas said. 'It was the place my father was educated and he was determined I should go there as well. So I suppose you could say that I grew up in England.'

'Were you homesick?' Penny asked curiously.

'I got used to it.' He shrugged. 'My mother, however, was never happy about it. But my father was a forceful character; he usually got his own way.'

'I can imagine,' Penny muttered with icy disdain, then noticed Lucas looking at her quizzically and realised she had probably sounded too vehement. 'I mean…I can imagine it was difficult for your mother. She must have missed you.' Quickly she tried to soften her tone.

'Yes, I suppose she did. I was an only child, and my father was away a lot on business.'

Yes, he was in Arbuda, having an affair, Penny thought disdainfully. She felt sorry for Lucas's mother. Not only had her husband been an overbearing tyrant but he had been unfaithful to her as well. She wondered if Isabella had known.

'I take it from what Mrs Gordon was saying that your mother is dead now?'

Lucas nodded. 'She died twelve years ago.'

'I'm sorry.' She wondered if Lucas had any idea about what had really gone on in Arbuda.

'And did you get on with your father?' she asked him curiously.

'We had our disagreements…' He shrugged. 'But thankfully we patched up our differences before he died. I'm glad of that.'

Which meant that he probably wouldn't want to hear

anything negative about his father now, Penny thought dryly.

'What about you?' Lucas asked. 'Did you have a good relationship with your parents?'

'Very. But my mother died when I was sixteen and Dad was low for a while after that. Unfortunately he made some bad decisions around that time. Got involved in a business deal with a very dodgy character…a man who had a hidden agenda…and from having a nice comfortable home things started to go downhill. I did what I could to help him, took over the running of the house and tried very hard to sort things out, but it was a difficult situation and it went from bad to worse.'

'So how is your father now?' Lucas asked.

'Financially he never recovered…' Penny hesitated. 'But he is still battling on and I'm hoping things will improve for him soon.'

'It sounds like he's had a tough time.' Lucas sounded sympathetic.

'Yes, and all because he was taken in by a confidence trickster.' Penny's eyes shimmered.

'Have you tried to redress the situation by law?'

'Oh, yes. Solicitors' letters have been flying backwards and forwards for years. All that happens is that the bills grow bigger. The debt piles up.'

'Maybe it's time he just cut his losses?' Lucas said quietly.

'I think he'd rather die than do that…'

'It's only money—and at least he has a loving and supportive daughter. That means a lot.'

A loving and supportive daughter who was dining with the enemy, Penny thought guiltily. And, what was worse, she was enjoying dining with the enemy. He seemed very easy to talk to, very charming. But then her mother had probably thought that about Lawrence Darien.

Outside in the hall the grandfather clock struck ten, the chimes echoing in the stillness of the house.

There was really no point sitting here telling Lucas about her father unless she told him the whole truth…and if she did that all hell might break loose. Speaking ill of the dead was a risky business, even under ordinary circumstances. And these were certainly not ordinary circumstances. She should have made her excuses and left ages ago, as she had planned.

'That was a delicious dinner, but I really should be going.' She straightened her cutlery on the plate.

'So soon?' He frowned. 'At least have coffee with me in the lounge first.'

Penny shook her head and got hastily to her feet. 'I'd better not. I didn't realise it was so late.'

'You must be tired.' Lucas also stood up, and walked around towards her. 'Don't worry about starting too early in the morning. Now that I've found those deeds some of the pressure is off. I might drop them over to Salvador's house in the morning. That way I could pick you up about eleven, if that's all right?'

'Fine.' The mention of those deeds made her tense up inside.

'And don't worry too much about your father, Milly,' he said softly. 'I know it's an old cliché, but if he has his health, really, at the end of the day, that is the most important thing.'

'You think so?' For some reason his matter-of-fact statement made her angry, especially as it was spoken in almost the same breath as his mentioning the deeds of her father's house.

It was easy for him to be so laid back, but what would

he say if it was his father in this situation? If it was his father who was going through hell? 'But money is important, Lucas,' she said with brittle emphasis. 'Let's face it, if it wasn't you wouldn't be getting ready to evict some old man from his home.'

For a second Lucas's eyes narrowed on her face. 'That's totally different.'

'I can't see that it is.' Her voice trembled slightly.

'Hey…' Lucas reached out and much to her consternation put a hand under her chin, tipping her face up towards his. 'Are you okay?'

'Of course I am.' She swallowed hard.

'This business in Arbuda is part of my father's last will and testament. He has requested specifically that I follow it through…' Lucas trailed off. 'Anyway, Salvador is looking in to all that for me. I assure you everything is being done decently.'

'Is it?' Penny was distracted suddenly as his hand seemed to trail upwards over her face in a butterfly caress.

And suddenly she wasn't thinking about her father any more. Instead her eyes were locked with his and she could feel small shivers of awareness shooting through her. She felt suddenly breathless with a strange kind of excitement…the kind that made her body tingle and her pulses quicken. His hand traced lightly across her cheekbones, setting her skin on fire, and then trailed through the soft silkiness of her hair.

Penny felt a thrill shooting through her that was so intense it was shocking, and there was a strange magnetic intensity between her body and his. He was standing only a few inches away, and yet she could feel the pull of his body inviting her closer. She wanted to move into his arms so badly that it was a physical effort not to sway closer.

His gaze moved to the softness of her mouth and she imagined she could almost feel his eyes touching her. She moistened her lips nervously as they tingled with the anticipation and the need for him to kiss her.

'Milly…' He breathed her name in an undertone.

Except it wasn't her name…she was here under false pretences. The fact flicked through her mind with lightning speed. She needed to back away from this quickly. Yet she couldn't seem to make herself. Her brain was logically telling her one thing but her body was saying something quite different, and with much more force.

Then, quite unexpectedly, Lucas was the one to step back. Penny wondered if she had misread the signs, if the chemistry that had flared between them had been all in her mind. She looked up at him wordlessly, and in the ensuing silence she could hear her heart hammering fiercely against her chest.

'Milly, I—' Whatever he had been about to say was interrupted by an almighty clatter coming from outside the room. 'What on earth was that?' he muttered in consternation, and hurried out to investigate.

Penny followed him into the hallway. There was the sound of someone moaning in pain and they quickly followed the noise down and into the kitchen. Mrs Gordon was lying on the kitchen floor, her leg twisted at an awkward angle beneath her, cutlery and pots and pans on the tiled floor around her.

'My God, are you all right?' Lucas was instantly beside her, his tone laced with deep concern.

'Yes…yes, I'm okay.' The woman moved and managed to sit up, but her face was white and her lips quivered as if she might burst into tears at any moment. 'What a mess,' she wailed as she looked around her at the floor. 'I tried to catch hold of the table to break my fall and everything came tumbling down on top of me.'

'Never mind the mess,' Lucas said impatiently. 'The most important thing is you. Do you think you've broken anything?'

'No.' The housekeeper moved her foot and winced. 'I can't believe I was so stupid. I spilt some water on the floor and forgot to mop it up immediately. Then the next thing I knew my legs just went beneath me... So silly...I'm always telling Isobel to be careful when these tiles are wet.' She flinched as she tried to get up.

'Maybe you'd better not move,' Lucas said gently. 'Where does it hurt?'

'I'll be all right.' With grim determination Mrs Gordon tried to hoist herself up, using the edge of the table.

'Okay...if you must get up, let me help you.' Hurriedly Lucas put an arm around her and lifted her to her feet.

'Thank you.' She smiled bravely as she leaned against the table. 'See—I'm fine.' But as soon as she put her foot down on the ground her face crumpled in agony.

'We should ring for an ambulance,' Lucas said firmly.

'No!' The woman looked horrified. 'I don't want all that fuss.'

'You need to get to hospital, Mrs Gordon,' Penny said gently.

'I'll be fine...really.' Even as she was speaking she was trying to gingerly test her foot on the floor again. But she was obviously in excruciating pain.

'I'll take you down to Casualty myself,' Lucas said determinedly. 'You've got to go and get checked out.' As he spoke Lucas moved to pick up a set of keys that were hanging by the back door. 'Will you keep an eye on Isobel for me while I'm gone?' He looked around at Penny and she nodded her head.

'Of course I will.'

'Thanks.' He smiled at her and then, ignoring his housekeeper's protests, scooped her up as if she were a mere lightweight and carried her towards the door.

Penny hurried to open it for him, and then followed them out through the night to open the passenger door of his car for them as well.

'All this fuss over a small fall,' Mrs Gordon said, her voice breaking on a sob. 'I'll be all right after a good night's sleep.'

'I'll feel better if you are properly checked over,' Lucas said soothingly. 'Please don't fret, Ethel.' Gently he tucked her skirt inside the car so that the door wouldn't catch it.

'We'll be back as soon as possible, Milly,' he said as he strode around to get into the car himself.

'That's okay. There's no hurry.' Penny stepped back and watched as he started the engine and the car pulled away down the driveway. Only when the lights had faded into the darkness did she return to the house.

CHAPTER FIVE

PENNY wandered back through the hallway and stood listening for any sound from Isobel. But all she could hear was the gentle rhythmic tick of the clock. Obviously the child was still fast asleep. She glanced through the doorway into the dining room, noting the dishes waiting to be cleared from the table. It seemed sensible to start tidying up. At least it would be one less worry for Lucas and Mrs Gordon when they returned from the hospital.

It didn't take long to clear the dining room, and then Penny started on the kitchen, lifting the debris from the floor and stacking the dishwasher before mopping and drying the tiles so that there would be no more accidents. The kitchen was a dream to work in. Every modern convenience was stowed away behind the shiny white units, and it was good to keep busy; it took her mind away from thinking about Lucas and the desire that had flared as soon as he had touched her. He seemed to have a strange power over her senses, a power that was extremely disconcerting.

She remembered how lovely he had been with Mrs Gordon, so gentle and concerned, and even that made her insides turn to gooey emotion. Ferociously she scrubbed at the kitchen counters until they gleamed. She wouldn't give those thoughts any space, she told herself angrily. Instead she would dwell on why she was here…and also poor Mrs Gordon. The woman had looked extremely shaken by that fall; she hoped that she hadn't broken anything.

The kitchen done, Penny meandered back into the hall. It seemed strange being alone in this house. She supposed she really should be making the most of the situation by going into the office and searching for those papers, but somehow it seemed a little too underhanded when Lucas was at a hospital on a mission of mercy.

On the other hand, the sooner she found those papers the sooner she could put all this behind her and get on with her own life. Penny paused by the door to the office. She had just reached out and turned the handle when a shrill ringing filled the silence. For a moment she imagined it was an alarm, then she realised that it was the phone. With a wry grin at her foolish imagination she hurried inside to answer it.

'Hi, it's me.' Lucas's voice sounded velvety-warm down the phone.

'Hi, how's Mrs Gordon?'

'Well, the good news is that she hasn't broken her ankle. The bad news is that there is a problem with her hip and they want to keep her in for observation.'

'Oh, no! The poor woman.'

'Yes, she's totally spooked. Hates hospitals. Anyway, I've rung her sister and she's on her way. But I think I'd better hang around until she arrives.'

'That's okay, Lucas. I'll just wait for you.'

'The thing is I might not be home for another couple of hours, and you must be exhausted. I was thinking it might be sensible if you bunk down in the spare bedroom. It's already made up.'

'I'm not that tired, Lucas,' she said quickly. 'I can wait up for you.'

'But then you'll have to get a taxi back to the hotel because I can't leave Isobel alone,' Lucas said calmly. 'Take the spare bedroom; it's the last door on the right upstairs. At least that way you'll get some sleep. Just make yourself at home.'

The phone went dead before she could argue further. Penny sat down on the edge of the office desk and glanced over at the filing cabinets. By the sounds of things she had a good few hours to go through them.

She stood up and opened the first drawer. *Make yourself at home…* Lucas's words echoed in her mind as she stared down at the papers inside. They had a warm ring to them and from nowhere she felt a fierce thrust of guilt.

'Damn it all,' she muttered vehemently, and slammed the drawer shut again. Then she turned and left the room. Somehow she didn't have the heart to go rummaging through files now.

Having these attacks of conscience wasn't helping her father, she told herself angrily as she went upstairs. She would have to get on with searching for those papers first thing tomorrow. It was either that or leave.

She paused by an open door halfway along the landing. It was Isobel's room. A small night lamp was on, highlighting the soft pink walls and the pink and white patchwork quilt that covered the bed. Penny crept in to check on the little girl. She was fast asleep, the covers thrown back slightly. Penny tucked them in around her and, noticing her teddy bear had slipped down between the bed and the side table, placed it in next to her again.

Poor little mite, she thought, watching over her for a moment. It couldn't be easy growing up without her mum. Quietly she slipped back out into the corridor.

The room next door was obviously Mrs Gordon's, judging by the voluminous purple dress hanging on the side of the wardrobe.

Lucas's room was across from that. She knew it was his room because it was so typically masculine. There was an enormous bed, with a pale grey cover on it, a computer in one corner with a stack of books sitting next to it, and a trouser press with a pair of jeans hanging over it.

She walked further on and opened the door at the end of the corridor. It was decorated in shades of lilac and white, with white wicker furniture, and had a country-fresh feel about it. The bed looked extremely inviting. Maybe she would take up Lucas's offer and bunk down for the night. At least that way she could get up early in the morning and get on with looking through those files. Closing the door behind her, she stripped off and slipped beneath the cool sheets.

As soon as her head hit the pillow she was asleep.

Her dreams that night were as troubled as her thoughts had been by day. One moment she was telling Lucas the truth…the next she was creeping out of the house, the deeds to her father's house tucked into her handbag. Stealing the papers had never been her intention, and she woke up in a cold panic, her heart thudding with fear.

The room was in pitch darkness, and for a few moments she couldn't remember where she was. There was a strange sound in the darkness, like a distant wailing. It took a moment for her to remember that she was at Lucas's house and that the noise was probably Isobel crying. Swiftly she threw back the covers, pulled on her trousers, buttoned up her top and hurried along to the child's room.

The little girl was sitting on the edge of her bed, sobbing uncontrollably.

'What's the matter, darling?' Penny said soothingly as she went across to her.

'Want my daddy.'

'Daddy will be here soon. He had to take Mrs Gordon

to the doctor because she had a sore leg.' Penny sat down beside her and put an arm around her. 'But it's nothing to worry about.'

Isobel looked up at her, her eyes brimming with tears. 'Why does Mrs Gordon have a sore leg?'

'Because she slipped on the kitchen floor.' Penny pulled back the bed covers. 'But she'll be better soon, and Daddy will be home. Now, why don't you get back into bed and try and get some sleep? You're going out with your grandma in the morning, aren't you?'

Isobel nodded, but made no move to get into the bed. 'Will Mrs Gordon have to go to heaven, like Mummy?' A huge tear spilled down her cheek.

'Oh, no, darling.' Penny's heart went out to the little girl and she wrapped her arms around her and held her tight. 'Mrs Gordon will be just fine.'

'Promise?' Isobel looked up at her, and when Penny nodded she snuggled happily back into her arms. Penny stroked the dark hair soothingly and rocked her for a few moments. It felt strangely comforting, holding the warmth of the child close in her arms.

'Now, let's have no more tears,' she whispered. 'There's nothing to be scared about.'

'There might be a bogeyman under the bed,' Isobel murmured solemnly. 'I'd be scared of that.'

'There's no such thing as bogeymen.'

'Sure?' Isobel looked up at her again with big wide eyes.

Penny grinned. 'I'm positive.'

Isobel cuddled in against her again.

'You really should be getting back to sleep. It must be very late…' Penny glanced up as a movement in the doorway caught her eye. Lucas was standing there watching them. He smiled at Penny as their eyes met.

'How long have you been there?' she asked in surprise.

'A few minutes. I've just got back from the hospital.'

Isobel looked up as she heard her father's voice. 'Daddy!' she squealed with delight, and flung herself off the bed to go and run into his arms.

'You should be in bed and asleep, young lady. It's three in the morning,' he said as he swung her up into his arms.

'I had a bad dream and I woke up. I thought there was a bogeyman under the bed.'

'As Milly said, there's no such thing as bogeymen,' Lucas told her gently. 'So back to bed with you.'

Penny moved out of the way as he carried the child back to her bed. She watched as he tucked her up.

'Sweet dreams, pumpkin,' he said.

'Night, Daddy,' Isobel snuggled down contentedly. 'Night, Milly.'

'Night, sweetheart.' Penny smiled.

Isobel looked as if she was fighting to keep her eyes open as they turned and left the room.

'So how is Mrs Gordon?' Penny asked as soon as they were out of earshot.

'Not good.' Lucas pulled the door closed behind them. 'Apparently she has been having a lot of pain in her hip for the last few months. But she's been too scared to go and see a doctor. This fall has just aggravated the problem further.'

'Poor woman.' Penny's face creased in concern. 'What do they think is wrong?'

'One of the doctors said it looked from the X-ray as if there was a problem with the hip joint which could have been caused by arthritis.' Lucas shrugged. 'But we'll know more tomorrow, when the consultant sees her.'

His eyes flicked down over her body. 'Did you get dressed in a hurry?' he asked with a grin.

She followed his eyes down and noticed her top was buttoned crookedly. Suddenly she was extremely conscious of her untidy appearance. Her blonde hair was tousled and loose around her shoulders, she was wearing no make-up and her clothes weren't even on correctly. 'I must look a mess...' Hurriedly she tried to rebutton her top. 'I was in bed asleep when I heard Isobel crying.'

'I don't think you could ever look a mess, Milly,' he said huskily. 'On the contrary, you are a very beautiful woman.'

The compliment and the way he was looking at her made her temperature suddenly shoot up. 'Thank you...I wasn't fishing for compliments.'

'I know that.' He noted that she was buttoning her top up crookedly again. 'Do you want a hand with that?' There was a hint of dry amusement in the darkness of his eyes.

'No, thank you.' She dropped her hands to her sides; they were far too unsteady to sort the problem out now. 'Anyway, it's late...I suppose we should turn in.'

'I suppose we should.'

He made no attempt to move away and neither did she; they just stood there looking at each other. To her consternation she could feel an intimate sense of awareness spiralling between them, just as it had earlier.

'Thanks for looking after Isobel for me tonight. You were great with her,' he said softly.

'It wasn't difficult. She's a lovely child.' She swallowed hard and tried to wrench her eyes away from the mesmerising force of his, but she couldn't. 'Anyway...you must be tired; it's been a long day.' She tried again to be strong and sensible and move away. The words sounded good, yet her body refused to put them into action.

'I'm not in the slightest bit tired,' he murmured. He reached out and smoothed a stray strand of her hair away from her face. The gentle touch of his hand against her skin sent a shivery erotic sensation flooding through her.

'Neither am I,' she whispered shakily.

'I know…' His eyes raked over her face, lingering on her lips. 'There is a certain chemistry between us…isn't there?'

It was more of a statement than a question, so she made no reply.

'And I've been wondering what to do about it ever since we were interrupted at this point earlier today.'

'Have you…?' She found herself swaying a little closer. What would it be like to kiss him? she wondered. Her heart thundered in her ears as if she had been running.

'And I've wondered how politically correct it would be to do this…' He bent closer and his lips connected with hers in a butterfly caress that set off an explosion of passionate sensation inside her. 'I keep trying to convince myself that this isn't a good idea,' he murmured, and he pulled back fractionally, his eyes on her lips, his breath soft against her skin. 'I keep telling myself that you work for me, and mixing business with pleasure can cause all kinds of complications…' As he spoke he brushed his lips lightly against hers again, in a featherlight provocative way that made her ache for so much more.

'You're right…' she murmured unsteadily. 'All kinds of complications…' And in more ways than one, she added silently, trying to make herself pull back from the situation. She was here under false pretences, for a start, so an affair of the heart was out of the question, and as she had never been a person who indulged in casual sex, it was time to move away now. Her mind registered the command but still she didn't move. She felt spellbound by his closeness.

'But then I thought…what the hell…?' As Lucas was speaking he traced the line of her mouth with one forefinger, sending shivery sensations of pure hunger racing through her. 'Maybe this is a risk worth taking…'

The rasping deep tones of his voice seemed to inflame her senses even more. 'Maybe it is…' she found herself agreeing softly.

He moved even closer then, lacing both hands through the softness of her hair, and held her in a possessive way as he kissed her again. Her resistance to him crumbled totally and this time she kissed him back, fire racing through her veins, adrenalin pumping. The kiss deepened and suddenly nothing mattered except the urgent demands of her body.

Penny wasn't even able to think straight any more. Everything was just a wild blur of complete and utter longing.

She felt his hands caressing up over her body, finding the aroused hard thrust of her naked breast through the cotton material of her blouse. The sensation of his fingers teasing her erect nipple through the light clothing was unbearably erotic. His tongue invaded the softness of her mouth, his kisses becoming more and more heated and demanding.

She stood on tiptoe, responding to him with equal passion, pressing closer against him.

'I've been wondering what this would feel like since the first moment you walked into my office,' he murmured.

'So have I,' she admitted shakily.

He smiled, and then, taking hold of her hand, he led her into his bedroom.

Penny's heart was thundering so heavily against her chest that it was like a wild animal trying to escape. The rational side of her brain told her that this was a mistake. But the voice of reason was a mere whisper against the hurricane force of her need for him.

He turned on the bedside lamp and it threw the room into a shadowy gold light.

Penny watched as he tore off his shirt. She noticed the way his muscles rippled with strength and vitality under the honey bronze of his skin, and she felt her stomach muscles contract into sharp knots of desire. She sat down on the edge of the bed, wondering if this was all a dream… Maybe she hadn't really woken up?

He reached for the buckle on his trousers and unfastened it. She had never really thought that a man's body was beautiful before…but his was. It was sheer perfection. From the broad, powerful shoulders to the narrow hips, he had the sort of body that could have belonged to an athlete, honed and tuned and in the peak of physical condition.

He glanced over at her, caught her watching him and grinned. Then he approached the bed, with a look of purpose in the dark eyes that made her heart beat even faster.

'Lucas, are we doing the right thing…?' she murmured, a note of panic in her voice.

He smiled and then reached out and unbuttoned her blouse, revealing the upward tilt of her breasts, the erect nipples. 'Your body seems to think so…and so does mine.'

As if to prove the point his fingers moved over her womanly curves and she closed her eyes as a burning wave of pleasure shot through her. She leaned back against the satin covers of the bed and helped him to remove the rest of her clothing, her fingers as frantic and feverish for him as his were for her.

CHAPTER SIX

WHEN Penny woke up the room was lit by a shadowy silver light cast from the outside landing. At some point Lucas must have switched off the bedside lamp, but Penny didn't remember that. All she remembered was the wild passion, the heat of his kisses, and the feel of his hands as they took her to heights she had never reached before. No one had ever made her feel like that before…not even Nick, and she had been deeply in love with him. The knowledge was deeply perturbing. Last night had been a mistake. Lucas Darien was the enemy.

She turned her head and looked across at him. He was fast asleep, lying on his side facing her. The covers had slipped from his shoulders, revealing the power of his body. Just looking at him made her stomach dip, as if she was on a swing and someone had pushed her too high, too hard. Her eyes drifted over the contours of his face, taking the opportunity to study him in sleep. His features were classically perfect: a strong, chiselled jawline, high cheekbones and a wide forehead. She noticed the length of his dark lashes, the sensual, soft curve of his mouth. And suddenly she wanted to reach out and touch him, cuddle into the protective curve of those arms, press her lips against his. She didn't want Lucas to be the enemy…she really didn't.

As if he sensed her watching him, he suddenly opened his eyes and their gaze connected.

He smiled lazily at her and her heart dipped with longing. 'Good morning.'

'Morning,' she murmured, thinking how formal and polite they sounded after a night of such intimacy.

'What time is it?'

'I don't know.' Trying to keep the covers over her nakedness, she stretched out her arm to peer at her watch. 'Five-thirty…I think.'

'Plenty of time, then.'

'Plenty of time for what?'

He gave a low laugh and rolled over so that he was pinning her against the mattress. 'What do you think?' he murmured playfully.

The sudden contact of his body against hers made her insides dissolve in longing. Then he kissed her, a long, lingering, warm kiss that sent her senses reeling into further chaos.

The feelings inside her were intensely conflicting. One part of her was telling her that this was wrong…that she was losing sight of the truth and her real reason for being here. The other part of her was recklessly trying to ignore all those warnings because she wanted him so much. It was a whole new experience for Penny; she had never had to fight with herself like this before—she had always been perfectly in control of her emotions.

'Being here with you like this is probably a big mistake,' she whispered, but at the same time she was running her fingers through the soft darkness of his hair almost wondrously, loving the texture of it against her hands, loving the freedom of being able to stroke him, touch him.

'Why is that?' he asked lazily, peppering her forehead and her cheeks and then the sides of her throat with kisses.

She hadn't even realised she had spoken aloud until he asked. 'I suppose for the same reasons you were expounding last night.' She murmured the excuse almost off-handedly, not wanting to think too deeply about anything except what he was doing to her.

Maybe it was the strange half-light of the room, or just the closeness of his naked body, but she had totally lost all inhibitions. She arched her back as his lips moved lower down to the hollow of her chest. Her body was clamouring wildly for him to touch her more intimately. She ached to feel his mouth against her breasts.

'Mmm…but after last night I think those worries have evaporated… What we shared was far too pleasurable to ever be classed as a mistake…' His hands travelled up over the curve of her hips, smoothing into her waist and then higher.

'Definitely,' she murmured breathlessly as his fingers moved over her breast, closing over the rosy hard peak of her desire. 'After all…' She gasped a little as his mouth followed the path of his hands. 'This is just sex—' She broke off as he pulled away from her slightly. 'What's the matter?' she asked throatily.

His dark eyes locked with hers in amusement. 'Nothing…I just didn't realise you were so modern in your approach to lovemaking.'

She felt herself colouring up with a different kind of heat now. The ironic thing was that she was anything but modern in her approach to lovemaking…she had never indulged in a one-night stand before in her life, had always needed to feel deeply involved with a man before going to bed with him. But she was enough of a realist to know that kind of a relationship was out of the question between them.

How could this ever be anything other than just a casual liaison when she had told him so many lies? And apart from that he was the one man in the world she should definitely not have taken to bed. She was betraying her father with every minute she was in his arms. She was sleeping with the enemy. The hard, cold facts thumped through her mind in unrelenting waves of condemnation.

There would never be a future for them as a couple.

'I just meant that there need be no recriminations between us tomorrow…' she murmured shakily, trying not to care too deeply. If all she could have of him was now then she would take what she could.

'Definitely no recriminations,' he agreed. His eyes moved over her heated countenance, taking in the vulnerable light in her green-gold eyes and the soft curve of her lips. He stroked his hand soothingly across her cheekbones, feeling the heat of her skin, and then threaded his hands through the silky cloud of her hair that was spread across the pillows around her. 'I learnt long ago not to worry about what might happen in the future…now is all that matters.'

'And this is just a bit of fun. Why shouldn't we enjoy ourselves…?' she whispered as his lips trailed up the column of her neck to the sensitive hollow of her throat.

'Why not, indeed?' he agreed lazily, moving further up to nibble on her ear.

Desperately she was trying to formulate sensible thoughts, whilst at the same time her body was driving her to new heights of need.

He found her lips and kissed her in a slow, intense way that drugged her senses even more. Then he pulled her closer and their bodies merged as one in a powerful, intoxicating rhythm.

Lucas was a masterful lover, totally skilled at turning a woman on, and she revelled in the warmth and passion of his body, meeting fire with fire. As she drowned in the heady experience the real world seemed to blur into insignificance. Nothing else mattered except here and now. Again and again he brought her to the brink of ecstasy, controlling her, playing with her until she was almost begging for release and total fulfilment. Then, just when she thought she couldn't wait any longer, he tipped her over the edge onto a rollercoaster of thunderous, joyful fulfilment.

She clung to him breathlessly afterwards. Neither of them spoke. There seemed no need for words; the way he cradled her close and stroked her hair seemed words enough.

Contentedly she drifted to sleep, secure in the powerful circle of his arms.

When Penny next opened her eyes, she felt warm and lazily content; she reached out across the bed, searching for Lucas, wanting to snuggle back into his arms, but her hands found only the cool empty space in the bed next to her. She sat up, brushing the weight of her hair back from her face as she glanced around. 'Lucas?'

There was no reply. She was alone in the room. Penny lay back against the pillows and looked at her watch. It was almost nine-thirty! She couldn't believe she had slept so late. Or maybe she could after the activity of the night… Her lips curved in a smile. Lucas had been the most incredible lover. Just thinking about what he had done to her made her insides melt all over again…made her want to do it all over again.

Sunlight was creeping into the room through a chink in the curtains. She watched the way it played over the satin bedcovers and felt warm and dreamy. She wished Lucas was here with her now—in fact she wished that every night could be spent like last night, wrapped in his arms…

Suddenly her thoughts froze as a swift surge of reality brutally attacked the wistful feelings inside her. She was being crazy. Sleeping with Lucas had been a one-off event. It could never happen again. Okay, last night had been wildly exciting and deeply satisfying, but it had also been incredibly reckless. She was here to help her father and there was no escaping that fact. And, what was more, if she didn't hurry and get out of here she would be exposed as a fraud by the real Mildred Bancroft—and she was damned sure Lucas wouldn't want to take her into his arms when that happened. He'd be livid and she couldn't honestly blame him.

Angry with herself for caring, she swung her legs out of bed and headed for the *en suite* bathroom. Her first loyalty had to be to her father.

What she needed to do today was find those papers, put them somewhere Lucas wouldn't think of looking for them, and then leave post haste. She couldn't afford to think about Lucas Darien on a personal level.

Penny stepped under the heavy jet of the shower and turned her face up towards the razor-sharp spray in an attempt to clear her mind of the confused warmth of last night. It had just been a pleasurable interlude, nothing more, she reassured herself sternly.

She felt a little better once she had showered and dressed. She continued to give herself a severe pep talk as she dried her hair, and by the time she left Lucas's bedroom had almost managed to convince herself that her priorities were back in order. Then she walked downstairs into the kitchen, her eyes connected with Lucas's and all her stern words counted for nothing.

'Good morning.' He smiled at her and she felt as if someone had pushed her into orbit, leaving her stomach behind.

'Morning.' She gave him the briefest of smiles and then wrenched her eyes away from his, trying very hard not to remember how they had wished each other good morning earlier… She was glad that they weren't alone in the room; Isobel was sitting at the breakfast bar, a glass of milk in front of her.

'How are you this morning, Isobel?' she asked, turning her attention to the child.

Isobel barely looked up. 'I'm okay,' she murmured.

'I'm making Isobel's favourite breakfast of pancakes,' Lucas said with a smile. 'Would you like some?'

'No, thank you. I never really eat much breakfast.'

'They won't be as good as Mrs Gordon makes anyway,' Isobel told her.

'Of course they will. Bet I make the best pancakes you've ever tasted,' Lucas said. 'Go on, try some, Milly. You must be hungry.'

Hidden in the softly spoken words was the husky reminder of why she should be hungry.

'No, I'm fine—really.' Penny hoped her cheeks hadn't just flared with colour. 'But I'll make some tea, if you don't mind.' Without waiting for him to reply she headed over for the kettle. She'd just have a quick drink and get back to the office. A cosy breakfast was definitely not what she needed right now.

'That would be great,' Lucas said cheerfully. 'But I'll have coffee.'

'Fine.' She busied herself opening cupboard doors to find cups.

Lucas poured some batter into a pan and the gentle sizzle of cooking filled the air. Surprisingly he looked quite at home in front of the stove, she thought as she glanced over at him. He was dressed in casual faded blue jeans and a blue T-shirt, and he had a teatowel strung over one shoulder, as if he spent most mornings whipping up some gastronomic delight. As Penny watched he scooped up the edges of the pancake and then flipped it over expertly.

'Mrs Gordon would be most impressed,' she remarked, and grinned over at Isobel, expecting her to smile back.

But Isobel was sitting at the breakfast bar looking totally unlike her usual sunny-natured self. She was resting her chin in her hands, a look of total dejection on her young face.

Penny looked questioningly over at Lucas and he shook his head.

'Isobel's grandma has had to cancel their outing today,' he explained in a light tone. 'She's a little disappointed.'

'Oh, dear.' Penny glanced back at Isobel. 'A little disappointed' was obviously the understatement of the year.

'Gran was going to take me to the beach,' Isobel said in a low tone.

And, judging by the pretty yellow pedal-pushers and matching top, she had been all ready to go when the news came. There was even a beach bag on the floor beside her, packed with a towel and her bucket and spade.

'That's a shame,' Penny said sympathetically. 'Maybe she'll take you another day instead.'

'Maybe…but she isn't feeling very well.' Isobel frowned, her young face suddenly creased with concern. 'I hope she doesn't have to go into hospital like Mrs Gordon.'

'I don't think she will, honey,' Lucas said quickly. 'Now, do me a favour—will you go outside and call Flint in?'

'Flint isn't allowed in the kitchen. Mrs Gordon says so,' the child told him solemnly.

'Well, we will make an exception today, as it is special circumstances,' Lucas said easily.

'Okay, Daddy.' The child slipped down off the high stool and ran out of the back door. A few seconds later they could hear her calling for the dog.

'That's better—thought we could do with a minute on our own.' Lucas smiled. He put the teatowel down and switched the cooker off, and in the ensuing silence Penny could feel her heart drumming erratically against her chest as he crossed purposefully towards her.

He looked so handsome and sure of himself, and suddenly she wasn't sure of anything any more…except the fact that all her strong words were like dust in the wind as soon as he came close.

He smiled at her. 'So, how are you feeling this morning?'

'Fine.' Vivid memories from last night flitted disturbingly through her mind as their eyes connected. His hands caressing over her waist and then sliding upwards towards her breast…his mouth hot and deeply possessive against her skin. 'Absolutely fine,' she reiterated brightly, trying to ignore the recollections. How did he manage to look so devastatingly handsome in just blue jeans and an open necked T-shirt? she wondered distractedly. But then Lucas would probably look good dressed in sackcloth, she thought, trying to switch her mind away from the dangerous attraction she felt for him.

'It's a pity Isobel's outing has had to be cancelled,' she said, trying desperately to keep her mind on more sensible things.

'Yes…it is.' He seemed to be studying her very intently; his eyes were moving over her face in a way that sent tingles of pure sensual awareness trickling through her.

Just the way he was looking at her made her want to forget everything and melt into his arms again; the need was like a raw ache inside her. With difficulty she made herself step back from him and forced herself to concentrate on Isobel. 'She seemed very disappointed.'

For a moment she thought he wasn't going to follow her lead, thought he was going to switch the subject back to what had happened between them last night again, but after a brief hesitation he took up the conversation. 'Yes, and unfortunately Pam is cancelling more and more frequently these days.'

'Is her health very bad?'

Lucas shook his head. 'Quite the contrary; she's in wonderful health. Pam's problem is that she has got a new boyfriend who is half her age and apparently she hasn't told him that she is a grandma. She's frightened it might put him off her.'

'I see.' Penny pulled a face. 'He wouldn't be a very nice person if a little thing like that put him off her. Grandmas are getting younger and younger these days anyway.'

'That's exactly what I told her, but she is completely besotted with him and doesn't want to take any risks with the relationship. So I'm afraid Isobel will have to take a back seat for the time being.' Lucas shrugged. 'That's her prerogative. And I wouldn't mind so much if she didn't keep letting Isobel down. She rings her up and makes promises and then at the last minute cancels them because he's arrived. You can't do that with young children; they don't understand. I've had to lie and tell Isobel she isn't well…and I don't like doing that.'

'It's a difficult situation, but you are right—you shouldn't make promises to children unless you are prepared to keep them.' Penny agreed completely. 'I'm surprised Isobel's grandma isn't more sensitive towards her. You'd think losing her daughter would make her granddaughter extra special.'

'You'd think so, wouldn't you?' Lucas agreed dryly.

'Maybe it's the grief of losing her daughter that has made her like that?' Penny suggested lightly. 'Grief can affect people in very different ways, you know.'

'Maybe.' Lucas smiled at her.

'What are you smiling at?' she asked curiously.

'You.' Lucas took a step closer to her, a gleam of humour in his dark eyes. 'You like to see the good in people, don't you?'

'I don't know…do I?' Her heart was starting to thump a heavy and irregular beat again.

'I think so.' To her consternation he suddenly reached out and pulled her into his arms. 'You have some very lovely traits.'

Penny wanted to pull away from him, but she couldn't. The merest touch of his body against hers made her feel weak with longing. She didn't know if she did see the good in people…all she knew was that she wanted to forget that he was her father's enemy and see the good in him.

He stroked the side of her face lightly with his fingers. 'And while we have this moment let me just tell you that last night was wonderful,' he murmured huskily.

Suddenly she didn't know if she could go on with her charade a moment longer. It was burning her away inside. 'Lucas, we need to talk—' She didn't know what she had been going to say, but whatever it was it was curtailed as the back door opened and Isobel came back in, with Flint skipping by her feet.

Lucas stepped back from Penny immediately, and then

bent to stroke Flint as the dog jumped up at him, wagging his tail.

'Look what I've got,' Isobel said, holding out a bunch of daisies in each hand. 'One is for Mrs Gordon and one for Grandma…and…' With difficulty she separated the bunch and held out a few blooms for Penny. 'These are for you.'

'They are lovely, Isobel,' Penny said, touched at the child's consideration. 'Thank you—it's a beautiful thought.' She took the daisies from her and put them to her nose. They had a peppery sweet smell.

'Daddy buys flowers for people sometimes,' Isobel said solemnly. 'He got roses for Emma.'

Penny wondered who Emma was… Some girlfriend, probably; in the language of flowers roses were for love. Was Lucas in love with someone else? She remembered Shauna telling her that he was cut up about a relationship that had just ended. Maybe he still was…maybe last night when he had been making love to her he had been wishing that he was with Emma. She was surprised to feel a sudden fierce surge of jealousy at the thought. The emotion shocked her. She had never been a jealous person and she had no right to feel that emotion now. Lucas could see whoever he wanted…send roses to whomever he wanted…it was none of her business.

'Let's put these flowers in water so they will stay fresh,' Penny said, turning her mind away from Lucas and his dalliances. He probably bought roses for lots of women…probably had a different girlfriend falling at his feet every week.

'There are jam jars under the sink,' Isobel offered helpfully.

Penny went to get them out. The white flowers made

charming posies in the jars. Penny lined them up on the kitchen window ledge and then returned to making Lucas some coffee and herself a cup of tea.

'Do you think Grandma might come and take me to the beach later today?' Isobel asked hopefully as she sat back at the breakfast bar.

'I don't think so, pumpkin.' Lucas put the plate of pancakes down in front of her.

'Oh.' Isobel stared at the plate of food in front of her dejectedly.

'Would you like maple syrup or lemon and sugar to go with those?' Lucas asked.

'Maple syrup, please. Do you think Gran will take me to the beach next week?'

'I don't know. I wouldn't bank on it, Issy.'

Isobel bit down on her bottom lip.

'Have you heard any news about Mrs Gordon?' Penny asked, changing the subject as she put Lucas's coffee down in front of him.

'Thanks, Milly. Yes—I rang this morning. She had a comfortable night and she is waiting for the specialist report this afternoon. Her sister is with her.'

'Can we go and see her, Daddy?' Isobel asked. 'I want to give her my flowers.'

'Not today, Issy. Mrs Gordon needs to have some rest.'

'Will Mrs Gordon still be able to take me shopping for my fairy outfit tomorrow after school?' Isobel asked suddenly.

'I don't think so, Isobel. I think you'll have to make do with my help for that shopping trip.'

Isobel looked shocked. 'Don't be silly, Daddy. You won't know what to buy. That's girls' stuff.'

'I think I might know a bit about what the more fashionable fairies will be wearing this season.' Lucas grinned. 'You can count on me.'

Penny laughed at the absurdity of the statement, but Isobel didn't look amused or impressed. 'You won't know anything! Everyone else will have the right clothes but I won't! Gina Fredrick will make fun of me and everyone will laugh.'

'Oh, come on, Isobel, you are blowing this thing out of proportion. It's a school play and you are six years of age. It doesn't really matter what you wear. All you need is a frilly frock and a wand; nobody is going to laugh at you.'

'Yes, they will—Gina Fredrick will.' Isobel suddenly looked as if she was going to cry. 'Gina won't be wearing a frilly dress. Her mummy takes her shopping all the time and she always looks good.'

'You always look good.'

'No, I don't. I had the wrong shoes for our school walking trip last Tuesday. Gina said they were old-fashioned.' Suddenly Isobel pushed her chair back from the breakfast bar and ran out of the room.

Lucas grimaced. 'Sorry about this, Milly. I think Isobel has had one disappointment too many for one day.'

'It's understandable,' Penny said lightly. 'But I don't think you should have told her that it doesn't matter what she wears for her big event. Even at the age of six a girl knows that's not true.'

Lucas raked a hand distractedly through his hair. 'It's a school play, Milly…'

'Even so, it's important that Isobel feels she is fitting in with her contemporaries. I remember when I went to school how important it was for me to fit in, and I think the pressures on children are even worse now.'

'I suppose you are right.' He shrugged. 'But, hell, if

she is worried like this at the age of six, what the heck will she be like when she becomes a teenager?'

Penny's heart went out to him; it couldn't be easy bringing up his daughter on his own. 'If you want, I'll take her shopping tomorrow.' She hadn't even realised she was going to make the offer until the words were out.

'Would you?' Lucas looked surprised—as well he might. She felt pretty surprised herself. 'That would be very kind of you, Milly. I'd really appreciate it.'

What the heck was she doing? Penny wondered dazedly. This was a real grey area. All right, she sympathised with Lucas's plight—being a one-parent family was not easy, and little Isobel's dejected face had tugged at her heartstrings; at the tender age of six she was obviously conscious of not having a mother, like the other girls in the class—but under the circumstances she couldn't afford to get involved here. This wasn't her problem. And yet…

'You really don't mind?' Lucas checked.

What if Mildred Bancroft turned up tomorrow? Penny's inner voice asked sternly. What then? Not only would she be in deep trouble, but Isobel would be let down yet again by another adult in her life. She should be concentrating on hiding those papers for her father and getting out of here—nothing else.

Penny glanced over at the doorway and saw Isobel's face peeping in; she had obviously heard Penny's offer and was waiting expectantly for her answer.

Penny took a deep breath. 'No, I don't mind,' she said gently. And, strangely enough, she really didn't. What that meant, she didn't know. At this point in time she didn't want to analyse anything too deeply.

She heard Isobel give a whoop of joy and then the

child came hurtling through the door to fling herself at Penny. 'Are you really going to come shopping with me?' she asked excitedly.

'Yes, Isobel. I'll take you tomorrow.' If she'd had any reservations about what she was doing they seemed to evaporate as the little girl climbed up on the stool beside her and flung her arms around her.

'Thank you…thank you,' she squealed excitedly.

'That's okay.' Penny felt quite overwhelmed by the child's response. After all, under different circumstances she wouldn't have thought twice about helping out.

'My dress is going to be far better than Gina Fredrick's now,' Isobel said with triumph.

'Well, I hope so.' Penny laughed. Over Isobel's shoulder her eyes connected with Lucas's. He smiled at her and she felt her heart dip, as if someone had opened a trap door and she had fallen through it.

She hoped he wasn't getting the wrong idea. All right, she liked his daughter, and wanted to help out, but she didn't want him to think that she was harbouring any serious thoughts about the nature of their relationship.

As the child pulled away Penny tried to get into a more businesslike frame of mind. She glanced at her watch. 'I could do with going back to my hotel for a change of clothes before we start work today, Lucas. I'll ring for a taxi—'

'I'll bring you down.' Lucas waved a hand as she started to object. 'I've got to go out anyway. I want to drop those papers at Salvador's house. Get him to check them out.'

Just thinking about those deeds nestling in Lucas's filing cabinet brought a sharp taste of reality into Penny's mouth.

'Tell you what—we'll have lunch at the Smugglers'

Inn and a walk along the beach while we are out,' Lucas continued, and smiled at Isobel. 'That way you can try out your bucket and spade after all.'

Isobel gave another whoop of delight that set Flint barking excitedly.

'Maybe you could give me a key for the house, Lucas,' Penny suggested tentatively over the noise. 'That way I can make my own way back here from the hotel after I've changed, and get on with finding the other documents you need.'

'Time enough for work later this afternoon,' Lucas said easily. 'Have lunch with us, Milly.'

Penny's heart thumped uneasily. Lunch sounded incredibly tempting. But she couldn't afford to relax; her ultimate goal had to be to find those papers. 'You really need those other papers, Lucas, and—'

'The other papers can wait a few more hours,' Lucas said, finishing his coffee.

She supposed he could afford to take a more relaxed view of things now he had the deeds to her father's property safely in his possession, Penny thought wryly. If only she had found them first. She could have been out of here before dinner last night and safely at the airport by now.

'So, what do you say? Will you have lunch with us?'

'Well, I…'

'Please come, Milly,' Isobel entreated, her eyes wide with excitement.

Penny glanced from the child back over at Lucas. 'You are on a time limit to find those papers,' she reminded him shakily, trying not to weaken but to think sensibly.

'I might not need them anyway. It will all depend on what Salvador tells me once he has gone through this other paperwork.'

'I see…' In which case her chance for helping her father might have passed, and it might be time to just cut her losses and book herself on the next flight back to Arbuda to help her father pack up his house.

She glanced from Isobel's earnest face to Lucas, who was patiently waiting for her to answer him. And suddenly the thought of leaving here was unbearable. She'd give herself two more days, she decided. And in that time she could see what the developments were with Lucas's solicitor and she could take Isobel shopping.

'Lunch sounds great,' she said decisively. 'I'd love to join you.'

CHAPTER SEVEN

IT WAS one of those halcyon days that came so often in the Caribbean. Clear blue skies and sizzling temperatures, with just a little edge of a cooling breeze from the trade winds. It was perfect—or rather it would have been if she'd been here under the right circumstances and the situation had been different.

Penny wondered what would have happened if she had told Lucas the truth this morning. Would she be sitting next to him in this car now as he drove her back to her hotel? Or would a taxi have been summoned and the door slammed behind her?

She glanced around at Isobel, who was sitting in the back. Flint was next to her on the car seat and she had her arm around him, happily telling him about their plans for the day. The dog was panting heavily, wagging his tail as if he understood exactly what she was saying.

'They're the best of friends,' Lucas said with a grin as she returned her attention frontward.

'Certainly seem to be,' Penny agreed. 'He's a great dog.'

'Yes, and a good guard dog—he's very protective of Isobel.'

They reached the outskirts of the city and drove down towards the old quarter. Bumping over the cobbled streets, Lucas pulled up a little way from her hotel.

'Do you want to go and see your solicitor and pick me up later?' Penny asked, reaching for the door handle.

'No, we'll wait. It will save me doubling back on myself—and anyway I'd like you to meet Salvador and his wife Maria; they are a nice couple.'

Under the circumstances Penny would have preferred not to meet Lucas's solicitor. 'Well, I might be a while, Lucas.'

'That's okay—we'll wait.'

Short of saying she just didn't want to meet Salvador there was nothing else she could do but nod her acceptance and climb out of the car.

Was it her imagination or was she getting more deeply embroiled in this charade with every passing minute? What with last night… Swiftly she tried to turn her mind away from that…and Isobel…and now Lucas's friends…

She turned into the cool air-conditioned foyer of the hotel and tried not to think too deeply about the situation.

'Morning, Ms Kennedy.' The woman behind the desk greeted her cordially, but it set Penny's nerves completely on edge. Just say Lucas had decided to come into the hotel with her—the game would definitely be up now.

With difficulty she put a smile on her face. 'Call me Milly,' she told her firmly. 'Everyone does.'

'Because of your writing name?'

Obviously the man she had spoken to yesterday had spread the word. 'Yes, that's right. Any messages for me?' she asked, quickly changing the subject. Not that she was expecting any messages. Her father thought she was working on board ship and she hadn't told her work colleagues or friends where she was going.

'No…no messages.'

'Okay, thanks. Could I have my room key, please?'

When she reached her bedroom she stripped off her clothes and hurriedly riffled through her wardrobe and found a cool blue summer dress to wear. Then she decided she'd better ring her father and see how he was.

So she took her mobile out of her bag and keyed in his number. As she waited for him to answer she walked through to the bathroom and brushed her teeth.

He still hadn't answered by the time she had finished. She hung up with a frown, wondering where he was. Maybe he was busy out in the fields. It was a little early, but he might be harvesting the sugar cane around now. She sincerely hoped so, because it would mean he could start paying Lucas some more money next month. And if the price of sugar had gone up and the harvest was good maybe he would get another year in his house. Of course if Lucas got his way and served his papers on time it wouldn't matter what the harvest was like; her father would be finished.

With those sobering thoughts ringing through her mind Penny returned outside to Lucas and Isobel.

'You weren't long at all,' Lucas said as she slipped back into the seat beside him.

'Well, I tried not to be.' She noticed the admiring glance he sent in her direction before he slipped the car into gear and pulled out into traffic. It had only been the briefest of looks but it had been purely sexual, and it sent an answering heat of desire racing through her.

Don't think about that, she told herself fiercely. Last night could never happen again. Her eyes were drawn to his hands on the steering wheel…large, capable hands that had caressed her so passionately, taking her to wild heights of exhilaration.

'We've had a slight change of plan while you've been in the hotel,' Lucas said, changing down a gear so that the powerful car could negotiate the winding roads more easily. 'I rang Salvador and he's just driving his mother-in-law home, so I said we'd have lunch and a walk first, then call on him for coffee on the way back.'

'That's fine,' Penny said, relieved that her meeting with his solicitor was being deferred, even if it was only for a few hours.

After travelling a few miles Lucas parked the car at the edge of a headland. 'The restaurant is over there,' he said, pointing to a white building in the distance that sat at the edge of a creamy white bay lined with palm trees. 'We can walk along the beach to it from here, if you are up to it?'

'Of course I'm up to it,' she said indignantly. 'It's not that far.'

He grinned. 'Just checking that you aren't too tired after your disturbed night's sleep.'

She felt herself blush to the roots of her hair and he laughed.

'I don't know what is so funny about that remark,' she said stiffly.

'Don't you?' His grin seemed to stretch even wider. 'You should see your face.' He reached for the door handle. 'So much for the modern, it-means-nothing remarks last night.'

'I meant what I said last night,' Penny replied, and her voice was quiet and steady but her heart was thumping with rapid disapproval.

'Whatever you say.' Lucas smiled. 'But I get the feeling you are more old-fashioned in your outlook than you like to let on.'

'Milly isn't old-fashioned,' Isobel piped up innocently from behind them, reminding them both of the young ears that might not have understood what they were talking about but were listening in just the same. 'She's cool.'

'Thank you, Isobel.' Penny smiled at the little girl, touched by her intervention. She glanced over at Lucas and couldn't resist grinning back at him and adding the childish words, 'So there.'

'You women always stick together, don't you?' he drawled with teasing amusement.

'That's because little girls are made of sugar and spice and all things nice, and little boys are made of slugs and snails and puppy dogs' tails,' Penny said with wink in Isobel's direction. 'So we have to stick together, don't we, Isobel?'

Isobel giggled. 'Yep, I reckon.' She nodded her head.

Together they got out of the car and walked towards the beach. 'Colin Sal is the naughtiest boy in our school, and he is definitely made of slugs and snails,' Isobel told Penny, taking hold of her hand as they walked down a winding path under the shade of palm trees. 'He brought a huge cockroach into school in a matchbox and let it loose in Miss Jenkins's desk and it ran up her sleeve.'

'Ugh.' Penny cringed. 'Poor Miss Jenkins!'

'I know.' Isobel nodded, pleased with Penny's shocked reaction. 'And it was huge,' she added dramatically. 'About that big…' She held up her hand to indicate a length of about six inches. 'Miss Jenkins was nearly crying.'

'I bet she was.'

'He's not a very nice boy,' Isobel added solemnly.

'Maybe you'd better keep your distance from him, then?' Penny suggested with a smile.

'Maybe…' Isobel let go of her hand as they reached the end of the path and ran ahead to cut across some rocks. Flint bounded across them with her, wagging his tail and waiting for her as he jumped down on the sand ahead of her.

'Be careful on the rocks,' Penny called after her.

'I will,' she called back merrily, without checking her speed.

'Slow down, Isobel,' Lucas called firmly as he watched her leap from rock to rock. She altered her stride slightly and jumped down onto the sand. 'I tell her to go carefully on there every time we come and she still insists on racing ahead.' Lucas reached out a hand to help Penny as they started to follow her across the rock surface.

'I'll be okay.' Penny slipped off her high-heeled sandals and, ignoring his hand, followed in Isobel's footsteps. Only when she reached the other side did she hesitate. The leap down onto the sand was quite steep.

Lucas jumped down ahead of her and then reached up to help her. Rather than topple down in an ungainly fashion she accepted the help, taking hold of his hand and then gingerly slipping down. He steadied her as her feet connected with the ground and for a moment she was held close against his body. Immediately her senses responded to that closeness. She was aware of the deliciously familiar tang of his cologne and the strength of his arms around her. She glanced up uncertainly and their eyes met. The yearning to be even closer and to feel his lips against hers was intense.

He was the one to step back from her. 'It's a bit of a step down, but worth it for the walk,' he said lightly, as if he hadn't been aware of the instant sexual chemistry that had flared.

Maybe he hadn't, she thought. Maybe last night he had enjoyed his fill of her and was now content to light-heartedly draw a line beneath the episode. She wished she was…but shockingly her traitorous body still seemed to be clamouring for more.

For a while they walked in silence, watching Isobel as she skipped ahead of them, her pink bucket and spade in one hand, the other resting lightly on Flint's head. The sand was warm under Penny's feet, the sun dazzling over the turquoise water. There wasn't another person around for miles.

'It's beautiful here,' Penny said, taking a deep breath of the salt-laced air.

'Just what we needed after being cooped up in that office,' Lucas agreed.

Isobel came running back to show them a shell she had picked up.

'That's very pretty.' Penny took it from her, admiring the pink mother-of-pearl sheen. 'You should keep it—put it on your dressing table and it will always remind you of our perfect day together on the beach.'

'I'll put it on top of my jewellery box,' Isobel said, pleased with the idea. 'Will you keep it safe for me?'

'I will indeed.' Penny opened her purse and put it in.

'You're very good with her,' Lucas remarked casually as they walked on again, Isobel skipping happily ahead. 'You seem a natural around children; I'm surprised you haven't got some of your own.'

'I would like a family one day,' Penny admitted, then, for some reason slightly embarrassed by the admission, added hastily, 'In the distant future, I mean…when I'm ready for settling down.'

'Of course.' He smiled over at her. 'So, tell me—have you ever come close to settling down?'

'Yes, once.'

'But you didn't love him enough to commit?' Lucas hazarded a guess when she didn't continue.

'No. I did love him.' Penny frowned. Usually when she talked about Nick or even thought about him there was a deep feeling of pain and regret inside her, but strangely this morning she felt no sharp jolt…no sadness at all. 'I was crazy about him,' she added. 'We lived together for over a year and were planning to get married.'

'So what happened?'

'Nick wasn't as committed to our relationship as I'd thought. He was seeing someone else.' Penny shrugged. 'So I moved out and she moved in.'

'How long ago was that?'

'Almost two years.'

'So, would you say you are over him now?' Lucas asked curiously.

'Yes, of course.'

Lucas noticed the way her green-gold eyes darkened as she spoke, the way her eyelashes flickered down, hiding the emotions within.

'I heard from a mutual friend not so long ago that they got married last Christmas.'

'And do you wish them well?'

Penny slanted a wry glance over at him and for a moment her eyes glinted with humour. 'I was a bit disappointed that they didn't invite me to the wedding. But apart from that there's no hard feelings.'

Lucas laughed. 'Well, obviously the guy is a total idiot.'

'Obviously,' Penny agreed dryly. 'Or maybe he just realised something I didn't...like we weren't meant for each other.' She looked away from Lucas, out across the sea. 'I used to think he was my perfect other half...that meeting him was kismet...'

'And then when it all fell apart you thought your chance for happiness has gone?' Lucas finished the sentence for her and she looked round at him in surprise.

'That's how I felt when Kay died. But life goes on, and surprisingly you can find happiness again. Although

I have to admit to the odd moment of feeling guilty about that…especially in the early days when I started to take a woman to my bed again.'

'I'm sorry, Lucas.' Penny shook her head. 'I'm talking about a mere affair and you've lost your wife.'

'You lived together; that's a lot more involved than a mere affair.'

'Yes…' Penny's heart slammed uncomfortably against her chest. Not a lot of people had understood that…but Lucas did. He seemed so honourable…so decent—and she was deceiving him. She swallowed hard on a lump in her throat.

They were reaching the other end of the beach now, and Penny could see the restaurant quite clearly. Tables with pristine white tablecloths were laid out on a long terrace under the shade of a vine-covered canopy.

'We get the best of both worlds here,' Lucas said as he allowed her to proceed up some steps ahead of him. 'The perfect service and food of a top restaurant along with the informality of beachside dining.'

Penny smiled, but inside she was thinking along much deeper lines—such as the fact there was no such thing as having the best of both worlds. At this moment her father was probably working hard in the fields, worrying that he was going to lose everything and that his efforts were going to be in vain. Meanwhile she was here, having lunch with the enemy. Guilt licked through her. Was she for or against Lucas? She wished she could make a decision and stick with it. All this changing her mind and her sympathies back and forward between the two men was tearing her apart.

All right, Lucas's father had been a rogue and a conman; there was no doubt about that. But that didn't mean Lucas was from the same mould. On the other hand, there was no doubt that her father didn't deserve to be in the mess he was in.

Lucas pulled out a chair for her, and then sat down opposite.

Isobel was still playing on the beach; she was busy making sandcastles by the water's edge, with Flint patiently watching her every move.

'Shall we leave Isobel to enjoy herself a little longer while we survey the menu?' Lucas asked, and she nodded in agreement.

'We won't leave her too long, though…' Lucas grinned. 'As you missed sampling my wonderful pancakes this morning you must be starving.'

'You're right—I am.' She looked across at him and smiled. 'I was impressed with your culinary skills this morning, by the way.'

'Maybe you'll stay and sample them next time,' he drawled teasingly.

Penny was glad that the waiter appeared beside them at that point, because she honestly didn't know how to respond to that remark. Okay, she knew Lucas was joking around, but she still found the subject of last night difficult to come to terms with. There wouldn't be a next time because it had probably been one of the most foolish moves of her life…it had also been the most pleasurable.

As the waiter greeted Lucas warmly and they talked for a little while her eyes moved over the lean, handsome lines of his face. Lucas was one of the most fascinating and most attractive men she had ever met. She liked the way his eyes lit up with warmth and humour as he talked, and the way there was a slight dimple in his chin when he smiled. Her eyes moved to the darkness of his hair and she remembered the way she had laced her fingers through it as his lips plundered against hers in a sensual moment of complete intimacy, their naked bodies entwined.

He looked over at her and smiled and her heart violently skipped a beat. 'What would you like to drink, Milly?'

'Er…a glass of white wine, please.' Hastily she lifted up the menu and pretended to study it.

Pull yourself together, she told herself furiously. Last night was just sex…don't dwell on it.

There was silence as the waiter disappeared to get their drinks. The only sound the gentle thud of the surf hitting the sand and the hissing as it withdrew.

'Have you made up your mind what you would like?' Lucas asked after a while.

What she would like was the impossible…she wanted more days like this, more nights like last night… She put the menu down, feeling annoyed with herself. 'I think I'll have the seafood.'

'It's good here—very fresh—'

Isobel came hurrying over to the table and interrupted them. 'Can I have pizza and chips, Daddy?'

Lucas considered the question for a moment. 'That's a bit of an unhealthy combination. Will you eat a side salad with it, and some fruit afterwards?'

Isobel wrinkled her nose. 'I suppose.'

Lucas shook his head as the child ran off again to continue making her sandcastles. 'She'd eat rubbish all day if I let her.'

Penny smiled. 'Wouldn't all children?'

'Probably, but I don't think Isobel would get away with half the things she does if Kay was here. She was always very health-conscious—worked out in the gym, did yoga, ate sensibly.'

'It's a big responsibility bringing her up on your own, isn't it?' Penny said softly.

'Being a single parent isn't easy. And of course with work I have to rely quite heavily on Mrs Gordon. But I enjoy being a dad.' He grinned suddenly as he looked over and saw Isobel paddling into the sea, getting the bottom of her pedal-pushers soaked in the process. 'Well, most days I do anyway.'

The waiter brought their drinks and they placed their order for food.

'You will find it difficult if Mrs Gordon is off work for too long,' Penny reflected. 'What will you do?'

Lucas shrugged. 'I suppose I'll need to hire someone to fill the gap. Not an easy task. Isobel adores her, and she is very reliable. But hopefully it won't be for long.'

Penny sipped her wine and wished she could offer to be of some help. She fought down the feeling, telling herself that she would be helping tomorrow, when she took Isobel shopping. That would have to be enough.

They spent an idyllic couple of hours over lunch. The food was wonderful and Lucas and Isobel were great company. Penny felt very at home with them. It was strange…it was as if she had known them all her life. When Lucas glanced at his watch and told them they should be heading off for Salvador's house it was as if a black thunderous cloud had rolled in over the heat of the day.

'Do we have to go, Daddy?' Even Isobel looked crest-fallen.

'Afraid so. And I've got work to do this afternoon, young lady, so you'll have to be good and play quietly.'

Isobel wrinkled her nose.

'Never mind—we are going shopping tomorrow,' Penny reminded her. 'That should be fun.'

Lucas got up to settle the bill and then they headed back across the beach.

'What did you do with the papers for Salvador?' Penny asked, her mind running ahead to the all-important meeting with his solicitor.

'I've locked them in the glove compartment of the car.'

Penny found herself hoping that the car might be gone when they got back. Then pulled herself up fiercely. It was hardly the wish of a decent upright citizen. All right, she wanted things to work out for her father—but not at any price.

And what about the price she was paying? Penny thought suddenly. She glanced across at Lucas. She didn't want to lose his friendship, but ultimately that was what was going to happen.

They arrived at the rocks and he reached out a hand to help her climb up towards the car. 'I really enjoyed lunch,' Penny said, trying to ignore the sensation of pleasure as his fingers curved firmly over hers. 'Thank you.'

'Maybe we can do it again some time. Next weekend we could take the yacht and sail around to a different bay.'

'Maybe.' Penny felt her heart thump painfully. Next week she would probably be back in Arbuda, helping her father. She pulled away from him and followed Isobel up towards the road.

They reached the car and Penny helped Isobel dust the sand off her feet and put her shoes on.

'Thanks, Milly.' Lucas picked up the child's bucket and spade. 'I'm just going to get Flint a drink of water from the back of the car. Will you check in the glove compartment and make sure those papers are all there?' He handed her a bunch of keys. 'It's the small gold one.'

Penny looked at the keys and felt her heart go into

overdrive. Finally she was going to get her hands on the deeds. Was it too late to do anything about it? Or was this the chance she had been waiting for?

Isobel ran around to the back of the car with her father, and Penny sat sideways in the passenger seat to open the compartment.

The papers were in a large brown envelope. She opened it and looked inside. There were reams of pages appertaining to her father's business partnership with Lawrence Darien. And then, behind them, the old yellowed deeds for the Kennedy estate. Just holding them in her hand sent Penny's mind reeling. Could she slip them into her handbag while Lucas and Isobel were occupied with the dog? She could simply tell Lucas they were missing, that he must have left them behind in the filing cabinet… He'd never suspect that she had them…would he?

'Everything in order?' Lucas's voice from the driver's door behind her made her jump nervously. She hadn't heard him coming around the side of the car.

'Yes…seems to be.'

'Great.' He flashed her a smile and then his eyes moved to the deeds in her hands. 'It was a bit remiss of me, leaving them in the car, I suppose.'

'Yes, very careless… But what is it they say? Easy come, easy go?' Penny couldn't keep the dry edge out of her tone.

Lucas's eyebrows lifted slightly. 'I wouldn't say those deeds were that easily come by,' he replied matter-of-factly. 'According to my father he had years of problems with William Kennedy, and gave the guy umpteen chances to pay back what he owes.'

'Really?' Penny had to bite back a terse reply, but there was a wealth of feeling loaded into that one word.

'Yes, really.' Lucas was distracted as Isobel started to giggle and mess about with Flint. 'Come on, Issy, back in the car now.'

Penny had no alternative but to put the deeds away in the envelope. She couldn't take them now that Lucas had seen them in her hand.

'Look, Milly, I know you don't like the thought of evicting someone from their home, and neither do I,' Lucas continued once the child had obeyed him. 'But this is business—not charity.'

'You are really quite cold, aren't you, Lucas?' she said brutally. 'In fact you remind me a bit of a shark circling in the water, the scent of blood around him.'

'It's all very well taking the moral high ground,' Lucas grated sardonically. 'But with respect you don't know the first thing about this case.'

Penny wanted to tell him that in fact she probably knew more than he did about it. But she fell silent.

A few minutes later they were driving back down the road. The light-hearted atmosphere that had accompanied lunch had disappeared.

Penny felt tense, and she could feel the beginning of a headache at the back of her eyes. She glanced surreptitiously over at Lucas. He looked stern and unapproachable now. Obviously her little outburst had not pleased him.

Not that she cared, she told herself. Lucas might be a nice guy, but he was his father's son and blood was thicker than water. And obviously he was going to follow Lawrence Darien's last instructions to the letter, no matter what.

Lucas slanted a look over at her. 'I don't know why we are arguing about this, Milly. I think we should agree to differ on the subject.'

'Fine.' Her tone was airily light.

She was aware that he looked at her rather strangely, and she had to force herself to smile and say lightly, 'As you said, it's none of my business.'

He turned the car through tall, impressive gateposts and up a long and winding drive. A little while later a white bungalow with blue shutters came into sight. It was built on the edge of a steep terraced garden that afforded magnificent views over the Caribbean. But it wasn't the sea view that held Penny's attention, it was the very beautiful young woman who was standing on the doorstep. She had long glossy hair the colour of copper beech and was wearing a flowing white summer dress that had crossover straps at the back and a split up the front, showing a provocative glimpse of tanned shapely legs.

She turned as their car pulled up beside her, and Penny wondered if it was her imagination or if the woman looked rattled at the sight of Lucas.

'Hi.' Her voice was slightly breathless. 'This is a surprise, Lucas. I didn't expect to see you here.'

'Hello, Emma,' Lucas replied as he got out of the car, and it suddenly became clear to Penny why the woman was looking a little uncomfortable. This was Lucas's ex-girlfriend. 'I didn't expect to see you either, but it's a pleasant surprise.' He reached her side and kissed her on the cheek. The woman's skin immediately flushed a bright rosy hue. However, it was the way she looked up at him that really caught Penny's attention.

She's still in love with him, Penny realised immediately. There was no mistaking that look of complete and utter adoration, even though the woman made a brave attempt to try and mask it by stepping back from him and looking hastily away. Where had Shauna got the idea that Emma had been the one to end the relationship?

Penny wondered. From where she was sitting it certainly didn't look that way. But then it was hard to read Lucas; it could be that behind that laid-back, relaxed demeanour he was also cut up about their break-up. Maybe he and Emma had just had a lovers' spat…and she was the consolation prize caught in the middle for one evening. The idea was deeply disturbing. Penny felt a thrust of pain inside her unlike anything she had ever experienced.

Furious with herself, she clenched her hands into tight fists in her lap. Lucas's love-life was nothing to do with her. And it didn't matter that their night together had meant nothing. She had known it could never lead to anything anyway, and was perfectly content for it to be exactly what it was…a pleasurable interlude.

Isobel got out of the back seat of the car and ran over to say hello to the woman.

'Hello, honey.' Emma smiled at her and the little girl smiled back, but stood slightly sheltered behind her father, reaching up to hold on to his hand.

'Maria invited me over for coffee at one-thirty,' Emma said as she reached to pat Flint, who had ambled over towards her.

'Did she?' Lucas looked amused for a second. 'She told me one-thirty for coffee as well.'

'Oh!' The woman looked totally uncomfortable now. 'Look, I had no idea she was planning anything like this.'

'Neither did I, but you know Maria—she has good intentions.'

'I suppose she does. But it's a bit embarrassing, isn't it?' Emma glanced over to the car at Penny. 'Look, I'll go. Tell Maria I'll ring her later.'

'Don't rush off.' Lucas frowned. 'I'm not staying long anyway. I've only come to see Salvador on a matter of business—I've got to get back to work this afternoon.'

'Some things don't change, do they?' She smiled at him wryly.

'No.' He smiled back at her. 'Well, you know me—'

'Focused and dedicated.' She cut across him and then grinned. 'Yes, I know you.'

There was silence between them for a few seconds and they just continued to look at each other.

Penny was starting to feel a bit awkward. She didn't know if she should stay in the car, so as not to intrude, or if she should get out and join them.

'Have you rung the doorbell?' Lucas asked Emma suddenly.

'Oh!' Flustered, the woman reached and pushed the button next to her. 'No! I forgot! I was just about to when you arrived.'

Lucas glanced back towards Penny, as if only just realising that she was still in the car. 'Bring the papers out of the glove compartment, will you, Milly?'

'Certainly, sir,' Penny murmured under her breath as she opened the glove compartment and took out the deeds for a second time that day.

She didn't know why but she felt a tinge annoyed that when Lucas had finally dragged his attention away from Emma it had just been to send a businesslike request in her direction. Maybe it was his way of letting Emma know that she was just a work colleague and nothing more. Well, that was his prerogative, she supposed. And as she wasn't planning on sticking around here for more than a few days more she had no right to feel annoyed by it.

As she got out of the car the front door swung open and an attractive brunette greeted them warmly. 'Lucas and Emma—how lovely that you should arrive together.'

'Well, I think that is more by your design than ours,'

Emma said, reaching to kiss the woman on the cheek. 'I'll forgive you just this once. But only because you are pregnant, Maria. Don't pull an outrageous stunt like this again.'

'Well, you know what they say—the course of true love never does run smooth. And as you two are my dearest friends I just thought you needed your heads banging together…' Maria trailed off in consternation as she suddenly saw Penny walking around the other side of the car. 'Oh…!'

'This is Milly Bancroft,' Lucas interjected smoothly. 'Milly, this is Maria Sandenio and Emma Johnson.'

Taking pity on Maria, who clearly thought she had made a major social gaffe, and to some extent on Emma, who looked as if she was wearing a hair shirt, Penny smiled brightly at them both. 'Pleased to meet you. I'm Lucas's PA.'

'Oh!' Maria looked marginally reassured, but Penny could tell that she still wasn't completely sure what the status was between her and Lucas. 'Well, it's good to meet you too. Come on in—let's not stand out here in the heat any longer.'

Penny handed Lucas the brown envelope as she passed him to go inside and their eyes met briefly. She wondered if he was thankful that she had introduced herself as his PA. After all, if he wanted a reconciliation with Emma it would help clear the path. But it was hard to tell what was going on behind that dark, steady gaze.

CHAPTER EIGHT

SALVADOR met them in the lounge. He was older than his wife; Maria only looked as if she was in her late twenties whilst Salvador was probably in his early forties. His dark hair was tinged with grey at the temples, and he was on the portly side, yet there was a warmth and vigour about him that was immensely attractive.

'Pleased to meet you,' he said, shaking Penny's hand firmly.

Penny smiled back, liking Lucas's friends and wishing again that she were not here under false pretences.

'So these are the infamous papers, are they?' Salvador said, turning to take the envelope from Lucas.

'Yes, we finally unearthed them yesterday.'

'Right—well, let's go through to my study and take a look at them, shall we?' Before anyone could say anything else Salvador had steered Lucas from the room. 'Won't be long, ladies,' he said as he closed the door behind them.

'Now, where have we heard that before?' Emma said to Maria with a grin. 'Do you remember the time when the four of us went to Vieques for the weekend and those two spent the whole afternoon going through some business papers?'

'Vaguely… Now, shall we have tea or coffee?' Maria smiled over at Penny and indicated that she should make herself comfortable on one of the cream leather armchairs.

'Gosh, you must remember that weekend, Maria,'

Emma continued, apparently blithely unaware that her friend was trying to change the subject in deference to Penny. 'We had the most wonderful time. It was such a romantic hotel, and Lucas bought me that picture I loved of the old lighthouse at Isabel Segunda.'

'Oh, yes…I kind of remember that.' Maria flicked a narrow-eyed look over at Emma. But she was totally oblivious to it and was settling herself at one end of the settee.

'We were both a bit put out about them bringing work with them, though…weren't we? But that's men for you. Honestly, I'm sure Lucas could stay cooped up quite happily in an office for days on end. When we were dating I used to refer to his work as the other woman…and I don't suppose he has changed any?' She glanced over at Penny for clarification.

'Well…I couldn't say,' Penny murmured. 'I haven't been working for him that long.'

Emma nodded and seemed pleased with the reply.

Penny wondered if the woman was trying to score points by drawing attention to their wonderful romantic weekend, or if she was just still smarting about their split-up and blamed a lot of it on Lucas's work.

'Now, then, what can I get you to drink?' Maria tried again to distract the conversation. 'Cola for you, Isobel?'

Isobel nodded.

'And what about you ladies…tea or coffee?'

'Whatever you are making is fine with me,' Penny said politely.

'Coffee would be great,' Emma said decisively.

As soon as Maria had headed out of the room Isobel sat on Penny's knee and cuddled close against her. 'Can I have lemonade instead?' she asked in a stage whisper.

'I don't know—maybe Maria doesn't have lemonade. Why don't you go after her and ask?'

Isobel shook her head shyly.

'Shall I go and ask for you?'

Isobel nodded, pleased by the suggestion. Emma, on the other hand, suddenly looked annoyed. What was the matter with her? Penny wondered, as she slipped Isobel from her knee.

'So, Isobel…tell me all the news. What's been happening since I've seen you last?' Emma asked in a cosy tone as Penny left the room.

She found Maria opening and closing cupboards in a kitchen that looked out onto a terrace with a spectacular view. 'Sorry to intrude, but Isobel was wondering if she could change her mind and have lemonade?' Penny asked as the woman turned.

'Yes, of course she can.' Maria turned and took a bottle from the fridge. 'Actually, I'm glad to have a moment alone with you. Sorry about before…you know…' The woman looked over at her and grimaced. 'Trying to fix Lucas back up with Emma was a wild idea. I'd no idea he was seeing someone else—'

'You've no need to apologise to me,' Penny said sincerely. 'Really, I'm not in the running where Lucas is concerned.'

Maria didn't look entirely convinced.

'He's a very attractive man, but…' Penny shrugged, and then for some reason—maybe because the woman seemed so genuinely upset at the situation—she found herself confiding in her. 'To be honest, I don't think I'll be staying around here for much longer,' she said, lowering her voice. 'Although I haven't told Lucas that yet.'

'That's a shame. He seems to think very highly of you. I just overheard him talking to Salvador about how invaluable you've been these last few days. How Isobel in particular has taken a shine to you.'

'Yes…I'm going to really miss Isobel.' Penny felt her heart bounce unevenly against her chest.

Maria glanced over at her.

'But things aren't particularly working out for me here,' Penny continued, trying to sound practical. 'So it's best I move on.'

Maria didn't probe further. 'Salvador will be furious with me for inviting Emma today. He is always telling me off for getting involved in other people's problems. It's just I felt sorry for her. She and Lucas seemed to be happy for a while; in fact I hadn't seen Lucas so relaxed since…well, since before Kay died, I suppose. Then with no apparent reason at all he just finished with her. And I was wondering if he really wanted to finish with her or if it was a case of cold feet—maybe he felt he was getting too close to her and panicked. I sometimes think he still feels a bit uncomfortable about dating other women…he was so in love with Kay, you see.' Maria finished loading the tray. 'Does that sound silly? Maybe he wanted to finish with Emma… I'm just guessing.'

'No, it doesn't sound silly,' Penny murmured, remembering how Lucas had that very afternoon admitted to feeling guilty when he'd started to take women to his bed again. 'He could very easily have ended it for those reasons.'

'Well, as Salvador would say, it is none of my business. But really I just want Lucas to be happy. I think he deserves it after all he's been through.'

Penny moved to take the heavy tray from her. 'Here—let me help. I think you are carrying enough around with you,' she added wryly, indicating the very evident bump of her pregnancy.

Maria laughed and patted her bump proudly. 'You're right.'

'When is the baby due?' Penny asked, glad to be able to move to a lighter subject. She didn't want to think about how much Lucas might be in love with Emma…the subject seemed to send her senses into disarray.

'Two weeks tomorrow.'

'Not long, then. Have you got everything packed and ready?'

'Oh, yes. The case is sitting by the bedroom door. Every time I so much as sigh Salvador is looking at me anxiously, wondering if he should run to pick it up and shoo me out to the car.'

Penny laughed. 'I take it nerves are running high?'

'Just a little. I think he's almost more nervous and excited than me.'

Maria opened the lounge door for her.

'Did you have lemonade, Aunty Maria?' Isobel asked shyly as they walked in.

'Yes, honey.' Maria took the glass off the tray and handed it over to her. 'Now, what have you two been talking about?'

'Isobel has been telling me that Mrs Gordon is in hospital,' Emma said, accepting the china cup and saucer that Maria passed over to her.

'No!' Maria looked over at Penny for confirmation.

'She slipped on the kitchen floor last night and Lucas took her down to Casualty,' Penny said with a nod. 'They are keeping her in for observation.'

'Poor woman.' Maria looked upset.

'I wonder how Lucas will manage without her,' Emma reflected, just as the door opened and the men returned.

'I take it you are talking about Mrs Gordon?' Lucas said as he crossed towards the mantelpiece.

'Yes, Milly was just telling us.' Emma looked over at him with concern. 'How will you manage without her?'

'I might have to employ someone else, but hopefully it won't be for long. Thank you, Maria.' He smiled at her as she handed him a cup of coffee.

'Does that mean someone else will be looking after me, Daddy?' Isobel's small voice cut into the conversation. She had a heavy frown across her brow.

'Maybe,' Lucas answered cautiously. 'But only until Mrs Gordon gets better.'

'Will it be somebody I know?'

Lucas shook his head. 'But you soon will know her.'

'But I don't want anybody else.' Isobel suddenly looked as if she was going to cry. 'Unless it is someone I know.' She glanced over at Penny. 'Will you look after me, Milly?' she asked, her eyes wide and pleading, her tone tearful.

Penny was very conscious of everyone's eyes on her, and at the same time her heart went out to the child. She would have given anything to have been able to say yes. 'Well, it's not quite as simple as that, Isobel,' she said instead, softly. 'But your daddy is very clever, and he will find someone really nice for you, I'm sure.'

'Of course I will.' Lucas put his coffee down and went to pick up the little girl and sit down with her on his knee. 'And Mrs Gordon will be back soon.'

Isobel nodded, but her bottom lip was trembling.

Penny wished she could have offered to do more. She glanced over and caught Emma's eyes on her. The woman was staring at her with a look of open resentment and it suddenly occurred to Penny that she wasn't at all pleased about Isobel requesting her help.

'So how is work going, Lucas?' Maria asked brightly, trying to change the subject once again. 'You weren't as long in that office as we'd thought.'

'That's because things are fairly much in order.' Lucas rocked Isobel on his knee soothingly. 'Salvador's help is invaluable. I can't thank him enough for squeezing me into his busy schedule.'

'No thanks necessary,' Salvador said swiftly. 'And there is no reason at all why everything shouldn't be settled by the end of the month. As I said earlier, Lucas, now you have those deeds I think you will definitely be taking possession of that land on time, and then the building work can begin. Under Arbuda law once building work has started they won't be able to revoke the permission for it. So if you make an agreement with the contractor who wants to buy the place and allow him access to start immediately there should be no problem.'

Penny felt the blood drain away from her face at those words. She had been worrying about Isobel...about stupid things like did Lucas really love Emma...and her father was about to lose his home. Where were her priorities?

'Are you all right, Milly?' Maria asked her suddenly. 'You look a bit pale.'

Aware that Lucas's eyes were on her, Penny forced herself to smile. 'I've got a bit of a headache, actually, but it's nothing. It will pass.'

'Shall I get you a couple of painkillers and a glass of water?' Maria asked kindly.

'No—really, I'm fine. Thank you.'

'I suppose we should make a move,' Lucas said, glancing at his watch. 'Leave you good folks in peace.'

'You don't have to,' Maria said immediately. 'We were hoping you'd all stay. Salvador was going to light the barbecue later.'

'Another time, Maria,' Lucas said, getting to his feet. 'But thank you for the invitation.'

Everyone stood up and walked with them through to the front door.

Penny noticed that Emma put a hand on Lucas's arm, detaining him. 'If you need any help, Lucas, don't hesitate to call me,' she said in a breathy undertone.

'Thank you, Emma, that's very kind.' Isobel wriggled to get out of his arms and he put her down, allowing her to run outside to where Flint was sitting waiting patiently for them.

'I mean it,' Emma continued earnestly. 'As you know, I finish work most days around four-thirty. I'd be happy to look after Isobel for you.'

Penny didn't hear what Lucas's reply was because Flint started to bark excitedly as Isobel ran around the lawn with him. But out of the corner of her eye she did see Lucas bend to kiss Emma lightly on the cheek. She put both hands on his arms and leaned closer and kissed him back.

Hastily Penny averted her gaze completely.

'It was lovely meeting you,' Maria said in a low tone as they stepped outside together. 'And I hope we get to see you again before you leave.'

Penny smiled. 'It was nice meeting you too. And I wish you all the best with your baby. Have you any idea if it is a he or a she?'

'No, it's going to be a surprise.'

'A wonderful surprise,' Salvador agreed, putting an arm around his wife.

As they drove away from the house Penny glanced

back and saw the couple still standing in the garden with their arms around each other, waving. Emma, on the other hand, was nowhere to be seen.

'Your friends are lovely,' Penny said as she settled back and fastened her seatbelt.

'Yes, I think so.' Lucas pulled out onto the road again and they followed the narrow lanes in silence for a while. 'How are you feeling now?' Lucas asked as they approached a junction.

'I've still got a bit of a headache,' Penny admitted, and it was the truth. Her head was pounding with a dull ache—due, no doubt, to tension.

'I'll take you back to your hotel and you can have the rest of the day off,' Lucas said immediately. 'You're probably tired.'

'What about the papers you were anxious to find?' she asked curiously. 'Don't you need them any more?'

Lucas shook his head. 'Salvador says we have enough with what I brought him today to proceed.'

'I see.' Her voice was bleak. So that was that. Her last chance to help her father had definitely passed. And she had squandered a couple of her chances…had been too busy thinking about Lucas when she should have been thinking about her father. Guilt settled like a heavy weight throughout her body. She might as well leave as soon as she could get a flight.

'Will you be well enough to come shopping with me tomorrow?' Isobel asked from the back of the car. And suddenly her guilt was twofold. She couldn't let Isobel down.

'Yes, I'll be fine, Isobel. I'll get a good night's sleep and everything will be better tomorrow.'

Even as she said the words she knew they were far from the truth. Things could only get worse tomorrow.

For a start it was Monday morning and the real Mildred Bancroft might very well turn up. Also, Salvador would probably post the letter of eviction tomorrow and that would end all her father's hopes for the future. Yes, tomorrow could be a very bad day indeed.

Penny fell silent, lost in her own thoughts of the future…a future without Lucas and Isobel.

As Lucas reached the outskirts of old San Juan he was caught up in heavy traffic. The streets were filled with people in colourful clothing and large floats were being brought down the narrow roads. 'There is obviously some kind of festival on today,' Lucas said with a shake of his head. 'We might be a while getting down to your hotel.'

'Just drop me here and I can walk,' Penny said quickly. 'I'd like the fresh air anyway.'

'Are you sure?' Lucas glanced over at her. 'If your head is bad you shouldn't be out in this heat.'

'Really, Lucas, just drop me here,' Penny insisted. 'A walk will do me good.'

Lucas pulled the car away from the crowds and stopped under the shade of an umbrella pine. 'Isobel and I will walk down with you.'

Penny looked into the back seat of the car. 'I think Isobel has had enough excitement for one day,' she said softly.

Lucas followed her gaze and noted that the child was asleep, with her head resting on Flint for a pillow.

'I think you are right.' Lucas smiled.

'Anyway, thank you for a lovely lunch and I'll see you tomorrow bright and early in the office.'

Lucas reached out and caught hold of her arm as she made to turn away. 'Haven't you forgotten something?'

'I don't think so.' Her heart seemed to slam against her chest as she looked back at him, her green eyes wide in her face. Was he going to kiss her? The thought was enough to send her blood pressure soaring.

'Your handbag.' He smiled and picked up her bag from the floor beside her. She couldn't believe that she had nearly forgotten it! It showed the state of her mind.

'Oh, yes! Sorry.' She took it from him, feeling flustered, wondering if he realised she had thought he meant a kiss. 'Thank you.' She reached again for the door handle.

'Milly?'

She looked around at him, wondering what she had forgotten this time. And that was when he leaned closer and kissed her. It was just a light touch of his lips against hers, but the sensation sent wild forces of desire shooting through her, made her senses swim in disarray. In that instant she wanted to move closer and be held in his arms, give herself up to the sheer pleasure of his caresses.

'Thank you for today, and for being so nice to Isobel,' he murmured as he pulled back.

'It wasn't hard,' she whispered in an unsteady tone, trying very hard to pull herself together. 'She's a wonderful child.'

'Well, I think so—but I'm biased.' He grinned.

Something about that lopsided grin made her heart lurch crazily. She stared into the darkness of his eyes. I'm in love with him, she thought suddenly.

The thought shocked her to her core. She couldn't love him—he was her father's enemy. Of all the people in the world to choose from he was the one she couldn't have. Maybe that was why the thought had crossed her mind. She always had been contrary, she reflected angrily.

'Anyway, I'd better go.' She swallowed hard and opened the door. 'I'll see you tomorrow at work.'

'Yes, see you tomorrow.' He watched her climb out

of the car. 'Hope your headache clears. Take some aspirin.'

It would take more than aspirin to clear what was wrong with her, she thought angrily as she walked away from him and merged with the crowds further down the street.

When Penny arrived at her hotel she was glad to find that it was the friendly woman receptionist on duty. She handed over her key without any pertinent remark or question and wished her a pleasant afternoon.

Penny escaped up to her room with a feeling of relief, and then lay on the bed looking up at the ceiling, trying to come to terms with the situation.

She wasn't in love with Lucas, she told herself over and over again. And to prove it she lifted the directory next to her and found the number for the airport. Her time here was over. She would book a flight for tomorrow. With determination she lifted the phone next to her bed.

The deed done, she lay back against the pillows. There... Tomorrow at a quarter to midnight she would get on a flight for Arbuda and go home to help and support her father.

The thought should have brought her some comfort. She was finally doing the right thing. She should never have come here in the first place. She imagined what her father would say if he knew...what he would think if he knew she had slept with the enemy! He would be devastated. No...Lucas had never been meant for her. He would be happier with Emma anyway...she was deeply in love with him and seemed genuinely fond of Isobel.

Penny rolled over and buried her head in the pillow, and tried to ignore the ache in her heart.

CHAPTER NINE

IT SEEMED unfair that the sun should still be shining when Penny had such a black hole in her heart. Even Shauna's bright, happy good morning grated on her.

'Morning, Shauna.' She gave the girl a strained smile.

'Are you okay? You look a bit pale,' the woman said.

'I'm fine,' Penny lied. In fact she felt anything but fine. 'Is Lucas in the office yet?'

'Oh, yes. He was in before me, as usual. He's not in a good mood, though, so I would advise you to keep your head down.'

'Really?' Penny frowned; Lucas didn't strike her as a moody person. 'What's wrong with him?'

'Beats me.' Shauna shrugged. 'He was on the phone when I arrived. Maybe it's something to do with that.'

Penny brushed a hand nervously down over her pale pink dress and tried to prepare herself for going into the inner sanctum to face him. She had decided that before she left she should come clean and tell him the truth. That meant saying something either this morning or later today, when she had taken Isobel shopping.

'There is a stack of mail this morning,' Shauna said, going through the pile with a frown. 'We are still very behind with things, thanks to the amount of sorting out since his father passed away.'

'Do you want me to help you go through those?' Penny asked, trying to put off the inevitable. If Lucas was in a bad mood, now was probably not the time to tell him the truth. And anyway, on reflection, maybe it would be best to tell him after her shopping trip with Isobel. If she told him before he might cancel the outing and Isobel would be devastated. Being out here with Shauna, keeping herself otherwise occupied, seemed an infinitely better idea.

'Thanks, Mildred.' Shauna passed her half of the correspondence. 'How was your weekend?'

'It was okay,' Penny answered lightly, trying not to think of the wonderful night of passion and the idyllic lunch at the Smugglers' Inn. 'What about you?'

Shauna waved her left hand in front of Penny's nose and she noticed for the first time the big diamond engagement ring on her finger. 'Paul proposed to me.'

'Oh, Shauna that's wonderful—congratulations.'

'Thank you.' The woman had a smile on her face that seemed to light up the entire room. 'I've never been so happy in all my life—I adore him.'

'I'm very happy for you,' Penny said with genuine warmth. 'Have you set a date yet?'

'We are talking about taking the first available one we can get at the church. I don't want to wait. My mother is a bit wary, though; she wants us to have a long engagement because we haven't known each other that long. But I said to her that when you meet the man you want to spend the rest of your life with you want the rest of your life to start straight away… And anyway, I just knew when I first met Paul that he was the right one for me. I just looked into his eyes and that was it. I was hooked.'

Penny thought back to when she had walked into this office last week and had first looked into Lucas's eyes. Something had happened in that moment, something momentous. Oh, she had tried to pretend otherwise…had tried to convince herself that the butterflies and the wild palpitations were all in her imagination. But they weren't. She was in love with him, had been from that first day. It was crazy and foolish and downright disloyal to her father, but she couldn't help herself. It was the reason she had gone to bed with him on Saturday…and it was the reason she didn't want to tell him who she was because then it would be over. And she didn't want it to be over.

Penny stared down at the envelopes in front of her and tried to be sensible and shut out the thoughts. But they were unfolding in her mind with a relentless certainty that refused to be ignored. Luckily Shauna didn't appear to notice that she had gone extremely quiet. She was telling Penny that she wanted a big white wedding with all the trimmings.

The phone rang, and as Shauna dealt with it Penny sat down on a stool at the far end of the desk and started to go through the mail.

'Lucas Shipping, how may I help?' Shauna said breezily. 'Sorry, he's not in his office at the moment. Can I take your details and get him to phone you back? Okay…no problem.' Shauna put the phone back down. 'Someone else trying to sell us insurance,' she muttered. 'So, anyway, as I was saying, my mother is adamant—' The outer door opened and she broke off as a woman walked in.

'How may I help?' Penny heard Shauna ask politely, but she didn't glance over. She was trying to sort out her priorities at the same time as sort through the mail. Her father had to be her main concern—

'Mildred Bancroft for Mr Darien,' a voice said briskly.

Penny felt her blood start to freeze in her veins and she looked up in horror.

'Sorry?' Shauna was looking at the woman blankly. 'Eh…did you want to see Mildred or Mr Darien?'

The woman frowned. She looked a little like an old-fashioned schoolmarm—the type who peered disapprovingly over heavy-rimmed glasses and gave detention if you so much as sneezed. Her grey hair was tied back in a severe style, away from her lined face, and she wore a plain white blouse and black skirt. 'I think you misunderstand, young woman,' she said in a tone that implied Shauna was slightly thick. 'I am Mildred Bancroft, here to see Mr Darien.'

Shauna's mouth literally dropped open and she looked helplessly around at Penny. If the situation hadn't been so grave the look on her face would have been comical. But Penny wasn't in any mood to laugh. 'You'd better tell Lucas she is here,' Penny murmured numbly.

Before either of them could move the office door opened and Lucas appeared. He looked formidable, his face drawn in a stern expression that Penny had never seen before—an expression that made her stomach knot with even more tension.

'Ah, you must be Mr Darien?' the woman said hopefully. 'I phoned you earlier.'

'Yes…Mildred Bancroft I presume?' Lucas said heavily.

'That's right.' The woman walked around the desk and held her hand out. 'Good to finally meet you.'

'Yes, likewise…' Lucas shook hands with her and then waved her through to his office. For a moment his eyes connected with Penny's. It was a cold, austere look that was a million miles from the way he had looked at her yesterday. 'You can come through as soon as I've dealt with Ms Bancroft,' he told her curtly. It was more of an order than an invitation, and then the door closed firmly behind him.

'Well!' Shauna swivelled around to look at Penny. 'What on earth is going on? And if that is Mildred Bancroft then who are you?'

'Sorry, Shauna.' Penny swept a shaking hand through the long length of her hair. 'It was just that you jumped to all the wrong conclusions when I came in to see Lucas that day, and I was so desperate that I just went along with it.'

'Golly!' Shauna's eyes were so wide they seemed to swamp her face. 'Had you been unemployed for a long time…was that it?'

'No… I just…' Penny shrugged helplessly. She didn't want to start explaining to Shauna before she had a chance to tell Lucas her side of things.

'Look, don't worry about it,' Shauna said softly. 'I'm sure Mr Darien will forgive you, because, let's face it, you're great at the job—things have been so much easier in this office since you arrived.'

'Thanks, Shauna.' Penny smiled at the woman gratefully and wished things were that simple.

'He'd never have employed that sourpuss anyway. At least I hope not!' Shauna made a face. 'Did you see the way she looked down her nose at me? Snooty woman—who did she think she was?'

'She thought she was Mildred Bancroft,' Penny answered dryly, her sense of humour coming briefly to her rescue.

Shauna met her eyes and giggled.

The office door opened at that moment and Mildred Bancroft appeared. Head held high, she marched through the office and without so much as a glance in their direction departed, leaving a freezing trail of mystery in her wake.

The door to Lucas's office was left wide open, but there was no sign of Lucas.

'What do you think happened?' Shauna mouthed silently.

Penny shrugged her shoulders.

'Milly, get yourself in here.' Lucas's voice boomed from within.

A sinking feeling in her stomach, Penny got to her feet.

'Good luck,' Shauna whispered.

'Thanks—I've got a feeling I'm going to need it.'

Lucas was sitting behind his desk, his dark head bent as he scribbled some notes on a form in front of him. 'Close the door,' he said bluntly, without looking up.

She did as he asked and then proceeded cautiously towards the desk. Still Lucas didn't glance up.

'Before you start tearing into me, I just want to say that I'm sorry.' She said the words quickly. 'I shouldn't have deceived you like that. It was wrong of me and I apologise unequivocally.'

Lucas threw his pen down and then leaned back in his chair. Their eyes met.

It was hard to tell what he was thinking. He looked very cool. But it was his silence that totally alarmed Penny. If he had shouted and ranted she probably could have coped better. But this steely look of complete disapproval tore into her like a knife. If he looked at her like this now, what would it be like when he discovered she was William Kennedy's daughter?

'Look, I really am sorry.' She tried again. 'I didn't set out to pretend to be someone else, and I'm not a dishonest person.'

He folded his arms in front of him. 'So who are you?' he asked quietly.

Her heart slammed against her chest and her knees suddenly felt weak. She sat down in the chair opposite to him. 'You can call me Penny,' she said, feebly backing away from telling him her surname.

'Oh, can I?' he grated sardonically. 'How kind. And is this another pseudonym? Is the real Penny about to march in to see me in a few days' time as well?'

'Don't be ridiculous,' she muttered with a flash of annoyance. 'Look, I'm sorry… I did try to tell you that I wasn't Mildred when I came in here last week, but you didn't give me a chance. You were really desperate for someone to help you out in here, don't forget.'

'Oh, and you were just being charitable, were you?' One eyebrow lifted disdainfully. 'Fancied a bit of social work? Hmm, was that it?'

'No…of course not.' She shrugged helplessly. 'I don't know what happened that day. You just looked at me and…I don't know… The next minute I was in this web of lies.'

'I think you've had plenty of chances since then to put me right,' he drawled softly. 'And you didn't take any of them.'

She felt her cheeks flare with colour. 'No…you're right. I didn't,' she admitted shakily. 'But I wanted to.'

'So what stopped you?' He stared at her with a cold, penetrating intensity.

'I suppose the fear that you'd look at me the way you are looking at me now,' she admitted huskily.

There was silence for a moment.

'I just…' She trailed off helplessly.

'Needed the job?' he finished for her wryly.

'Well…I was going to say I just got caught up in the

moment. You asked me if I'd start straight away and I found myself agreeing.' She shrugged. 'It was crazy—I knew the real Mildred would probably turn up sooner or later, but—'

'But you figured you would prove yourself and make yourself indispensable in the meantime?'

'I wasn't going to say that,' she replied, and sent him a fulminating glare from sea-green eyes as her old spirit kicked in. 'Stop finishing my sentences for me.'

'Hey, you are in no position to start dictating terms,' he reminded her crisply, but there was a brief flicker of amusement in his eyes now. 'So I take it the agency sent you and when you got here you discovered the job had already gone. I can understand you being annoyed. You'd travelled a long way to get here. You should have just told me the truth. That agency doesn't seem to know what the hell it's doing. I've been on the phone to them this morning and talked to some woman who was totally clueless. Couldn't even find my file and kept me on hold for twenty minutes. I hung up in the end.'

'They don't seem very professional,' Penny murmured uncomfortably. 'But they are not completely to blame here—'

'Well, they may have a good reputation but I won't be using them again.' Lucas shook his head. 'But you should have been honest. You didn't need to go to so much trouble to get the damn job, as it turns out.' He leaned forwards suddenly. 'Because, given the choice between you and the real Mildred, I would have given you the job anyway.'

'Would you?' She felt her heart speeding up as conflicting emotions spun through her. There was a part of her that didn't want him to start being nice about this—

it just made it even more difficult to tell him the whole truth.

'Where has she been anyway?' she asked distractedly.

'Family commitments kept her in Barbados for longer than she had anticipated.' Lucas shook his head. 'Can you imagine? She actually thought she could waltz in here and start work days late without so much as a phone call of explanation. Anyway, I told her that the agency had sent someone else and that I couldn't afford to sit around waiting for her.'

'Oh!' Penny stared at him in consternation. 'You mean you sent her packing!'

'Well, I wouldn't use those words exactly.' Lucas shrugged. 'We had an amicable meeting. She understood my dilemma. She tried to say that she had written to me, telling me the date she would arrive. But I didn't receive the letter—and anyway, frankly, it's just too late now.'

He tapped his fingers on the desk impatiently. 'Then she had the nerve to tell me that my receptionist wasn't as efficient as she should be.' He frowned. 'A bit of a nerve, don't you think, when she was late for her job? She wouldn't have fitted in here anyway.'

Penny bit down on her lip. 'So…she's not coming back, then?' she ventured cautiously.

'No.' He smiled. 'She's not coming back. I just told you that.'

'I see.' Penny stared at him guiltily. Now she had lost the woman her job! 'Do you think that maybe you've been a bit hasty? Have you got a contact number for her?'

'I don't need a number for her because I won't be contacting her,' Lucas said flatly, and then sat back in his seat. 'So…I suppose what I'm saying is, if you want the job here it's yours.'

Penny sat in stunned silence for a moment. She hadn't expected this. As soon as Mildred Bancroft had arrived she'd envisaged him telling her to pack up her stuff and leave.

'I don't like dishonesty in any form…Penny,' he continued briskly. 'But I've thought about it and I can see you must have been very upset, travelling all that way for a job that had been allocated to someone else. So…' He stood up from behind the desk and walked around towards her. 'I'll overlook your propensity for shady behaviour just this once.' The words were said with a shade of wry humour. He perched on the edge of the desk beside her. 'What do you say? Shall we start from the beginning again?'

Penny would have given anything to just say yes… But how could she? She didn't belong here. She belonged in Arbuda, with her father, or on board the cruise liner doing her own job… This was all a lie. 'It's a bit more complicated than that,' she said huskily.

'No, it's not. You just should have told me the truth up front…Penny…'

The sound of her name on his lips made her heart leap. It sounded so warm and delicious and… She pulled her thoughts back from that dangerous abyss.

'I know I should.' There was a long silence where she tried to pull herself together. She needed to tell him everything. Maybe if she threw herself at his mercy he'd be lenient with her father. And maybe he wouldn't… Maybe it would make things worse for her father. The thought froze her. Lying about her name was bad…lying about what she was doing here was a lot worse. Maybe she should tell him as little as possible and just exit gracefully from the situation. At least that way he wouldn't hate her. She couldn't stand for him to hate her.

'The thing is I'm feeling tremendously guilty that I've lost Mildred Bancroft her job.'

'I wouldn't waste your energy with that,' Lucas said firmly. 'If you hadn't come along when you did I'd have got someone else. I was at the end of my tether waiting for her anyway.' His eyes flicked over her assessingly. 'So, now we have all that cleared up, will you stay on here as my PA?'

Her heart was beating furiously against her ribcage. She moistened her lips nervously and then took a deep breath. 'I can't, Lucas,' she said softly. 'I'm sorry.'

He frowned, and there was a long pause before he said heavily, 'Do you mind telling me why not?'

'I have personal reasons. But I don't think it's working out here for me anyway.' She forced herself to say the words, but her voice was husky and anything but sure.

'Has this got anything to do with what happened between us on Saturday night?'

The direct question and the way his eyes were searching over her face made her blush uncontrollably. 'No...of course not.'

'Are you sure?' he asked gently.

'Of course I'm sure.' His closeness was a little unnerving. If she moved a fraction of an inch her leg would be touching his. And she could smell the evocative tang of his cologne. It brought back memories of being in his arms, running her fingers through his hair, their naked bodies pressed close.

'I suppose businesswise what happened between us was a mistake. But—' He broke off as the phone rang on his desk. 'Shauna, will you hold my calls?' he called impatiently through to the outer office. But the phone continued to ring. 'Shauna—the phone.' He raised his voice an octave and the ringing stopped.

'This is nothing to do with what happened on Saturday night,' she cut in quickly, before he could say anything more. 'I told you…that was just a bit of fun. I've forgotten it already.'

He raised one eyebrow. 'Is that a fact?' he drawled coolly.

'Yes.' Her eyes connected with his for a second before she rapidly looked away.

'I think you are wrong about that,' he said softly. 'It wasn't just a bit of fun.'

The calm, husky timbre of his tone set her pulses racing. She looked back up at him uncertainly.

'It was a lot of fun,' he finished distinctly.

The flare of disappointment inside her was acute, and she realised that deep down she had been hoping he was going to say something else. Stupid of her, really, but in that heartbeat of a moment a whole load of romantic notions had raced through her head—notions of him telling her that their lovemaking had affected him as profoundly as it had her.

Idiot, she berated herself angrily. Their night together had just been a passing distraction, and a man as attractive and as sexy as Lucas probably had a lot of them. If Lucas was going to get serious about anyone it would be Emma.

'Penny?' As she looked away from him he put a hand under her chin and gently tipped her face so that she was forced to meet his gaze again. His eyes held hers, steady and somehow intense. They seemed to reach straight into her soul.

'Will you at least stay on until I can find someone to replace you?' The businesslike question was very much at odds with the gentle tone of his voice, the touch of his hand against her skin.

'I don't think I can,' she whispered helplessly, and pulled away from his touch. But even though she had broken the contact with him her skin seemed to burn from his touch.

There was a tap on the office door. 'Mr Darien, it's the call you have been waiting for from Arbuda,' Shauna said apologetically as she stuck her head around the door. Her glance moved from Penny to Lucas, noting the fact that he wasn't behind the desk but sitting quite close to her.

'Tell him I'll phone him back,' Lucas said calmly.

'I think it's important. He sounded agitated and demanded to speak to you.'

'Tell him I'll phone him back.' This time Lucas's tone brooked no argument and Shauna hurriedly closed the door.

'So, do you want to tell me why not?' he asked Penny, as if there had been no interruption.

Penny took a deep breath and stuck as closely to the truth as she dared. 'My father is in trouble and I need to go home and help him.'

Lucas said nothing for a moment, and the way he was looking at her was unnerving.

'I told you about him, if you remember...'

'Yes, I remember.' He stood up from the desk and returned to his seat. 'Okay I'll give you a couple of weeks off to sort the problem out with your father. But then I need you back here.' Lucas was flicking through some pages in his diary and he spoke like a man who was used to getting his own way. 'I've got an extremely busy period towards the middle of next month. Can you be back by then?' He glanced over at her sharply.

Penny hesitated, then inclined her head. There was no

point in discussing this. She was booked on a flight to Arbuda tonight and she wouldn't be coming back.

'What time do you want me to take Isobel shopping?' she asked instead.

Lucas glanced up. 'I thought we'd finish early and collect her straight from school.'

'Are you coming?' she asked in surprise.

'Of course I'm coming. You need someone to drive and carry shopping bags, don't you?' He grinned.

The phone rang again, and then went dead as Shauna answered it. 'It's the builder again,' she called, a note of desperation in her voice.

Lucas snatched up the receiver. 'Hi, John, how's it going?' he asked jovially. 'Yeah, sorry about that—I was in a business meeting with a wayward member of staff.' He glanced over at Penny with amusement lurking in his dark eyes.

Penny didn't smile back. She was feeling desperately guilty for lying to Lucas, but he didn't feel in the slightest bit guilty about what he was doing to her father. He said he didn't like dishonesty of any kind, but what he was doing was downright wicked.

She scraped her chair back from the desk. The sooner she got away from him and forgot all about him the better.

CHAPTER TEN

ISOBEL spun around and around, her arms outstretched, the white dress billowing out around her legs, her dark hair swinging.

'What do you think, Milly?' she asked excitedly.

'I think you are going to get dizzy and fall over. Stand still for a minute.' Penny grinned.

The child did as she asked and the dress fell in soft folds around her. She looked like a little cherub. The ragged handkerchief hem was perfect and the short sleeves trimmed with strands of seed pearls looked just right. She lifted her face expectantly towards Penny, and her cheeks were rosy and her eyes shone as she gave a cheeky grin. 'What do you think?' she asked again.

'I think you look like the most perfect fairy princess in the whole world.' Penny smiled and then impulsively bent and kissed the child on her forehead.

Isobel threw her arms around her neck and hugged her. 'Wait until Gina Fredrick sees this!'

'She'll be impressed,' Penny agreed. 'And I think your daddy will be impressed too.'

'I am impressed,' Lucas said from behind them, taking them both by surprise. He had poked his head around the door leading to the changing rooms and was looking down the corridor at them.

'You're not allowed in here, Daddy. It's girls only,' Isobel said, wagging a finger at him in disapproval.

'It's only the corridor, Isobel,' Lucas said with a grin.

'I don't think I'll see anything I shouldn't. Come on out so I can look at the dress properly. I'm getting lonely out here.'

Dutifully Isobel trotted outside, into the main body of the shop, whereupon she caused quite a sensation with the assistants who came over to admire her in the dress.

'She looks gorgeous, doesn't she?' Penny remarked quietly to Lucas as she stood next to him and watched the little girl twirling happily in front of the mirrors.

'Yes, she does,' Lucas agreed softly, and then grinned at Penny. 'And you were right—that dress is definitely worth traipsing into every shop in town for.'

'You are learning fast.' Penny laughed. Lucas had been starting to flag as they had rejected one dress after another. In typical male fashion he had been ready to call it a day as they had tried shop after shop. But Penny had been determined that Isobel would get her dress today. She wanted to get on that plane tonight knowing that at least she had achieved something on her trip here…even if it was something as small as making a child happy.

'You've got to have stamina when you go shopping with the girls,' Penny said lightly. 'Isn't that right, Isobel?'

Isobel nodded happily.

'Okay, you've made your point, but it's time to eat now,' Lucas said firmly. 'There is a great little restaurant just down from here—'

'But I haven't got my wings yet, Daddy,' Isobel said. 'I can't be a fairy princess without wings.'

'I don't think we will be able to buy them in a shop, Issy,' Penny said. 'Tell you what—we'll find a haberdashery and buy some wire and some gossamer material and I'll construct you a wonderful pair of wings.'

'There's no end to your talents, is there?' Lucas remarked lightly.

'Not really, no,' Penny agreed with a teasing smile.

He smiled back, and as their eyes locked Penny felt her heart go into freefall. Hurriedly she looked away. She couldn't allow herself to think how handsome he was…how much she wanted him. Because he was out of bounds. She could never have a relationship with Lucas Darien. A gnawing ache caught at her heart, but she firmly tried to ignore it, reminding herself instead that he had spent several hours at the office today looking into the business of evicting her father from his home.

'When will you make my wings?' Isobel asked anxiously.

'I'll do it tonight,' Penny promised.

'You don't have to do it so soon. The play isn't for another three weeks,' Lucas told her.

'Even so, it would be better to get it done now.' Penny smiled at Isobel. 'Then you can relax, knowing you are organised—isn't that right?'

The child nodded happily.

'Okay, well, as you are kindly going to create a costume for my daughter, how about I create some dinner for us back at home while you are busy?' Lucas suggested.

Penny hesitated. Her plan had been to run the wings up in her hotel bedroom and then leave them by Lucas's front door on her way out to the airport. But it seemed much more sensible to make them at his house and then just leave.

Penny nodded. 'You've got yourself a deal.'

Half an hour later they arrived back at Lucas's house, laden down with bags.

'I don't know about you, but I could use a drink,' Lucas said as he put the shopping down in the kitchen.

'You can't take the pace, Daddy.' Isobel giggled.

'You're right—I can't.' He smiled over at Penny. 'How about a glass of wine?'

'Thanks—I'd love one.' Penny took the bag with Isobel's dress in it and handed it over to the little girl. 'Better go and hang that up before it gets creased.'

'Yes, Milly,' the child said happily.

'Isobel?' Penny stopped her as she ran towards the door. 'You can call me Penny, if you like…because all my friends do.'

The child seemed to think about that for a moment. 'I like the name Milly better,' she said. 'Can I still call you Milly?'

'Yes, if you like,' Penny said, puzzled by the request.

'Good.' The child smiled and ran out.

'I wonder what is behind that,' Lucas murmured.

'Beats me.' Penny shrugged. 'Maybe she just thinks it's a bit strange, calling me by a different name.'

'I thought it was a bit strange myself,' Lucas said, a glint of humour in his dark eyes.

'Yes, well, I am sorry about that, Lucas,' she said briskly.

'That's okay.' He uncorked a bottle of white wine and for a moment the only sound was the plump glug of liquid as he filled two glasses. 'I just hope you don't mind if I slip occasionally and call you Milly myself.' He passed the glass over to her and her hand brushed against his as she accepted it. The contact sent an immediate rush of adrenalin racing through her. 'You see, I tend to think of you as Milly. Thoroughly modern Milly.'

She tried to pretend that she didn't know what he was

referring to, but the teasing, sexy tone of his voice sent her senses racing.

'If you slip and call me Milly I won't hold it against you,' she assured him with a half-smile, trying to feign indifference. But when she met his eyes she felt her heart dip as if she had suddenly lost all sense of gravity. If only he knew, she thought poignantly, that there was nothing casual or modern about her feelings for him. That she had slept with him for the most age-old of reasons. She was in love with him.

He smiled and touched his glass against hers. 'And thanks for helping out with Isobel today. I don't know what we would have done without you.'

'I'm sure you would have managed.' She turned and tried to busy herself looking through the bags on the table. 'Now, I suppose I should get on with Isobel's costume.'

'You can work in here on the table, if you'd like,' he said, helping to clear a space for her by taking some of the bags away.

'I don't want to get in the way of your cooking,' she said quickly, thinking it might be easier to concentrate on what she was doing if she was in another room from him.

'Don't worry—you won't be in the way,' he said with a grin. 'And anyway, I could do with some moral support. I'm afraid my cooking is a little rusty. I actually burnt dinner last night, and we were only having hamburgers and salad.'

Penny smiled mischievously. 'Was it the lettuce or the hamburgers that you burnt?'

'Hey, I'm not that clueless.' Lucas took off the jacket of his business suit and rolled up the sleeves of his white shirt. 'And to prove it I shall create a masterpiece,' he assured her. 'I just want a witness, that's all…' He slanted a wry grin in her direction. 'And maybe a bit of advice as I go along.'

'You might be asking the wrong person,' Penny joked. 'My cooking isn't that marvellous either.'

She busied herself emptying the material and the wire onto the table, trying not to notice how attractive Lucas looked. There was something about his casual informality and the teasing smile that just set her senses racing. Out of the corner of her eye she saw him loosening his tie to take it off. She noticed the strong column of his neck, the powerful forearms…

'How's Mrs Gordon?' she asked, trying firmly to steer her mind away from dangerous ground.

'She's okay. I rang the hospital this morning and they said she'd had a comfortable night. The good news is that they are saying now she might not need surgery on her hip, that physiotherapy might fix her up. But she is going to have to take it easy for a few weeks.'

'You'll miss her.'

'You're not kidding.' Lucas opened the fridge and took some vegetables out. 'I'm going to take Isobel in to see her tomorrow night. Come with us, if you'd like.'

'It might not be a good idea, Lucas,' Penny answered carefully. 'She might not be up to having so many visitors at once.'

'Well, I'll check and tell you tomorrow.'

She'd be back in Arbuda tomorrow, Penny thought bleakly. And she would probably never see Lucas or Isobel again.

'How's the repossession order going with the house on Arbuda?' she asked him, firmly trying to concentrate on the reason why she couldn't stay here. She had tried to monitor the situation as she continued to go through files today, but a lot of her work had taken her to the outer office. 'You seemed to be on the phone a lot.'

'That's because there's a lot to sort out.'

'Has Salvador sent out the letter of eviction yet?'

'You sound very disapproving, Penny.' He paused by the table, and when she didn't answer him or look over at him he reached out and put one finger under her chin, forcing her to look at him.

'I am disapproving,' she said cautiously. 'I've told you that already.'

'And I've told you it's just business, Penny. Repossession isn't pleasant, but it happens.'

She stepped back from him angrily. But she was angrier with herself than with him, because despite the unpleasant subject she felt a flare of sexual need inside her at the touch of his hand, the closeness of his body. The fact that she could still feel like that at the same time as talking about her father's downfall was shocking, and she hated herself for it...but she just couldn't seem to help herself.

'Anyway, as you said before, we'll agree to disagree about it, shall we?' she said shakily, trying to cover up her emotions by starting to unravel the roll of netting on the table.

'I suppose you feel strongly about this because you are worried about your own father and his financial problems,' Lucas said suddenly.

The sentence caused her to look over at him sharply. Did he have any idea how close he was to the truth? she wondered, and her heart hammered wildly against her chest. 'I feel strongly about it because I think what you are doing is wrong.'

'For someone who has been...shall we say...

economical with the truth, you can be quite sanctimonious, can't you?'

She frowned. 'Yes, well, I've said I'm sorry,' she muttered shakily. 'And I didn't set out deliberately to lie or to hurt anybody.'

'Look, Penny, my father left me a job to do and I'm doing it.'

And blood was thicker than water at the end of the day, she thought grimly. If she told him his father was a cheat it would not further the cause of softening his attitude in any way. She was frankly wasting her time.

Luckily at that moment Isobel ran back into the room. 'What are we having for dinner, Daddy?' she asked happily.

'Stir-fried vegetables and steak.'

'Can I have chips?'

'No, you can't.' Lucas said.

Isobel made a face. 'Daddy burnt dinner last night,' she told Penny as she climbed up on the stool next to her. 'It tasted horrible.'

'Yes, thank you, snitch.' Lucas ruffled her hair and she grinned.

There was silence for a while as Lucas carried on with the preparations for the meal and Isobel watched Penny. She had probably gone too far in her condemnation of him, she thought as she snipped the wire to size. She wondered if it was her imagination or was there a bit of an atmosphere between them now?

'Do you like my daddy?' Isobel asked Penny suddenly.

The question took Penny very much by surprise. 'Well…yes…'

'He likes you too,' she said happily. 'Don't you, Daddy?'

Penny glanced over at Lucas and met his eyes.

Whereas she felt deeply embarrassed by the line of questioning, he merely looked amused. 'Yes—well, most of the time anyway. I could have done without the surprise this morning.'

'What surprise?' Isobel asked.

'Never you mind.' Lucas turned off the stove. 'I'm going to serve dinner now. How long will you be, Penny?'

'I'm just about finished.' Penny glued the last piece of net in place.

'We'll adjourn to the dining room, then. Come and help me lay the table, Issy.'

Lucas was just in the process of carrying the food through to the other room when the phone rang. 'Will you pick that up for me, Penny?' he called back over his shoulder. 'Tell whoever it is I'll call them back after dinner.'

It was Emma, and she sounded distinctly put out when she heard Penny's voice answering the phone. 'You're working late,' she remarked stiffly.

'I was just helping Isobel with a costume for her school play,' Penny told her.

'I see.'

'Lucas is just in the process of preparing dinner—can he ring you back, Emma?'

'I just wanted to tell him that Maria has gone into labour. Salvador took her into hospital this afternoon.'

'That's great news. Although she is a bit early, isn't she? I hope everything goes okay for them.'

'Yes, so do I. Oh, and will you tell Lucas that I said thank you for the beautiful bouquet of flowers? Tell him they were fabulous. I'll call him tomorrow—I'm just on my way to the cinema now.'

'Okay, I'll tell him.' Penny put the phone down

thoughtfully. If Lucas was sending Emma flowers did that mean he wanted to get back with her? She tried to tell herself that it would probably be a good thing if he did. It would mean he had finally put the past and Kay behind him, and Isobel clearly needed a mother figure in her life.

'Penny, your dinner is getting cold,' Lucas called through from the other room.

'Sorry about that,' she said as she went through and took her seat at the candlelit table opposite to Lucas. 'That was Emma; she said that Maria has gone into labour. Salvador is with her at the hospital.'

Lucas grinned. 'Well, that's exciting news. I hope she has an easy time and it all goes well.'

'Yes, so do I.' Penny looked down at the food in front of her. 'This looks very nice.'

'Chips would have been better,' Isobel piped in. 'They are my favourite. Chips and tomato sauce.'

'My daughter has a wonderful taste in fine cuisine, don't you think, Penny?' Lucas said with a shake of his head.

'She certainly does.' Penny winked at Isobel, and then returned her attention to Lucas. 'Oh, and Emma said to say thank you for the flowers. She said they were fabulous. She'll ring you tomorrow; she's going to the cinema tonight.'

Lucas nodded. 'I'm glad she liked them,' he said casually.

Penny pushed the food around on her plate. She had been feeling hungry earlier, but now her appetite seemed to have completely deserted her. The thought of Lucas with Emma was like a knife twisting inside her. The fact that she knew she was being ridiculous just made it all the worse. She was leaving Puerto Rico. There was no way a relationship between her and Lucas would ever work out. Even if he did forgive her for lying to him—and that was a big if—it would certainly break her father's heart if he found out she was involved with Lawrence Darien's son. The whole situation was a complete no-go.

'How's my cooking?' Lucas asked, reaching over to top up her wine glass.

'Surprisingly good.' She smiled over at him. It was a lovely meal; it was just a pity she couldn't enjoy it. 'Mrs Gordon would be proud of you.'

'It's raining, Daddy,' Isobel said suddenly. They all looked towards the window. A torrential tropical downpour was almost obscuring the greenery of the garden.

'Wow! I hope that doesn't stay around for long, otherwise I'll get soaked just running into the hotel.'

'You can always stay here tonight,' Lucas suggested.

The invitation was issued in a casual way but it sent Penny's senses into wild disarray. 'No, I'll be fine, Lucas,' she said hastily. But she couldn't bring herself to look across at him as she replied. Was he inviting her to share his bed again? Or was he simply offering her the spare room? She wasn't sure. But whichever it was she had to remain strong and refuse.

'In fact, I'll help you clear these dishes away and then I really must ring for a taxi. I've got a few phone calls I want to make from my hotel.' She forced herself to say the words, and to sound cool and practical, even though the thought of sleeping with him again was making her blood thunder through her veins with excitement and longing.

'Fair enough.' Lucas nodded his head.

'Daddy, can I be excused now?' Isobel asked.

Lucas glanced down the table, checking how much of

her dinner she had eaten. 'Okay. But it's getting late now, Issy, so you have to start getting ready for bed.'

'Will you come and tuck me in?' Isobel asked.

'Don't I always?' Lucas said with a smile.

'No, I meant Milly...will you tuck me in tonight, Milly?'

'If you like,' Penny agreed softly, touched by the child's request.

'Meantime, it's into the shower with you,' Lucas said as he got to his feet and started to clear the dishes from the table.

'I'll do this, Lucas. You see to Isobel,' Penny said, standing up to help him.

'Thanks, Penny.'

As father and daughter disappeared upstairs Penny carried the dishes through to the kitchen. She could hear Isobel's laughter drifting down and it made her smile as she stacked the dishwasher.

What would it be like to be a part of their lives? she wondered. To live here as a family? If only she didn't know anything about Lawrence Darien...if only she was here for all the right reasons instead of all the wrong ones. She allowed herself to daydream for a little while and watched the rain outside. It was coming down in thunderous sheets, bouncing off the steps that led up to the veranda.

Flint ambled up to the back door and distracted her as he started whining to get out. 'Are you sure you want to go out there?' Penny asked him. 'It's pretty grim.'

The dog whined again, so she opened the door. Flint took a step back as he saw the rain. 'I did try to warn you.' Penny smiled.

After a moment's hesitation the dog wandered out onto the porch, and a few seconds later he ventured down the steps into the garden. The rain was so heavy it obscured him from view as soon as he had walked a few yards. Penny could hardly even see the car on the drive—it was just a blur of colour against the green grass.

'Flint, come on, boy. Better come back in,' Penny called. But there was no sign of the animal. She stepped out onto the porch. 'Flint!' she called again.

The light was fading now, and darkness was dropping fast. The smell of rain was fresh and heavy in the air, and although it was still warm it was a more bearable temperature than it had been all day.

Penny leaned against the railing and took deep breaths.

'Pleasant out here when it rains, isn't it?' Lucas said from behind her.

She turned and found him watching her from the doorway. 'Yes, it's fresh and quite exhilarating, isn't it? I was just waiting for Flint—he very bravely headed out into the garden.'

'He likes the coolness of this weather.' Lucas walked over to stand beside her. 'I like it myself. It's as if everything is being washed clean, isn't it?'

There was silence for a while, except for the rumble of rain on the roof over their heads. Penny watched as it fell like a watery blanket, enclosing them from the darkness of the world outside.

'Shall we forget our disagreement earlier?' he asked suddenly.

She nodded.

'I don't really think you are sanctimonious. Just a bit irritating and stubborn at times.' He grinned.

'Stubborn?' She turned and looked at him with a raised eyebrow. 'How do you arrive at that conclusion?'

'Well, you won't admit that I'm right—which, of course, I nearly always am,' he said teasingly.

'You wish.' Penny shook her head and looked away from him.

'Penny?'

She looked over at him questioningly.

'Are you okay?'

'Yes—why?'

'You just looked so serious for a moment.'

'I'm fine.'

'Good…I'm glad we are still friends.' The half teasing smile made her heart dip crazily. Maybe here in this house they were friends, but outside in the real world he could never be anything other than her father's enemy. As she looked into his eyes she found herself wishing that they could stay like this for ever, cocooned from reality, that time could stand still and she wouldn't have to leave.

Flint came hurrying back up the steps to the veranda, and then, before they could move out of his way, shook himself vigorously. 'Flint!' they both shouted in dismay as water flew all over them in icy droplets.

'Thanks a bunch, fella,' Lucas said, brushing himself down.

Flint looked up at him with unconcerned eyes and shook himself again, which made Penny laugh because she had wisely moved further away.

'Very funny.' Lucas looked over at her and smiled wryly. 'Look at me—I'm soaked!' He brushed at his white shirt, which was now sticking to him in damp patches.

'That will teach you to think you are always right,' Penny said, laughing again.

'Hey, take that back immediately. I expect a little more meekness and subordination from my employees,' he said laughingly.

'Then I think you've got the wrong employee,' she said with a grin.

'You might be right.' He advanced towards her, a wicked light of indignation in his eyes.

'Anyway, I'd better go and tuck Isobel up,' she said with a smile as she backed away from him.

'Oh, no, you don't...' He caught up with her before she had reached the door and put a hand on the wall behind her, effectively trapping her close to him. 'Before I let you escape I think an apology might be in order.'

'An apology for what?' She smiled. 'Siding with Flint?'

'No, an apology for being volatile and difficult.'

'Difficult! You're the difficult one.' She raised her chin slightly.

'Last chance—you'd better start saying you are sorry, otherwise I just might have to kiss you senseless.' His eyes moved towards her lips and suddenly the mood between them changed dramatically. The laughter and the teasing disappeared, replaced by a powerful surge of sexual awareness.

She moistened her lips nervously; her heart was racing out of control. She wanted him to kiss her...wanted him so much it was as if every inch, every nerve in her body was crying out for him.

As he lowered his head she closed her eyes. The touch of his lips against hers was electric; it sent shivery waves of delight shooting through her. She reached her hands up tentatively and rested them against his shoulders, then slid them higher around his neck and kissed him back with heated passion.

All coherent thought slipped away in those few moments of ecstasy. She felt his hands around her waist and longed for them to caress her, longed to get even closer into his arms.

The sound of the rain seemed to drown out all the voices inside her that said this was wrong.

He was the one to pull back from her, leaving her breathless and filled with a gnawing ache of need inside.

'I suppose we shouldn't have done that,' she whispered unsteadily.

'Why not?' He smiled at her.

'Because…' *Because this was wrong,* her mind screamed. *Because she was lying to him about who she was and they could never have a relationship in any real sense…* The knowledge washed through her in cold waves of torment. 'Because…this will complicate our working relationship,' she finished weakly. 'And, anyway, didn't you just send Emma some flowers? Do you really think it's right to kiss me and pursue her at the same time?'

He smiled. 'Are you jealous, by any chance?'

'No, of course not.' The arrogant question set her blood on fire. But the annoying thing was that he was right. She was jealous of Emma even though she had no earthly right to be.

'Anyway, I'd better go…' She ducked away from him, under his arm. 'I don't want to keep Isobel waiting. Will you ring for a taxi for me while I tuck her in?'

'If that's what you want.'

It wasn't what she wanted; she looked over at him and felt as if her heart was truly breaking. Then hurriedly she went inside.

Isobel was cuddled down beneath the sheets, her teddy bear held tight in her arms. Penny sat down on the bed beside her.

'Thanks for coming shopping with me, Milly,' she said.

'I enjoyed it,' Penny said truthfully. 'And you looked gorgeous in your dress.'

The child nodded. 'I got the best dress in the whole world,' she said solemnly.

'I think you did,' Penny agreed with a smile. She reached out and tenderly stroked a stray strand of hair back from the little girl's face, and as she did so the knowledge that this wasn't goodnight but goodbye swamped her with sadness. 'I'm sure you will be the most beautiful girl in the play.' She bent and kissed her on the forehead. 'Now, time for sleep.'

'Milly, will you come and see me in my play?' The child asked suddenly, before she could stand up.

Penny bit down on her lip. 'I don't think I can, Isobel.'

'Why?' A frown creased the smooth lines of the child's forehead.

'Because...' Penny paused, and then decided it was best to tell the little girl the truth. 'I have to go home and see my dad for a while because he needs me.'

'Oh!' Isobel looked as if she might cry suddenly.

'But that doesn't mean I don't want to come, Issy,' Penny said gently. 'Given the chance I would love to see you in your school play. But sometimes things just aren't possible. I'm worried about my dad, you see, because he's on his own. You do understand, don't you?'

Isobel nodded. 'Like me and my daddy?'

'Yes. A bit like that.' Penny smiled at her. 'But I will be thinking about you and wondering how you are getting on.'

'I'll think about you too,' Isobel said, and cuddled further down next to her teddy bear.

'Shall I switch off this light?' Penny asked as she moved away.

'No…I like the light on.' The child's eyes were growing heavy now. 'See you tomorrow, Milly.'

'Goodnight, Isobel. Sweet dreams.' As she crept from the room she saw Lucas standing in the shadows outside the doorway.

'Why won't you be here for her play?' he asked quietly as he closed the door behind her.

'I told you—I've got to go home.' She started to move away from him towards the stairs. She really felt that she needed to get out of here fairly quickly—because if she didn't she might start crying. Saying goodbye to Isobel had been even harder than she had expected. But before she could move very far Lucas caught hold of her arm.

'You know Isobel's play isn't for another three weeks,' he said crisply. 'I thought you said you'd be back by then?'

'Is it three weeks away?' Penny feigned puzzlement. 'Well, then, I probably will make it. I just didn't want to make promises I might not be able to keep.'

He pulled her around so that she was forced to look at him. 'But you don't mind making promises to me that you can't keep?' His eyes moved searchingly over her face. 'What is going on, Penny?'

'I told you—I'm worried about my father.'

'And that's all?'

'It's enough…believe me.' For a moment her voice was unsteady, and her eyes lingered on his mouth for longer than they should have. 'Did you ring for a taxi for me?'

'What do you think?' he murmured dryly.

'I think you should have done,' she said huskily, but

at the same time she could feel herself swaying closer towards him.

'No, you don't. You think that we have some unfinished business.'

'Down in the office, you mean? Looking through those files…?' She tried to make light of the situation. 'Emma is right about you. You've got a one-track mind for business…'

He ignored the flippant statement and instead leaned closer and touched his lips against hers, tasting her as if she were some rare delicacy that needed savouring. The sensations that flowed through her were bittersweet. She wanted him so much.

'My one-track mind at the moment is firmly focused on you…' he murmured as he pulled back fractionally. 'And don't tell me you don't want me to do this…because I know that you do…you want me as badly as I want you.'

The arrogant confidence of his words was punctuated by the feel of his hands as they moved over her body with assured, masterful strokes. She told herself that she should push him away, but she couldn't. His caresses were sending her body wild with need. She wanted so much more. He was right—she did want him as much as he wanted her.

He bent to take possession of her lips again, and she kissed him back with hungry approval. She felt his hands moving to undress her; the zip at the back of her dress was pulled down, his hand moving beneath to find the cool softness of her skin.

Then he lifted her up and carried her through to the bedroom.

'Now, where were we…?' he said as he placed her down on the bed.

Even as she was telling herself that this was wrong she was reaching to unbutton his shirt with feverish fingers. What difference would one more night make? she asked herself weakly. She just wanted to feel his body against her, relish the heady bliss of his kisses and his caresses one last time. Was that really so wrong? Then she would walk away and put this episode in her life behind her—forget it as best she could…

CHAPTER ELEVEN

PENNY lay in the warm circle of Lucas's arms, her head against his chest, listening to the steady sound of his breathing, the regular beat of his heart. Their passion had been wild and gloriously fulfilling; now, sleepy and sated, they lay wrapped in each other's arms. Outside the rain was still thundering down in relentless torrents. To Penny it sounded like tumultuous applause—probably the heavens' sarcastic approval for another spectacular mistake, she thought with dry irony. She should never have stayed; all she had succeeded in doing was proving to herself how much she loved him, how much she was giving up by walking away.

She would never be able to forget Lucas...never. Turning her head slightly, she looked at the illuminated numbers on the alarm clock next to the bed. If she was to have any chance of catching her flight she would have to leave now.

'Lucas?' She whispered his name, her voice husky in the darkness.

There was no reply.

Cautiously she pulled away from him. His arm tightened around her for a moment and she stopped, fearing he had woken up. But the pattern of his breathing didn't alter. She slipped out from his arms and then looked back at him. The light from the landing was slanting over the bed; the covers were low on his waist, revealing the powerful shoulders, the broad chest. But it was his face that held her attention. She drank in the lean, handsome features for one last time.

Then impulsively she leaned over and kissed him on the lips. He smiled sleepily and reached out, stroking his hand through the silky softness of her hair, pulling her in close against him. For a moment she allowed herself one last luxury of being held by him. Then, taking a deep breath, she moved away.

He didn't stir. Hurriedly she picked up her clothes from the floor, searching under the bed for a shoe that was mysteriously missing. She found it after a few frantic minutes and then tiptoed quietly away.

She got dressed in the lounge at the same time as phoning for a taxi. Then she spent an anxious half an hour waiting for it to arrive whilst penning a short note to Lucas, which she put on the hall table by the phone. It was almost ten by the time she left, closing the door quietly behind her. She had a last glimpse of Lucas's house through the rain-splattered windows of the taxi as it pulled away.

Then she turned and stared resolutely in front of her at the darkness of the country roads. Her father needed her, and her first loyalty had to be to him. There could be no more looking back now. Lucas and Isobel were in the past.

Her flight was delayed, which was good news because otherwise she might have missed it. She arrived at the airport with minutes to spare, but ended up spending nearly the whole night in the departure lounge, staring up at the screens.

It was daylight when she finally touched down in Arbuda. It felt really weird, coming out of the familiar terminal into the heat of the morning. Nothing much changed on this small island—it was as if time had stood still and she had never been away. Even the same taxi drivers sat outside, smoking and laughing as they waited for a fare.

As she climbed into the taxi that would take her on the last leg of her journey she felt tired and edgy. She leaned back and closed her eyes, and memories of Lucas making love to her filtered through her mind. His hands on her body, his lips heated and passionate against hers. What would he think when he woke this morning to find her gone? When he read her note telling him she wouldn't be back and that she was sorry?

She squeezed her eyes tight in an effort not to think about it. At least he would never find out how she had deceived him and who she really was… She had made sure all traces of her name had been scrubbed out of the hotel register before she left. The woman receptionist had been very understanding when she had told her she was running away from a possessive boyfriend and didn't want him to trace her. The man who worked there had looked rather more suspicious when she had said the same thing to him earlier that morning, but she had slipped him a few dollars and he had nodded and shrugged his shoulders. And as they had never had her Arbuda address anyway, just her Miami base address for work, she supposed that her secret was now safe.

Not that Lucas would give her a lot of thought. He'd probably be more bothered that she had left him in the lurch at work than anything else.

As she opened her eyes the taxi pulled into the driveway of her father's house. She noticed the sugar cane was still in the fields.

The house came into view after a few minutes. It looked sadly neglected—the railing to the front door was hanging off and the blue paint that had once looked so pretty on the shutters was fading.

'Have you seen anything of my father recently, Joshua?' Penny asked, leaning forwards to talk to the taxi driver.

'No, miss. He had to lay off some of his labourers, and I heard from Mrs Gillingham that he's been in a bad way. She's been bringing him in a little of her chicken soup, trying to do her best for him.'

Penny's heart missed a beat. If her father was accepting Mrs Gillingham's help he must indeed be in a bad way. Mrs Gillingham was her father's neighbour, a kindly widow who sometimes popped over to see him—much to his annoyance. He couldn't stick her, and complained loudly about her being a very annoying woman.

'Thanks, Joshua.' As soon as the taxi pulled to a halt she jumped out and paid him, and practically ran up to the front door.

'Dad?' she called loudly as she walked through the front door. The place looked surprisingly clean and tidy. Usually when she came home on leave she spent her time cleaning and organising. 'Dad, are you okay?'

The door through to the kitchen opened and Mrs Gillingham came out. She was a plump woman in her sixties, with a pleasant smiling face. 'Oh, it's you, dear; I wondered what the commotion was. Your father is upstairs in his bed. He had an accident a couple of days ago—'

'What kind of an accident? Is he okay?' Penny asked in consternation.

'He had a car crash and broke his leg. Poor man has been in a bit of a state.'

'Oh, no! Thanks, Mrs Gillingham.' Penny took the stairs two at a time to go up and see him.

She found him lying on top of the patchwork counterpane in his bedroom reading a newspaper. He put it down as she came in and she was shocked to see how frail he looked. All colour had gone from his face and he had lost a lot of weight in the few months since she had last been home.

'Dad, are you okay?' She went over to put her arms around him.

He smiled tenderly at her as she pulled back. 'I'm all the better for seeing you. Where have you been? I tried to get in contact with you via your company and they said you were off on leave.'

'I had a bit of business to deal with,' Penny said guiltily. 'You could have phoned me on my mobile.'

'I've lost the number—don't know what the heck I've done with my address book.'

'Oh, Dad, what am I going to do with you?'

'Worse than that, I think I've lost the house, Penny,' he said sadly.

'Have you received the eviction order?'

Her father shook his head. 'But it's only a matter of time. I can't afford these massive repayments that Darien insisted on. And I've had to lay off workers, which means I won't get the sugar crop in time, which means I'm even further behind.'

'I'm sorry, Dad,' Penny said softly, her heart going out to him.

'It's not your fault.' He smiled sadly. 'It's my own, for getting involved with Lawrence Darien. That man never forgave me for stealing your mother away from him.'

'Well, you didn't exactly steal her. She found out he was married and finished with him.'

William Kennedy inclined his head. 'But she found out

he was married because I told her.' His lips twisted wryly. 'I played a bit dirty, I suppose.'

'He was still married—he was the one playing dirty.'

'Well, whatever… He never did forgive me. And now it seems his son is just as cold as he was.'

Penny thought about Lucas. 'Cold' wasn't how she would ever describe him. 'You don't really know that for a fact, Dad.'

Her father looked at her with sceptical eyes. 'That guy is a chip off the old block. If I ever saw him I'd—' For a moment her father's face seemed to heat up to a shade of purple that wasn't healthy.

'Now, now, William…' Mrs Gillingham strolled in with a tray. 'You're not upsetting yourself, are you?' She put the tray down beside him and reached to plump up the pillows at his back.

'Don't fuss, woman,' he said with agitation. 'I'm fine.'

'No, you're not—you are getting your blood pressure up for no reason at all.'

'Your blood pressure would be up if you were losing your house,' William muttered.

Rona Gillingham rolled her eyes at Penny. 'You just concentrate on eating that sandwich and getting well. I'll pop back later to see how you are going on.'

'I'll be fine now that Penny is here,' William said in a low tone.

'Well, I'll pop in later anyway.' With a smile, the woman retreated.

'Thanks, Mrs Gillingham,' Penny called after her, but she had already gone.

'You shouldn't be so tetchy, Dad. You are very lucky to have such a nice neighbour,' she said crossly as she passed him over his tray.

'She's never been away from here, you know…

morning, noon and night.' He reached to pick up the sandwich on the tray, then added softly. 'Fine woman, though…fine woman.'

'Dad?' Penny looked over at him in surprise and then smiled. 'There's life in the old dog yet, isn't there? Despite that plaster on your leg.'

Her father grinned. 'If I could just forget about Darien I'd be happy,' he muttered dryly.

'I don't think there is much chance of that, Dad. But I'm home now, and I have another few weeks leave ahead of me. I'll help you pack everything up.'

'You will not. I'm not packing anything until I have to.' William leaned back against the pillows. 'But if you'd organise the remainder of my workforce to help bring the sugar in, I'd be very grateful. Who knows? We might get the harvest in on time after all.'

'You mean if I work day and night?' Penny looked over at him and shook her head.

'Oh, go on, Pen…for your dear old dad. Just think—we might be able to teach that Darien ogre a thing or two after all, like don't underestimate a Kennedy.'

Despite the breeze, the temperature was sizzling. Penny had brought drinks down to the workers in the fields, and now she sat down in the field of sugar cane and looked up at the blue sky.

It was nearly two weeks now since she had left Puerto Rico, and surprisingly no eviction notice had arrived. In fact, no communication from Lucas had arrived at all. Planning permission would be revoked in two days. She wondered what on earth was going on. Had something happened to Lucas? Maybe he was ill…? Maybe Isobel was ill and everything was just forgotten as he dealt with the problem?

She closed her eyes and tried to rid herself of the idea that had been lurking in the cold depths of her thoughts for a few days now. Lucas would be fine…and so would Isobel, she tried to reassure herself. They would probably hear from him today, and by tomorrow a JCB would arrive to start digging foundations.

A breeze rustled through the sugar cane around her. God, she missed him… Every day she thought of him, remembered the way he had kissed her, held her…looked at her. As a treat she allowed herself to conjure him up in her mind, tall and lithe, with those powerful shoulders. She remembered how it had felt to be held in the tenderness of his embrace. The way he'd half smiled sometimes, and the way he'd watched her with those dark, incredibly sexy eyes.

There was the sound of a car pulling up by the gates further down from her. Penny didn't stand up to investigate. She was dreamily imagining she was lying in Lucas's arms.

Somebody got out of the car and called to one of the workmen standing nearby.

'Afternoon—I'm looking for the William Kennedy residence.'

The familiar husky timbre of the voice made Penny's heart stop beating for an instant. It sounded like Lucas! Was she conjuring him up so vividly in her mind that she was imagining his voice?

She sat up, and through the dense screen of sugar cane she could just make out a tall man standing by the side of the road. He had his back to her, but he had a similar build to Lucas and dark hair. He was wearing khaki trousers and a matching short-sleeved shirt.

She saw her co-worker Matthew pointing up the drive towards her father's house. The man turned to get back in his car, and Penny felt the world tip at a dizzying crazy angle as she realised it was indeed Lucas Darien. For a moment she was just so incredibly pleased to see him that she couldn't think of anything else. But as he got back into the red sports car and turned up the drive her brain suddenly started to click into gear again.

What on earth did he want? Was he coming to take possession of the property in person, rather than sending in the bailiffs? The notion made fear zing through her veins. That would be enough to give her father a heart attack.

She scrambled quickly to her feet to try and stop him, but she was too late. He had already driven past her, leaving a white trail of dust in his wake.

'Matthew!' She called across to her colleague as he turned his attention back to lancing through the cane. 'What did that man want?'

'He was looking for your father. Has some business with him.' Matthew shook his head. 'He didn't say what it was about.'

'Damn!' Penny took a deep breath. She was going to have to get back to the house, and quick. Only trouble was their other colleague Jim had just driven off with the truck ten minutes earlier. There was nothing else for it—she had to set off at a run up the drive. She took a short-cut across the fields halfway up, but it still took her half an hour to reach the house.

Just in time to see Lucas driving off looking rather grim-faced. He didn't see her, however; he was too busy turning the car before heading back down the drive.

Penny entered the house, her heart racing, her mouth dry with fear as she wondered what kind of state she would find her father in.

He was sitting in the lounge, staring out of the window with a strangely silent look about him.

'Dad?' Penny approached cautiously. 'What was that all about? Is everything all right?'

'Hmm?' William Kennedy looked over at his daughter with a faraway expression on his face.

'Was that Lucas Darien?'

'Yes…very strange…'

'What's strange?' Penny came closer. 'What happened, Dad?'

'He apologised to me.' Her father raised his eyes towards hers. 'Can you believe it? Told me that he was calling off his solicitor and that the house was mine.'

Penny sat down on the adjacent chair, her legs weak with relief. 'Why?'

'Seems when he was going through his father's files he found a codicil to the will. Lawrence had had second thoughts about pursuing his vendetta against me.' William held up a letter. 'He'd even left a letter for me, written to me on his deathbed, telling me he regretted his actions…that he had been obsessed with Clara and had never got over losing her…'

'Really?' Penny was stunned. 'What did Lucas say?'

'Well, he hadn't read the letter. It was sealed and addressed to me, and he said he felt he should deliver it in person. He also handed me a cheque to cover my losses and he apologised profusely.' William shrugged. 'I was going to make a fuss—tell him what I thought…but I found I couldn't because… Well, he is a very decent chap, actually…who'd have thought it…eh?'

'Did he mention me?' Penny asked, her heart thundering nervously.

'You?' William frowned. 'Why would he mention you?'

Why, indeed, when he didn't even know of her connection here? Penny bit down on her lip. 'I didn't tell you, Dad, but I went to see him.'

Her father looked at her as if only just seeing her for the first time. 'Oh!' Then he smiled. 'Is he the reason you've been looking so damn miserable these last few weeks?'

Penny nodded.

'Well, you'd better get after him, hadn't you? He's staying in town tonight, at the Sheraton hotel. He leaves first thing tomorrow morning.'

Penny scrambled to her feet and ran out of the room. It was only when she got into the hall that she caught sight of herself in the mirror. She was wearing faded blue jeans and a rather clingy old white T-shirt. Maybe she had better change first, she thought.

It was strange whilst she was showering and changing and getting ready to go after Lucas. Her adrenalin was running high with feverish excitement. It was only after she had parked her father's battered old pick-up truck a few blocks down from the swish hotel building that she started to have doubts…that excitement turned to nerves.

Going after Lucas was all very well, but just say he wasn't interested… Maybe he hadn't even missed her. He might even be back with Emma by now.

She stepped out of the car and brushed a nervous hand down over her blue dress. What should she say to him? Even though he had discovered the truth about his father it couldn't be easy for him. He probably wasn't in the best of moods, and finding out that she was William Kennedy's daughter might really infuriate him.

The sun was setting in a flamingo-pink sky as Penny walked slowly up to the front entrance to the hotel. Gold lights illuminated the impressive lobby. It's now or never,

Penny told herself firmly. If she didn't go in and talk to Lucas she would always wonder about what might have been.

As she walked in towards the reception desk a man walked out from one of the lounges and preceded her to the desk. Penny was so busy rehearsing in her mind what she would say to Lucas that she didn't pay him much attention.

It was only when the receptionist smiled and said, 'Evening, Mr Darien,' that Penny realised it was Lucas, who was now standing with his back to her a few yards away.

'Evening, Dominique—any messages for me?' He sounded his usual nonchalant self, but just the deep, familiar resonances of his tone made Penny's emotions dissolve with longing.

'Two phone calls, sir.' The woman handed across a piece of paper from one of the pigeonholes behind him.

'Thanks.' Smiling, Lucas turned—and that was when his gaze connected with Penny's.

The first thing Penny noted was the look of complete surprise in his dark eyes.

'Penny—what the heck are you doing here?' he grated, a raw tone to his voice.

'I live here,' she said quietly 'I—'

'What? In the Sheraton Hotel, Arbuda?' he said sarcastically. 'What do you do? Skip around the Caribbean using different aliases for different islands?'

'Don't be silly—'

'Silly?' His eyes narrowed on her and she realised she had said the wrong thing. He advanced slowly and with each step she felt her heart thudding with nerves. There was no mistaking the fact that he was angry with her…blazing, in fact. 'What the hell are you playing at?

Have you any idea how I felt when I found that damn note you left?'

'I had to go, Lucas…' She shook her head helplessly.

'Without even a word?' He shook his head and then he grabbed hold of her arm, his fingers squeezing into her skin.

'I tried to tell you I had to leave, but you didn't want to listen—'

'Well, I'm listening now.' He marched her firmly across the foyer.

'Where are we going?'

'We're going somewhere private, where you can explain yourself.' He stopped by the lifts and pushed a button for the doors to open. Then he marched her into the mirrored interior.

Another couple stepped in beside them just as the door was about to close. There was silence as the elevator swept smoothly up towards the top floor. Surreptitiously Penny studied Lucas in the smoked mirrors. She had never seen him look so tense. Even on the morning when Mildred Bancroft arrived he hadn't seemed this formidable!

The lift stopped and the other couple got out. They continued upwards.

'Lucas, will you let go of me?' she murmured, looking down at the hand on her arm.

'I don't feel like letting go of you,' he grated. 'You've got some explaining to do.' The doors swished open and he steered her outside into the long, empty corridor.

'Look, I know I've got explaining to do—that's why I'm here… You don't need to frog-march me like this.'

But still Lucas didn't let go of her. She watched as he put a security card into one of the doors and pushed it open. Then they walked in to a sumptuous apartment. It had gold carpets and deep sofas in heavy brocade material. There were double patio doors at one end, that were open to a balcony overlooking the velvet darkness of the Caribbean Sea. The tranquil scene, bathed by the silvery light of a full moon, was very much at odds with the tense atmosphere between them in the room.

'Okay, you said you wanted to explain—now explain,' Lucas said tersely as he released her.

'Lucas, don't be like this.' She rubbed at her arm absently.

'How do you expect me to be?' His eyes were cold.

She pushed a shaking hand through her long blonde hair. 'You've got every right to be angry, I know that.'

'Good.' His eyes flicked over her, taking in the high heels, the tanned long legs and the stylish way her dress emphasised the perfect proportions of her figure. 'Because I'm not just angry, I'm furious. So where the hell have you been?'

'I told you I had to come home, that my father needed me.' There was a heartbeat of a pause before she added softly, 'My father is William Kennedy. You came to see him today. I'm Penny Kennedy.'

'You are William Kennedy's daughter?' His eyes narrowed on her face in a moment of disbelief.

'Yes.' She sat down on the arm of one of the sofas. 'The real reason I came to see you in Puerto Rico was to beg for some leniency for my father.' She flicked an uncertain glance over at him to see how he was taking this, but it was hard to tell. It was as if shutters had come down across his features, leaving just a steely aloofness.

'I never intended to stay…or to deceive you,' she added quickly. 'It was just when you accused my dad of being a no-hoper…a useless reprobate—'

'I never said that,' Lucas cut in, his tone heavy.

'You may as well have.' She glanced over at him. 'It was what you thought, and it made me so damned mad.'

'Indeed,' Lucas murmured coolly.

'Anyway…' Penny carried on uncertainly, flicking an imaginary crease from her dress, not able to look at him properly now. 'When you told me you had to find the deeds to the property before the end of the month I had this idea that if I could find them first it would stop the building work, and also give my father more time to make an interim payment and take some of the pressure off.'

'So you were doing a bit of conservation work as well as a bit of spying for your father?' he grated sardonically.

'Come on, Lucas, give me a break here.' She glanced over at him pleadingly. 'In the end I didn't do anything wrong… In fact, I was more of a help than a hindrance—you've got to admit that.'

'Do I?' Lucas shook his head. 'On the contrary, I think you have been a damned hindrance.'

She bit down on her lip. 'Well, I am sorry you feel like that…but what you were doing was wrong—'

'I was simply following the terms of my father's will. He had made me an executor and I was fulfilling my final obligation to him.'

'Yes, well, your motives weren't completely altruistic; you did stand to make a lot of money from the sale of my father's property to a builder.'

'Is that what you think of me? That my main concern is money?' His voice was cold.

Penny frowned. 'No…' She admitted softly. 'It's not what I think of you at all.'

'You've got to understand, Penny, that my father and I never really saw eye to eye. I knew he was a womaniser…knew also that he had indulged in some shady deals over the years. But we had patched up our differences before he died and I was glad of that.' Lucas pushed a hand through the darkness of his hair. 'He apologised to me before he died, said how much he regretted some of his actions. He asked me to take charge of his business affairs, said he wanted to leave most of his fortune to me. When I said I didn't want it or need it, he said that I was to accept it for Isobel. That he wanted to make amends for not being around much for her.' He shrugged helplessly. 'What could I say to that? So I agreed, and I tried to do everything strictly by the book. I got rid of his shady solicitor, looked into every aspect of his finances. I had no idea that the repossession order was a personal matter.'

'I know you didn't.'

He met her eyes levelly. 'You should have said something.'

'I didn't think it would do any good. And it wasn't just because you stood to make a lot of money out of the deal. How could I tell you that your father was...?' She glanced over at him warily. It was one thing for him to criticise his father, but quite another for her to do it. 'That he hadn't been particularly kind...' She finished weakly. 'I couldn't do it, Lucas, and then I got firmly enmeshed in the lies and became too nervous about telling you the truth.'

'Really?' One dark eyebrow lifted wryly.

'Yes, really.' She looked over at him steadily. 'I didn't want you to hate me...'

'So you just ran away?'

'I didn't run away. I just had to leave.' She swallowed hard. 'Don't you understand, Lucas? You were my father's enemy. And I'm all he's got.' Her green eyes held his earnestly. 'He's been through hell, worrying about losing his house, how could I tell him he was also losing me—that I'd taken up with the enemy?' Her voice trembled. 'The state he was in, it would have finished him off.'

'He's a lucky man to have someone so loyal to him,' Lucas said quietly.

'I didn't feel very loyal sometimes,' she murmured huskily, and then blushed as he looked over and met her eyes. 'Anyway…' She looked away from him hastily. 'I hope you'll forgive me.'

Lucas didn't say anything for a long moment, and Penny felt her nerves twist with unmerciful anxiety. 'Would you like a drink?' he asked finally, and turned away to the mini-bar behind him.

Was that all he was going to say? Penny stared at him in frustration. 'No. I've got to drive home.'

She watched as he poured himself a whisky.

'So this is home, is it?' he asked, turning to look at her again.

For a second Penny had a vivid image of sitting at Lucas's dining table, with the candlelight flickering between them and Isobel complaining that she would have preferred chips. She remembered standing in the kitchen, looking out at the rain and listening to the child's laughter upstairs as Lucas teased her about something. There had been a warm feeling of belonging in that house, the feeling of being a part of a family. She ached for that almost as much as she ached for Lucas to put his arms around her.

'This is home sometimes,' she said huskily. 'But I don't live here. I'm manageress of a beauty spa on board a cruise ship.'

Lucas watched the golden liquid swirl around the crystal glass. 'You are full of surprises, Ms Kennedy.'

Penny felt a lump wedge in her throat. It didn't sound as if Lucas would ever forgive her.

'And you made a hell of a PA,' he remarked casually.

Penny frowned. 'I was good at that job,' she said with a flash of annoyance, her old spirit returning. She glared at him. 'You know I was. I'm computer literate, and I can run an office like yours no problem.'

'Yes. That's what I said; you were a hell of a PA. How come you were so proficient in an office when it's not really your line?'

'I did an office management course years ago.' She shrugged, not really wanting to talk about such mundane things. But as silence stretched between them she found herself filling the space with more mundane conversation. 'Have you got someone else to replace me?'

'Why? Do you want your job back?' He grinned suddenly.

'No, I just wondered.' She frowned, wishing she hadn't asked. 'I've got my own job, and it's very rewarding. Honestly, you can be damned arrogant sometimes,' she muttered.

'If you really want to know I've missed you like crazy.' He finished his drink and put the empty glass down.

She glanced over at him, her heart unsteady now as she wondered if he was talking in a business sense or a personal one. 'Even though a moment ago you were telling me I was a damned hindrance?' She managed to sound slightly sardonic.

'You were.' He met her eyes levelly. 'You were a damn distraction.'

Her heart started to race as he walked across towards

her. 'You are a distraction now. Sometimes I can hardly think straight when I look at you…do you know that?'

She looked up at him, unsure what direction his words were taking.

'You see, that's exactly what I'm talking about.' He shook his head. 'You look at me with those gorgeous eyes and things start to fragment in my mind… It happened the first day you walked into my office.' He reached out and caught hold of her hand, pulling her to her feet. 'I knew I should have asked you more questions—especially as I knew full well your CV wasn't right. But all I could think was…I want this woman to stay.'

Penny's heart leapt wildly.

'That feeling hasn't happened to me in a very long time,' he finished huskily, his eyes on her lips.

'Hasn't it?' She took a deep breath. 'If you want to know the truth, something happened to me that day too. I walked in and you looked at me and I almost forgot why I was there. I think that was part of the reason why I fell so easily into the lie of being Mildred Bancroft.'

'And then you left with equal ease. Have you any idea how I felt when I woke up and found you were gone? When I found that note?' His voice hardened.

She opened her mouth to answer, but suddenly she was in his arms and he was kissing her with a punishing degree of passion. She clung to him, excitement and need racing like fire through her veins as she kissed him back.

'I didn't want to go, Lucas…I really didn't,' she breathed unsteadily, wrapping her arms up around his neck, hardly daring to believe that he was kissing her, that he seemed to have forgiven her. 'I'm sorry…I'm sorry.' She punctuated the words with kisses, trailing her fingers through the soft darkness of his hair, loving the feeling of being so close, of being able to touch him…love him.

'No, I'm sorry,' he murmured, kissing her back, his hands travelling up and over her body with slow, sensuous strokes. 'Sorry I ever let you escape so easily. I can see now that I'm going to have to do something very radical about that…'

She pulled away from him, a small frown over her eyes.

'And I can also see that I'm going to have to do something about the fact that you keep changing your name.'

'I'm not going to change my name again, Lucas. Penny Kennedy is my name—I thought we'd cleared the air—'

'We have.' He kissed the tip of her nose, and then the frown from between her eyes. 'I just think that to be on the safe side we should change it again—this time more permanently.'

'Lucas, what are you talking about?' She pulled further away from him.

'I'm talking about changing your name to Mrs Lucas Darien,' he said softly. 'I want you to marry me, Penny…that way I hope that I can ensure you will stay around every day and every night for the rest of my life.'

She was so stunned she could hardly speak. He watched as the colour drained from her face.

'Penny?'

'Why are you asking me this?' she asked huskily.

'Because I'm in love with you.' He answered her with deep sincerity. 'And I don't want to lose you ever again.'

The words made her mind reel with happiness, with disbelief. She stared up at him wordlessly for a few seconds and then her eyes filled with tears. 'I thought…I wondered if you were seeing Emma again…'

'Why would you think that?'

Penny shrugged awkwardly. 'Because you sent her flowers…because Maria said you'd been the happiest she had known you in a long time when you were dating her.'

'Emma was only ever just a friend. She wanted more from me than I could give her. The flowers were sent out of friendship, for her birthday, and I made it clear there was no other motive.' He said the words steadily and reached to pull her close again. 'She's a very nice person, but just not right for me. In fact I had given up ever finding the right person again…until you walked into my office.'

A tear trickled down the smooth paleness of her skin. In these weeks apart from him she had dreamed of this, yearned for it, but she had never dared hope it would ever be possible.

'Look, I know you have a fabulous job…and I know you value your freedom…but if you say yes, Penny, I will do everything in my power to make you happy. The fact is I'm crazy about you…no other reason in the world would make me propose.'

'Oh, Lucas.' Her voice wobbled precariously. 'I'm crazy about you too…I adore you. I think I fell in love with you the first moment I saw you.'

She saw the light of happiness in his eyes as she said those words, and suddenly she was crushed in his arms and he was kissing her with such passion that it took her breath away. She clung to him, kissing him back, joy flooding through her with fierce intensity.

'I can't believe this is happening,' she whispered as he pulled back slightly to look at her.

'Neither can I. I didn't think I could ever feel this happy again.'

'I know.' She bit down on her lip.

'Hey, wait until Isobel hears our news—she's going to be ecstatic.'

The words caused a flood of warmth and excitement to rush through her. 'I've missed Isobel so much…how is she?'

'Fine—she's spending time with her grandma, but I've got to be back tomorrow.' He looked down at her earnestly. 'You will come back with me, won't you?'

She nodded. 'Try and stop me,' she whispered softly. 'As Shauna said, when you meet the man you want to spend the rest of your life with you want the rest of your life to start straight away…'

0109/05a

MILLS & BOON

BY REQUEST

3

NOVELS ONLY

£5.49

On sale
6th February 2009

In February 2009
Mills & Boon present
two bestselling collections,
each featuring three
fabulous romances
by favourite authors...

At Her Latin Lover's Command

Featuring

The Italian Count's Command by Sara Wood
The French Count's Mistress by Susan Stephens
At the Spanish Duke's Command by Fiona Hood-Stewart

Available at WHSmith, Tesco, ASDA, and all good bookshops
www.millsandboon.co.uk

0109/01b

209/10/MB199

THESE MILLIONAIRES WANT TO GET MARRIED…

Three passionate romances from bestselling Australian author MIRANDA LEE, featuring:

Bought: One Bride

The Tycoon's Trophy Wife

A Scandalous Marriage

Available 16th January 2009